A MAGICAL COLLECTION OF SHORT STORIES

ENCHANTED FORESTS

ASTRID V.J. ALICE IVINYA LYNDSEY HALL

N.D.T. CASALE JENNIFER KROPF BEN LANG DONNA WHITE

SKY SOMMERS ELENA SHELEST XANDER CROSS

ENCHANTED FORESTS

A Magical Collection of Short Stories

Published July 2022
ISBN (e-book): 978-91-987442-5-5
ISBN (paperback): 978-91-987442-4-8

Illustrations by Elena Shelest

Edited by Carolyn Gent, Melissa Cole, Amanda Nicoler, Kereah Keller, and Dr Edith A. Kostka

Proofread by Astrid V.J.

Cover Design by Emily's World of Design

Formatting by Astrid V.J.

❀ Created with Vellum

Dedicated in honour of Justin Sather who, at the age of ten years, raised over $20 000 for the protection of frogs and has founded For the Love of Frogs, an organisation whose mission is to conserve 30 percent of the planet by 2030.

The rainforests hold answers to questions we have yet to ask.

— Mark Plotkin

Gems of Fae and Foolery

Alice Ivinya

I chewed on the dried, salted meat until my jaw ached, waiting for it to soften enough to swallow. Fi slumped down beside me, her tattooed face streaked with dirt from the mine. She stretched her gloved hands out to the fire, most of her grubby fingers sticking through the holes, and made a big show of yawning. Her blue eyes flicked back and forth, making sure nobody was in earshot before she leaned in.

"We should go tonight." She paused as another dwarf strode past. "I've got it all figured out."

"Fi..." I sighed. I finally managed to swallow a chunk of the meat without choking. "Where would we go? We've got nothing." I chewed off another strip of meat and offered some to Fi.

She grimaced and held up her hand. "Na-ah. I won't eat another mouthful of that." She wiped her nose with her knuckles and folded her arms. "Come on, Andie. We continue here, we'll be worked half to death in five years. We're treated worse than the donkeys. We should go to the Red Forest. There are lots of dwarves there. We'll find respect and be able to work for ourselves. Unlike this death hole." She waved her hand dismissively at the camp and the humans who lazed around, all at least a head taller than us. She scowled, her long black fringe hiding her eyes. One half of her head was shaved, the other braided back. "They'll never let us go until we're so broken, we can no longer work."

She fell quiet as we heard the heavy stomp of Master Greg. He loomed over Fi first and wiggled his fat finger that strained the seams of his gloves. His ragged wide-brimmed hat covered his face up to his messy beard. "Gem count," he ordered in his low, phlegm-filled voice.

Fi didn't meet the older dwarf's eyes as she scowled into the fire. Not even Fi was that stupid. She handed over a sack, and Master Greg opened its glowing contents into his scarred leather glove. He sniffed the fragments of rock and crystal and grunted. "Three grade twos and a grade three. Might even be a hint of sapphire in this last one." He studied the fifth rock with greedy eyes.

Her scowl deepened. "That's four grade *threes*, and one grade *one*. That's sapphire, no doubt. There's nothing wrong with my nose. Ain't no grade twos."

Master Greg's eyes darkened. He put one hand on Fi's shoulder. "You saying I'm wrong, girl?"

"Fi," I hissed in warning, pulling her sleeve back as her fists clenched.

"I'm saying you're trying to cheat me of my rations."

Around me there was a collective gasp as everyone held their breath. I cursed too quietly for Master Greg to hear.

The older dwarf pocketed Fi's gems, and just like that, they were gone. Fear for my friend tightened my chest. The overseer raised his voice. "Seems like you've come back to me empty handed, girl."

Fi leaped to her feet and pushed herself right up into his face. Master Greg took a step back. I grabbed her hand and tried to pull her away, but she had always been so much stronger than me, especially when in a rage. My heart pounded in my ears as my friend yelled spittle-flecked words. "You thief! Call yourself a dwarf when you cheat your own people? You're nothing but a fat toad with his head stuffed up the humans'..."

Her voice was cut off as a human guard hit her head from behind with a club. The blow would have knocked many people out cold, but Fi merely dropped to one knee, gasping and shaking her head. She rose with one fist clenched and it caught Master Greg full under his chin with a crack that made me wince.

She'd really done it now.

I reached to pull Fi away, to stop her making things worse, but the human guard grabbed my jacket and yanked me back, sending me sprawling to the edges of the fire. I screamed as one of my fingers touched the embers, burning away my skin. I rolled clear and saw three guards holding Fi between them. Her nose was bleeding. She crumpled as one punched her in the chest.

No, no, no!

A hand pulled me away from the fire as I screamed Fi's name. It forced me down on one of the logs that served as seats for the mine workers. Another dwarf, one eye covered by a dirty rag wrapped around her head, put her hands on my shoulders and obscured my vision of Fi.

"Don't watch, girl. It will just make it worse. Let me treat your hand, or you'll struggle to find enough gems in the mine tomorrow."

Numbness washed over me as I heard Fi cry out and swear. I could do nothing to help her. I'd never felt such a coward in my life.

The dwarf, I remembered her name was Magda, poured the water from her flask over the burn, and I hissed in pain. Over her shoulder, I watched as they dragged Fi away to the wooden cages that formed a wall down one side of the camp, far away from the warmth of the fires.

"If that girl doesn't learn to bite her tongue, she will be dead next time. Everyone knows Master Greg lines his own pockets. It's just the way it is." She chuckled, surprising me. "Still, it was good to see her plant a good 'un on his face."

I couldn't smile. Fi was stupid but also very brave, and I hadn't managed to help her at all.

Master Greg's roar behind us made us all flinch. "She stays in there for a week. No food. If I catch any one of you going up to her, you will be flogged and on half-rations for a month."

I wanted to glare at him, but instead stared at my boots like everyone else until he stomped away. I let out a sigh, then my breath caught as I felt the heavy weight in my pocket. Fi's distraction had stopped him collecting my gems for the day. I'd had a good day, and more than a few of them glowed with traces of magic. They would work well as currency.

Fi was right. It was time for us to go.

As the coldness of night forced everyone to huddle near each other, wrapped in their thin blankets, noise grew on the other side of the camp. We had a fae peddler tonight, here to trade potions and jewelry in return for the raw magic gems from the mines. He only spoke to the humans, of course, and the sounds of their bartering bounced off the sides of the tents that ringed us.

The humans loved the fae, despite their disdain and their trickery. I agreed with Fi on this subject: the humans were absolute idiots. Nothing good ever came from the fae. Looks were deceiving, and they were all too preened and dainty for me anyway.

As the sales came to a close, I listened as the humans begged the fae to stay the night and treat them to a song, causing many dwarves trying to sleep to mutter and roll their eyes. The fae would never say no to flattery, and if they complemented him now, he might be hollering all night.

The peddler took up his lute and sang above the dainty plucking of strings for several hours while the humans got drunk. For once, I didn't mind. My heart was pounding too fast for me to sleep, and the humans would fall into deep, drink-addled slumber soon. I twisted my necklace, the only memory I had of my mother, over and over in my hand, listening as the dwarves ripped the air with their snores.

Long after midnight, the camp had quietened, and there was only the pop of the dying fire and the piercing cries of owls and bats.

I stood up and pulled the hood of my cloak over my head far enough to cast my face into shadow from the firelight, pushing my light brown hair behind my ears out of sight. I snuck as quietly as I could to the edge of the camp and was relieved to see even the guards were asleep, slumped on their tree stumps.

Fi's thin body was huddled in a corner in a cage under her thin cloak. I wrestled the metal hair pins from my unruly frizzy hair and looked back to check the guards were still sleeping. The camp remained still. It took me less than a minute to unpick the lock, all the while checking over my shoulder, certain I would see Master Greg looming over me. My mouth was so dry that I couldn't swallow, and the burn on my finger throbbed with my racing heartbeat, but still the night was quiet.

I eased the creaking door open and slipped in. "Fi?" I whispered. I crept over to her and shook her shoulder.

She groaned and rolled over toward me. Despite the fact her braids were tied back, she still had to flick her fringe from her eyes to see me. "Andie?" Her eyes widened in surprise as she sat up and looked around, her hand clutching her middle. She grinned through split lips when she saw the open door, dried blood still on her chin, hiding the dots of her tattoo. "You actually did it. Here was I thinking you wouldn't take the opportunity, and all this was gonna be for nothing."

"We're not free yet," I hissed. "Can you walk?"

"'Course." She eased herself into a crouch, wincing. "Lead the way."

"Just don't do anything stupid." I turned and crept back to the door.

Fi chuckled softly in the darkness. "You worry too much."

I strongly disagreed with the statement as far as Fi was concerned, but swallowed my rebuttal to creep out of the cage and past the sleeping guard.

My friend limped after me as we dived into the shadows of the fae's wagon.

We sat with our backs to the large wheels, catching our breath for a moment. I noticed that even the spokes were painted with gold oak leaves. But of course they were. Gaudy, ostentatious fae.

We crawled to the last wheel, and the darkness of the trees loomed ahead, invitingly close.

"Well, well, what do we have here?"

The voice was soft deep velvet in the dark. I bit back a scream as I wheeled around. Sat on the arched roof of the wooden wagon was the fae, his eyes glowing silver in the starlight. His full lips were pulled into a smirk. Fi hissed a curse.

"Nothing that concerns you," I whispered. "Leave us alone."

I knew that fae liked it when you begged, but that they liked bargains more. I had nothing with me to trade. That was, except for the raw gems in my pocket and we would likely need those later. Though fae liked strange things in stories, like the color of your hair or a memory. Well he could have all the memories of mine he wanted. None of them were happy.

"What will you give me if I don't raise the alarm?" He asked, his thoughts on the same path as mine. He let one leg dangle close to my face, the other crossed beneath him in a relaxed posture. He stretched absentmindedly, making me imagine Fi punching him in the face. That stupid slender face with high cheek bones and a strong jaw, typical of all the fae and the origin of their arrogance. His hair fell in silky golden waves over broad shoulders and down his lithe back. He looked ridiculous.

But still I had to play his silly game. "I have..."

Before I could finish the sentence, Fi whipped her hand back from where it had been searching under the canvas and threw something at the fae. Something she'd grabbed from inside his wagon. His eyes had a split second to widen before a glass vial shattered in his face.

I gaped aghast. A glass bottle wasn't going to do much more than anger him, especially if it had marred his precious face. Let alone the fact he would see it as stealing. "Fi! What have you done? He'll raise the alarm!"

She grabbed my hand and pulled me into a run for the trees. "We're dwarves. We die before we make bargains with the fae." She spat, almost making us stumble.

We reached the nearest gnarled oak tree, and looked back at the caravan, silhouetted against the dying light of the camp. The fae had vanished, but no alarm sounded. Instead, something glittered in the grass with the drifting specks of gem-magic.

Curiosity seized me, and I freed my grasp from Fi to creep back. She cursed and stayed in the shadows, hunting for something. A weapon, I guessed.

I came closer to the softly glowing object, the light already fading from its skin. It was a frog. Fi had somehow grabbed a vial that had turned the fae into a frog. And the most fat, disgusting one I had ever seen, at that.

I couldn't help a snorting laugh escape from my throat. The frog seemed dazed and weak. It lay on its back, lifting its limbs in uncoordinated motion. The final light of gem-magic dimmed, and with it went the last signs the frog had ever been something else.

Fi bumped into my back as she peered over my shoulder. She laughed under her breath. "So there is some justice in the world. Bargain your way out of that one!" She prodded the frog with a sharpened stick.

I looked at the helpless thing which couldn't even move its own body. I took in the width of the wagon wheels, the nearness of the camp, and all the people who would happily spit and roast a fat frog for their breakfast. Guilt twisted my stomach.

I scooped up the frog and put him in my pocket, buttoning it shut.

"Andie, what are you doing?" asked Fi dryly. She folded her arms. "Nah-ah. We don't need a fae anywhere near us."

"But he's a frog," I muttered and took off at a run back to the trees. Behind us the camp slept on. We had probably three hours before dawn, maybe less, and we needed to be far away by then.

Fi caught my shoulder. "Leave him, Andie."

I didn't meet her eyes, but kept my attention forward. "I will. Just, as soon as we're far enough away that he won't be able to raise the alarm. We don't know when he might turn back into a fae."

"Ugh, just throw him in a pond somewhere, then."

I didn't reply and concentrated on weaving through the trees and avoiding brambles. A pond sounded like a good idea. But what if he got eaten by a big fish or something? A heron? "Not my problem," I muttered under my breath. He'd probably lived several hundred years already.

As dawn rose, every part of me ached and Fi was faring even worse, limping behind me, clutching her bruised side. Her face was rigid but I knew she wouldn't complain. Neither of us really knew where we were headed. For now, it was enough to simply put distance between us and the mines.

It was cold enough for our breaths to fog and frost to glitter across the ferns. We had no warm clothing, making us eager for the sun to rise higher and give us some warmth. After an hour, we stumbled onto a dirt road in the woods and followed the easier route to a junction. A weathered sign declared the way to two different human cities. Beneath them, carved into the post, was a single dwarvish rune.

"Sanctuary," I read out loud for Fi's benefit. Below was an arrow pointing down a deer path I would have overlooked. Fi limped up behind me and her face was pale, her breath ragged. I pulled her arm over my shoulder and pointed into the trees. "Come on. Maybe we can rest there until we recover?"

Fi didn't reply which worried me, and I pulled her up the path to a squat cottage with smoke curling from its chimney. A small trout pond nestled to one side, which looked like a good place for me to leave the frog. I had felt it squirming weakly in my pocket all night.

I knocked on the door and took a few steps back, ready to run.

We could hear shuffling steps behind the wood and Fi tensed beside me as it opened. An old human lady dressed in a nightgown opened the door and held up a lantern, causing us to squint. In her other hand she brandished a kitchen knife, making me stumble back further.

She looked down at us, and her lined face broke into a smile. "Ah, it's just you. Come in, come in." She turned and hobbled back inside, leaving the door gaping open. Fi and I shared an incredulous look before following her into the delicious warmth of her cottage. We had hoped for a dwarf, not another human, but it looked like this old lady would be easy enough to outrun if we had to, even with a kitchen knife.

The woman closed and bolted the door and placed the lantern on a bulky table. The room was large but cluttered with every object imaginable, from bundles of herbs to a pickaxe, to many trinkets and jewelry which were undoubtedly of dwarvish craftsmanship.

"I'm Margery." The old woman hobbled to the far end of the room and thumped on the door half concealed by a heavy curtain. "Brux, you can come out. It's friends."

Our eyes turned to the door, and we both breathed a sigh of relief as a grizzled dwarf came out, a magnifying eye loupe strapped to his forehead. He had to be the one who had made all the jewelry and trinkets that surrounded us. His long white beard reached his knees.

He placed his hands on his hips. "Welcome, girls. Are you runaways?"

We didn't reply, and Fi placed a hand on my arm in warning as I took a breath. At last I said, "Could we trouble you for a place to sleep and some food?"

He chuckled. "Of course, of course. My wife here loves to cook for guests." He gestured to the old lady. I tried not to gape. They were married? A dwarf and a human? No wonder they lived alone in the forest. "Everyone is welcome here, no matter your story. Well, except for the fae, of course." He snorted. My hand rested on my pocket.

Margery showed us to a small bedroom cramped by twin beds

covered in colorful patchwork quilts. "You rest here, my dears, and I will cook."

I eased my swollen feet from my boots and stretched out on the bed, my feet tingling at being free. Fi sat with her ear to the door, listening. Now we had proper candlelight, I could see her cut lip and matching black eyes. "I need to make sure they don't leave the cottage to alert anyone that we're here. It could be a trap."

I sighed and fished the frog from my pocket. He was still an ungainly tangle of limbs. I wondered if his brain had become that of a frog too. His skin was becoming dry and sticky so I dribbled some water over him from a jug on the floor between our beds. Hopefully he wasn't too squished.

The frog squinted round gold eyes at me. "What have you done?" he croaked. I dropped him onto the quilt in shock and barely stopped myself from screaming.

Fi's eyes flicked over to me and she scoffed. "Told you, you should have left him." She snorted a laugh.

"Change me back right now, and I will give you wealth beyond your dreams," gurgled the fae-frog.

Fi laughed freely now, coming to flop onto the bed next to me. She grimaced and clutched her side as she settled. "Hard luck, for you. Dwarves don't make bargains with fae. You're stuck."

I raised an eyebrow, lifting up the frog, who had finally got himself into a sitting position. He was yellow with brown speckles, and neither color was pretty on him. He looked like a moldy leaf.

I brought him close to my face. "How would I turn you back?"

The frog managed to glare. "Take me to a pretty maiden and get her to kiss me."

Fi and I looked at each other, then both rolled back, hollering with laughter. The frog squirmed free back onto the bed.

"No pretty maidens here," I gasped. "Just us ugly dwarves."

"Or the human outside," suggested Fi, dropping her chin onto her forearms on the bed for a better look. "Though she's no maiden."

We laughed again, though the frog was becoming increasingly agitated. "Well, find one then, you fools. What are you two even doing?"

Fi poked him in the side. "Escaping from the mines."

The frog's eyes widened, and his voice was heavy with disbelieving accusation. "You kidnapped me!"

I folded my arms. "Well, we couldn't leave you to raise the alarm or get squished by a horse."

"Or roasted and eaten by Master Greg," snorted Fi.

The fae looked back from one of us to the other and just opened and closed his mouth. "Take me back at once, and I can give you..."

Fi poked his side even harder. "Not happening, mate."

"...beauty," he finished, undeterred. "You know the fae cannot speak lies."

Fi snorted. "Have *you* looked in the mirror recently?"

I giggled and fluttered my eyelashes. "We're dwarves, what would we do with beauty?"

The frog lifted his feet impatiently. "Name your terms then. What do you want in return for taking me to a pretty maiden or back to my wagon."

I copied Fi and poked his side. "You realize if we took you to a pretty maiden, she'd just shriek and run?"

"Or hit you with a broom?" Tears were streaking down Fi's cheeks now.

He licked his mouth with his thick pink tongue and turned his back to me. "They'd run from you maybe. We fae are immortal representations of power, beauty and wit. I never have any trouble kissing maidens. I will explain who I am, and she will be more than eager to kiss me. You know people have bargained away things of great value for a single kiss from me."

His last words sent me into a fit of laughter so violent, I could barely breathe. I couldn't imagine anyone ever kissing a slimy frog, whatever they promised.

The frog was growing indignant. "You don't seem to understand the seriousness of the situation. My wagon has been left unattended. Do you have any idea the chaos that could ensue when the humans start rooting through it? There are many vials of gem-magic in there. Not to mention the squandered wealth... My collection is valuable beyond your wildest dreams."

A knock interrupted our laughter. The old lady's voice came

from behind the door. "Breakfast is served. I'm glad you two are relaxing, but I honestly expected you to sleep."

I scooped the frog into my pocket despite his protests and opened the door with a smile. "It's the nerves, Margery. Now we're finally somewhere safe, they're coming to the surface. It's hard not to laugh."

"And cry," added Fi, wiping her cheeks with the palms of her hands.

Margery didn't know what to make of the confessions and just bustled us to the table where her dwarf husband was already sitting, fiddling with a contraption. His beard was draped back over one shoulder.

The smells were wonderful: sausages, eggs, bacon and toast. I hadn't eaten these sorts of foods for years. My stomach contracted and my mouth watered.

"I think I'm going to be sick," came a muffled voice from my pocket. I squished it.

We sat down and dug into the food, both of us heaping as much onto our plates as we could fit.

Margery nodded approvingly, loading a far smaller amount onto her own plate. "Ah, what it is to have young growing appetites."

"Where are you two headed?" asked the dwarf as he fitted a polished magic gem in the center of a charm.

"The Red Forest," I said around a mouthful of food. "We've heard there are many dwarves there, and it's a good place to earn an honest living." I glanced at Fi. "Though we don't know the way."

The dwarf nodded, his eyes never leaving his work. "Ah, the Red Forest. Good, good. It's not a kind time for dwarves to be wandering these parts alone. The Red Forest is a place you can disappear into and find safety from your past." His fingers searched over the table for a miniature screwdriver, which his wife handed to him without thought. "And no fae sets foot in the Red Forest. They're a scourge upon this country, I tell you, and they're walking more and more in the lands of men, playing their dangerous games. Watch your back."

Fi and I shared a look.

"There was a fae peddler in the camp the night we left." Fi paused to drink the fresh milk. "He was there to buy gemstones."

"Thieving cowards," muttered the dwarf. "They never do any of the hard work themselves, yet are more than happy to rob us of our hard-earned gems." His knuckles clenched white around the screwdriver.

The old woman nodded. "I heard at the market two days ago that the peddler passing through is from the High Court. Somebody important, but bored enough to play games in the mortal realm."

Great.

"If I got my hands on him, I would show him what I thought of them spiriting away our gems for their pathetic decorations in their mysterious realms." He stabbed his screwdriver into the table hard enough for it to pierce the wood. "Meanwhile, we who actually need them are left with barely enough for our work. Our work, which actually matters; making things folk need."

A cold shiver ran down my spine. My hand went to my pocket, and I was alarmed to not feel the shape of the frog inside. I pushed back my chair and saw the frog stumbling across the floor on slippery feet. Could he be any more idiotic?

I dropped to my hands and knees and grabbed him before he could get us killed. I pushed him into my gem pouch that fastened tightly and took out my best find from the mines yesterday.

I poked my head back up. Fi was gaping at me and shook her head, incredulous, as if to ask what on earth I was doing. I put the raw gem next to the dwarf. "Sorry, I dropped this. Take it as a gesture of our thanks for your hospitality. I'm afraid it's not been refined."

The dwarf took the gem and sniffed it before studying it through his single eye loupe. "Well, well, if that's not a hint of amethyst and ruby. And that smell... I could do a few clever things with this."

He grinned at me. "Our hospitality is free, yet I wouldn't turn down a gift such as this. Here, let me give you something in return."

He got up and collected a pendant hanging from a nail in a ceiling beam. Inside it, a tiny cut ruby glowed with magic. It sat in a miniature cage. On one side was the dwarvish rune for 'sanctuary'. On the other was the rune for 'forest'.

He handed me the pendant. "That gem will guide you to the Red Forest. That is where its paired sister resides, and the necklaces will always call to each other."

In my pouch a muffled voice sounded. "It stinks in here, let me out." I coughed to cover up the voice and hoped the dwarf's ears were dulled with age.

"Thank you," I managed. "This is very kind of you."

He grinned and held out his hand. "Don't mention it."

A croaking voice cried out, "Let me out!" The pouch vibrated against my hand. I broke into coughing again to cover it up. Fi's eyebrows rose as she stared at me.

"My, my, that is a bad cough you have, dear," said Margery. "I've heard there are bad gases down in the mines."

I nodded in agreement and shook my pouch to keep the frog quiet. I stood up. "May I use your toilet?"

"Out the back, dear."

I hurried outside into the still-cold midday air and shivered to the outhouse. I closed the rickety door and pulled out the frog. "What are you playing at?"

The frog glared at me. "I was suffocating in there. Have you ever washed that pouch? No? I didn't think so. Do you, in fact, wash at all?"

I hissed at him. "If that couple discovers that you're a fae, they will kill you. Most likely with a screwdriver."

He sniffed. "I'd rather be dead than stuck in your stinking pouch."

Irritation swelled within me. "Fine, just get out and go. Good luck surviving on your own."

He hesitated for a moment. "You're freeing me in a lavatory? I never thought I'd say this, but it smells worse than your pouch."

"Just get out of my life."

The frog leaped up my arm, closer to my face. "Excuse me, you kidnapped me, not the other way around."

"Well, you tried to ruin our escape."

"You're dwarves. You belong in mines. It's what you're built for."

I picked him up by his back leg and dangled him over the hole in the plank, right over where the sewage had piled beneath. "I think I'll let you go right here."

A fist hammered on the door. "Time to go, Andie. The dwarf

has this telescope thing. He's spotted Master Greg coming up the path from the road." It was Fi.

I cursed and stuffed the frog back into the pouch. I did not want him finding Master Greg and telling him where we were headed.

"Margery said to follow the stream uphill and she would delay them as long as possible and cover our tracks. She's given us food too."

I opened the door and peered down the path. Cracking branches sounded over the gurgle of the bubbling stream. Real fear made my blood run cold. If Master Greg caught us...

I took the bag Fi handed me and hurried behind the house.

Fi rubbed her split lip. "Andie, please tell me you got rid of the fae? Dropped him down the toilet? Preferably before you used it?"

I chuckled despite my nerves and shook my head. "He might give us away."

We started climbing over boulders slick with moss. "You won't even throw him in the pond?"

I grimaced. "The trout look huge. They'll eat him."

"Good!"

We hushed our voices as the cracking branches came closer and quickened our pace over the rocks next to the stream.

"Hey, I'm in here!" croaked the frog from my pouch. I wrapped it in my cloak to muffle his voice further.

Fi looked murderous so I hurried us along and kept shaking the bundle to keep him quiet.

The climb was steep and slow in places, but the trees quickly obscured the cottage below, and the rocks hid our tracks.

As the stream twisted into a rocky ravine, we reached another road, little more than a dirt track too narrow for wagons, and made quicker progress up the hill. I pulled the pendant from my baggy top and swung it in front of me. The gem inside the tiny cage tugged to the east. I grinned and squeezed Fi's hand. "Look, look, it's actually working! We're going to find it."

She grinned at me, light dancing in her eyes, and we walked as fast as we could with Fi's aching side. Our bellies were full of the massive breakfast, making our minds sluggish as we imagined what true freedom might look like.

An hour or two passed before I registered the muffled voice of the frog. "If you don't let me out right now, I'm going to die. It is hot and smelly and there is no air. Seriously, I will die."

I unwrapped the bundle and opened the pouch. The frog climbed out onto my hand with uncoordinated long limbs. He gasped in the cold air. "You almost killed me."

Fi scoffed. "I thought fae were meant to be immortal and powerful and all that."

The frog turned to face her. "Well, I would be if you'd not turned me into a frog."

She lifted her eyebrows, hands on hips. "Why do you even have such a potion in your wagon? And most likely for sale? Surely there must be laws against turning people into helpless animals? If you were willing to do that to others, surely you deserve a taste of your own medicine?"

He sniffed and turned away from her. "I'm not to blame for the horrible things humans will do to each other. I just find them entertaining to watch. Life can be ever so boring at times."

"Andie, let him go by this rock. He can live out the rest of his miserable life in a remote area of forest until something eats him."

I bit my lip, looking around at how overgrown the path had become. "But, Fi, don't you think that's a little harsh? Maybe we could set him free near a village when we're close to the Red Forest?"

"Ugh, even your names are ugly. Are you sure neither of you will accept a bargain for beauty? I mean even making your noses a little smaller, will do you the world of good." He squinted up at me. "And your hair, well, has a bird ever tried to nest in it?"

I sighed, shaking my head at how oblivious he was. "Fine, let's leave him here."

The frog was leaning toward Fi's face now. "I thought women wore jewelry to enhance their beauty? You've just stuck plain metal rings through your eyebrows. How do you even blow your nose with that metal bar through it? And your poor ears..."

I dropped him on the ground, wiped my hands, and walked off without a backward glance. It was clearly what he wanted, so I wasn't going to feel sorry for him anymore.

A howl echoed through the trees, deep and melancholic. Fi and I froze. She raised a bread knife she must have swiped from the cottage. I suppressed a spike of annoyance that she had stolen from the sweet couple who had helped us so much. I could deal with that later, but right now, I was glad we had some sort of weapon.

"What was that?" came a quiet croak from behind.

"Sounded like a savage monster to me." Fi shrugged. "Probably looking for something or someone to eat."

Another howl ripped through the air, closer this time. A cold finger of fear ran down my spine. The frog hopped to my feet.

"All right, all right, I've changed my mind. I retract everything I said. Take me with you."

I glared down at him. "Why should we?"

"Because if you don't, I will follow you screaming as loudly as I can until the monsters come. They'll decide to eat you over me."

Fi and I looked at each other in exasperation. I scooped him up. "You know what, fae? I'll make you a deal. I'll take you with us if you promise not to speak unless we ask you a direct question. This deal holds for the duration of our travels together."

The frog nodded as a howl sent shudders through my whole body. I stuffed him in my pocket, and we started running. All manner of creatures, magical and mundane, lived in these woods. It's why the mining camp had guards at night.

We crested the hill and skidded down a scree slope on the other side, the sharp shale biting into our skin through the holes in our gloves. Dust rose up and cloaked us both. When we hit the bottom, we both stumbled on through the undergrowth. Every now and again, I held out the pendant to check we were going in the right direction.

Howls echoed near and far, seemingly from every direction, and I was horribly aware that the sun was starting to set.

As evening drew in, we made a makeshift shelter of leaves and bark over large branches. We didn't dare light a fire, and we had no food to eat, just water in our flasks. I was glad of the bread knife as Fi and I took turns on watch while the other tried to sleep in the shivering dampness.

The woods were full of shadows in the measly starlight, and the howling never stopped.

We rose with the first light of dawn, neither of us having had more than a few snatched moments of delirious sleep, and forced our stiff limbs to walk. The sooner we were safely in the Red Forest, the better. Here the pine, ash and beech seemed to stretch forever, full of things we wanted to avoid.

We followed an eastern road with weary feet until Fi grabbed me roughly. A strangled sound left my throat as she pulled me down into a ditch before I could realize what was going on. I hit the rocky side and gasped, but Fi pressed her finger to my lips and pointed ahead though vibrant ferns.

Three fae sat on gleaming white horses, their golden bridles set with gemstones. They rode with no haste in colorful embroidered cloaks that were completely impractical for a hack through the cold, muddy woods.

I didn't notice the frog had wormed his way free to get a better look until I felt his cool skin against my neck. He leaped off my shoulder and hopped to the middle of the road.

"I am no longer traveling with you, and thus our deal is broken," he called out over his shoulder. "It was distinctly not pleasurable. Now, if you would excuse me, I have a wagon to save."

Fi put an arm on my shoulder. "Finally. Good riddance."

The frog leaped toward the mounted fae at an impressive pace. He started yelling and calling for his kinsmen to stop. As the frog neared the hind hooves of the closest horse, the long, pointed ears of its rider twitched. He tilted his head, frowned, and dismounted in one smooth movement. He flourished his cloak as he did so which made me roll my eyes at Fi.

Quicker than humans or dwarves could move, the fae swooped up the frog, and his companions dismounted behind him.

I tensed and squeezed Fi's arm. She looked at me and nodded. We both adjusted our stances, ready to run if needed. Surely the frog wouldn't give us away after we had helped him? But I didn't trust him at all.

The fae holding the frog tutted, pushing his silver hair back over his shoulders with deathly pale hands. "Well, well, well, if it isn't Lord Clovance. You look a little worse for wear."

A female fae with dark skin and black hair in gold bands swayed up beside the first. "So it is. You're a little shorter than I remember."

They laughed. The third fae, another woman with tan skin and feathers and gems woven in her hair, peered down at the frog. "Hmm, you stink of dwarf." Her heavily painted eyes darted up and somehow looked straight at us. "Shall we collect your friends, Clovance?"

Fi swore. We turned and broke into a run down the bottom of the ditch, our feet stumbling on the uneven, boggy ground. To my dismay, the two female Fae caught up within moments, slipping into the ditch with their mouths twisted in disgust. I felt hands grip my hair, and then both Fi and I were on the floor, our arms twisted behind us.

I struggled, and got a knee in my back for the effort.

A voice tinkled over my head. "My, my, I think this pair smells even worse than normal, don't you think, Mycerilla?"

"Have some pity, the pathetic creatures are dressed in rags. Life can't have been kind to them."

Fi spat, but the fae didn't seem to notice. They hauled us to our feet in unison, keeping our arms twisted behind us so we couldn't struggle without dislocating our shoulders. Each one was almost twice our height, and easily prodded us forward back to where they had left their horses.

Fi winced as she tried to wriggle free. "Let us go. We want no part in your stupid games."

Our captors ignored her as they forced us to stand next to their male companion.

The frog looked up at the silver-haired fae in whose hands he sat. "My wagon is still with the humans at the mining camp. I need to get a beautiful maiden to kiss me so I can return and retrieve it before they mess up all the spells."

I yanked my arms free of the fae holding me and glared at her over my shoulder. She smiled like a wolf. "Frog, tell them to let us go. We've got no part in this."

The male fae didn't even glance at me and raised the frog up to his face. "Fear not, we'll retrieve your wagon, Clovance. I'm sure the miners will like the return of their dwarves too."

My chest tightened at his words, and I made to run again, only to be roughly grabbed by the fae who had held me before. She was too fast and strong. I wished we had been armed with axes.

The frog sighed. "Let the dwarves go. They're not into bargains or games. They bored me; they'll bore you too."

I looked at him incredulously. Had he just stood up for us?

The male fae tutted. "Be that as it may, I suspect the humans will pay gemstones for their return. We'll bring them too."

He returned to his horse and unhooked a tiny filigree cage. He pushed the frog inside. "I much prefer you as a frog, Clovance. The Faery King has favored you for far too long. I think it's time to give others a chance to shine, don't you?"

He chuckled, hooked the cage back to the saddle and untied a bottle. He grinned as he drank a liquid that stained his lips purple. Faery wine.

The frog jumped agitated around the cage. "Tine, I will make you a bargain." There was an uncertain undertone to his voice.

The fae mounted his horse with a victorious expression that

made my blood run cold. The female fae tied Fi and my hands with ropes attached to their saddles. Had we come so far, only to be returned to Master Greg? Fi had been right. I should have dropped that frog down the toilet.

"I'm listening, Clovance" said the male fae. The females mounted their steeds, and the three set off at a leisurely pace, dragging us behind them.

"You can have my wagon and the dwarves if you leave me in a village with at least one pretty maiden."

My heart sank. So much for standing up for us.

The male fae shrugged, making his silver hair ripple down his back. "Really, Clovance. I already have the dwarves, and the means to claim your wagon. Why would I make such a bargain?"

"Fine, I will arrange a marriage between yourself and the King's second daughter. Just reverse this curse."

The fae chuckled. "So much confidence for a little frog to have in himself. I think I might gift you to Lord Ashen. He would be thrilled to have you as his plaything, I am sure. He'd pay a hefty price."

I dragged my feet, struggling to fight my growing despair. Everything had been going so well. I hunched over as I thought about what Master Greg and the humans would do to us when we returned. I doubted we would get the cages. He had once hung an escapee upside down for two days by their ankles. He hated Fi already. He might not let her survive even a day. No, we had to escape.

I looked at Fi, but all her attention was focused on glaring at the fae's backs. The breadknife was no longer at her belt.

The fae pulled us west through the woods, and I felt the life of the Red Forests fall farther away.

Fi shook me awake in the darkness, a finger to her lips. She was free, her ropes cut. I looked down and watched her saw through my rope with her bread knife. I had assumed she had lost it, but she must have been hiding it from the fae. My whole body sagged in relief. She motioned for me to lift my hands so she could untie the rest, and excitement awoke in my belly.

The moon was out, but the heavy canopy dappled the light so it was hard to see anything. In the darkness, I couldn't see any movements to suggest the fae were still awake. I pushed the final coils of rope from my body and eased my limbs to standing. The woods were silent.

Fi put her finger to her lips and then pointed east. I nodded and placed each foot carefully amongst the leaves so as not to make even a rustle as we edged away. I was so tired and so desperate, my hands trembled.

"Psssst!"

My heart sank and tears pressed behind my eyes. I couldn't deal with anything more from that confounded frog!

"Pssst! Please, Andie, listen to me."

I looked in the direction of the sound and saw the cage hanging from a branch in the moonlight. I put my finger to my lips.

The frog stretched out a leg through the bars. "Take me with you, and I'll do a deal."

I grabbed his cage, unhooking it soundlessly from the tree, and edged away from the camp so we could talk at a safer distance without waking the fae.

"You have to be kidding me," muttered Fi. She jabbed at the cage. "Let me guess you'll holler and wake the fae unless we rescue you?"

The frog shook his head. "Better than that. I know how you can transport yourselves to the Red Forest in the blink of an eye. I only ask that you take me with you."

I frowned. Fae couldn't lie. Why couldn't he have told us about this earlier? I supposed he had just wanted to go back to his stupid wagon which was the opposite direction.

"We can transport ourselves from here?" I hissed, thinking through his words carefully. "We have everything we need?"

He nodded emphatically, his webbed feet curling around the filagree bars.

"Tell us," hissed Fi.

The frog cocked his head. "I thought you didn't make deals with..."

She shook the cage. "Just tell us, slime ball."

He was silent for a moment as if enjoying our suspense. "That pendant you have around your neck, is magically paired to another ruby in the Red Forest, correct?"

I nodded, freeing the necklace from my shirt so it could hang free, pulsing softly in the darkness.

"Well, fae can sense and follow all magical bonds and agreements. We that are powerful enough, can even use those links as a method of transport. In my true form, I can pull the three of us down the bond, and we'll end up instantly in the Red Forest. It is powerful magic, but I believe I have just enough strength for the three of us. It is the ancient way we could ensure all bargains are fulfilled."

I sighed, lowering the cage. "I thought you said we had everything we needed here? How are we going to give you back your true form? There are no pretty maidens that I've seen, unless either of those fae count."

He sniffed. "They've not been maidens for hundreds of years."

Fi rattled his cage. "You said everything was here to transport us. So do it."

The frog leveled its liquid-gold eyes at me. "You just have to drink a beauty potion, and all will be over."

I gaped at him. "You have to be joking. I don't want to look like you fae. I'm a dwarf and proud of it."

He hopped around his cage. "Fine, we'll stay here then. The fae will catch us as soon as they wake. You dwarves leave a stinking trail for our noses." He pushed his face through the gap in the bars. "Every fae carries a beauty potion in their bags so they may stay eternally young. Steal one, drink it, kiss me, and this will all be over."

I hesitated. I didn't like this idea one bit. Why should I have to be beautiful by the fae's standard for my kiss to break curses? I didn't like the way they looked. I wanted to look like me.

Fi clasped my arm. "Just leave him with the fae, Andie, and we'll make our own way back just fine."

Only we wouldn't. I knew we wouldn't.

But I wasn't going to drink any stinking fae potion. How I looked was just fine.

I opened the latch on the tiny cage and helped the frog out. Before he could object, I pressed my lips to his speckled back. I pulled back quickly and wiped my mouth. He was seriously gross.

The frog slipped from my jerking hands and fell amongst the leaves. A soft glow surrounded him.

Behind me, a voice cried out. I looked over my shoulder and saw gemstones flaring through the trees. I looked back at Clovance and saw his shape elongating, stretching, until the fae lay shivering in the leaf litter.

It had worked.

Footsteps rang behind us as our captors located our trial.

Clovance grabbed the pendant without standing. Sitting, his face was already level with my chest. He wrapped one arm around my waist, and I grabbed Fi's hand. He swung the ruby in the air and breathed in sharply.

His grip tightened around my middle. I exhaled. Everything around us blurred.

We landed in a tangle of limbs, a canvas roof giving way beneath us until we all rolled into a dip in its center. We were on top of some form of tent. I squinted up in the faint early light of dawn and could see the second pendant hung from a branch above us, glinting in the light of torches.

All around us, dwarven faces appeared around the corners of the canvas and squinted down at us in wonder and confusion.

"Fae!" one called out. A dozen axes and clubs appeared in hands. Tattooed faces twisted into snarls.

"He's with us," I called, shaking the dizziness away.

I rolled to the edge of the canvas, the tent collapsing even further, and brushed down my clothes before helping Clovance to his feet behind me. He towered over us all, yet somehow seemed smaller than before. I grinned up at him. "Well fancy that. Perhaps I am not as ugly as you thought after all."

The fae blinked at me in confusion. "But... that..."

Fi sprung up behind us and grabbed my shoulder with a giddy smile. "Nah, the ugly ones have always been the fae with their complete inability to grow decent facial hair. I could never kiss some-body without a good beard."

The fae's cheeks reddened. I had no idea the fae could even feel embarrassed.

I giggled as more dwarves came to inspect us, and their suspicion turned to welcome as the fae lingered behind us without trying to boss anyone around. Fi and I were patted on the back and flagons of ale were shoved into our hands.

I grabbed Clovance by the hand and he didn't flinch or try to pull free, his expression dumbfounded and maybe a little horror-struck. "It's time for you to enjoy the hospitality of the free dwarves."

He grimaced at the ale I offered him without taking it and rubbed the back of his neck. "I need to get my wagon, Andie. I can't let the humans at your mining camp play around with all that gem magic."

My joy dimmed slightly. We were a long way away from the mining camp now. Even farther because of the magic he used to help us. Maybe there was some good in him after all.

He looked at me hopefully. "Do you have anything magically linked to the camp? Made any magical bargains with anyone there? And linked objects?"

I shook my head. Behind us Fi was animated as she told a crowd of dwarves where we had come from and our adventure here. She'd added a troll and a giant wolf fight by the sound of it as she pointed to her black eyes.

A broad dwarf with two axes across his back strode toward me with a scowl on his scarred face directed at Clovance. He clamped a meaty hand on my shoulder. "You from the gemstone mines, lass?"

I nodded, a trickle of apprehension rippling down my spine.

He grunted. "Good. We were hoping to get somebody from there. You see those mines should belong to the dwarves like the times of old. We need inside information. How many guards and their routines. How deep the mines are and whether we can tunnel in from the side."

I smiled broadly. "We can help, can't we, Clovance? Then you can get your wagon back. We just need to kick the humans out and Master Greg."

The fae lord sighed dramatically. "Fates help me. Fine. But this does not make us friends."

The large dwarf raised an eyebrow. "A fae willing to help without a bargain, what did you do to him, lass?"

I grinned. "I kissed him."

ABOUT THE AUTHOR

Alice is a USA Today bestselling author. She is also an award winning international and Barnes and Noble bestseller.

She lives in Bristol, England. She is wife to Sam, mummy to their toddler and owns the best dog in the world, Summer. She has loved fantasy all her life and is currently writing three fairytale retellings. When she's not off galavanting in other worlds, she loves walking the dog and spending time with her church family.

Find out more about Alice here: http://alicegent.com

The Lucky Tortoise

Ben Lang

The palace had a garden. The garden had a pond. The pond had a tortoise.

The tortoise had a new friend.

Her new friend, a young boy, had come crashing through the bushes, brandishing a bamboo cane as if it were a sword. Deep in a world of his own, saving it from evil the tortoise didn't doubt.

He stopped in his tracks on seeing her huge shell, its peak as far from the ground as the hair on his head. After his staring he approached the great tortoise cautiously. Soon they were playing a new game that delighted them both. It was a team game. The boy's role was to climb into the apple tree, to take the choicest apples, and throw them down to the tortoise. Her job was to eat them. Bonus points if she caught the falling apples in her mouth without letting them touch the ground.

Crunch, crunch, crunch went the apples. Giggle went the boy at the sound of their demise. Burp went the happy old tortoise, to further giggles from the boy.

All too soon the sky turned pink and the boy was forced to leave.

But the next day and every day thereafter, as soon as his duties were finished and his lessons ended, he rushed straight back to the pond and the tortoise.

They devised new games to play together. For example the peach-tree game. This tree was not suited to the boy's climbing, but, standing on the tortoise's domed back, his young hands could tear the fuzzy pink fruit down to appreciative mouths.

Tortoise spat out a peach stone. Ping! Quickly the contest of stone-spitting became well established. Boy gave some good shots, but the best distance always went to Tortoise.

As the fruit passed out of season, they found other ways to play. Sometimes they would both take water from the pond, turn their heads back and gurgle together in chorus. Boy laughed at the gurgles, but it turned to a splutter as he choked on the gurgle-water. Tortoise, ever the more sensible of the two, laughed with her eyes.

In the cleaning game Boy would wet his sleeve and use the sodden silk to polish Tortoise's big shell. He loved how her smooth shell gleamed in the sun when he had polished it. It looked so different to her leathery skin, even though both were brown. She reciprocated by chomping at tufts of Boy's hair to style it.

Sometimes the boy would talk about the world of men. Especially the parts of it that worried him. Tortoise was a very good listener. She never once interrupted him or asked distracting questions. She allowed Boy's ramblings to find their own way to the point.

He told her about his wonderful mother, who read him stories and sometimes baked delicious cinnamon buns. But, he confided, she wasn't all good. Sometimes she combed his hair or made him eat spinach. The combing was yanky, and the spinach slimy. He spoke proudly about his distant father, the king, no less. Although beyond the fact that he was proud to have a king for a father he had nothing to say about him. They had never spoken.

He had much more to say about the other children, his half-brothers and sisters. None of it was good. They were always saying that his mother was the king's least-favourite wife. They said she was ugly and he was strange and stupid. They spat at him and called him names.

His tutors were stern, but not mean. Actually, Boy corrected, one tutor was mean. He had told Boy he had to paint his entire picture and leave no white spaces left on the entire page! No white at all, that would take forever and ever. So yes, *that* tutor was mean.

Tortoise did not pry and ask what the boy had painted. But the next day when he finished painting all the empty space he brought it to show her.

It was a painting of Tortoise. Boy was very self-critical. By making him paint the blue sky all the way to the ground the tutor had made him accidentally get blue all over the shell, ruining the whole picture. But you could still sort of see what it would have looked like before, with Tortoise's shell here in dark brown and her head and neck coming up here. Tortoise gave the picture a smell, then licked it, presumably trying to get the blue spill off the shell. It didn't work, but Boy thought it was kind of her to try.

Tortoise didn't criticise the painting at all, so Boy proudly hung it in his room. He found a convenient hook on the wall for it behind some boring black-and-white painting that was just words anyway.

When his tutors found out they told him off. The old painting had been good luck, they said. Good auspices. Boy wasn't just any child, he was a prince, they lectured. If he accrued bad luck it could damage the harvest or bring plague. He had to always remember and be very careful. It was his role as a prince to bring luck to his people —the good kind.

When the lecture was over the tutor smiled kindly over his catfish whiskers and smoke-wisp of a beard. They walked to Boy's room and a geomancer was called to find an auspicious place on the wall for the painting of Tortoise. It was even closer to Boy's bed than the old place where the boring poem had been put back.

As Boy grew older his responsibilities towards the kingdom's luck became more onerous. At the tea ceremonies he had to remember which way to pass the pot and he had to sit still sipping the yucky stuff all afternoon. He was warned that if he carelessly used the wrong spoon for his soup, a ship might sink and its crew drown. If he walked through another man's shadow, foreign powers might gain unwanted influence over the land. During prayers he had to remain completely still and silent, and not fall asleep. Too much movement invited disunity and chaos upon the state-church, while falling asleep put it in danger of fading from relevance. Rearranging the stones, raking the sand, washing down the altar with scented water, all these tasks had to be done in very specific ways that frustrated the energetic child.

The adults were never happy, the other children always mean. They seemed to find their duties so easy. They never spilled their tea and when they raked the sand the patterns were neat. While the tutors called Boy careless the other children said he was a useless twitchy freak. It didn't help that he had no full-siblings to stick up for him.

Boy increasingly felt the burdens of his position even when he was alone, but never when he was with Tortoise.

One day Boy and one of his older half-sisters were to carry water for the Tree of Wisdom. The old tree was of a species associated with great thinkers past. The tutors said the species, peredexions, had silver bark and fruit that dismissed despair. They said that all serpent-kind feared the shadow of the peredexion tree. The particular specimen in the palace was long dead, its bark turned disappointingly black and its branches empty of fruit. However, watering the dead tree was still good fortune: it would bring success to the children's education and help learning flourish throughout the land.

Boy and the older girl started the ritual at the sacred well, to gather water into an ornate painted vase which they would then carry to the tree itself. She wore her pink silks like a second skin, moved like a dancer and lifted the bucket chain with fluid grace. Without pause she poured the water into the waiting urn, and spilt not one drop. When it was Boy's turn to lift a bucket, his nerves made his hands shake as he pulled the chain. What if he pulled too quickly? Would rushing invite crafted tools to fail? What if he spilt water? Wastage, loss of knowledge? Drought? Hand over hand he pulled the chain and worried about all the harm he could cause.

When finally the bucket emerged, he tilted it to the urn, and poured. He felt a shake in his arm, an involuntary flutter of movement, but it came near the end, and he was able to get all the water into the vase.

His sister raised an eyebrow and gave him a pointed look.

Boy went to the two bamboo poles that they would slide into the urn's handles to carry it. He lifted one but then saw his sister bowing to the well to thank it for its kindness.

Boy felt his hands ball to fists in frustration. How could he forget?! He dropped the pole on the ground and hastily bowed to the well. He hoped it wouldn't go dry because of his rudeness.

His sister frowned at the clattering of the pole he had dropped. With her usual poise she passed her pole though one of the urn's handles so that Boy could take the other end of it. He then reciprocated, passing his pole to her through the other handle.

They walked towards the Tree of Wisdom, Boy marching as smartly as he could with one pole in each hand, following behind his sister who walked with effortless poise. The vase rode between them, painted serpents spiralling around it, with the water within sloshing far more than Boy liked. The noise was bad. Boy felt they should have been walking smoother. Actually, *he* should have been walking smoother, she was doing well already.

He put his shoulders back and adjusted his grip on a pole. It twisted slightly, his arm gave a spontaneous quiver, and then the vase fell. Fragments of pottery in a puddle of water.

Boy screwed up his eyes and stamped his foot on the ground. His sister's mask of tranquillity broke, and through it he could see her fury.

The worst bit, as always, was what they said afterwards. They asked if Boy cared about the kingdom. If he wanted learning to wither or for floods to assault the coasts. How many people had he killed with his clumsiness? Why wasn't he just more careful?

His sister was the meanest. Just after the pot shattered, he made the mistake of telling her that his arm had just shaken by itself, that he hadn't been able to stop it. She said that proved he was a twitchy freak. She speculated about how bad an omen it was for a prince to be unable to control his own arms. A sickness in the royal family.

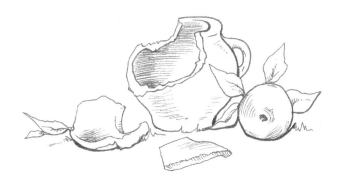

The next day Boy found Tortoise. She was munching leaves as if nothing had happened. As if Boy had not cursed his own chances of finding higher knowledge and those of his innocent sister. As if he had not invited floods on some poor commoners he had never met.

But to Tortoise it was like none of those things had happened. Together they played a story-game where the willow-tree was Runjknau, the king of the demons. Tortoise was a shapeshifting dragon. Boy was a mighty hero, the greatest swordsman in the world! The bushes became an army of awful demons, but Boy's bamboo stick became a sword and, with Tortoise's help, he fought against them all. Swing, swing, swing went his stick. He swung it so fast that he could hear the air breaking in its path with a "quaaaaar-rrk" noise. He swung it so hard that leaves and twigs went flying. Correction: demon's heads went flying. One demon after another fell as the swordsman and the dragon charged fearlessly deeper into the dark forest, into Runjknau's domain where the sun never shone. The demons intended to destroy the Scales of Destiny, upon which fortune was weighed and fate determined. The heroes needed to stop them, else all the world would be thrown into chaos.

They fought all the way to Runjknau himself. Here, the game did not go quite the direction he had expected, and Runjknau surprised Boy with the offer of an alliance. The demon said that the gods of men had been cruel to give them control of destiny. Such control treated people too harshly for the most minor of mistakes. He promised to make a world without luck. One where none could influence their fortunes through ritual. Where plague or flood would either occur or not and mankind would bear no part of the responsibility. A world where auspices granted no power of prediction. Boy stopped, stupefied by the strange turn of the story. After he collected himself, he finished the game the only way he could think of. He shooed off the demon's lies and attacked with his sword.

The duel was hard fought, but in the end Tortoise distracted Runjknau at just the right moment for Boy to decapitate the awful demon.

As the demon's head landed on the ground it transformed back into the cut vine of a willow tree. Tortoise even began to eat it! But Boy supposed that was okay, she was a dragon after all.

Boy's days became ever more ritualised, making him increasingly dependent on Tortoise's support. At night he had nightmares where delicate glass sculptures were balanced all over his body and, no matter how hard he tried, they would fall and shatter on the floor. The hopes of his hapless subjects ruined by his inability to just be careful.

As the months passed, his mother started to become morose, quick to tears and tantrums. This scared the young child who preferred the solemn stability of Tortoise.

It wasn't just his mother. All the people were starting to act strange. His whiskered tutor patted Boy on the shoulder after lessons and told him that things were going to be all right in the end. This failed to comfort, serving only to confirm that things were not all right at the moment.

A servant told him not to be scared. They told him the king was too wise to give up a smart woman like his mum "to make room for a trollop like that". The boy didn't know what a trollop was. Everyone was acting so weird. Only Tortoise stayed normal.

He found Mother sobbing again. Distressed, he tried to flee to Tortoise, but Mother held him back.

She said that the two of them would have to leave the palace. Tomorrow. He would have to wear his best formal clothes and comb his hair. Then the two of them would go together to the temple and from there they would go to a brighter, better place. They were being given to the gods. It was a very high honour. He should not be scared no matter what people said.

The boy let Mother hug him, but her distress was scary, so, as soon as he could, he ran for Tortoise. On his way to the gardens he passed a group of older half-siblings who sat gossiping and sipping tea. The other children looked at him funny. His older sister, who, since the water incident, had always called him names just stared at him sadly. Another boy remarked, "That's the sacrifice."

He found Tortoise eating at the lower leaves of a bay tree by her pond.

Boy snapped a good-looking branch and placed it in front of her to save her old neck the stretch. Then he sat. The sky was already evening pink. Boy had arrived about the time he would normally be leaving for his dinner and bedtime story.

He told her that he would be going away. He told her how much he was going to miss her. He sobbed, but she reassured him with her familiar munching.

When he had told Tortoise everything and cried himself out, she finally spoke.

"Climb into my shell," said Tortoise. "You can squeeze in under here. We can leave tonight. Then we can stay together."

Tortoise took in a deep, deep breath. Under her shell she pulled in her back as far as it would go, then kept pulling. She opened a gap above her neck, which she told Boy to get into.

So, in he climbed. Out of the twilight garden and into the darker place above Tortoise's back, under her huge shell. He had to curl himself into a tight little ball to fit in that cramped place.

"What about Mother?" he asked, now inside the smooth confines of the shell.

Tortoise sadly pointed out that she would not fit under her shell. Her voice rumbled ever so much deeper and stronger heard from inside.

Tortoise had lived more than ten years for every one of Boy's, but like him, she had never left the palace and its gardens. Nevertheless she trod between flowerbeds and willows until she found the garden's wall and gate, two ornate brass doors flanked by a pair of torches and a pair of mailed soldiers with spears.

The soldiers were surprised to see a tortoise wandering right up to them at night. She nosed the bright doors to signal her intent.

They made expressions at one another.

"This is very inauspicious," said one.

"Should we let it out?" asked the other.

"Taking lucky animals by force turns the luck bad. Everyone knows that. So, I suppose we let it go?"

"Yes. We wouldn't want to bring misfortune on the king the day before one of his weddings."

"Agreed."

They shouted out to their colleagues that guarded the way from the outside. The reliefs of brass pulled outwards. Tortoise thanked the soldiers with a bob of her head and made her slow way out into the world beyond the palace.

A new world for them both.

eyond those doors the tranquil gardens gave way to busy torchlit streets. Fire-eaters and jugglers performed before plates pleading for coins. Children charged hither and thither in excited gaggles.

Tortoise knew people well enough to see the carnival for what it was. The king encouraged the common people to revel in his weddings with alms, pageants and circuses.

Boy remained hidden in her shell as she walked the streets. None accosted or obstructed Tortoise, although many palmed her shell for luck. A man selling bangles and beads gave Tortoise a necklace. This was much less appreciated than the candied apple given by another seller.

They came to the city walls with gates of their own. Beside the gate sat a grandly painted royal carriage and a troop of mounted soldiers. The horses had the striped patterning and orange-black of tigers, while their riders wore armoured uniforms in the king's own colours

"Who leaves tonight?" came a ritualised call from the gatehouse.

"Royal guard of the Tygermark," replied the leader of the riders. "We bring ten-score weight in silver for the great Lord Hushtenhan as a royal gift to compensate for the loss of his daughter and grandson, who shall tomorrow join the gods." While he shouted his orange-black striped horse pawed the ground eagerly, ready to be off into the night.

"Then let this gate be opened for you!" came the reply. The wooden gates of the city began to creak open.

"He'll be mighty pleased with his compensation I don't doubt," said one rider to another. "I escorted the dowry he paid the king all those years ago. This is over fifty times what he gave!"

"I just hope it doesn't rain tonight," muttered another.

"There is not a cloud in the sky to make rain. Besides, look, an auspicious tortoise has given us luck."

The carriage and riders filed out into the countryside while Tortoise followed unimpeded behind them.

Tortoise walked the countryside for a long time. Indeed, the sun was once again tinting the sky when Tortoise finally stopped her plodding. She sucked herself tight, and Boy came climbing out. With relief they both stretched. Boy's limbs and Tortoise's back ached.

Boy thought for a second he was right where they had started. But after a few blinks he noticed the trees were different. They were uglier, more haphazardly spaced, less fruit-bearing. Wild trees were disappointing.

He cast about. No people. No buildings. Just trees dressed with yellow foliage and a carpet of soggy brown leaves.

They found a stream to drink from. Boy tried to start the gurgling game but his heart wasn't in it. He cast his eyes back towards home and worried about his mother. She had said they were going somewhere nice, but it had also been scary. Maybe she would be sad to not have him with her? He didn't want to make her sad.

"You will be with her again in the end," said Tortoise, as if reading his mind.

Boy nodded glumly. Try as he might, he could not remain fully ignorant of his mother's fate. After all he had cleaned the red stains from the sacred altar himself on occasion. He didn't want to talk about it.

They tracked the water downriver. The forest had many trees, but all of them were bad trees. No fruit. No flowers. Tortoise didn't even think much of their leaves.

By afternoon sleep caught them both. They nestled together in a chamber-like space, surrounded but not filled by branches.

I n the palace was Hurdain, sceptre-captain of the Tygermark. It had been a most inauspicious morning. First, his guards at the garden gate had reported that a lucky tortoise had left the palace. A very bad sign.

Second, they had not yet found the prince. They had searched the whole palace three times now, but he was not here. Hurdain had got nothing useful from the mother. Maybe if he had been allowed to interrogate her for longer they would have learned something. But the king had insisted that the sacrifice could not be delayed.

It was not Hurdain's place to wonder if the king's impatience was driven by devotion to the kingdom's fortune or an eagerness to marry that new woman who had so caught his eye.

He marched through the palace corridors, glancing into decorative vases as he passed just in case. He made his way to the prince's room. A nice room of course, auspicious poems as expected and a painting of a... brown blob? He let the sniffers off their leads and blew his whistle.

Hideous creatures sniffers. Like pigs for the most part, except for their snouts. The head, torso and front-limbs of a rat stuck out of the place where the pig's snout would be. Black rat fur giving way to the equally black bristles of the boarish pigs.

The sniffers eagerly entered the room, their split hooves clomping on the wooden floor. They bent their pig-necks down to place their tiny little rat paws on the floor. Big mean red eyes in the pig face, tiny mean red eyes in the rat face. Sniff, sniff sniff. Sniffers were good at sniffing.

Hurdain followed them to a bay tree by a pond in the garden. He had never known sniffers to lose a scent before, but here they had. They snuffled in confusion about this spot in the garden.

He scanned for foot prints. Round prints, big prints. Tortoise prints? Maybe. A tortoise had left the palace last night, which seemed an odd coincidence. Oh, a tortoise! That is what the painting had been of.

Hurdain frowned. Could the boy be with the tortoise? It seemed implausible, but the sniffers had led him here. He blew his whistle and indicated the tortoise print. The sniffers lowered their rat-noses down to drink in the scent of tortoise.

Hurdain frowned at the sun. Time was running out. Depriving the gods of a promised gift was awful fortune. The kind of bad luck that could shatter a kingdom with war or strife. Hurdain feared that the cost could well be the collapse of the nation itself. He had nothing against the poor runaway boy, but if sacrificing the child could save the kingdom, then it needed to be done.

I n another place was Rekkacoaton.

He blinked red lids over green eyes. He rolled over on the desert sand to warm himself in the sun. His shape was reptilian: serpentine and crocodilian together. His colours were red and orange. His scale was elephantine. This was how he chose to incarnate himself. He flapped the frilled mane about his neck and lashed the air with his forked tongue. He tasted the scent of an approaching cat.

The black cat came skulking to him across the desert, but kept some distance. Rekkacoaton could be accidentally lethal: his scales stung like thousand-fold nettles and the caustic scent of his breath triggered spasms in man and beast alike.

With a purr the cat told Rekkacoaton about a prince-child. A lamb stolen from the gods.

Rekkacoaton's truth-whiskers quivered in confirmation and he smiled wide at the cat's report. A child stolen from the powers of heaven? What feast could ever compare to food stolen from the table of the gods themselves? The food of heaven. A step toward immortality.

Rekkacoaton had known that recruiting spies was wise. But he had never hoped for such fortuitous news. He bade the cat tell him all it knew about this prince.

T he next morning Boy and Tortoise crept from their hollow and drank again from the stream. They were both getting very hungry, and the forest did not see fit to remedy this situation.

They continued, as best they could, away from their home city. They followed the river vaguely downhill, and as they did the river both widened and became less distinct. Its muddy banks gave way to a kind of puddly mess. It started to flow less, smell more, and it became impossible to really tell where the wet mud ended and the river began.

Boy took his shoes off to keep them clean. Tortoise grumbled her annoyance.

The trees themselves seemed to disdain the deepening water, and started to stand over it on stilt-like roots. The water reached Boy's calves and Tortoise began to move with something that was half-walk, half swim.

"This is gross. Why don't we go another way?" asked Boy as his foot sank unexpectedly deep into the earth below the water.

"They will have sniffers", answered Tortoise, "they can't track us through this water."

"Because it stinks?" asked Boy.

Tortoise nodded, but Boy barely noticed as he had just spotted fruit. Not apples, but not that different looking. They were growing on some of the stilted trees.

"Apples," he cried, pointing.

They knew this game well. Boy pulled himself up onto the roots of the trees and then further into the lower branches. He threw the first fruit he found to Tortoise.

She snapped it out of the air with her distinctive crunch.

"How is it?" asked Boy.

"The best I can say is that it is food," replied Tortoise. Boy thought the same as he bit into his first of the fruits. It had an oddly sandy texture, with hard little white spots spread throughout the squishy grey flesh. It tasted mildly sour, in a way that reminded Boy of the smell of wet dog. He was never going to complain about spinach again.

Boy climbed from one tree to another, sampling mangrove apples and tossing most down to Tortoise. The trees were good for climbing, and the birds that Boy scared from their perches wheeled away in colourful circles.

"Let's keep moving", said Tortoise. "I am sure there will be more fruits on the way."

"The way where?" asked Boy, reluctantly climbing down to lower his just-dried feet back into the stinky water.

"The way to something better than these to eat. They used to have a tree in the palace that stood over water like these ones. But that one was silver, and it had great fruit. Hopefully we can find one of those."

"The tutors said that one was called something like a pered-ered-onian."

"It would be good to find one like that."

Boy, newly returned to the water, scratched his calves. The brackish water was irritating, he worried it was probably worse for poor Tortoise who had more of her body submerged.

They wandered for the rest of the day, stopping on a few more occasions for more of the not-really-apples. The tide rose as the day wore on and by early evening it was so high that they had to swim.

They found a place where the roots matted together into a mesh at about the high-water mark. Tortoise tried to heave her way out, but she was exhausted from swimming and slid back in.

"Take this bit in your mouth to help pull with your neck," suggested Boy, pointing to a particularly sturdy root. "I will get in to give you a push from behind."

Tortoise bit hard and flexed her neck. Her front feet clawed up at the matted roots while her hind feet paddled. Boy tried stretching tall, with his feet on the ground and his hands on Tortoise. But the mud was too slippery for him to get a good purchase. Giving up on that he pushed at Tortoise with his strongest frog-kicks, and she slowly dragged herself up out of the water.

He splashed out after her. Tortoise panted; Boy spluttered.

It was a good place to spend the night. They had space to lie up out of the water and there was more fruit overhead. Boy lay against Tortoise's big shell, while she curved her neck around to place her chin on his lap.

The two fell asleep listening to the cries of the bats and the distant sound of the sea beating against the trees. As his mind slipped towards sleep, Boy's last thought was of Runjknau, the demon king Tortoise and he had defeated together in the garden. He remembered the demon's plan to make a world without luck, and he wondered if, in such a world, his mother would have been spared.

The next day began much as the one before. They waded, Boy climbed for fruit and they made their slow way through the forest.

Some time after midday they stopped for a snack. Boy was high in the trees, throwing fruit down to Tortoise, when the creature attacked.

It slithered into sight at speed. Huge and red. A snake-crocodile with a head as long as Tortoise's shell. Without hesitation the beast leaped up towards Boy.

He was quite high in the tree, and the beast was no great jumper. Its huge jaws snapped shut beneath him, cracking off a branch underneath.

No sooner had the creature failed its first jump, than it took in a big breath and leaped up again. This time it exhaled at the peak of its arc, straight towards the perched boy. Its breath stung. It burned up Boy's nose like spice. He spluttered and gave a choking cough. He felt a quivering coming upon him. The same kind of shiver that made him drop tea at the ceremonies or mess up his calligraphy. A kind of involuntary tremor.

But Boy had spent a lifetime practising how to suppress such shakes. He steadied his mind, and that steadied his body. He froze, petrified by choice, fear or both and gripped his branch with his whole will.

The huge creature stood on all fours below. It held Boy's stare in its green eyes, daring him to fall, challenging him to keep his composure after inhaling its spasm-inducing breath.

"Climb away!" shouted Tortoise. "Get away. Don't believe a word it says! A silver tree, you will be safe in a silver tree!"

The crocodile beast turned to consider Tortoise.

"Your Tortoise can live, it's only you I want," the creature said. Its voice was so deep and croaky that Boy could barely make out the words.

"But if you make me wait", the creature slithered so that its body implied a crescent about Tortoise, "I may need a snack."

Boy's knuckles ached as his fingers held the branch so hard it hurt. He realised with misplaced shame that he had wet himself. He couldn't breathe properly, his chest was too tight. It was like cold water, the feeling of not being able to open his lungs and draw in air.

"Please..." he cried. He didn't even know what he was going to ask. He looked into Tortoise's dark eyes over the creature's flat forehead and furled flap of a mane.

"A silver-barked tree. You will be safe there," said Tortoise. "You will be safe," she repeated. Then she bit the monster.

One of its forefeet had been perched on a stone. Tortoise stretched her head in with surprising suddenness and took a pair of reptilian toes between her molars. She bit down with all of her strength. All her practice chomping apples had given her quite the bite.

The beast roared in anger and furiously turned to attack Tortoise. Boy saw his chance, and climbed sobbing towards the next tree. Hoping to get from one tree to another through the canopy.

Hand over hand he climbed. One branch then another. He strove for height, but often to get from one tree to the next, he needed to get lower. Sometimes as low as the roots, barely his own height above the water. He heard growls and splashes at first, but the sound was soon gone.

The sun turned orange in the sky and he kept climbing through the twilight. At long last it became too dark for Boy to see where he was going. Too dark to choose the right branches. He went as high as he could in the tree he was in, curled himself up into a ball and cried. He scolded himself for not doing more to save Tortoise. He pleaded to all the gods he could name that she might still be alive. He wished he were back in his room with his painting, his mum and Tortoise.

"I can hear you, human." It was the voice of the creature, the great crocodile-like-thing. "It's still too dark to see, but I hear your breath. I sense the warmth of your blood."

Boy awoke in his tree. He had fallen asleep clinging to the unseen trunk. The thing's voice came from somewhere below in the absolute dark.

"I am Rekkacoaton. You escaped your people and your gods, but me you shall not evade. Climb down. It will be painless. You will no longer be cold. No longer scared. You will find your Tortoise."

"You killed her!" Boy accused.

"Yes," it replied. "You have been the cause of so many deaths. First your mother; sacrificed because you shamed her with your clumsiness, shakes and your failure to be careful.

"Then your Tortoise; killed while you fled to protect your own skin.

"And, even as we speak, others die because of you. Your grandfather, Lord Hushtenhan, has made rebellion and war. My agents report that he sent the king's silver back to him, along with the heads of the men who carried it. It is a futile war, he knows he cannot win. But his anger drives him to fight nonetheless. His horsemen will pillage and burn for some time before they are ultimately defeated. How many hundreds will his rage kill? But of course", the creature paused, "It is not your grandfather's rage that is the root of the problem. It is your escape. By stealing yourself from the gods you inflicted terrible damage on your kingdom's luck. That is the true cause of the coming war. You chose to save yourself knowing that it was awful luck. Your selfishness could kill thousands of your people. The people you were supposed to serve.

"It's best if you climb down. It will be quick. It will be *just*."

Boy's guilt felt heavy in his stomach. So heavy, he felt like his arms were straining to hold himself against a fall. His people, he had failed them once again. So much failure. Tortoise. Mother.

"There is no atonement for what you have done," came the voice. "But I offer release from the pain."

Boy began feeling his way down to a lower branch. Maybe the creature was right. What would he do far from home without Tortoise to guide him anyway? He lowered himself a branch.

Precious little moonlight made it through the leaves above, but in one small gap Boy could see some stars. Stars were nice. He had seen them many times, but had never really looked at them before. Now seemed a bit late. The bark against his palms was nice. He had touched bark so many times, but had never really just stopped to feel it. Even the croak of distant frogs suddenly sounded good. The world was saying goodbye.

As he lowered himself over another limb of the tree, he felt a hard lump break from the branch. Oh, another one of the apples. He had dislodged it as he slid himself lower. Might as well eat it now rather than let it go to waste.

Mortality heightened every sense, but taste more than the others. And, it was not the same type of fruit. It was something else. This was not "at best, food", this was sumptuous and sweet. It had a tanginess and as each bite fell down into his stomach it burned hot. Licking his fingers Boy wished he had another such fruit. Or that he had the time to find and eat more.

But he *could* have the time. He could wait till morning to find more to eat, then go down the tree later. All of a sudden it seemed incredibly stupid to go down at all. If another few minutes to enjoy a snack was good, then how much better to take all the time he could get?

He climbed up a branch.

A snarl came from the darkness below, and the tree shook. He reached to climb higher and heard the thump of Rekkacoaton throwing his weight against the tree again. Roots below snapped, and the tree thrashed again.

Boy clung on to a firm branch.

Crash. Crash. Crash! Rekkacoaton slammed himself against the tree. Unseen in the dark. Boy winced at every shake.

The creature paused its attacks, panting.

Boy thought for a moment that he was turning on his branch. But soon realised it was far worse: the tree was beginning to tilt. He adjusted his grip and looked about. The darkness was weakening. Enough light for him to make out a stronger looking branch.

The crashing resumed. Rekkacoaton throwing himself against the tree.

Dawn lit the sky. Looking up, Boy saw the upper branches of the tree glow red in the reflected sun. It glowed so bright. For the first time he had light enough to see the tree was shiny with silver bark.

The scene below was still darkness, a deeper shadow putting its head down to ram the sagging tree with its forehead.

Another crash. The beast moved further away, aiming for a longer run-up this time.

It charged. The darkness in which it ran was beginning to dapple. The overall darkness lessened with the shadows of the branches criss-crossing.

And the running creature passed into the shadow of the silver tree. The part of the shadow that fell across the creature inverted, becoming a brightness. The creature screamed. And it dropped lifeless into the water.

This, Boy supposed, was why serpents feared the shadow of a pered-ered-onian.

H urdain pushed his horse as hard as it would go through the mangroves. It disliked the mud but it was a dutiful beast and pushed onward.

The sniffers he had left behind. They were useless here. Hurdain cursed. He was supposed to be a tracker, but in this place he was doing little more than picking directions at random and hoping.

His leg throbbed in pain. Intervening had been a mistake, in hindsight. The day before, his riders had chanced upon a village in the process of being attacked by the rebels. The smoke on the horizon had drawn them. The intervention had been timely, they had caught the rebels by surprise while they were piling fuel on a burning barn. The Tygermark had won and had even been able to open the barn in time to save some of the hapless citizens bolted inside.

But it had still been a mistake. The root of the problem was the prince. Catching him would save the whole kingdom, not just one village. The distraction had lost them time. It had also cost soldiers. Of Hurdain's original unit of twenty, they were down to fifteen; two dead and three so wounded they needed to be left behind to heal.

By rights Hurdain should be with the wounded. If any of his men had taken a crossbow bolt to the shin he would have left them to heal. But he held himself to stricter standards. It hurt, of course. And maybe it would turn to gangrene.

That didn't matter. The prince mattered. Bringing back the prince to finish the ceremony would save his homeland.

His tiger-striped horse kept its pace through the sloshing water. The mid-morning sun came through the trees, illuminating small glinting fish that fled from his horse's wake.

He found the remains of the tortoise bobbing in the water. A broken shell still clinging to some bloody limbs. Flies everywhere. Some of the small fish crowding about for a nibble. Its wounds appeared to be tears and bites from some enormous beast.

He had not yet made sense of the corpse when he heard a horn sounded from nearby. One of his party had found the boy.

He turned his horse towards the sound and pushed it even harder.

It was not far to the silver tree, its magnificent brightness standing it out from the other plants of the mangrove. This forest was known for having a few peredexion trees, but Hurdain had never seen one and was struck by how silver it really was.

The boy sat in the tree, eating a peredexion fruit. At the foot of the tree lay a dead monster. A huge red lizard.

Nearby one of Hurdain's riders sat on his own tiger-striped horse. His horn was lowered and his eyes flicked between the dead dragon and the boy.

"I won't go back", said the boy.

Hurdain shook his head. He had lured a dragon into the shadow of a peredexion tree? That was... incredible. It was auspicious. The prince had outwitted a dragon? Incredibly, spectacularly, good luck. Dynasties had been founded on less. Certainly far more than the luck of the planned sacrifice. More than a lifetime of auspicious acts.

Hurdain felt himself smiling. His homeland was saved, not by his hand but by the child's.

"You don't have to. You have done enough for the kingdom," said Hurdain, smiling at the dead dragon. "More than enough. More than anyone."

"I won't come with you," said the boy. "I don't trust you."

"Understandable," replied Hurdain. "But please take my rations," he hooked the belt of his rationbag on a root of the sagging peredexion, "and may fortune smile upon you."

He beckoned to his comrade. With considerable effort, and not a few burns from its caustic scales, they took the monster's head. Then, bowing farewell, they left the prince to make his own life.

L eft on his own in the silver tree, Boy's mind wandered, for some reason, back to the demon Runjknau he had battled in his game all that time ago. He remembered the demon's imagined words, its offer to make the world a place of chance and chaos. He remembered how, at the time, he had been unsure which was worse: a world where fate could be controlled through ceremony or one where it could not.

In a flash of insight he saw that there was a third possibility far worse than either. A world of actual random chance, but one where people *believed* it was all in their power, so berated themselves for every misstep, wracked themselves with guilt over every natural disaster and offered up their lives for no purpose.

If bad things kept happening in the kingdom, they would blame Boy and come looking for him again. So he decided he had better move on.

About the Author

Ben Lang is a fantasy and myth obsessive who loves monsters, adventures and exotic lands. His stories aim to include an awesome setting, a great monster and an emotive plot. He lives in Nottingham, UK at the sufferance of Megan who tolerates his over-consumption of tea and eternal state of foggy optimism.

Thanks for reading, good luck outwitting any monsters that find you.

FEATHER GREEN

JENNIFER KROPF

PART 1

DANGERS OF THE FOREST

The first time Estheryn Peretz set foot in the Murmuring Forest, she'd been handed a bow carved by her father and a quiver of arrows with soft emerald feathers. When she'd asked why the feathers were so green, her father had responded, "They're from a special bird of this forest; one whose spirit will teach your hands to be steady and train your eyes to spot a target."

Estheryn sensed the forest's energy below her toes, felt the whispers of the forest's breath in her hair. She giggled, and in return the Murmuring Forest ruffled its leaves in affection for the little girl of olive skin and auburn hair who raced through its wild grasses with bare feet.

When Greecia—the kingdom of the North—locked their borders and refused to trade with Persianna, Estheryn's father brought her to the forest often. "Father," she said one sunkissed morning. "Will you teach me how to avoid the deadly hands of the bitter trees, and the rippling soils that swallow travellers whole? And will you show me how to make a remedy for a bite from the poison glow bugs living beneath the roots?" she asked.

Her father smiled as he fastened the last of the green feathers onto a new batch of arrows. "How about I teach you the magic tune to whistle to draw down the birds? And how to hold her hand so they'll donate their feathers and sing you a blessing of safety? And how about I teach you wise sermons from the old scriptures of the Adriel God whom we serve, along with verses, prayers, and hymns? You must not always live in fear, Estheryn. Sometimes it's alright to forget the dangers and study the good things, instead."

Estheryn was only twelve years old the day she spotted a dozen royal Persianna horses in the brush, and crept closer to listen to the voices of the men atop them.

These men were polished and rich. Growing up in a family of butchers in a coastal village far from the kingdom's capital, Estheryn had never seen men like these.

"It's tradition, Xerxes. You must kill a stag of the Murmuring Forest if you want to impress the court, and your future wife. It's perfectly safe to hunt with the guards here. My men won't let you drown in the rippling soils." The voice was dark and raspy, like ash.

"I don't want to impress anyone, Father. Especially that Greecia girl you're forcing me to unite with."

Estheryn halted her steps when she saw the boy who spoke— tanned skin, hair black as onyx, eyes green like the moss between her toes. "I won't marry that girl. I'm thirteen years old. I won't marry *anyone*," he added.

The threads of his jacket glimmered with magic—it was as though they moved all on their own without needing sunlight. It was so perplexing, Estheryn didn't notice her father approaching. She didn't realize he was behind her until his hand came around and cupped her mouth.

"Silence, Daughter," he whispered against her ear. "You're eavesdropping on the Shah of Persianna. Back away. Watch your step."

Estheryn's eyes rounded. The *king*?

"Do you think your brutality to the villagers intimidates me, Father?" the boy on the horse spoke again.

"Xerxes, you will do what I command. And keep your voice down! We vowed to keep your union with Greecia a secret until the treaty has been signed. You're going to ruin the alliance with your complaints."

The argument went on as Estheryn's father pulled her away, but she stole one last look at the boy wearing magic threads and at the coronet atop his dark hair. But the glance cost her, and she snapped a twig below her heel.

"Who goes there?"

Estheryn felt her father flinch, and she was shoved into the forest.

She caught herself against a rock as her father eased through the purple maple brush toward the horses. "It is I." His voice was tense. "I apologize. I was passing by and—"

"You were eavesdropping," the ashy voice said. Estheryn could barely make out the face of the man through all the foliage, but she held her breath at the sight of the wreath of golden spears around the king's head.

"Please, I was just—"

"Kill him. He's heard our secrets." The king's command pierced Estheryn's chest like a cold blade. She sprang forward but the snap of a bowstring sounded, and her heels skidded to a halt before the purple shrubs.

Something slammed into the forest floor.

She couldn't breathe.

Ducking to see through the leaves, Estheryn saw her father on his back, craning his neck in her direction. Though a silver arrow protruded from his chest, he caught her eye and gave her a look; one with a simple message: *Run.*

"Shall we interrogate him to see what he knows? Perhaps he's a Greecian spy?" one of the men said.

"First we ought to split up and see if there are others."

Estheryn didn't wait to watch which directions the men would go. She sprinted back the way she had come, leaping over tree roots and swinging from branches. The arrows rattled in the quiver at her back, their green feathers brushing her hair.

With a pounding chest and an aching spirit, she rounded a trunk as the thundering of horse hooves reached her ears. She glanced back to see if she was followed.

An arm swung around her waist and tore her from the air.

Estheryn was thrust back against the trunk and pinned by a body —a boy. A boy with onyx hair, a golden coronet, and magic threads. She tore the silk headband from her hair and covered the top half of her face with it.

Through the thin fabric, she could see the boy's green eyes swimming as they took her in—her tousled hair, her trembling lips, the mask she'd pulled over half her face. "Spy," he whispered, though Estheryn couldn't imagine why he didn't shout it.

"I'm not a spy," she promised, wincing at the quiver crushing against her back. "I'm a hunter. And a—*forest expert.*"

The boy looked doubtful. "And I'm a prince. But neither one of us can save you after what you overheard." His gaze darted to the half-dozen arrows with bright feathers peeking over her shoulder.

Tears sprang into Estheryn's eyes. Though her capture meant she was facing imprisonment at best, all she could see in her mind's eye was her father lying on that bed of moss. The men on horses had spoken of an interrogation, but Estheryn had shot enough animals to know the silver arrow had gone into her father's body where it mattered. Her father was already dead.

Something flickered in the boy's eyes when a glittering tear slipped from beneath Estheryn's mask and dripped off her jaw. It landed on his magic-threaded sleeve. "Tell me your name," he demanded, eyeing the spill.

She could not tell him. He might track her down if she did.

"Aleah," she lied.

"Your *full* name, Peasant."

Estheryn swallowed. "Aleah Mizrahi."

"And you're a *forest expert?*" That look of doubt returned, but Estheryn nodded.

The prince removed his hold on her and pulled himself back from the tree. His brows tugged together, his coronet slightly off tilt from their collision. "My father will kill you if he finds you here. This forest is owned by the Persianna royal family for hunting. Get out of it, and don't set foot in it again."

The boy marched to the great brown mare waiting in a glow of sunlight. "And if you ever tell a soul that I saw you, or that we spoke, or if I ever hear that you've come back here, Aleah Mizrahi, I'll find you, and I will kill you myself."

The numbness left Estheryn's fingertips. She took off into the trees, leaving the Prince of Persianna behind, along with his murderous father, and the body of the father she would never see again.

Turn left, a voice in her mind made her jump. She caught a branch and used it to make a new course.

Shouts emerged from her right; the grunts of horses and the stomping of hooves filled the forest where she would have been caught if she hadn't turned. She spun to search for the owner of the voice, but she saw no one.

"There! Someone is escaping!" a man called from the bushes.

Estheryn crossed a vine bridge and leapt to scale an orange-rock cliffside. She had just broken into a run through the lush tongue-blossoms when the voice spoke again.

Go right.

She tore right and scurried up a hill as the sounds of shrieks reverberated through the trees. The moment she set foot on a patch of stone, the soil of the hill she'd climbed began to melt, streaming down like liquid chocolate and tumbling over the forest floor. Estheryn gasped. She'd seen the edges of the soils ripple before, but she had never seen them come alive.

Trees began tipping inward, collapsing into walls of branches and capturing the men on the horses as they appeared. Birds spiralled down from the skies: emerald, violet, and cerulean creatures with a shouting birdsong in their beaks. The horses sank in the soil; the men in royal leathers started to scream.

Large stones rolled from the hills, crushing grass and branches as they neared the sinking group.

Estheryn's gaze fired to a boy in the distance who had been split off from the others. He fell against a thick root, which tore his magic jacket. The root coiled at his ankle and dragged him against a tree to pin him there.

Save him, the new voice told Estheryn.

"Who are you?" she breathed, searching the skies, and rocks, the woods. "Are you the forest? Have you learned to speak?"

I am the creator of the forest. The Adriel God, whom your father knew.

She turned back toward the Prince of Persianna who was being squeezed by the winding root. The surrounding trees began to stir. It was an impossible shot for most—much too far away.

You must save him, the voice said again.

The hand of a slender tree came down to crush the boy where he was trapped, stretching its spindly fingers to pierce through flesh, and in the next heartbeat, Estheryn had drawn an arrow and let it fly.

Green feathers ruffled as the arrow spiralled through leaf and wind, soared past branches and chaos, plunged by horses and terror, and pierced the root gripping the prince's throat.

The root fell limp. The prince gasped and rolled away as the slender tree's hand stabbed where he had just been. The boy stared with wide eyes as the bony branch tried to pull its hand back, but found itself stuck in the bark.

Estheryn watched the prince's gaze fall on the arrow where the delicate green feathers blew in the wind. He plucked a single feather and held it before his face.

She didn't wait to see what he did with it. She sprinted over the rocks on bare toes.

PART 2

VOICES OF THE FOREST

E stheryn didn't go home. She couldn't face her mother after what had happened to her father. She didn't know how to convey such dreadful things out loud.

She wandered the streets of the coastal villages for many hours, ignoring the merchants. She forgot where she was going as she put one foot in front of the other.

Estheryn only realized it had started to rain when a man hollered from his fence and asked if she was alright. She realized her hair was drenched, her feet were caked with mud, and her heart was as gray as the Salt Sea off the cliffs.

"Adriel God," she whispered as she drifted toward the cliff's sharp edge. Her watery gaze wandered the cliff's slope, down to the pointed rocks below, down into the dark depths of the sea where she imagined herself sinking if she were to jump. "I have served you and studied your scriptures since I could read." Slightly closer to that edge, she tilted. "So why has this bad thing happened?"

Silence.

The Salt Sea sang a coaxing lullaby, inviting her to swim. But she had to tell her mother the dreadful news. She had to be there to hold her mother when the tears began to roll down the frail woman's cheeks.

And so, she went home after all.

The closed-casket funeral was short and not attended by many.

"What happened?" Mordecai whispered to Estheryn as the priest spoke his final words. "There was an arrow in your father's chest. I took it out and hid it before the rest of the boys came to help me fetch the body, but I saw it, Estheryn. Who shot my uncle?"

"I cannot say, Cousin." Estheryn swallowed, hearing the king's ashy voice in her mind again, and again.

Kill him. Kill him. Kill him.

Mordecai's jaw hardened. He stood up straight to listen. Even though she and Mordecai had been apart for the last two years, Estheryn was relieved he had come home from his studies with the priest-sages to stand by her side for her father's funeral.

She wished she could tell him everything, but Prince Xerxes's threat lingered in her ears—that she could not tell a soul, lest he come to find her and kill her for it. Even though she'd given the prince a false name, she did not doubt his ability to track her down.

The village gossiped that her father had been killed by the angry trees of the Murmuring Forest, and Estheryn let them believe it.

Three years passed before it was announced to the villages that Xerxes, Prince of Persianna, would be wedded to Vashti—a well-loved Greecian princess. The very secret her father had been killed for, was now set free across all of Persianna.

Estheryn tried to forget about the forest, but she heard it in her sleep: the whispers in the branches, the trees cracking their spines, the flutters of birdwings, the songs of the wind in the purple leaves. She heard the snap of a bowstring, and the glide of a silver arrow. She heard a body thumping to the forest floor.

The voice of ash lingered in her ears all the while.

Estheryn chiselled new arrows and tightened the string on her bow one evening, before heading home from the cliffs to practice her shots behind their village house. Her mother was off trying to find someone generous enough to donate food now that their butchers business had gone belly up.

Without being allowed to go into the forest, Estheryn couldn't hunt. And without meat, they had nothing to trade. Nothing but a pile of useless, green-feathered arrows.

As she fired her shots, she winced at the circle of chalk she'd drawn on the barrel at the end of the yard. Her aim was getting sloppy. She needed real prey. She needed the forest.

There were parades and dancers and feasts all throughout the kingdom on the day the Persianna prince was wed. Gossip surged through the cities and villages; it was all Estheryn heard about for weeks afterward. She imagined the prince in the jacket with magic threads, far too young to be married off, waiting at the end of an aisle for a beautiful Greecian girl in white; a girl he did not want to marry. The constant chatter of the prince was a gong being struck in her head, reminding her of that horrid day. The day her father had been stolen, the day her forest had been stolen. The day that had ruined her life and taken food off her mother's table.

One month later, she couldn't stand to be away anymore.

Estheryn dared a visit to the forest. Her nerves buzzed, her palms grew warm. If she was quiet and quick, no one would have to know she had been there.

A new sign hung on the Murmuring Forest's outermost tree. It had the royal Persianna seal upon it and a strict warning that all peasants must keep out.

Estheryn crept in slowly, worried the forest might not remember her after all this time. She knocked against a trunk to ask permission to enter.

When a sugar-scented breeze lifted her hair in greeting, she rushed in; a smile cracking her face. The birds circled overhead, casting reflections off their emerald and grape feathers and sending scatters of coloured, prismed light into the shadows of the forest like drops of glowing honey-gems.

She raced and climbed and hunted and sang. Estheryn spent the evening watching the sky melt into the orange cliffs and waited until diamond stars twinkled overhead.

She carried a large hare on her shoulder when she left, its blood leaking into her clothes. She could hardly wait to see the look that would appear on her mother's face when—

Estheryn staggered to a stop on the road.

The porch candles were lit. They flickered in the night breeze and turned the faces of the half-dozen guardsmen at the door to liquid gold. Amidst the group, her mother cried, her arms held tight by a pair in royal leathers—the same outfits worn by the group in the Murmuring Forest with the king all those years ago.

Estheryn dropped the hare and lifted an arrow from her quiver. She had no fabric to mask her face now, only the midnight shadows.

"Don't!" her mother cried from the porch when she saw, turning the attention of the guards. And so, Estheryn held her finger on the arrow. "Find your cousin! Don't come back here!" But Estheryn kept her stance, weapon pointed, breath held, even as the guards drew their swords at the sight of her. She watched down the line of her arrow as the men pulled her mother from the porch and forced her into a carriage.

Estheryn was still in that same position when the guards put their weapons away, climbed into the carriage, and drove it up the hill where it disappeared over the other side.

She tossed her bow to the ground and raced for the porch stairs, eyeing the fluttering notice that had been pegged to her front door.

The owner of this house has been caught stealing from the market.
By Persianna law, thieves shall be tried, and their belongings
confiscated by the Crown.

Tears stung Estheryn's eyes.

Her mother? Stealing?

Estheryn thought back to the countless nights of an empty table and a hungry belly. She thought of those rare occasions where her mother had shown up at home with a satchel of grain or a basket of pink apples.

Estheryn's chest filled with rage. She turned and faced the night, listening to the distant roar of the Salt Sea as it crashed against the cliffside. The moonlight painted her silver.

"Find your cousin," her mother had said.

But Estheryn wanted to do a wicked thing. And maybe after, Mordecai and his priest allies could grant her forgiveness for it.

PART 3

SCREAMS OF THE FOREST

The capital of Persianna was a buzzing hive of scarlet ribbons, sapphire cloaks, and shimmering translucent scarves. Bronze bracelets clapped together on women's wrists, and metallic shawl-fringes added to the music. Yellow and violet powders fired into the sky from rooftops, blanketing the streets in a chalky haze. Somewhere within these colours and noises, her mother was imprisoned.

Estheryn tugged the hood of her cloak further over her eyes, slipping through the crowded streets on light toes. The quiver and bow at her back gave her a hunchback look beneath the fabric, and people avoided eye contact, likely assuming her to be a cripple.

She waded through the bodies, searching for a street sign for the monastery where her cousin worked during the day. She wondered what she might say to Mordecai when she saw him, how she might explain all that had happened.

When she finally found the duo of monastery buildings—wide and pale and not spectacular in the slightest—Estheryn moved on past them. She marked the turns of the streets so she would remember which way to run once she did her terrible thing, and she weaved through the winding paths toward the glittering palace in the distance. She hummed an old tune her father used to sing about a river of life coming down from heaven, and she silently prayed for a miracle to find her mother, wherever she was.

With all the crowds and merchants, it took Estheryn until late afternoon before she reached the palace gate. And there, tucked beneath the shade of a wide fig tree hidden from the main street, she waited.

T he morning came with the sound of clanking horse hooves, and Estheryn rubbed her eyes, wincing at the dust. She scrambled behind the fig tree when she saw the royal carriages leaving the palace gates, surrounded by dozens of men on horses with their weapons drawn. Gilded statues balanced atop the carriage roofs, visions of the royal family.

She spotted the Prince of Persianna first—the curtains of his oval window were open, and he stared out at the people who rushed to flock the street sides as they passed. Prince Xerxes looked different than when Estheryn had crossed him in the Murmuring Forest all those years ago. He wore a white imperial jacket now with no magic threads. His jaw was solid, his gaze pointed, his expression—unpleasant.

Estheryn drew her bow and slipped an arrow from her quiver. The green feathers brushed her cheekbone as she pulled the bowstring tight, arrow sliding back over the notch. She was as silent as the soil, as still as the rocks, and as watchful as the forest trees— just like her father had taught her. She could almost hear the murmuring of the leaves, and the whispers of the wind as though she was back in her forest, not in this sparkling capital city.

But she did not take aim at the prince that had left her with a threat. Estheryn took aim at the carriage that followed—the one glowing with glass spindles and wide, copper wheels. She took in a long breath and let it out gently.

But a voice filled her head: *Be still.*

Estheryn nearly choked as she tightened the grip on her arrow and let out an ancient Persianna curse.

A carriage of guards swept in behind the king's carriage, blocking off her line of sight. Estheryn stood, shoving her bow away, her gaze hopping from face to face in the street to see who it was that had spotted her and told her to *be still*. But she had a feeling no Persianna citizen was responsible.

"Adriel God," she whispered a moment later. "Am I not your servant?" she asked.

Silence.

So, she went on. "Have I not learned your scriptures? Am I not an Adriel?" She swallowed and flitted into the street to follow the carriages, tugging her hood back up as she did. "The answer is, *yes*," she muttered to the wind. "I am one of your people. So let me fulfill my purpose."

Estheryn followed the carriages to the edge of the city, gliding by bodies and buildings to keep the royal family in her line of sight. They trekked so far, she thought her legs might give out. The sun was halfway across the sky by the time the carriages slowed, but her feet came together when she realized where they were.

Beyond the hazy treeline, a great forest filled the valley with purple leaves. Orange cliffs peeked from the treetops, and emerald, cerulean, and violet birds floated along with the distant mist.

The Murmuring Forest was quiet. *Too* quiet. Something was different about the spirit of the woods and Estheryn discarded her boots. Sweat glittered on her brow as she scaled the glassy rocks and slipped from tree to tree.

She was rounding an orange wall of stone when an ashy voice caught her like a fishhook, "The Greecians want me to meet with them alone first. The rest of you stay here with Xerxes. Make sure he doesn't run off."

A series of chuckles followed. The prince's wasn't one of them.

Estheryn's heart thumped in her chest. She scurried around a patch of thistle weeds and ducked below a canopy of sleeping vines. She took in a heavy breath and placed her hand against the nearest trunk of a slender black tree. "Please," she begged the forest. "Help me do this."

The tree shifted and stretched its branches, a low yawn fluttering on the wind. But something else responded: *This is not the moment for which you were created.*

Estheryn shut her mouth, nostrils flared. "This *is* my purpose," she said back to her God.

She looked up at the dark tree that seemed to narrow two knot-eyes at her. Perhaps the tree agreed with its creator.

Estheryn huffed and ignored the warning, ripping her bow from her shoulder and drawing an arrow. She padded over the moss and brushed past a purple maple bush as she came to a clearing, stepping out into a beam of sunlight breaking through the mist, arrow ready.

The King of Persianna strutted into the clearing. He'd been moving quickly but he halted when he noticed her. His eyes widened —green eyes that matched his son's. He opened his mouth to yell, but Estheryn cut him off, "Don't."

She yanked her hood off and returned to her ready stance.

The king studied her, then scowled as though realizing she was nothing more than a Persianna peasant. "Do you not know who I am? I'm the Shah. You'll be *hanged* for this," he promised.

"So be it."

Maybe Mordecai would pray for her soul once she was gone. "You murdered my father in these woods," a tear fattened at the corner of her eye, "Now I shall do the same to you, Shah."

The king's face was blank. Estheryn realized he didn't remember who her father was, and her jaw hardened. How many people had this king killed in this forest?

The king's hand inched toward his sword. Estheryn moved to fire, but her finger gripped the arrow and would not let go.

This is not the moment for which you were created.

What did that mean?

What other moment was there?

Suddenly, a flock of black arrows spiralled through the branches, speckling the clearing like porcupine quills. Estheryn redirected her aim and fired into the trees as four soldiers in Greecian leathers drifted from the shadows. Her arrow caught the shoulder of the closest one, lurching him backward off his feet. She spun to run, but halted.

The King of Persianna lay flat on the forest moss, four foreign arrows protruding from his chest.

It was a returned memory, with a different body.

She bolted into the Murmuring Forest. She swung from a branch and trampled over the brush until she spotted the group of Persianna men waiting on their horses a short distance away. "Run! The Greecians are coming!" she shouted, but they looked around in confusion. With an exasperated huff, Estheryn ripped her arrows from her quiver and mounted her bow. It would make her appear guilty, but it was the only way to get the men to move.

The first arrow she fired split through the edge of a trunk, sending wood chips exploding over the group.

Her next arrow captured the hat off a rider's head.

The third caught a sword being drawn and tore it from the wielder's hand.

And the last one she saved for the prince. Estheryn swallowed as the group panicked and shuffled, drawing their weapons and retreating back to the carriages at the edge of the forest. She aimed for Prince Xerxes's saddlebag, praying to the Adriel God that she wouldn't pierce the horse. It was her last arrow—the last one with emerald feathers and the blessing of the birds that had donated them.

She let the arrow fly and tossed her bow to the ground. She watched the chaos over her shoulder as she left it all behind—the king's body, the young Prince of Persianna, the Murmuring Forest waking up.

But a fresh Persianna curse slipped from her lips when she realized the prince had not tried to escape.

Prince Xerxes's horse screeched and staggered. He slid off the creature's back and ripped the arrow from his saddlebag, while his men shouted at him to follow. The prince stared at the wood spindle with three emerald feathers. His horse trotted off after the men, but the prince still remained, blinking at the feathers. Slowly, he plucked one from the arrow.

Estheryn padded over on bare toes, snatching half a broken arrow from the moss as she did. Her arm came around the prince's body, the arrow tip pressing against his throat. She felt him flex in her grip, felt him hold his breath.

"*Forest expert*," he guessed, a cautious and unexpected greeting. Prince Xerxes tilted his head, but her hood covered her face. "I see you disobeyed me and came back. You should be killed for attacking the Prince of Persianna with your arrows." His words were cold.

Estheryn pressed the arrow in harder, and he shut his mouth. "You watched my father die in this forest, Prince. Now I've watched yours die." Xerxes's moss-green eyes widened, but Estheryn went on, "This is *my* forest. And it will kill you if I ask it to. So, get out of it. And don't allow your family to set foot in it again."

She stepped back, spinning to put her back to him as she left so he wouldn't catch a glimpse of her bright eyes.

"Aleah Mizrahi." Estheryn's ears filled with the sound of the prince's boots crunching twigs as he turned around. "If you've really killed my father, you'll die for it. I will find you," he swore.

She opened her mouth to deny it, to warn him of his own wife. But she closed it again. Maybe this prince deserved to be fooled. A smile tugged at the edge of Estheryn's mouth and she broke into a sprint. "Not in this forest, you won't."

Deep in the purple maples of the Murmuring Forest, Estheryn waited for the moment for which she was created, praying for her mother, and sending messages to the priest sages. She crept to the city's edge to watch from the branches as the Adriel people grew hated in Persianna, persecuted for their faith. She watched corruption grow, and as time went on, she felt that moment drawing nearer and nearer.

She could only pray that her purpose had nothing to do with Xerxes, King of Persianna.

When she was brave enough, Esteryn decided she would find Mordecai, and aid the priest sages in their work to help the Adriel people stand against the Persianna corruption. But until then, Estheryn Peretz would sing with the wind, eat from the forest, race through the grasses, and drink the dew from the purple maple leaves. For, sometimes you must not live in fear. Sometimes it's alright to forget the dangers and study the good things instead.

AUTHOR'S NOTE

Sign up for Jennifer Kropf's emails to learn about her upcoming books, including a historical fantasy retelling of Queen Esther from the Hebrew Bible featuring Estheryn and King Xerxes. Discover what happens when the Adriel God calls Estheryn back—back to her true destiny, back to the capitol, and back before the Persianna prince she hoped she would never see again.

Email signup: http://www.JenniferKropf.com

ABOUT THE AUTHOR

Jennifer Kropf is the author of *The Winter Souls Series* and was a finalist for the *Indie Fantasy Book of the Year* award with Caffeinated Fantasy in 2020. She lives amidst lush Canadian farmland with her husband and three kids, and writes Christmas themed fantasy stories meant to inspire family traditions in households at Christmas time.

She is the founder of Winter Publishing House, and always loved The Chronicles of Narnia by C. S. Lewis growing up.

Learn more about Jennifer here: https://linktr.ee/JenniferKropf

Apple and the Dead Forest

Xander Cross

Píngguǒ hé Sǐ Sēnlín
平果和死森林
Apple and the Dead Forest

Every story begins inside the heart of another story.

E veryone was gathering in the central building of the tulou to keep warm. The merciless wind howled outside the round, mud-brick fortress and whistled through its narrow streets. Píngguǒ wrapped the ragged, old blanket tighter around his arms like a cloak and slipped inside the dark room, already filled to capacity.

The scrawny boy dodged hips and elbows to creep close to the center, pressing his blanket to his nose to filter the smells of people who had not bathed in a long time. There was little clean water to do so between the ground pollution and continual droughts. Every drop had to be filtered through a five-step process. Water was far too precious to squander on vanity.

"And that day, fire lit up the sky!" the ancient storyteller said, bony arms flung wide. A baby cried in the silence that ensued her proclamation. The mother jostled the child up and down, shushing it with intermittent success.

Píngguǒ remembered when the night had turned to day. It had been the Year of the Fire Dragon when the lights went out and never came back on. The Carrington Event of 2156 occurred just over two years prior, during the Lunar New Year when he was a little kid. Píngguǒ was older now, thirteen, although no less awkward.

The entire city had howled louder than the wind. His father and mother got him and his older sister out, but it was a near thing. Father died saving them from a group of men, or so the family presumed. He never saw his bàba again after he told them to run. When the sun set, the sky remained stained with blood, and for two days, the night was morning bright.

"The finger of the sun proclaimed the Age of Dragons is over," the storyteller continued. "The reign of darkness is nearly complete."

It certainly felt that way. The smog was heavy at times and made it difficult to breathe. Sandstorms still hailed out of the great western desert, and ice winds laden with dirty snow swept down from Northern Mongolia. After years of extreme flooding, which had claimed most of the low-lying areas, the polarity shifted. No rain had fallen since Píngguǒ could remember. Months? Over a year now? It seemed like forever.

"Hi, Píngguǒ," Lǐ Lín whispered.

He ducked around legs and crawled along the floor until he reached Lín's side. Lín was pretty, even with soot smudged across her nose and cheeks. Píngguǒ really liked her, but she only thought of him as a friend. That hurt, but Píngguǒ understood. She was a year older, and he was nobody special. Not many people liked him, so he accepted the situation for what it was simply to be close to her.

Still, he dreamed of what it might be like to kiss Lín. He never cared about that sort of thing before he met her, but after, it was all he could think about. Sadly, Píngguǒ knew it was a lost cause. Lín liked Min, of course, their other friend, who was already sitting beside her.

Wáng Min was the kind of boy everyone liked: tall, athletic, and muscled despite the lack of nourishment. Min pulled his long hair into a ponytail, the bit of scruff on his chin and upper lip giving him a manly air. At the ripe old age of fifteen going on sixteen, Min was handsome. All the girls liked him, and the women doted on him, too. He always helped out, was good at hunting and gathering firewood, *and* he could fight.

Píngguǒ was none of these things.

Píngguǒ's real name was Zheng Ping, but no one ever called him that, not even his mother. To her, he was just "érzi," meaning 'son,' and his sister called him "dìdi," or little brother. When they made it to the tulou, he hadn't shed the weight from his city life yet. The other kids started calling him "Apple," and the elders took it up, too. The humiliating name stuck, and so whether or not he was thin, he was still Píngguǒ.

Sometimes he was jealous of Min. But Min had been the first to be kind to Píngguǒ when the other boys bullied him. After that, Min let Píngguǒ follow him around without chasing him off. Min was so heroic and likable that Píngguǒ felt lucky to be near the older boy.

"Hey, Píngguǒ." Min grunted.

"Nǐ hǎo!" he greeted back.

An annoyed adult shushed them, and Píngguǒ remembered there was a story in progress. He quieted, becoming overheated in the mass press of Hakka and refugees. He pulled off his blanket and crushed it between his sweaty palms.

"The dragons are no more and all the demons roam free, but that is not the worst! On the other side of the shadows, the great old ones are stirring, and their minions with them! Woe betide us, for we dwell in the Age of Suffering. Without the dragons to protect the light, nothing can stop the dread evil from coming to devour us all!"

A dramatic pause followed, with only the gurgling of the comforted baby and a few muffled adult coughs in the ensuing silence.

"But there is still hope. They say one dragon yet lives," the old woman whispered.

Everyone leaned in.

"Hiding deep in the mountains to protect the last seed vault, awaits Lord Bái for the day a brave soul will come to distribute the seeds to the world and make it live and grow once more. A loving soul with the heart of a phoenix! And in flame, this young prince shall be reborn to protect the realm of light."

"Do you think any of that's true?" Píngguǒ asked later when they shuffled out with everyone else. The streets inside the tulou were narrow, with its many residences crowded together. The structure was a miniature fortress in the round, built by the Hakka people on the shores and mountains of Fujian. Amidst Climate Upheaval following the Carrington, the tulous had become a sanctuary for any human who abided by the rules of the communal Hakka.

"Real dragons?" Min scoffed. "Have you ever heard of such a thing?"

"I dunno," Lín said. "The dinosaurs were real, right? There's bones to prove it."

"Dinosaurs are dinosaurs. They are *not* dragons," Min affirmed.

Píngguǒ didn't know anything about dragons, but he had seen a demon once, although he knew better than to say so. He did not want to be made fun of or defend what he knew was the truth to his friends.

"Not that dragon stuff, the seed vault," Píngguǒ clarified.

"Here's where we split," Min said. The crowd had thinned out considerably by then, leaving the three teenagers almost alone in the street. "Unless, you need an escort?"

"No!" Píngguǒ said a shade too quick. "I'll be okay. Hurry on before Lín's dad gets mad."

Min nodded, his expression stiff and serious. "All right. See you tomorrow."

"Zàijiàn!" Lín waved over her shoulder.

"See you later," Píngguǒ said, his tone mournful.

Píngguǒ watched them leave, wanting to call them back, that he'd changed his mind. A pit of fear lodged in Píngguǒ's stomach as he turned and walked to the small room that housed him, his sister, and their mother. Trudging back alone was always daunting in the narrow confines of the tulou. The roofs of the circular buildings overhung the dark streets, making almost a turtle shell to protect the village. One could run from rooftop to rooftop if they wished, but Píngguǒ was too afraid of slipping and falling to try. It looked like fun, though, and Píngguǒ dreamed of working up the courage.

The problem was, that's where *they* waited for him.

On cue, something cold, hard, and wet slapped his face. He touched his stinging cheek, his fingers wet with mud and ice. Jeering laughter filled the night air. "Hey! Useless rich boy, you like food? You look hungry, Apple. Eat *this*!"

Another mud cake thudded down.

Píngguǒ dodged it. The dark ooze splattered on the packed earth, this time smelling of dung. Píngguǒ ran, the echo of feet running across the rooftop, giving chase. His door was down a dark, dead end alley, and he'd been laid out on the ground there before on nights he wasn't quick enough. The alley door was just ahead, if he could make it...

His heart pounded, the cold air searing his lungs with blazing pain, the mist coming so fast from his mouth that it obscured his vision. He heard shouting, but never turned to look. Then a hand clamped down on his shoulder before he could open the door, just within reach. Píngguǒ jumped, waiting to feel the accustomed blows. He was prepared to hit the ground and curl up to protect himself around his blanket to keep them from destroying it. It was the only cover he had left, and without it, he would freeze to death.

"Steady, boy," an elder's voice said. "I'm not taking the hide out of you." By his manner of speech, it was one of the Hakka. "They're gone."

"Thank y-you, m-mister..." Píngguŏ could not tell if he was shivering from the cold or the adrenaline.

"No need to thank me. Some lads just got the mean in them. Already too many mean people in the world. Don't end up like them, and that'll be thanks enough."

Píngguŏ nodded and went inside, climbing the narrow stairs to their tiny, two-room apartment on the third floor. He found his sister preparing to go out.

"Where were you?" his jiĕjiĕ asked, pulling on her sweater. "You know I have to go." To qualify for their meager portion of rice and eggs, Mai did weaving and other communal chores by day. At night, she made rounds to the elderly, reading, sewing and other small tasks. There was no such thing as currency any longer, only service.

"There was a story in the public house. Is mom better?"

"Of course not. She isn't going to get better, either. Best for all of us if she just dies in her sleep," his sister whispered. Mai didn't really mean it, but they were all tired and frustrated. Worse, Píngguŏ suspected Mai was right. Lots of people had fallen sick, and none of them were getting better, especially the older ones.

"Time was, people could collect herbs in the forest to make medicine and heal themselves," he said, the verbatim imitation of an elder he had heard lamenting about all the illness.

"There are no forests," Mai said. "None living, anyway, and there never will be again. The only things out there are demons and blight." His sister's eyes were haunted by their reality, and she looked older than she should, a real adult. She dipped a rag in a precious bit of water and wiped the dirt smearing his cheek. She didn't ask how it happened, and he was grateful. "Watch mom, all right?"

"I don't want you to go," Píngguŏ said.

"I know, but we need to eat. I made some rice. It's not much. I gave mom her share already, what she could get down." A knock on the door meant her friends were there to make their rounds together. Mai grabbed her coat and left.

Píngguǒ wished he could help. He had been raised with the notion that he was the man of the house now, but he seemed incapable of doing anything. It shamed him, and he felt as useless as the bullies said he was. His stomach gurgled. He was almost hungry enough to eat that mud.

His father had been a doctor, and so they lived better than others, though not so well as the top percent. Píngguǒ had not known what it was like to be truly hungry back then, the kind of hunger that ate a body from the inside out. Now that raw, burning sensation was a constant companion. The softness from a life of sitting and affording to eat had long melted away.

But I'm still not strong.

Píngguǒ ate his two spoonfuls of rice very sparingly. There was not much left, and the way they had to grow it was difficult at best. Soon there might not even be this much to eat, and what would the people do then? Píngguǒ was educated enough to know that without proper nourishment, they would all die.

"How did it get like this?" he asked his empty spoon. But he knew the answer. People had taken and taken until the earth had nothing left to give. He had seen the images of green forests that stretched forever, and although he had never laid eyes on them himself, he had traveled through parts of the Dead Forest when they fled the city, so he knew it had been true.

His mother moaned and he went to check on her. He gave her a little water, but she waved him away.

"Píngguǒ," she said, saying his name instead of calling him 'son.' She passed out, looking worse than he'd ever seen her. For the first time, she appeared...old.

Remembering his mother as she had been, Píngguǒ could stand it no longer. "Don't worry, mama. I'm going to fix you," he said with so much conviction, he knew he must make it happen or die trying.

But what can I do? I'm a nobody.

He remembered the story from earlier, and the seed silo in particular. Plants could be used to make medicine. Perhaps they could grow a cure.

I need to go talk to Min. Maybe he'll know what to do.

Scary as it was to go out on his own at night, it felt good to make a decision and act on it. He only hoped he would be back before Mai got home, or she'd scold him. It was early enough to risk it, so he tied his tattered blanket around his shoulders and snuck out.

Píngguǒ crept down to the alleyway exit. He closed the door quietly and turned to head out to the street when he heard voices. The group of teens was lingering near the mouth of the alley!

In near silence, lest even a scuff of his thin shoe alert them, Píngguǒ ducked back. His heart beat so hard that he could hear nothing else. His breath was misty and cold. He glanced around wildly, knowing the sound of the door would alert them. He wondered if he could hide among the buckets. It was no good. He would make too much noise. His eyes peered over and saw the ladder.

There was nothing for it, he would have to climb up to the roof.

For you, mama...

He managed to pull himself up and over when the boys walked past and moved down the street, joking amongst themselves. They never glanced up.

Píngguǒ clung to the tiles, too afraid to move. Shivering, he forced himself to stand. The view was almost beautiful, the hazy moonlight casting its wan glow across the black tiles. The outer ring wall and its balconies towered above him, while the squat, multistory buildings spread below.

With trepidation, he made his way along, trying not to slide off the high, steep, slippery slope. Little by little, however, he grew more confident, and made his way to Min's home. The hard part was climbing down to Min's balcony on the third floor.

His feet slid on the icy surface as his toes just barely touched the rail. For a moment, Píngguǒ thought he was going to die! After a moment of scuffling, his fingers aching, the door shuffled aside.

"Píngguǒ? What in the world—?" Then Min had his legs and helped him get down to the wooden planks.

"I know it's late, but I need to run something by you, and I don't think it can wait," Píngguǒ said in between pants, trying not to think about his near brush with death.

He peered past Min into a room as narrow and sparse as his own. Lín was sitting on a crude stool within, a red handprint staining her cheek. That meant her father was in a sour mood tonight. There was nothing any of them could do about it except give her shelter when it got bad. In the morning, it was like it never happened. No one acknowledged it and life went on.

"You okay, Lín?" Píngguǒ asked.

"Yeah," she whispered. "I wish I could get out of here, anywhere. But there's nowhere left to go, is there?"

"Maybe there is," Píngguǒ offered, and he launched into his absurd plan to leave the compound, travel across the mountains to find a seed silo without a proper map to guide them. By the time he was done, he realized how stupid it all sounded.

Min shook his head. "I know where it is, if I remember correctly. My father pointed out the mountain with the silo when I was younger than you. There's no way to know for sure that old vault still has anything worthwhile left in it," he said, the weight of his deeper voice giving him more conviction than Píngguǒ's higher, strained tones.

"But it *has* to," Píngguǒ said. "How else can we go on?"

Something troubled filled Min's eyes.

"What is it?" Píngguǒ asked.

"I shouldn't be talking about this, but the truth is, there's less food than anyone knows. The elders aren't letting on, but I know from working on bringing in the harvests. A lot did not make it, and the seeds, the few that matured, are poor. We're having more trouble finding any game, too."

Lín sat up straighter. "According to the aunties, if the spring does not come soon, and we can't start planting... if the rains don't fall again...I heard one tell another this morning that if it comes to that, they should kill the children in their sleep to keep them from the pain of starving to death."

Min swiped a hand through the long hair framing his face. A cold pit of fear lodged in Píngguǒ's stomach. That included him. And if they were willing to murder children?

"What about the people who are sick? Like my mother!"

"This sounds crazy, but maybe I *should* go after these fool's seeds," Min said, his lips pressed tight. "Any chance is better than none."

"You can't go alone, Min. What if you break a leg? Or get mauled by wild animals?" Lín asked.

"I'll take Píngguŏ."

"And what about me?" Lín asked, indignant.

"You can't come," Min said.

"If you say it's because I'm a girl..."

"Don't take this wrong, Lín, but you *are* a girl. It's not that you aren't strong or capable, I've seen you carry the water buckets on your harness."

"Then..."

"There's a lot of bad people out there, Lín. They'll hurt you."

"Think I don't know that! I've been hurt!" She touched her swollen cheek.

"They'll hurt you worse, and never stop until you're dead," Min said, staring into her defiant eyes.

"Girls know that better than boys," she snarled, fiercer than ever. "I can't stay here without you, Min. I'd rather go out and take my chances than stay another day under my father's roof. Besides, how are you going to carry all that seed back by yourself?"

Min sighed. "Then you gotta dress and act like a boy."

They all looked at her clothes, which were layers of mismatched garments from whatever could be salvaged. She had no shape under it, nothing about her that said male or female either way.

"We have to leave tonight," Min continued. "Sooner the better, before anyone knows what we're doing. The elders have known about that old silo for decades, but so far as they're concerned, it's just a thieves' den, and if there was seed, it's long gone. They'll stop us."

"We need supplies," Lín said.

Min nodded. "I can get what we need. You both wait here." And with that, he left.

Now Píngguŏ's doubts crept in. "What happens if we get out there and it's nothing? Or we can't find our way back?" he wondered aloud.

"Hey, it's your plan, right?" Lín kissed him on the cheek, the first he'd ever received from a girl who was not his relative. His skin tingled, the warmth remaining long after she set about making one of Min's blankets into a knapsack.

hirty minutes later, Min was back with a map and less food than they needed, for he had no wish to steal when the supply was so low. But there was no way they could subsist on the Dead Forest, either. He, too, had a makeshift pack on his back, filled with things required for venturing out into the wilderness.

Quietly, they slipped out into the night. Fortunately by this time, most of the residents were either asleep or preoccupied. No one stopped them as they made their way through the maze of dark streets. Píngguǒ felt a thrill of fear as Min lead them to a short, thick wooden door at the end of a narrow passage. It was unnerving to watch Min unlatch the protective barrier that kept the bad things out.

Darkness yawned before them, but when nothing rushed inside other than the wind, Min ducked his head and stepped beyond the tulou's safety, followed by Lín. Píngguǒ swallowed his fear and followed them.

The cold was far more intense without the round wall for a windbreak. Píngguǒ wanted to go back inside, where his flat bedroll no longer seemed so hard and frigid. The only sounds were the wind and the creaking branches of the dead sentinels who watched their passage with blind eyes.

Hours passed without a word spoken, the cluster of squat, round dwellings receding from view behind. The path atop the ridge was narrow and rocky, with darkness all around. Píngguǒ's toes turned painfully numb. He thought of his sister, surely home by now and furious with him, maybe worried, too. He envied her. Píngguǒ's calves burned, his thighs ached, and there were sharp pains in his shins. To top it off, the cold was lodged inside of him now.

Píngguǒ fought to be brave and said nothing of his discomfort, so as not to shame himself before the others. Neither Min nor Lín were complaining, after all. And although Min had taken the lead of their expedition, it had been Píngguǒ's idea to begin with, so he forced himself to be strong.

One foot in front of the other, he told himself, and concentrated on just that. The rocky earth underfoot hypnotized him, however, and he wobbled a few times, almost falling once if not for Min grabbing him by the scruff of his collar. It was only then that he realized the others had stopped to wait for him, and that he had passed by them without realizing it.

Min's face was clear. Dawn was upon them. As the sky lightened, Lín spotted a little rocky alcove for them to climb beneath. There, they huddled together, shivering in the cold, damp air.

"H-h-how l-long d-do you think it will take?" Lín asked in the middle of the two boys, her teeth chattering.

"At this pace? A couple days at least," Min observed, rubbing his arms to generate heat.

A yawning pit of despair opened in Píngguǒ's gut. How could they make it? The full reality of their situation descended over Píngguǒ's heart, crushing it inside his chest.

I'm not alone, he reminded himself. *My friends are here.* And that was part of the problem—he felt guilty, too. What if this was a stupid idea after all, and he went and stuck it in Min's head?

He said we were running out of food anyway, and Lín said that the elders might kill us in our sleep rather than let us starve. Isn't a chance —any chance—better?

Although they were huddled together under a tarp and two blankets, it was still cold. The earth emanated it and robbed the heat from their bodies along with the bite of the wind. Píngguǒ didn't think he could rest, but he blinked, and a second later, Min was shaking his shoulder.

"Píngguǒ, wake up already. Wow, you're a heavy sleeper."

Píngguǒ rubbed his eyes, yawning, blinking back tears at the bright grey white light.

"Come on, time's wasting," Min said. "We have to keep going."

Píngguǒ remembered where he was, and what they were doing. He got up to find it was much colder outside their makeshift nest.

"Do you think they'll send a search party for us?" Lín asked when they struck out again.

"Maybe once we don't show up for our duties. They might strike out a little ways, but they won't know which direction to go in," Min said. "There's no resources or energy to sustain a prolonged search. Even so, we shouldn't linger."

That sent a new flash of fear stabbing through Píngguǒ's heart. The idea of being caught and punished with nothing to show for it was too shameful for words. "How long have we been asleep?"

Min chuckled. "Don't worry, just a few hours. They have to discover we've all gone missing together to sort it out. Anyway, we need short bursts of rest, or we're not going to make it."

Píngguǒ understood, and he didn't complain when Min stopped to pass out bits of stale rice cake, either. The hard, crumbly meal woke up his stomach rather than alleviating his hunger, though. And if he felt stiff and sore before his nap, it was nothing compared to the pain in his legs and back now that he'd rested.

By the gloomy light of day, the uneven path atop the ridge was narrower than it seemed in the dark. To either side, the slopes were steep, worn to gravel and sand by erosion with the loss of plant life. Every step was treacherous and terrifying. It was enough to make his doubts lance through him all over again. Had he been alone, he would have turned back. But he wasn't alone. So, single-file, Píngguǒ brought up the rear behind Lín, and he wasn't going to desert her or Min. He was going to protect their backs no matter what.

Min gazed upward as a sudden gust of cold wind cut through their layers. "We need to make up for some time. Can you smell it?"

Píngguǒ sniffed the air. There was a sharp tang, the scent of cold and moisture with thick, oily smog.

"Snow," Lín said, concern constricting her voice. Ordinary snow from the olden days would have been bad enough. The snow that fell now was the color of ash, cloying and smelly.

"We have to move fast and hope it passes to the north," Min said, and by the tension in his tone, Píngguǒ could tell Min was worried.

An hour later, that concern proved justified when the first grey, fat flakes fell like cold ash from the leaden sky.

Píngguǒ had another fear as he wound his blanket around his face against the shrieking wind. The mountain path was sloping on the decline, and soon they would descend to the Dead Forest. There were lots of tales about the horrors that dwelled within that skeletal decay. Before they had found the tulou, his group of refugees was attacked by very real demons within it.

Min stopped, pulled out his map, and pointed. "We need to get to that mountain over there." And the way was through the Dead Forest, where ghosts surely haunted. Even the elders said so.

Píngguǒ gulped. "Do we have to?"

"There's no other way," Min affirmed.

When they reached the outskirts of the trees, a gruff, deep voice shouted, "Hey! You kids! What are you doing there?"

The three looked over to see a man in rags. Behind him, another emerged, then a third. A group of men could spell disaster.

"Run!" Min shouted.

"Hey, get back here!" one of the men yelled.

Píngguǒ did not know if the men were friends or foes, but he did not want to find out. Píngguǒ ran as fast as he could, adrenaline making him fleet of foot where before he could hardly keep up. He concentrated on Min's and Lín's backs, to the point he nearly ran up on Lín when they plunged headlong into a patch of dark, leafless thickets. The thin branches whipped and scratched his body, tearing his clothes.

Píngguǒ was more afraid than when the bullies chased him, for there was no one out here to stop somebody stronger from doing whatever they pleased with the weak. His heart thudded, lungs burning, but he did not stop.

Then, Min did.

The three leaned against the dead trees, breathing hard.

"They're not following," Min said.

Píngguǒ listened beyond his pounding heart. It was true. There was too much brush and debris not to make noise in a headlong chase.

"They might be afraid of something in here, or they know a

better path. Either way, we need to stop and figure out where we are."

"There's no sunlight or moss on the trees." Lín frowned.

Píngguǒ looked up. "That mountain over there, is that the one?"

Min's gaze followed Píngguǒ's outstretched arm. "Yeah. Good work. Looks like this path might be a shortcut."

"We should be quiet, in case someone-or-*thing* else is out here," Píngguǒ suggested, thinking of demons as well as men and feral dogs. He wasn't sure which he was more afraid of.

It was difficult to be quiet, though. Píngguǒ winced with each twig he broke, which was every other step. The more he tried, the worse it was. The deep, low-lying smog did not make it easier as it obscured the path ahead. And night was falling.

"I have to stop," Lín admitted. "I'm sorry."

Píngguǒ was glad she said it, because he was desperate for a rest. He'd almost fallen asleep walking.

"We've come pretty far," Min said. "We'll set up a lean-to with these old branches."

"Even dead, the forest takes care of us," Lín whispered, her voice ethereal in the deepening twilight. "I hope we can fix it, so everything can live again, and the animals return. That's why I came."

"I can't see anyone starve," Min said. "And time is running out. Planting season is upon us."

Píngguǒ hadn't considered why the others had come, only his own reasons. Although they were for his mother, he realized this was a selfish desire in a way. He also didn't want to be murdered in his sleep. While he resolved these were good reasons, it was not just for her or himself that he must see it through to the end. It had to be for everyone, or no one could be saved.

They gathered enough branches to lean against a leafless thicket until the night grew too dark to make anything out. Min spread the tarp on the ground and they crawled underneath. It was growing colder with the nightfall, but at least it was not snowing in the valley. They ate a little and drank sparingly. Their food was almost gone, and Píngguǒ wondered how they would make it back.

Píngguǒ awoke to grunting.

"I smells 'em, I do! Younglin's, all virgin, ripe, an' sweet," the brusque voice said, as if around a mouthful of grinding rocks.

Píngguǒ heard Lín's breathing change beside him. He was too scared to move. No one said anything.

"Can't see nuthin', yeh sure?" a rougher voice inquired.

"Yeah. And we best eat 'em quick! Soon the worst of our kind will rip across the veil! There'll be nothin' left for us when that happens."

It was an èmó, a demon! These were the big, scary kind, too, with tusks like boars and the horns of goats and oxen. Píngguǒ was terrified stiff. Worse, the monsters were stumbling through the dark toward them.

"How long, ya think? Before the Dark Lords break through?"

"Bah, not long. As soon as the last dragon dies. Any day now."

"Hope he lives long enough to let us have these little treats, and find out where they came from. Could be a proper store of humans to eat!"

So it was true! The storyteller had been right, and disguised as fantasy was the naked truth, too appalling to be believed. There was a dragon, and he was dying.

Heavy, flat feet approached, crunching through the brush without care. It was nearly on top of them when the èmó stopped. Lín squeezed his hand in the dark.

"Smell's strongest here." It breathed in deep. "One's a female. Soft, juicy meat!"

"Now!" Min yelled, jumping up and thrusting one of the branches into the èmó's throat.

Lín threw her force behind Min's. The creature fell back and gurgled, clutching at the thick stick lodged in it. The other beast roared, and the trio took off toward the mountain. Píngguǒ realized he could see somewhat, that the clouds were thin enough to allow moonlight.

The remaining èmó crashed through the woods behind them. "Ya slew m'uh older brother! I'll rip yeh limb from limb!"

Píngguǒ did not know where he found the energy, but he ran harder than he ever had in his life. It was like a nightmare he could not wake up from. His legs ached, his chest burned, but it did not matter. The thunderous crashing of the brush behind him was coming closer stride by stride!

Then a brilliant glow lit up the forest, blinding Píngguǒ. He stopped, confused. The èmó screamed, followed by an abrupt silence.

When Píngguǒ could see again, a pale demon stood in front of them. This one was different from the horned èmó, who lay dead and smoldering in the dirt. It was more serpent-like, with gold eyes, long, white hair, and narrow features tinged with snake scales.

"Is this what disturbs my Lord's sacred rest?" The demon sniffed in disdain.

"Your... Lord?" Min asked between breaths.

"Lord Bái," the snake demon said, as if they should know. "Come. Lord Bai has seen no humans in a long time. Maybe he will want to see you."

Píngguǒ was the first to follow, not Min or Lín. Píngguǒ looked back at where they stood and shrugged. "We're here. Isn't this where we were heading, why we left? Besides, didn't the storyteller say the dragon's name was Bái?"

The three followed the albino demon to a hidden door at the base of the mountain and down a long corridor into its secret heart. When they reached the central chamber, Lín gasped. When Píngguǒ saw why, his heart leapt to his throat, and the muscles at the backs of his knees turned to jelly. For there, not in a vault of gold, but a treasure far more precious, lay the last dragon.

Lord Bái was nearly a corpse, such a sad state the ancient creature was in. The white scales may once have been luminous as the moon, but they were a dingy pearl now, encrusted with dust. The beast's white mane hung lank, its long neck and flank scarred from many battles.

The sight of such suffering made Píngguǒ sad. He wanted to cry.

The dragon was as large as legend promised, its body coiled tight.

The huge head, the size of a small bus, roused, the most beautiful liquid blue eyes opening. A great sigh issued from the beast, warm and smelling of brimstone.

"Ah, at last." His was the weary voice of cracked honey, and like the rest of him, must have been beautiful and magnificent before its ruin. Like the earth itself.

The serpentine neck lifted, a cascade of dust raining down upon them. Min coughed, and Lín gave a polite "a-choo."

Poor Píngguǒ honked like a goose, the vault echoing his sneeze at an alarming volume. The demon glared at him, and even his friends were embarrassed on his behalf. He covered his nose, but it took a full minute for the violent storm to abate.

"Sorry!" He wheezed, falling to the floor in supplication, for dragons did not suffer fools, and Píngguǒ knew himself to be nothing else.

"Long have I waited for you," the dragon addressed them.

"How did you know we would come?" Min asked.

"Humans always come. Your species' tenacious need for survival made it inevitable. Others have come, too, of course, to loot or find thieves' shelter."

"Like the ogres!" Píngguǒ chirped, still on his knees.

The gigantic head nodded, but this time Píngguǒ smartly covered his face before the allergens fell.

"We have destroyed those whose hearts are impure." The great, blue eye fixed them. "Are *you* worthy of this treasure?"

The teenagers looked at one another, but it was Min who spoke. "We come from a tulou north of here. Things are bad. We're starving..."

"Everyone is starving, including my servant," the dragon said. "Three children would feed him well."

Píngguǒ glanced at the serpent demon and gulped.

"Please, sir, we mean no trouble," Lin begged. "There aren't many of us left, and Píngguǒ's mother is sick."

Píngguǒ found himself the sudden, unwanted center of attention. He cringed, his shoulders hunching to his ears.

"Is that true?" the dragon asked.

Píngguǒ nodded, trying to find his tongue. "Y-y-yes," he squeaked.

"What was that?" The huge head craned down, and now Píngguǒ was eye to eye with the dragon. If he hadn't been so dehydrated, he would surely have wet himself. He felt small, a tiny, insignificant thing barely worth eating, shaking from the effort of trying to stand.

"Yes, sir. I'm not here to loot. We just want the elders not to kill the kids to keep them from starving!" By the end, Píngguǒ was shouting. *This is why I really came*, and he knew it was true. "Please, sir, *please* let us have good seeds!" He bowed, shaking all the while.

"Well, then," the dragon said. "You have an excellent reason to be here." He called to the demon who had saved them. "Cheng, procure the human children water and rations. I dare say they'll die upon my floor, otherwise."

The white-haired demon bowed stiffly. "As you say, it will be done, Lord Bái." He went off without looking at them.

"So we can have the seeds?" Lín asked hopefully.

"We shall see," the dragon replied. "But first you eat and I will explain what comes next," he said with a tinge of sorrow.

Rations were brought to them in vacuum-sealed aluminum bags. The scent of meat and gravy were mouth watering, although by this point, Píngguǒ would have eaten poison. He ate as if he had never seen food before, not caring that his manners were so uncouth.

Min and Lín were not much better in the wake of famine and exhaustion.

All the while, Lord Bái spoke. "Darkness and Light were born together, eternal twins, dancing in harmony amid their rivalry. Sometimes this balance tips and must be corrected by the proper players, as is the case now. I could lay our recent grievance at the feet of so many sources, not the least of which mankind itself, who preferred impermanent and gaudy baubles to clean air and water.

"But in the end, it is we dragons who must bear the blame. We were charged to keep the balance between Light and Dark, no more or less, a divine task set by the gods. For our protection, we behaved as emperors over mankind and demonkind alike, and told ourselves it was not our place to meddle, though we were pleased to reap kingly rewards for our 'service.'"

"What happened?" Lín asked when the creature fell to silent rumination.

"Not so very long ago, one of our ancient order was felled by a younger, more ambitious dragon. We sought to bring this errant creature low, for we knew he sought to rule over us, and a dictatorship would prevail. But one of his own menagerie, a demon fox, did him in. Would that one of us had done the deed properly in battle, for that dragon would have replaced the vanquished one by right of fire, fang, and claw.

"Alas, a power vacuum was created, and each dragon sought the opportunity to claim the prize for themselves, the lordship of an entire megapolis. In the end, we destroyed one another in our greed and vanity. Only when the aurora lit up the sky with the bloody light of the Phoenix, and the electricity cut out, did I know the extent of our foolishness. Our world order collapsed within hours. We dragons had destroyed too many of our own kind, you see, and those of us who remained were weakened."

To prove it so, a glowing pearl appeared in Lord Bái's talons, casting the large room in an eerie light. "Once this was as brilliant as the sun, but now it is less than the moon," the dragon said. "We could not stop the destruction of the cities when the lower castes and the demons we once kept in check rose up. Some of them took the white fox's example and turned on their masters.

"Now I am the last and the denizens of the dark have grown bolder, their intrusions penetrating into our world every day. That is the nature of the dark, after all, and we were too close to becoming as they are to stop the inevitable turn of the tide. So, the perpetual gloom creeps in day by day. Only my presence keeps the Dark Lords from crossing over, but soon my light, too, shall fade from this world. I am dying."

"I am sorry for you, Lord Bái," Lín said, her voice soft with sadness.

"Do not be, little one. It is for you I fear. What will happen to the last of you when my own eternal night comes? Not much longer,

I think," the heavy head rested on the floor, eyelids lowering under the exhaustion of speaking so long. "No, not much longer now."

"No, you can't!" Min shouted. "You have to fight! We all have to fight!"

The dragon chuckled, a dry and raspy sound. "And fight you will, and I, too. But what is fated is inevitable. Everything's time comes to an end, even the lives of ancient dragons." Its reptilian lips drew back in a draconic smile. "Every Age must pass for a new one to be born."

A great rumble rent the earth and Píngguǒ was knocked off his feet.

The dragon, however, was not perturbed by this turn of events."Listen, and heed me," Lord Bái said when the quake ceased. "My time is nearly done. When the heart of the last dragon ceases to beat, the Lords of the Dark will cross the veil and seek to take this land. They are coming now. Can you feel it?"

Píngguǒ did. All the hair on his body was raised from it, goose-prickles standing out all over his skin. He wanted to run away from the creeping shadow, but there was nowhere to go, no hole deep or safe enough. He shivered, the rich food he'd just eaten turning over in his stomach.

Min and Lín looked at one another uneasily, but Píngguǒ nodded vigorously. "*I* do. It makes me want to be sick!"

The dragon scrutinized him and made a *hum* in his throat. "I see. Then perhaps you are the key."

"What? How?" Píngguǒ blurted.

"Begin by believing in yourself."

"How do I do that?"

"By doing what you know you can do. As you learn to trust yourself, you will gain strength and confidence. Know yourself, and don't let anyone define you. This is the only path to the light within."

The earth shook again, thunder rumbled. A shrieking cry pierced the sky, and Píngguǒ clamped his hands over his ears. The Dark had broken through.

"It is time," Lord Bái said with great dignity. He stood, and with a deep, rattling sigh, crawled out through the corridor like a snake from its hole, the demon attendant beside him.

Píngguǒ followed.

"What are you doing?" Lín asked.

"I have to," Píngguǒ answered, unable to explain. "Where is there to go anyway?"

Min shook his head, but together they left the silo. Outside, the sky turned blacker than Píngguǒ had ever seen it. The earth rumbled and jumped, and lightning arced as a black cloud rushed toward them, engulfing everything in its path. Píngguǒ would have run, no matter his brave words, except that he was frozen.

The dragon waited calmly, his pearl glowing white, and the cloud stopped short of them. Out of the roiling smoke stepped first one claw, then another, until another dragon, this one with obsidian scales emerged.

"Today you draw your last breath," the Lord of the Darkverse declared. "You cannot stop us this time."

"I am not here to stop you," Bái said, his voice deep and steady. "I am merely preparing the way. Meet me now in the old way if you wish. Face me with fire, fang, and claw."

Píngguǒ saw the dragon had no fear. He accepted his fate with majesty. The last dragon drew in a deep breath and took to the air, his sinuous body glowing as a cloud of dust and seed grit flew off. For a moment, Lord Bái was beautiful again.

The sleek, jet black monster met Lord Bái's challenge. The two serpentine creatures whorled around one another in a spiral that tightened until they grappled, hopelessly intertwined. The jewel of the white dragon's pearl glowed so bright that Píngguǒ could not see. It was indeed as blinding as the sun!

The dark beast screamed and shielded its eyes, the white going for the other's throat. For a moment, Píngguǒ had hope! Perhaps Lord Bái had strength enough to vanquish his enemy!

But the victory was short-lived. The black dragon evaded the worst of that savage bite and tore into Lord Bái. The white dragon's claws and fangs let go and he screamed, the wail piercing Píngguǒ's skull. The enemy unleashed his eldritch fire into Bái's open jaws, and dropped the white dragon to the ground like rubbish. Violet flames poured from the dead dragon's eyes and throat, roasting his organs inside the oven of his scales.

The pearl's light abruptly winked out of existence. The world turned to grim dusk.

The black dragon landed, and when the snake demon charged it to avenge his master, the beast flicked him aside like an ant. The demon's sword flew in the opposite direction, clanging near the three teens. Píngguǒ was too frightened to do anything, fight or flee. He stood rooted in place, his brain screaming at him to run.

"Don't, Min!" Lín shouted.

"I have to," Min shouted over a gust of roaring wind. "Píngguǒ, take care of Lin! Get her out of here! Hurry!"

But they did not go. Instead, Min picked up the snake demon's fallen sword, though he had never wielded one before, and made his stand.

The monster laughed. "Pathetic excuse for a man-thing!" The beast casually brushed him aside. Min landed on his knees. "Is this what you protect? Then I will begin here." The onyx beast inhaled and prepared to blow its flame into the open steel door of the silo.

"NO!" Píngguǒ thought, but it was Min who yelled it.

The young would-be hero jumped up and ran forward again. The monster tilted his head and *thwacked* Min across the torso with its tail. Min was thrown back, landing hard on the packed earth.

Píngguǒ covered his mouth in horror.

Lín ran to Min's side, heedless of her own imminent danger. It was clear to Píngguǒ she loved Min, and always had. The pain of it stabbed his heart.

I won't hate her, or him, he swore. *It hurts, but I'm happy for them.*

That was if Min was even still alive. Píngguǒ couldn't tell. Lín cradled Min's head on her lap, clutching him as if it were in her power to make him wake up. At the very least, she was prepared to die with him.

The monster trod toward them. "Foolish pests. I will eat you now, then set your world afire!"

Píngguǒ felt himself stir. *No, better me than them!*

He thought of his father, willing to die to save him. Faced with losing those he loved, he understood his father's sacrifice. It wasn't a choice. Somewhere within himself, Píngguǒ found a well of strength he never knew he possessed.

He stood and ran full force at the dragon, past Lín and Min, who was blinking, unfocused. Píngguǒ squeezed his own eyes shut as he faced the beast that was generating the black fog. The inky cloud was moving again, and it threatened to engulf them all.

Forgive me, Mai...

Screaming, fists balled tight, Píngguǒ flung himself in front of his friends. The darkness swept over him as his arms spread wide to protect them.

At first, there was nothing.

"What did you expect?" a voice answered, warm with a high masculine tenor.

"I don't know," Píngguǒ replied. He could see nothing, even though his eyes were open, or he thought they were. He couldn't feel them, or anything else either, not his arms, legs, hands, or feet. He experienced panic before a tremendous sensation of peace engulfed him. "I'm dead."

"Yes," the voice responded.

"I thought it would hurt."

"It did, but you can't remember."

"Oh, good. Um—will it always be this dark?"

"That depends."

"On?"

"You."

Píngguǒ wasn't sure what to do with that information. "I died trying to save my friends. Did I do that much?"

"Oh, Ping, you were very brave and very foolish. How can your sacrifice save them?"

"It was better than doing nothing," Píngguǒ said. "And it would have come for me anyway. I didn't have the energy to run away and there was nowhere left to hide." Píngguǒ wondered when he had gotten so pragmatic. Maybe it was this whole death thing. "I'm just sorry it didn't help."

"I did not say that."

Píngguǒ saw past the darkness, at Min and Lín clinging together as the monster came for them in slow motion.

They were still alive!

Hope blossomed anew in Píngguǒ like a candle flame in a dark room. Its sudden warmth sprang from his wise-mind, the center between his heart and his gut, and flooded through his 'body.' In his vision, the flame traced the symbol of a Yin Yang. Never static, the fiery wheel turned, one side always giving way to but never over-taking the other. It made Píngguǒ think of a clock.

"The balance was destroyed long ago," the voice said. "To be restored, it was necessary to remove the corrupt foundations of the old and build anew."

"I don't understand."

"No, but you will."

"Who are you?" Píngguǒ asked.

The flames changed shape and became the form of a bird with a long neck, its fiery likeness a cross between a peacock and a swan, only more beautiful. The boy was overcome by awe. The creature's singing cry pierced his soul; the flaming wings surrounded him. Píngguǒ expected scorching pain, but instead, there was warmth. The fire purified him, filling him with strength and vitality.

"What do you desire, Ping?" the phoenix asked.

"To protect my friends, heal my mother, and maybe this world, too, as much as I can. I want to make the forest live again. For Lín."

"Now that the last dragon of light has perished, the corruption of avarice and sloth in his species dies with him. The task to keep the balance between light and dark falls to another, whose heart is true. Someone must carry this burden on behalf of mankind. Ping of the ancient line of Zheng, will it be you?"

Píngguǒ gulped, knowing his answer. He shoved his fear aside. "Yes," Zheng Ping said in a voice stronger and bolder than he had ever heard it.

"Then..."

Everything went black.

"...be reborn."

Fire bloomed, and he knew that he was not just at its center. He had become the fire itself, the heart that kept the Dread Lords on their side of the Veil. He spread his arms, only to find they were wings! *He* was a phoenix!

The soul of Lord Bái rode the currents of warm wind toward him across the golden sky. The dragon was as resplendent as he must have been in his youth. The sight of Lord Bái restored brought hot tears to Ping's eyes, which sizzled off into mist.

"Come," the spectral dragon said, and Ping obeyed.

In his phoenix body, he and the dragon flew in a wide spiral around a celestial temple that emerged from the brilliant light. A manifestation of spiritual energy, Lord Bái's pearl drifted upward and glowed bright as the sun above them.

"The Age of the Dragons is over. It is your turn now," Bái told him. "Protect them. Protect your world and make it grow." With those final words, the dragon flew off into the Great Light, the wholeness that is Source.

Pangs of reunion emanated from the Light, and he knew his father was there, and so many others. "I want to, but I can't, not yet. I have to go back now. I love you, bàba. I understand why you chose to be a doctor, and why you saved us. I can do no less. It's in my blood."

He turned away and flew high, toward the dragon's pearl. He

captured the glowing orb with his beak and swallowed the relic of pure Source. It joined its strength to his, and together, they pressed against the preternatural dark overtaking the world, shoving it back. With an outrush of flame, he burned his way through.

Ping blinked and found himself standing on the dry earth in front of his stunned friends. He did not hold a sword, or any weapon, but for this he did not need one. All that was required was to embrace the entirety of himself and shine forth.

The Dark Lord writhed away from him, holding the scorched hole over its stomach, unable to attack. "How? I devoured you!"

Ping stood tall, unafraid of the monster in front of him. It held no terror for him any longer. He thought of the love he bore Lín and Min, his mother and sister, his father and grandparents. He approached the creature calmly, shoulders back.

"Return to your domain. This world does not belong to you and it is still guarded," Ping and the Phoenix spoke as one.

The light inside him illumined forth, the nimbus of which bore the graceful shape of a bird. The clouds opened and the sun shone upon him in the same instant. Unlike his friends, Ping did not need to shield his eyes from the brilliance any longer. With a smile he stepped forward and the monster fell back, slithering into the shadows until they, too, disappeared.

Although the landscape remained desolate, there was a feeling of newness in the air, the possibility for a real future. However, it was easier to face monsters and the unknown than his friends.

"Hey," Ping smiled sheepishly.

Lín ran over and threw her arms around him, and Min, holding his ribs, joined her a minute later. They squeezed him between them. Lín was shaking, and it occurred to Ping that she was crying.

"How could you do that to me! I thought you were dead!" She sobbed.

"I had to save you," Ping mumbled. "Both of you."

"Píngguǒ..." Lín said.

"It's just Ping, now." Ping grinned with confidence.

"Oh, okay." Lín said. "But how? How did you do that?"

Ping smiled. "I couldn't stand by and do nothing. It turns out, I'm not an apple at all, but a phoenix."

Min nodded although it was clear he did not understand. "So what now, Pínggu—uh, Ping?"

"We do what we came for. We have to gather as much as we can, and those rations, too. We can come back for the rest. Before we go, we should begin planting here," Ping said with unaccustomed authority. "For Lord Bái."

"All right," Lín said. "For Lord Bái."

Of the snake demon, there remained neither corpse nor sword, so they presumed the creature had survived and moved on of its own accord. Ping decided they should bury the remains of the great dragon, to which Min and Lín agreed. With picks and spades, they cleared the dead brush outside and set to work digging. It took longer than they wanted, deep into the following afternoon, but Ping was adamant. Afterward, they planted a field of flower seeds over the dragon's grave.

Next came the daunting task of preparing to return to the tulou. The problem was, there were a lot of seeds, all different kinds sealed in aluminum pouches deep down inside the mountain where it was coldest. The pouches were kept in plastic bins stacked inside steel cages.

The task almost seemed impossible, but Lín and Min knew what they needed most in food and medicine from working with the elders, so they started with that. It took a few days to sort everything into baskets to haul on poles over their shoulders.

"I didn't realize it would be quite *this* heavy!" Lín lamented on the day they set out for home. Heavy or not, there was nothing for it but transport as much as they could bear.

"It will get easier," Ping said. "It's not just for us, or for the Hakka. It's for everyone. So we have to plant some along the way, wherever we go."

Carrying their loads, the three teens emerged into the daylight. It was warmer, brighter, like spring had found them at last. The change helped make the burden less cumbersome. For a moment the clouds gave way, and fingers of sunlight spilled over the landscape. Thunder rumbled, and the clouds dispensed rain across the mountain range in the distance, heading for the tulou village.

"I think the weather is turning," Lín observed.

"Oh yes," Ping said. "It is."

"You're so weird now," Min commented. "I hope whatever magic you've got going, it can get us back in one piece. We still have men and demons to get through."

Ping smiled enigmatically as they set off into the Dead Forest. "We'll make it. I know we will."

Unseen to their eyes, Ping felt the energy of his spirit's tail and wings spread over the land as he walked. Where the sunlight fell over the dragon's grave, a few tiny, green sprouts struggled toward the sun. Not everything they planted would take root, of course, or survive, but it was a beginning.

And that was enough.

AUTHOR'S NOTE

Thank you for reading this artifact of The Atlas Dystopia Apocalyptica by Xander Cross. In fact, it contains quite a few spoilers for the entire TADA-verse! For more information on Lord Bái, the other dragons, and most especially that "white fox" he mentioned, please visit here: http://www.ayakashifox.com

About the Author

Xander Cross lives a quiet life with his spouse in Maryland. He holds a bachelor's in History, which he uses to write paranormal fiction. A lifelong enthusiast of Japanese culture and folklore, Xander cosplays as a kitsune yōkai on occasion. In addition to the supernatural cyberpunk series, "The Atlas Dystopia Apocalyptica," he has also published a paranormal romance novella trilogy entitled "Come by Night" on Wattpad.

For additional information or to contact the author, please visit here: https://www.ayakashifox.com

To Snare a Prince

Sky Sommers

"You can stop following me, I'm not going to give you any food," Greta told the raccoon that had been tailing her from the outskirts of Borough village. Everyone knew that if you gave a wild critter as much as a scrap, they were yours forever, and forest dwellers needed to be self-sufficient.

There was a flash of a bushy tail with a striped tip above the nearby copse of ferns.

Greta *hunhed* and clutched her wicker basket closer. She had to get to Granny's hut with all the leftovers from The Duchess or there would be hell to pay.

The dusty road led her farther and farther into the woods. She remembered the first time Grace, their stepmother, made her and Hans come into the woods. Oh, how they hadn't wanted to go. After all, they had known Grizelda to be the wicked witch who had wanted to eat them when they were five. Greta smiled, remembering how their "wicked" stepmother had dragged her and Hans into the woods, asking them questions about being lost in the woods. Mostly about how their mother had made them remember. As it turned out, the witch was their maternal grandmother who had rescued them. And when Greta realized who the bad guy was, she didn't want to believe it at first. Yeah, that had been a day full of surprises: step-mother stereotype—overturned; grandmother—found; mother—cursed to hell and back.

Greta stopped underneath a familiar pine tree when she saw the log hut across the meadow. Just a few more steps.

"*Eez-bush-ka, eez-bush-ka,*" was all Greta managed to shout before the hut staggered onto its chicken leg stilts and turned around. The porch swing creaked as its chains rattled.

When the hut sat down with an *oomph*, Greta was happy she hadn't gotten too close. Otherwise, she would have had to receive Granny's visitors covered in dirt and coated in dust.

A climbing rope unraveled and Greta had to dodge to avoid being buried under it. Greta shook her finger at her grandmother's house and the hut retracted the rope as if it were a tongue sticking out. The hut pushed out its logs as makeshift stairs for Greta to climb. "Thank you, hut," Greta said and headed inside.

"Now I know you think I don't need to bring food here," she

told the ratty cloth splayed across the long table, "but some villagers who dine at the Duchess can come by and they'd prefer restaurant food to what I might cook here. You've heard the expression, "Don't craft where you eat, right? Well, in my case, don't let your paying customers catch you mixing potions in the same kitchen you cook their pricey food in."

The tablecloth flipped a corner and a cup of tea appeared out of nowhere.

"Oh, bless you," Greta said and gulped down the tea. "Mm, chamomile, nice! I'm sure someone will be here any minute now. Granny said she got most visitors on Friday evenings and on Saturdays."

The door creaked and Greta tensed. When nobody appeared, she exhaled and hastened to transfer the last of the things from her basket to Granny's kitchen shelves.

There was a tug at her skirts and Greta yelped when she looked down.

It was that raccoon again.

"What are you doing here? Shoo! I have Granny's customers coming any minute now, I can't have you here," Greta hissed.

The raccoon sat and extended its hind leg towards her.

"You think I'll give you food so you'll go away? No. Bad raccoon. Bad. Go away!"

The critter drew its head into its shoulders at her tirade, but stayed put.

"Oh, I wish you were sentient and would just tell me what it is you want if it's not food!" Greta said and stomped to put the cauldron on. Granny's guests always expected the cauldron to bubble and steam to be rising from it when they came in. They never suspected it was just water.

Greta did a quick inventory of the glass jars housing various herbs when she heard a gurgle that sounded an awful lot like the "please" of a dying man.

When she turned around to see who had come in and needed urgent help she saw the raccoon, its front paws extended towards her in a silent plea.

"Who said that?" Greta asked the room.

"Ph-leee-se," gurgled the raccoon, its eyes wide as saucers. The critter clapped one of its front paws over its snout while the other paw pointed at its extended hind leg.

Greta froze for a second. "I didn't know the animals in these woods could talk," she finally managed. "Is something wrong with your paw?"

She got a nod.

Greta sighed, extended her hands towards the raccoon, then thought better of it and asked, "May I?"

The animal nodded. Greta scooped it up and lifted it onto the table, closer to the window and the light. "Show me."

The critter extended its hind leg again and Greta saw a splinter the size of her finger protruding from the largest pad.

"Oh. You walked all this way from the village with that in your paw?" she asked and the critter nodded.

"You poor dear. Ok, I'll fix it, but it'll hurt a little," Greta said, mumbling, "It'll probably hurt like hell, but it's not like I can offer you tea or use a numbing salve."

The raccoon retracted its paw and pointed at Granny's cupboard. "Salve."

Greta eyed the cupboard with Granny's secret stash and then the raccoon. "You want the salve?"

The racoon nodded.

"Ok, but then you'll go? I have Granny's patients coming soon and I don't think they'd like it if they saw wild animals here."

The raccoon nodded vigorously.

"Not that you're a wild animal any more. Sentient and able to speak. Darn those wishes. Granny did warn me and look where I am," Greta muttered as she fetched the numbing paste and applied it.

A yank, a yelp and a scurry later, Greta observed as the striped tip of the raccoon's tail swished out the door.

"Don't tell your friends!" she yelled after it.

A whole day of pregnant prissy ladies and pimply awkward youths later, Greta seriously thought that the highlight of her Friday night had been the raccoon.

The tablecloth produced tea after tea and, when her stomach growled, a slice of Granny's apple pie, which Greta gobbled down regardless of it being close to midnight.

Just her luck that Granny decided to leave for another dimension. Not only did she lose the only person who was pretending to run The Duchess, Cinderella's stepmother's restaurant instead of her, but now she got to listen to the villagers complain that the local witch had gone missing. Right after they doubted a minor could help them at all. At the tender age of sixteen, Greta had decided that if Granny wasn't seeing patients, someone had to, so she had scheduled all the appointments for this weekend.

Trial run, she thought.

Let's see if this will work out, she thought.

If it doesn't, I can always use the time to enhance Grace's recipes magically and The Duchess will practically run itself.

Greta looked up at the full moon, sighed, thankful for the silence and headed off to bed.

S he woke to strange sounds coming from the half-open window. It sounded like braying, spitting, scratching, twittering and then some. Greta opened her eyes. By the position of the sun, it was early. Only the birds should be tweeting anything.

The door squeaked and Greta groaned. "Not this early. I don't want to see anyone yet." She made a mental note to ask Hans to fix the door the next time he was around and snuck into her dress. "I haven't even had breakfast yet," she grumbled and yawned.

"You again!" she said as she spotted the familiar black snout peeking at her.

"You said 'tell your friends'," the raccoon said and looked out the door.

"I said *don't* tell your friends," Greta retorted and shuffled over, "but I guess I can help a couple of animal patients before the humans come."

She wasn't quite prepared for what awaited her outside. "No, no I can't," Greta said and closed the door.

The raccoon looked at her with reproach.

Greta shuffled over to the table and whispered to the tablecloth, "Coffee, please. Black with lots and lots and lots of sugar. And a cinnamon bun. Please."

The requested items materialized in seconds. Greta inhaled the coffee and the bun and braved the door.

It was worse than before. In the five minutes that she had taken for breakfast, the queue had doubled.

There was a moose, standing on the top stair with birds flying around its head, foxes peeking between its legs, rabbits trying to squeeze between hedgehogs and the foxes while trying to tell off the blind bear behind them.

The queue snaked from the door across the entire meadow to the edge of the forest.

Greta blinked. "I'm not a vet. I never wanted to be a vet. I only ever wanted to mix potions and come up with fun stuff like the alternative colors of the rainbow and..."

"You're babbling," the raccoon said.

"What?"

"You're nervous. You're babbling," the critter repeated.

"Yeah. I wonder why. Ever treated a bear? Or a moose? Me neither!" Greta told it and rolled her eyes. She was arguing with a raccoon, a raccoon for cripes' sakes!

"So, don't argue. Help them!" The raccoon pointed at her queue of patients.

Greta sighed and knew that she wouldn't be able to turn them away. "Just this once."

When Greta was done for the day, the raccoon handed her a cup of tea the tablecloth had produced. Greta was so tired she only growled her thanks and dove nose-first into the cup.

As soon as the empty cup touched the cloth, it refilled. Greta downed that one as well. When it refilled the third time Greta coughed and waved for the honey jar. It came zooming and trickled a healthy dollop over the edge and into the cup.

"Thank you," Greta rasped and thought: *never again*.

She had tended to animals in the morning, and then people from noon to midnight, half of them in the past two hours.

Why did people think the remedy would be more potent if they came and got it after sundown?

The raccoon sat in the corner and watched her.

She waved a finger at it. "Don't do that again."

The racoon nodded. "I won't. They might."

Greta rolled her eyes. "Listen, we need to establish some ground rules, you and I," Greta told the raccoon. "First, unless it is life or death, I only see the animals late in the evenings after I'm done at The Duchess. I see people on the weekend because someone has to."

The raccoon nodded.

"Now if we could only figure out how to register all the patients to avoid wounded animals trekking here in vain or me healing everyone who has turned up until early morning..." Greta extended her feet and sighed.

"I can tell those who should come." The raccoon went scurrying and brought a pail, then darted to the shelf with Granny's herbs and picked out lavender and when it reached for a small pot and dipped it into the cauldron with boiling water.

"Are you making me a foot soak?" Greta asked.

The raccoon froze and nodded.

Greta rolled her eyes again and let the raccoon pour scalding water into the pail and then pour the jug of cold drinking water after it.

Greta relaxed in Granny's only armchair, thanked the raccoon and saw the critter slip out the door minutes after midnight.

Except it came back the next day. And the day after that. And the day after that.

"It figures, with a cannibal for a grandmother and an evil stepmother, you'd end up as the local witch," spat the woman who came through the door.

"She smells funny," the raccoon whispered to Greta who sniggered.

"I do not smell, you varmint!" the woman protested. "Why do you have varmint in the hut? Grizelda never had…"

"Betty Bonfleur, how may I help you?" Greta asked without really meaning it, but motioned for her visitor to come in and take a seat nevertheless.

"It's Countess DeVille now—John and I are married," the woman said, thrusting her chin up and her bejeweled hand out. When she moved, the light on the door frame chose this moment to turn green.

"What? Again?" Betty sighed. "Well, John won't be happy, it's our fourth already. I guess when I made a wish that we should have more babies to cover for the ones he made me get rid of, my wish did come true."

"You're…you're going to have a child?" Greta asked, eyes agoggle.

The raccoon and Betty nodded.

"That's what I meant. She smells different than females who are not with babies," the raccoon told Greta.

That Saturday Greta was up to her elbows in unrequited love, unwanted pregnancies and an occasional request from the men who were few and far between to remove the hex their mother-in-law had vexed them with. Greta handed out love potions to the first kind of customers, suggested adoption to the second kind and insinuated the men needed to be kinder to their kin so they'd remove the hex. At least it wasn't all pimples and boils.

Weeks turned to months, but Greta had still not come to grips with her new reality—restaurant by day, tending to the humans on the weekend and to the animals from dusk till the witching hour. Greta rose early, fell into bed after midnight and there was no end in sight.

She slurped her tea and looked longingly at her wand right there on the shelf where she had left it months, months(!) ago when the first critters arrived. She hadn't found a smidgen of time to practice her spells and the wand was gathering dust. Greta sighed and went to work.

"Hey, sis, how are..." the tall red-headed hulk of a man with a ginger crew cut and hardly any clothes on froze in the doorway at the sight of Greta bandaging a fox's paw.

"Hans, we've talked about your attire. Tight pants and leather straps housing various weapons across your bare chest do not count as clothes," Greta told her dizygotic twin. "I'll find you a shirt."

The russet lady flicked her white-tipped tail and bowed to the girl.

"Missus Bean's hens are off limits, you hear, she's got mouths to feed," Greta told the fox who streaked between Hans' legs; and gone she was.

"Are you running an animal hospital now?" Hans asked and put his scabbard on the table.

"Weapons off the table," Greta nudged the sword. "Nah, this is just temporary," she said as the raccoon ushered in another limping beast.

"Yeah, I can see that," Hans smirked, taking up a seat on the long bench.

"You don't seem very fazed by this," Greta gestured at the raccoon bringing her water in a pail and a clean towel for the hare Greta was consoling and trying not to picture its best cuts and how she'd prepare it at her restaurant.

"I've seen worse," Hans said and patted the tatty tablecloth. It hesitated for a full minute and then produced a medium rare steak with mash and a glass of water. "Thank you muchly."

"I believe you have, but I'm in a bit of a pickle here and I don't really know how to go about it. Any ideas?" Greta asked.

Hans gnawed on his steak, the child's bib dangling around his bulging neck being the only thing standing in between the blood spatter and his pristine white shirt. When he was done chewing, Hans said, "Give me a minute to think about it."

Greta finished bandaging the hare and offered the raccoon a seat at the table. The cloth produced a hard-boiled egg, a fresh fish and a bowl of nuts for the raccoon. Greta poured some water into a bowl. The raccoon nodded and started on its dinner.

"I see you have a live-in partner," Hans smirked. "I would go for a human male, if I were you, but suit yourself."

"I don't see you wooing any belles either. We're sixteen, it's too early for meaningful relationships!" Greta said. When Hans smirked, she added hastily, "And unmeaningful ones either."

Hans ruffled her hair, making Greta's red mane look like a fiery dandelion. "What I meant was—you bonding with someone, anyone and allowing them to help—that's a good start."

"No, that was not a good start. He's the one who caused it all."

"I'm a she, actually," the raccoon said, "and if you could find a way for me not to be a walking-talking appointments register and an usher, I could spend my evenings with my babies."

Greta gawked while Hans looked at the critter as if appraising her.

"Tell me, what are your main problems?" Hans asked Greta.

Half an hour later, Hans threw the door to the hut wide open. "Listen up, everybody," Hans bellowed and the forest dwellers fell silent at the sight of a warrior in leather getup with a sword strapped to his back. "New rules. Rule number one: you only come here on Sundays. Rule number..."

The raccoon coughed behind him, "Sundays? They're animals."

"Hans, they can't talk. Only the raccoon can, I wished she was sentient and would tell me what it...she wanted and..."

"Don't you know better than to say your wishes out loud?" Hans looked at his sister like she was a child and Greta bristled.

"Listen, I was tired, worked the whole week at The Duchess, alone and then she appeared and wanted something and then..."

Hans raised up his hands. "I get it, I get it. One problem at a time."

"Listen up! Can anybody count to seven?" Hans asked the animals.

One of the rabbits raised its paw.

"Anybody else?" Hans scoured the meadow for more admissions. "Geesh, this is worse than recruits from the Dark territories. Fine."

He trudged down the steps and upended a small garden cart. As he touched his hand to the wood, it sprouted vines that arranged themselves into a green flower on the bottom of the cart.

"Look! Green flower means you can come," Hans bellowed and a bear sat down at his tone. Hans waved his hand over the flower and the vines turned orange. "Orange means do not come. Got it?"

Hans stared every critter down until they all nodded.

"Good."

The animals just stood there.

Hans motioned to the orange flower. "You see the color. Do you know what you need to do?"

The animals just stood there.

"Which one's orange again?" the raccoon piped up. "Is that the same color as the earth or is it the color of the leaves? Or is it more like the sky?"

Hans blinked. "You don't see colors like I do?"

A few hedgehogs shrugged as the rabbits nodded.

Hans sighed and made the flower mutate into a thumbs up sign.

"When the separate appendage points up at the sky—this way," he demonstrated, "means you can queue and wait to be let in. When it points to the ground," he twirled the sign, "means today is no good. Now, leave, come back tomorrow, when the sign points sky-high," Hans explained.

The raccoon waved them off. Slowly, the animals started dispersing.

When the meadow emptied, Hans turned and went back in. "I've agreed with the sign to do a thumbs up every seven days on Sundays. Now you only need the raccoon on Sundays, right? You can agree to see people on Saturdays and you have the evenings to yourself."

Greta nodded. The raccoon bowed and snuck out.

"The question is—is that enough?" Seeing Greta's fallen face, Hans softened. "I remember how some nights at The Duchess get with our pernickety guests. You must be dead on your feet. Where do you find time to study? And how's your apprenticeship with the Blue Fairy?"

Greta hung her head. "She kind of disappeared. I haven't seen her in months."

Hans sighed. "I could put some feelers out to try and find her. Meanwhile, I suggest you close the restaurant on Mondays. People can cook for themselves, they'll appreciate you more. Besides, Monday was the least busy day anyway, you won't lose much money. Tell me, what else can I do to help this instant?"

Greta hugged him. "Thank gods for brothers!"

The rest of the day, he helped her clean the hut. Greta was grateful for him bringing the water from the well, soaping the windows, taking down the curtains. She couldn't help noticing how he kept whispering with the tablecloth. When she caught them yet another time, a slice of apple pie with whipped cream on top appeared next to Hans. He clutched the plate a little bit too quickly. "Want one?"

Greta shook her head. "You and your secrets. I eat well, no need to conspire behind my back with the tablecloth to feed me better."

Hans smiled and nodded. "I'm not."

Despite asking Hans in one hundred and one ways what he'd been whispering about with Granny's favorite magical artifact, Greta didn't get a peep out of him. She wondered about the fact that even tablecloths might have and can keep secrets.

When Hans left to rejoin his merry band of Warriors, Greta sensed all her dishes were made with butter. She had to tell the table-cloth off for trying to fatten her up as per her brother's orders, but promised to tell Hans that the cloth had tried.

Things returned to relative normality for a while.

A week after Hans left, Greta stood in her doorway and marveled at the queue that she was almost accustomed to by now. Almost, but not quite.

"Shall I let someone in?" the raccoon asked next to her, rubbing her paws together as the sky darkened and gales of storm wind ripped at Greta's dress.

"What the..." was all Greta managed to say before the dust got to her. She squinted her eyes, coughed up the lungful of dirt she had caught and saw the animals disperse every which way.

With a loud *thunk* a golden-bellied dragon descended onto the meadow, bending a few trees outwards as it landed.

"I don't think that one will fit inside," the raccoon whispered and hid behind Greta's skirts.

"Cousin told me the landing pad was tight, but this is awful," Greta heard in her mind as three of the dragon's heads swerved towards her.

"Would you please keep yourself out of my head, it's polite to ask first if you are allowed to do that, you know," Greta said out loud while thinking, "If someone would ease up on the yummies, my trees would still be alive."

"Yummies? Did you say yummies? Where are the yummies?" Greta heard in her mind again as a fourth head started sniffing the air.

"Ah, so you're the glutton," Greta said.

"Watch it, human, do you know who you're speaking to?" another head hovered by the railing, eyeing her up and down with its amber iris.

"No, but I bet you're one of the dragons that Ella keeps yakking about," Greta offered.

"Ella? Ella? Who said Ella?" another head appeared, so Greta started counting.

"Six, you have six heads. Great! Try not to spit fire or you'll burn down my forest!"

"Who is Ella to you?" asked the interrogating head.

"She's my sister. You said your cousin mentioned this place?"

"Yes, our three-headed cousin. He said the human was kind here. I highly doubted it and now I see he lied," the interrogating head huffed, making Greta's skirts billow.

"Watch it! Remember what I said about NOT setting things on fire? That includes the hut. Your cousin must have meant my Granny. She left."

"No, he said a small human was kind to him. A boy," the hungry head said.

"A boy? You confused me with a boy?" Greta gestured at her skirts and her long auburn hair.

The interrogating head smirked.

"Oh, this was you being funny. Nice one! Granny often had Henry over..."

"Yes, Henry. Where is he?"

Greta eyed the dragon warily. "Like I'd tell you where my six-year-old stepbrother is so you can eat him."

All of the heads started rolling their eyes and mumbling protestations.

"Shut it!" Greta yelled at the top of her lungs.

When the dragon hissed and all six heads started snaking towards her with slits for eyes. "You dare to..."

"*Shhh*, I can't hear the birds," Greta said and raised her finger, making the dragon go quiet. "You spooked off all of my patients with your arrival and I guess I'm thankful, but the fact that the birds aren't singing is worrying."

"There is no bigger predator than us in these woods. We would sense it," one of the heads said as a raven-haired boy darted from the underbrush, running at them, yelling "Gretaaaaa!!!!!"

"Everyone is entitled to their misconceptions," said a familiar ginger hulk emerging from the trees, and the dragon stilled. Armed to the teeth, yet again, Hans leaned on one of the pine-trees lining the meadow as the raven-haired boy raced up the stairs. "You claim to be a predator? You like salads. Eddie, old bud, how have you been?"

"Hans!" All the heads that had been making their way to Greta looked down at Hans.

Greta shuddered. "You can't eat him. He's my brother."

One of the dragon's heads swiveled down and smiled rapaciously at the boy who started running towards Greta.

"You can't eat him either. He's my other brother. *Ooomph*, Henry!" she staggered back, almost missing her footing when the boy lunged into her embrace.

"Henry, stop smothering Greta, you only see her every day at The Duchess," Hans said while Greta looked down to check why she had slipped. She noticed a wet patch on the wooden floorboards.

The raccoon hid her snout behind her paws. "I'm sorry, I got scared. After the kids, I've got bladder issues."

Greta patted her assistant on the head and asked Hans, hugging Henry. "What brings you around twice in a fortnight? You forgot me for years and now you're here again? What gives?"

"Wife?" one of the heads asked Hans.

"Jilted lover?" supposed the interrogating one.

"Sister," Hans said.

"Twin," Greta corrected him.

"Aaaah," came from five heads as the interrogating sceptic looked from Hans to Greta. "I fail to see the resemblance," it said.

"You would, wouldn't you. Stop judging," Greta waved her finger at the dragon, a little braver now that her twin was there. "If you want food, go inside, you know what to do," she whispered to Henry.

"She insults us. Has been from the start. We are royally dismayed," one of the heads told Hans.

"Royally?" Greta eyed the golden giant. "I thought all royal dragons were black?"

Four of the heads huffed. "That's after we reach puberty."

Greta's jaw dropped. "You're a child? Colorful dragons are children?"

Hans threw his head back and laughed. "Yeah, if you call a five-hundred-year-old dragon a kid, then yes, he's a child. Come on, stop taking everything personally, Eddie."

"Eddie?" Greta asked. "How well do you know him?" she asked her brother.

"You didn't even introduce yourself and you're mad at her?" Hans *tsk-tsk-ed* at the dragon. Five of the heads had the decency to look ashamed. "What did I teach you about humans? You need to introduce yourself first and ask questions later."

"That's what Ella said as well. Introduce, find out what the problem is, then burn down the village, not the other way around," one of the heads nodded.

Greta gulped. "That sounds like good advice. Wait, Ella taught you that? Are you one of the dragons who she has the cultural exchange with? You guys teach her telepathy and she teaches you how to be around humans again?"

The cautious head nodded slowly. "Correct. *She* didn't introduce herself either," he tattled to Hans. "Pot, kettle, all that."

Greta rolled her eyes. "I'm Greta, pleased to meet you, Eddie," she said. "What brings you here?"

All of the heads looked at her reproachfully and the dragon nudged the thumbs up sign with its tail.

"You have an ailment? Is that it?" Greta asked and got a nod from three heads. "Wait, let me guess," Greta eyed head number four who was sniffing her pumpkin patch, "you ate something you shouldn't have and now you have indigestion?"

Two heads head-butted the glutton. "Hey, I'm not at fault that he smelled so good."

"He? Who did you eat?" Greta paled, bracing herself for having to deal with extracting chewed human remains.

"Don't worry, he doesn't eat sentient beasts or humans," Hans patted her arm.

"Who said all humans are sentient, and the glutton head would care to know the difference when it's hungry," Greta mumbled to herself. Out loud she said, "So, who or what did you eat, when and what happened afterwards?"

The glutton head turned its snout towards the woods. "I'm not telling you. You're rude!"

"I'm rude? I'm rude?" Greta asked. "You land here, without so much as an invitation or a warning. You scare off all my patients and muscle up in the queue, so now maybe someone who has a more critical condition will die because you decided that you're more important. You didn't introduce yourself and just assumed you're due a red-carpet roll? You didn't ask for help, you ordered me to help you. Now, which one of us is rude?"

The heads eyed each other and seemed to be in caucus. One of them snaked out and sniffed the air a short distance away from Greta. "Definitely Ella's sister." The interrogating head *hunhed* and said, "As if there were any doubt, based on the mouth work."

Refusing to be subjected to any more insults, Greta *huffed* and went into the underbrush in search of her patients, mumbling, "He shows up and I'm pretty sure it's a he, yeah, he shows up, scares everyone, including me to death and he's in the right? Just because he's bigger and meaner doesn't mean..."

"We're sorry," said one of the heads, snaking up to her from behind and making her jump.

"Sheesh! You should give fair warning about your approach! And intentions! And..."

The black slits of his irises narrowed. "And how exactly do you propose I do that? Start whispering, "Hey little girl, I wanna talk to you? I wanna apologize, please, please let me apologize?" something like that maybe?"

Greta's hands went to her hips. "Yes, for instance. You're bigger than everyone else..."

"Not where I come from," the head mumbled.

"Well, you are the biggest one here. Don't you know that animals and humans are wary of things bigger than them?"

"I'm not a thing!"

"You know what I mean," Greta said.

"You don't seem to be wary of me and you're just a tiny human," the dragon head said.

"Well, in my line of work, where would I be if I gave in to every bully who towers over me?" Greta looked up at the head that was hovering near the treetops. "Pretty much everyone is bigger than me," she said.

"I'm no bully!" the dragon protested as Greta found a wounded hare and crouched, turning her back to the dragon so she could hide it from the hare's view.

"Uh-huh," Greta said, trying to see where the critter's wound originated.

"No, really. Back home I'm the youngest and smallest. Everybody laughs at me," the head sniffled. "I'm the one being bullied."

"So, to compensate, you come here and lord it over those who are smaller than you? Fui! Shame on you," Greta said and picked the hare up. "Now please retreat before this poor creature has a heart attack. I'll treat this one and then I'll need to go find the others. You know, everybody who you scared off when you arrived?" Greta looked at the dragon's head pointedly.

"Would you like some help? I can call them back mentally. Explain things, tell them to form a line and wait," the head said, lowering its snout to Greta's height.

"And will you wait until I'm done with everyone else who came before you?" Greta asked, looking into the dragon's right eye. She saw her reflection in his giant pupil and gulped. *it's not every day you see yourself in full height in something other than a mirror.*

The dragon's head seemed to pause for a second. "Yes, I think we can wait. The one we ate is amenable to it, too."

Horrified, Greta realized the cause of the dragon's indigestion might still be alive in there, somewhere.

"Erm... what will you do while I..." Greta asked, trying to still the animal in her grasp.

"I'll wait. Speak to Hans and Henry. We love Henry, we hear he has lovely stories to tell," the head said, soaring for the treetops.

Not all of those in need came back despite the dragon's call. Maybe some of them were afraid of his bulk, maybe some were accompanying relatives and didn't need to be there.

Greta was done in two hours and when the raccoon had ushered the last of the foxes away, her stomach grumbled.

"Best to get this out of the way before I have lunch," Greta said and ventured to see the dragon. She didn't want her food to come back up when she freed the dragon's accidental breakfast.

The beast was resting its heads in the meadow grass and Hans was lying next to its huge belly.

"How is our patient? The... he that you ate was alive when you ate him, I hope?" Greta asked, trying to sound professional.

"I ate a plant. I didn't know it was sentient. Then he informed me from my bowels that it was a *he* and demanded to be let out," the dragon complained.

"Why didn't you?" Greta asked.

"Do you know how things come out of dragons?" one of the heads asked.

Greta had to admit that she didn't.

"Well, one way is how the remnants of everyone's food leaves, but no, *he* didn't want to be digested and pooped out. No, *he* insisted *he* can't be digested, that *he's* indigestible!"

"Is there another way?" Greta asked.

"Yes, but that didn't suit him either. If dragons regurgitate, we hiccough fire," one of Eddie's heads said and got a hissy head-butt from another. "We're not supposed to tell."

Greta noticed Henry had come back outside and was scribbling like mad into his leather-bound notebook.

"She's our doctor," one head said to another, "she's supposed to keep things secret."

"He's not," the other head nodded at Hans.

"They're twins, it's unavoidable. One will know what the other one thinks."

Greta and Hans exchanged looks. Nobody was supposed to know their best kept secret.

The chatty head kept explaining, "As I was saying, the other way is out. *He* didn't want to be burnt to a crisp. So here we are," three of Eddie's heads sighed and Hans held on for dear life not to be blown five feet away.

"What do you expect me to do?" Greta looked flabbergasted.

"Help," Eddie said.

Greta sat on her porch steps. "Let me think a bit. Laxatives won't work, neither will an emetic, besides," she eyed the meadow. "I don't want to clean it up later. So, either we approach surgically or magically."

"Surgically?" Hans echoed.

"We cut Eddie open," Greta said. "Eddie, whereabouts do you feel that the *he* you ate is placed at the moment?"

"Cut? Cut?? Muahhaaahaaa," Eddie roared with laughter. "You can't cut me, I'm a dragon, only the claws of other dragons or St. George's spear..." five heads hissed at the blabbermouth. The cautious head rolled its eyes, and swiveled down to Henry's height. "Fine, I'll only tell the storyteller then."

Greta went to stand in-between Eddie and Henry. "Another secret, I presume. Very well, where do I get a dragon's claw or that spear?" Greta asked.

Hans looked at her like she was insane. He ruffled around in his sack. "Here, let me find it." He came up empty-handed. "Are you insane? Nobody has ever got a dragon's claw that is not attached to a dragon. Such a thing doesn't exist!"

"Well, technically," the blabbermouth said and got another hiss from his fellow heads, "fine, fine, I won't say anything."

"Well, if you don't want to share your secret claw, then you'd better fly home to where other dragons are so that we can try to cut you open with the help of one of your relatives and then we can let Mister Plant out."

"Can we leave this as a remedy of the last resort?" the blabbermouth said. "There would be no coming back from that kind of shame."

"Understood," Greta said. "That leaves just one remedy—a magical one. I need to consult my books. Wait here." She stood up. "You," she pointed at Hans, "guard Henry and you," she pointed at Henry, "try not to get eaten." Ignoring Eddie's lament, Greta turned and went inside.

The tablecloth had a steaming bowl of soup ready for her.

Greta walked over to the book shelf and picked up a volume, 'Inside Out: A Defensive Guide to Magic'. Nope, not that. 'Outside In: Directing the Elements'. Nope. 'Internal Elemental Magic'. This looked promising. Dragon fire was fire and fire was one of the elements.

Greta took the volume, sat down and started ladling soup into her mouth. When she found the right passage, the spoon froze in mid-air. She released the spoon and it disappeared before it hit the table. Next, Greta gulped the remnants of the soup over the edge of the bowl and ran out, holding the book.

"I think I figured it out! We need to put you to sleep!" she yelled.

"Shhhh... you'll wake Eddie," Hans hissed at her as Henry kept scribbling in his notebook, ignoring the world around him.

"He's asleep?" Greta blinked back her surprise. "But he said he had indigestion! Never mind. Even better, now all we have to do is tell Mister Plant to climb out."

"How do you propose we tell him? Our telepathic conveyor is fast asleep," Hans said pointing at Eddie. Two of whose heads snored loudly at the same time.

"I can hear you, you know," someone spoke in both their minds.

"Everyone's a telepath these days?" Greta mumbled and thought, *Well then you already know what you have to do. You have to exit while the dragon is asleep so as not to get fried in the blast. Start climbing back the way you went down.*

"Is she always this bossy?" Mister Plant asked so that both of them could hear.

Hans snorted and Greta huffed.

"Look, do you want my help or not?" Greta asked, heading over to the glutton head and making sure its maw was open.

Greta thought she saw movement and then something black covered in green goo slithered out and fell to the ground. The head just snorted, licked its nose and slept on.

The blob ambled to stand up. Greta discerned two arms, two legs, one head and a lot of green goo.

"Mister Plant? You're Mister Plant?" Greta's eyebrows shot up to her hairline.

"Actually, I'm Nefarious Russelbulb the Seventh. As in seventh cousin to the ruling Elven King of Windermere, on the Dark side, of course," the blob of green goo bowed.

"Mister Russelbulb..." Greta started.

"Nefarious to you, dear lady," the blob said.

"Nefarious, you said the Dark side, does that mean Windermere has an inhabited Light side as well?" Greta asked. "And why were you masquerading as a plant? Were you spying in the Dragon Kingdom?"

Hans looked at the gooey elf and crossed his arms. "Spy, eh? Wait 'til Eddie wakes up. He eats spies for breakfast. So, I guess he was right to gobble you up."

"How come you know Eddie eats spies?" Greta asked her brother.

"We hang out. Who do you think told him to come see you?" Hans winked.

"Are you quite finished bickering?" Nefarious asked, wiping his face with the tip of the dragon's wing. "I'm not a spy. I was experimenting. Testing out a supposition on how carnivorous dragons really are. Turns out, the not eating humans thing..."

"You're an elf," Greta pointed out.

Nefarious shrugged. "So? As I was saying. It seems that for dragons, eating humanoids is more of an ethical taboo. If they didn't know you're an elf or human..."

"Meaning if you pretended to be something else," Greta interjected.

"Yes," Nefarious said, grinding his teeth. "When I pretended to be a plant, but smelled like an elf, then the dragon still attempted to eat me." He raised his finger and looked victorious.

Greta nodded. "Uh-uh, uh-uh. Mister experimenter, how were you planning on getting out of there, given that the two natural ways did not suit Your Highness?"

Henry looked up and kept scribbling furiously.

"How do you know?" Nefarious asked.

"What do you mean? Eddie told us of the two ways and that you had qualms. You must have heard him, if you were able to hear us two," Greta said. Only someone as dim as this guy could have experimented alone and without a back-up plan.

"No, I meant about the Highness," Nefarious said and noticed the green goo dripping from his sleeve. "Oh, dear. This just won't do."

There was a *whoosh* and a raven-haired man with deep-set gray eyes dressed all in black velvet stood before the twins.

Greta narrowed her eyes at him. "You look familiar. Have we met before?"

Nefarious bowed, but didn't answer.

"Dude, are you wearing eye-liner?" Hans asked.

"Erm, so you really are an elf?" Greta asked.

"He was an elf fifteen minutes ago, in case you missed it," Hans said and Greta elbowed him in the ribs. "What was that for?"

Nefarious smiled an enigmatic smile. "I owe you my life, sweet maiden, and I'm at your service." He bowed with flourish, his long hair nearly touching the forest floor.

"Please call me Greta," she said, wondering what was wrong with her stomach and where had the butterflies come from.

"What an enchanting name for such an enchanting...hm...Fairy Godmother, I believe?" Nefarious inclined his head as if listening to something.

"Godmother already? How do you manage that on top of running a restaurant and an animal shelter?" Hans smirked.

"You're forgetting the witch's hut on Saturdays. Thanks, Granny, for dumping everything on me!" Greta growled, then remembered she was just called charming and smiled at Nefarious.

Hans leaned down and took Greta by her chin. "You have black circles under your eyes. The improved regimen doesn't seem to be helping, you look tired. Been working yourself to the bone with studies and everything, have you?" Hans asked and shook his head. He pointed at the raccoon anxiously washing her paws. "See, even your helper is worried about you. If you had only confined yourself to 'the people to tend to' as you said, then the dragon wouldn't have come here and you wouldn't have rescued me and we would never have met," Nefarious said and took a few steps towards Greta.

There was a loud snort and one of the heads opened one eye. "Did someone say my name?" Eddie asked and all of his heads yawned in unison.

"It'll be wanting real food next and then what'll I do," Greta mumbled and tried to avoid looking at Nefarious. The elf was making her heart skip, her palms sweat and her thoughts muddy and she didn't like it.

"I can be without food for days," the glutton head told Greta.

Greta inhaled sharply, regretting it instantly as her heart palpitations increased. *The dragon heard me. Botheration!*

"Considering he nearly ate me, he must be hungry." Nefarious kept advancing on Greta and trying to catch her eye. "Permit me to assist you in a getaway," the elf bowed low, never taking his eyes off her.

Greta thought she saw him smirk and backed away, tripping on a tree branch. She would have landed on her bum if one of Eddie's heads hadn't caught her. The rest of them snaked around sniffing for something.

Leaning on the scaly neck, Greta said, "You're quite chivalrous for a beast. I'm sorry I accidentally called you a thing back there. And a beast just now," she said and got a curt nod from one of the heads.

"We forgive you," the hoity-toity one said while the rest of them kept searching for something.

Now that sounded like the royal 'we', Greta thought. "Oh, I hope you're not sniffing around for some poor critter to gobble up," she told Eddie. "You know, I wish..." Greta said and clapped her hand over her mouth. "Oh no, I'm not wishing for anything."

Two of the heads encircled her. "Yeeees, but if you *could* wish, what would you wish for?" they whispered.

"If I could wish, then I would wish for you to have just one head, not six, it's rather disorienting, you know," Greta said and noticed Henry smiling at his journal.

The glutton head peered over Henry's shoulder and *hunhed*. "I can do that."

"Do what?" Greta asked.

The dragon disintegrated into a million golden particles that kept condensing until moments later, the particles reassembled into a golden-haired lad in a white shirt and dark blue jeans. "Darius Edward Goldencrest, at your service," the godlike young man said, flashing white teeth on his bronze face.

"You forgot prince," Hans said as Nefarious cringed.

"Prince? I think I liked you more when you had six heads and were just Eddie," Greta told him and noticed that the young man had amber eyes. Just like Eddie.

"But you liked Eddie, didn't you?" Henry asked Greta.

Nefarious was the only one who looked at Darius like he was snot. "Well, well, well."

Greta glanced at the elf when he spoke and felt her heart go *kathump* again. The more she looked, the more she wanted to go over to Nefarious and touch him. Greta balled her hands into fists and used her last resolve to stay put.

"I'll have none of your underhanded pheromone seduction ploys, thank you very much," the dragon prince waved his hand at Nefarious. Greta's urge to run to the elf disappeared and she felt her heartbeat steadying.

She bit her lip.

"Why did you do that?" Nefarious said to Darius. "Aren't dragons always saying, finders, keepers? So, what if I enhanced my charm a little. In human form, I saw her first!" Nefarious said haughtily.

"Technically, I saw her first," Darius said. "You were still food at that point. If only you had had the good sense to be digested when you had the chance, she wouldn't have met you at all."

"And you wouldn't have needed her help, so neither of us would be vying for her attention," the elf said.

"Would you please stop it! I'm right here and I'm not interested in either one of you!" Greta shouted.

Both men turned to her, looking genuinely puzzled. "Whyever not? Are you not of marriageable age?" Darius asked.

"She is," Hans said.

Henry sniggered, took the pencil out of his mouth and started writing again.

"And which one of her male relatives should be addressed for her hand in marriage?" Darius asked.

"Marriage? Now, wait a minute! I have a restaurant to run, a witch's practice to tend to and lots of animals to doctor, not to mention magic to learn! I don't have time for marriage!" Greta protested.

"You can learn magic with me," Darius said and moved close enough for Greta to smell him. *Pineapple. The dude smells of pineapple.*

"She could learn in the Dark territories," Nefarious said, looking doubtful and flanking Greta from the other side.

"Yes, but you'd have to marry her, and even then she wouldn't be accepted in your kingdom. She's not a dark elf or a dark witch, she's as light as they come. She heals people and creatures of the forest," Darius said, moving closer to Greta.

"I'd be amenable to marriage if she could keep her sharp tongue in check," the dark elf said.

Greta huffed. "If you subjugate women, no way I'd marry you even if you begged."

"Me? Beg?" Nefarious looked scandalized.

"I'd beg," Darius offered, stroking Greta's hair. "And marry."

"Stop that!" Greta swatted at his hand, earning herself a brain-melting smile and being pulled closer into an embrace.

Nefarious opened his mouth to protest, but closed it again. "You're right, dragon, as the negotiations have progressed from fun to marriage proposals, I'm bowing out. My King can tame her if he likes. I prefer my women pliant." The elf bowed to Greta and vanished.

Greta's mouth formed a neat 'O'. "The gall!"

"Eddie, old bud, that last bit about the elven King sounded like "You can expect our declarations of war in the morning". I think you've got competition."

Darius cringed and held Greta closer.

"Watch it, Eddie, you're cutting off my air supply," she snapped.

"Greta, if you need time to be wooed and need someone else to care for the animals on weekends, talk to Mama, she likes animals, she has always wanted to heal them, not cook them," Henry piped up, hardly lifting his head from his notebook.

"I don't need to be wooed," Greta said when Darius interjected. "With your stepmother's help, the restaurant will sort itself out as well, I'm sure. Now who do I have to ask for her hand?" Darius pressed Hans, yanking Greta back by her waist when she tried to slip away.

"Our father, Oz is in another dimension and not in his right mind to consent to anything important. Our granddad is off galli-vanting somewhere, so that makes *me* her closest male relative." Hans crossed his arms and smirked.

"You're enjoying yourself, aren't you? Just you wait 'till you need advice on how to woo a girl." Greta narrowed her eyes at her brother, disentangling herself from Darius' arms in one swift stroke, just like

Hans had taught her. She backed off towards the hut with as tiny steps as possible to get away from the jesting loons.

"Hans can always ask his in-laws, we're legendary in wooing women," Darius said.

"If this is you wooing, then I definitely liked you more when you were Eddie," Greta said.

Darius and Hans were having a staring contest.

"What? What are they doing?" Greta whispered to Henry who had found a seat on the bottom log of the staircase to the hut.

"They're talking. About you," Henry whispered back.

"Hey, don't talk about me as if I'm not present, I'm right here!" Greta shouted. "First the tablecloth, now your buddy. Gods grant me the serenity..." she mumbled. The men ignored her.

"Are you sure she'll forgive?" Darius asked, casting a glance Greta's way.

"Forgive what? What are you going to do that needs forgiveness? Don't decimate the hut when you turn back into a dragon!" Greta exclaimed as the prince bowed to Hans and disintegrated into a giant golden cloud of particles. "Look, if you have to ask," Greta told the cloud, "then you already know..." The cloud shaped itself into a flying dragon. "Weird, I didn't know dragons could transform like that, mid-flight," Greta mused. "As I was saying, Eddie, if you have to ask for someone's forgiveness, then you already know the aaaaans-weeeeer," Greta yelped when she was already airborne. In the meadow beneath them Hans and Henry high-fived each other. Greta rolled her eyes, watching the treetops speed by and ordered, "Eddie... Darius...Your Highness...put me down. Bad dragon, bad..."

"No," the dragon roared.

"What do you mean "no"? You're not taking me where I think you're taking me?"

"Yes," rumbled the beast. *Consider this a royal invite*, Eddie said in her mind and Greta thought she heard him chuckle. As they ascended to strata above the birds and the clouds, all Greta could do was try to make herself comfortable in the giant claws of a six-headed golden dragon. That and plan her revenge.

Author's Note

If you want to know what becomes of Greta, you'll have to wait a year and read To Steal A Kiss in Enchanted Flames (out June 18, 2023).

Meanwhile, you can read up on Hans & Greta in Cinders: Necessary Evil available here: https://storyoriginapp.com/universalbooklinks/ f507caaa-2f49-11eb-802a-db85264fdfe0

ABOUT THE AUTHOR

For most of her life, Sky has lived and worked in Tallinn, Estonia, with brief escapes all over the world in search of her muse. Penguins and polar bears, beware, I will get there. Eventually.

Sky's debut e-book was about ancient goddesses running amok, trying to get their wilted powers back. She then proceeded to publishing her own books and found her way from Greek and Arthurian myths and legends to fairytales retold for young adult and adult audiences. So far, Thumbelina has been updated for suspicious adults, more sinister versions of Cinderella, Red Riding Hood and

The Wizard of Oz were released in 2020-2021 (Cinders-Embers-Ash aka the Magic Mirrors Saga) and a dystopian book made a blip in October 2021. All her books are peppered with dry humour, linked by some character or another and usually she loves making you choose at the end—depending on whether you are an optimist or a pessimist.

Sky lives in a house with a small garden with her husband and mostly one, but on occasion plus four kids. No dog.

You can best find & interact with Sky on Instagram: @sommers_sky/

Blood of the Unicorn

N.D.T. Casale

"I do not want to become Queen of West Ivoria, Elspeth!" shouted Princess Calypso as she yanked the crown from her dark curls. The coronet clattered to the marble floor.

Her handmaiden's wrinkled hands picked up the circlet of diamond and gold. She clutched her back. "My dear, you are sixteen and your grandmother cannot remain on the throne forever."

Calypso crossed her arms and felt tears brim in the corners of her eyes. In this moment she would have given anything to be anyone but herself. What was the point in governing a kingdom when she herself had no freedom?

"What is all this ruckus?" declared a regal voice.

Through her blurred vision, Calypso saw her grandmother Queen Hylzarie enter the throne room. Her long white hair was pulled into a low chignon, diamonds dangled from her earlobes, and the diadem that signified her status as queen sparkled in the light. The collar of her red dress framed her elegant neckline and was fitted at the top then widened into ruffles.

"Nothing, Your Majesty," replied Elspeth, hiding Calypso's coronet behind her back. She brushed a lock of her gray hair behind her ears.

"Of course it was not nothing," grumbled the queen, her long black fingernails wrapped around her staff. "It was my grand-daughter complaining about being queen again." She narrowed her eyes and turned to look at Calypso. "All she wants to do is play in the dirt all day and speak to objects that don't talk back."

"That is not true! I am a gardener!" replied Calypso.

"Queens are not gardeners. That is why we hire botanists. It was a fun hobby when you were a child, but now you must accept your royal duty. If your parents were still alive, you would have more time. I am old, and a ruler of West Ivoria cannot reign past her seventieth year of life. A strong leader must remain on the throne, otherwise evil will creep in. You must be responsible and do what is right."

"What if I don't want to accept my destiny?"

"You have no choice."

"I hate you!"

Calypso turned and ran out of the throne room, slamming the door behind her. With tears dripping over her face, she raced down the winding staircases and narrow hallways until she reached the place that was her peace. Yanking open the heavy oak doors, the princess stepped into the solarium.

The room housed a dome ceiling with wood pillars that framed the sanctuary in an octagonal shape. There were built-in shelves that housed plants of all kinds. Each pot held a unique species that Calypso had grown from seed to stem. Glass windows revealed the castle gardens, and beyond the property line were the Enchanted Woods. At the center of the room was the mosaic of a rose in a circle surrounded by ivy.

Calypso stood in the center of the circle and looked around. Like the rose, she felt herself surrounded by the ivy and the green plants that made her happy. Since she was a child, she and her mother would garden together. Like her mother, Calypso loved the feel of the dirt and the satisfaction of watching the beautiful plants grow and blossom. Her grandmother had loved to garden too, but after Calypso's mother had died, the queen wanted nothing to do with flowers.

"Your Highness."

The princess turned and saw Elspeth. The older woman's wrinkled palms held her crown. Calypso lowered her eyes and gave the handmaiden a wan smile. When her parents died, Elspeth had helped raise her while her grandmother had been occupied with royal duties. The elder handmaiden was her closest confidante.

"You know that change is not easy, my dear," stated Elspeth as she placed the crown onto the princess's head. The handmaiden then walked over to the shelves and touched the leaves of the various potted flora. "A long time ago, Ivoria used to be one realm, ruled by a noble king. When he died, his twin daughters Estelle and Willa both desired the throne. They could not agree on who should be queen. When Estelle tried to poison Willa, it was decided by the advisor to divide Ivoria into East and West. The Enchanted Woods would be the divider separating the realm in half. Willa took the west and Estelle took the east. While each sister had their own domain, neither one was satisfied. They looked for any opportunity to overtake the other and join the two realms together again.

"It has been stated that a ruler must remain on each throne at all times, for if one domain lacks a leader, the descendants of the opposing side will try to overtake the kingdom. Then there will be a vicious war.

Calypso groaned. "Why couldn't I have had a sibling!"

"My dear, we cannot wish for what we know we will never have. If you do not become Queen of West Ivoria, the Queen of East Ivoria will try to conquer our monarchy. East Ivoria has become a cold and evil place throughout the centuries. West Ivoria is a place of good. We cannot let our dominion become evil." The wrinkles in Elspeth's face crinkled as she smiled. "Forgive your grandmother. It was as difficult for her as it was for you when your parents died. Grief hardened her heart. Despite her harsh tones, she means well."

Calypso's eyes caught a glimpse of the weaponry covered in dust hanging on the opposite wall. Archery was her father's favorite sport just like gardening was her mother's passion. At times, it felt like the solarium was the only place where she felt connected to her parents.

No gardening. No archery. A queen does not have time. Her grandmother's voice filled her brain.

"I need some air. I think I am going to take a walk into town," replied Calypso.

Worry reflected in Elspeth's eyes. "You know how I feel about you going into town without protection."

"Elspeth, I have done this thousands of times. You know I need to do this. I need freedom from the stuffy walls of this place."

The old woman sighed. "Very well. Be wary of strangers."

The princess took her coronet and placed it on the shelf in-between two potted plants. She reached for a cloak. Covering her head, she stepped out the door.

S neaking off to the village had always been Calypso's way of rebelling against her royal title. Since her grandmother was the face of West Ivoria, many of the villagers did not know what the princess looked like. Without her crown, and adorned in her gardening garments, she fit in with the rest of the people.

Ah how wonderful it feels to be a normal citizen, thought Calypso as she practically danced into the hamlet. Her grandmother would never allow her to leave the palace walls for fear something might happen. The only people Calypso interacted with were other royals. Over time she got sick of attending regal courts, fancy balls, and formal dinner meetings. Here in the town square she could be humble Calypso instead of Princess Calypso of West Ivoria.

She believed her visits were worthwhile too, for she got to listen to the conversations among the townsfolk about West Ivoria. She got to hear their concerns, their opinions, their joys, and sadnesses. Her mother had always taught her that a good ruler listens to the people. For a kingdom is nothing without its loyal citizens. In her heart, Calypso felt this was the right thing to do. More royals should take the people's views into consideration when making decisions.

The princess made her way through the colorful displays in the marketplace. She was admiring some trinkets at one of the booths, when she felt a hand on her arm. Looking up she saw a peddler woman dressed in green. The lass was not much older than herself with pretty eyes and blonde hair wrapped loosely with a brightly colored scarf around her head. She seemed friendly in a curious kind of way.

"Ah, how is it that a beautiful girl like yourself has eyes that are so sad?" asked the maiden in green.

Calypso smiled politely and ignored her. On her visits to town, she made it a priority not to speak. For she did not want her royal speech to give her identity away.

"Your soul is troubled and your heart bears the weight of a destiny you do not wish to carry."

Why is this intruder so persistent? The princess looked up. "I do not know what you are talking about. I am fine."

The peddler woman reached into her basket and pulled out a golden pear. "What is your heart's desire?"

Seeing the fruit sparkling in the sunlight sent a chill through Calypso's spine. "Freedom..." she whispered. The word escaped her lips before she could stop herself.

Taking her hand, the blonde woman placed the golden pear into her palm. "A lonely heart's desire shall be fulfilled from eating this pear. Take a bite and the heart shall have everything it wishes for," she whispered.

Calypso stared at the golden pear, "I don't understand." She looked up, but the lady was gone.

"Odd woman," muttered Calypso as she continued to walk through the market. "Magic pear, heart's desire." She shook her head. "That woman is out of her mind." She sighed, "I wish not to be queen, so I may take care of my plants that I love. Flowers bring joy to others. What is the point of being royal if I cannot make myself and others happy?" In her heart, she knew a wish like hers could never be granted. As an only child, it was fated that she would take the throne. Sometimes the greatest wishes could never be fulfilled.

Her stomach growled. Absent-mindedly, Calypso took a bite of the delicious pear and headed back to the castle.

The next morning, the rising sun was accompanied by a scream that echoed throughout the castle. Calypso awoke and tumbled out of bed. She struggled out of the tangle of blankets, grabbed her robe, and hurried towards the sounds of distress.

The castle was in chaos. Servants ran past her and the advisors were bumping into one another. The princess ran down the hall to find Elspeth standing outside her grandmother's bedroom. Her shaking hands clasped to her chest, and her eyes widened.

"Elspeth! What is wrong?" cried Calypso putting her arms around the older woman.

"I-I...went to check on the queen..." stuttered the handmaiden.

"Is Grandma alright? Why hasn't a doctor been fetched?"

"Oh...dear..see for yourself..."

Her heartbeat increased and Calypso felt her palms grow sweaty. What was wrong with her grandmother?

She clasped her slender fingers around the door knob.

"Be careful," heaved Elspeth, "I-I do not know how *it* will react."

With her breath coming in rasps and tension filling each muscle,

Calypso threw open the door. A scream escaped her lips and then was stifled by her hands upon her mouth, for sitting there among the satin sheets and pillows was not her grandmother but a unicorn!

The unicorn lay partially on its side with its legs folded comfortably among the blankets, while its chin rested on the feathered cushions. The hair of the majestic equine was white like the snow on the mountaintops. Its long mane was embroidered with flowers. A long golden horn protruded out of its forehead, and just behind the horn between the ears a crown was perched on its head. Her grandmother's crown.

"Grandma?" gulped Calypso, stepping forward toward the creature.

Lifting its head, the unicorn snorted, nostrils flaring. For a second, the princess thought she saw the glow of human intelligence in the unicorn's eyes. The warmth reminded her of the kindness that had existed in her grandmother's eyes long ago before her parents' deaths. But it had been years since she had witnessed that kind of love. However, the glimmer of recognition quickly became a fleeting shadow as the creature's animalistic nature came forth.

Neighing, the unicorn struggled to get out of bed. The frame collapsed as the equine got to its feet and hopped to the floor. Pawing the ground, the frightened unicorn began to pace the small area, lifting its front hooves while snorting. Its hindquarters slammed into the dresser causing the large cabinet to topple over. Drawers containing her grandmother's clothes opened, spilling their royal contents. Kicking backwards, the beast's hooves shattered the mirror spewing pieces of glass every which way. Calypso could see the confusion and distress in the wide eyes of the startled grandmother. Finally, realizing that Calypso was standing in front of an open door, the horned being fled to freedom.

Screaming, Calypso jumped out of the way as pounding hooves clicked on the marble floor.

"Princess! Are you alright?" asked Elspeth, helping her up.

Calypso did not respond and began to run after the unicorn whose flight was causing chaos throughout the entire palace.

"Stop that unicorn! That's the queen!" she yelled, following the trail of overturned pedestals, smashed statues, and broken frames of portraits.

Willing her body to move faster, the princess ran through the winding twists and turns of the castle until the open front doors greeted her.

The cool wind blew her messy curls across her face. She struggled to put them behind her ears.

"Who opened the doors!" she yelled.

"I did," replied the castle steward. "The unicorn was destroying the castle, and I did not wish the creature to hurt itself."

"Where did it go?"

"Why, into the Enchanted Woods, of course," continued the steward, "That is where all the unicorns live, they say. Although I have no idea how one found its way into the castle." He walked off leaving Calypso alone in the grand hall.

The princess took in the waves of destruction. Broken vases, overturned furniture, and more portraits knocked off the walls. She sank to her knees as her brain tried to process what had just happened. The queen's crown and human glow of the eyes flashed through her mind.

Her grandmother was a unicorn! But how?

Take a bite of the pear and the heart's desire will be fulfilled. The words of the peddler woman sang through her reflection. She remembered the juiciness of the pear and the taste of its flesh on her tongue. Her stomach twisted in knots, and she felt sick. Could the pear have been bewitched? What sort of magic had been released from her greedy bite? She had no idea how such a transformation could have twisted her heart's desire into her worst nightmare.

"What have I done?" she whispered.

Her revelation was interrupted by the chambermaid's voice. "The queen is missing!"

"So, you are telling us that Queen Hylzarle has been turned into a unicorn?" asked the first advisor.

It was later that morning. Calypso had changed into her royal attire and met with the council.

"Yes. The animal was in her bed wearing her crown," replied the princess. She had left out the part about the golden pear and her wish.

"Where is the unicorn now?" asked the first advisor.

"It ran into the Enchanted Woods," replied the second advisor.

"So no one has any idea of the location of Queen Hylzarie?" continued the first advisor.

"No, sir," replied the third advisor.

"Well, then, until the queen appears in her designated form, we must continue to have a ruler on the throne. Princess Calypso, you are now the queen," stated the first advisor.

The color drained from the princess's face.

"What?" whispered Calypso, her heartbeat in her throat.

"You are the only heir to the throne. Of course, a formal coronation will have to take place, but we can always do that later. In the meantime, you must rule West Ivoria."

"What about my grandmother?" replied Calypso, her voice thick with disgust. "You're not going to go look for her?"

"My dear, of course we are, but you do not understand. No one is going to believe the queen is a unicorn as you say. Besides, the queen was set to retire anyway. Who knows, maybe she decided she needed some time to herself?"

"I do not want to be queen," replied Calypso.

"You have no choice," replied the first advisor. "The existence of West Ivoria relies on a ruler sitting on the throne."

So much for the heart's desire, thought Calypso. The bite of the fruit had done nothing but make her life more miserable. That was not her intention when she had made her wish.

A hand rested on her shoulder. It was Elspeth. "Come on, Princess, let's get you ready for duty."

"We must think of a proclamation for the townsfolk," mused the first advisor to the other people at the table. "We can state the queen is not well and has decided to retire early from her duties as monarch. With new blood on the throne, we may now bring prosperity to the lands."

Calypso brushed off Elspeth's touch. "No!" She shouted. "I will not be queen! This is not what I wished for! I wish to be a botanist!" Ripping the crown off her head, she threw the symbol of royalty to the ground. Then she raced out of the room, down the stairs, and out the front doors, vanishing into the Enchanted Woods after her grandmother.

Twigs snapped under her slippers, and the branches cracked as she thrashed her way into the forest. Tears streamed down her face, and her lungs heaved. Her thoughts were jumbled.

When her feet could run no farther, she stopped. Panting, Calypso looked up to see she was surrounded by woods. The branches of the sturdy oaks and hickory trees covered most of the sky. The gaps in the branches exposed small patches of blue. Tall pines and maples were scattered throughout the forest. Catching her breath, the princess looked around and saw wildflowers, shrubs, ferns, sedges, and mosses.

Crack!

A flash of white flickered in between the thick vegetation.

Crack! Crack! Twigs snapped. Calypso gasped and drew her hands to her mouth. She had failed to think about what lived in the forest before she entered it. Who knew what called the trees their home? What dangers lurked behind the rocks? How would she defend herself?

A hearty snort came from the underbrush. The princess stepped back as a large unicorn trotted into the clearing where she stood.

"Grandma?" she asked quickly, then realized the unicorn was not wearing a crown. White like newfallen snow; entwined in its mane were diamonds, emeralds, and sapphires. Its eyes were full of light,and its long golden horn caught the sunlight. The princess backed away from the majestic creature.

"I am not a grandmother," the unicorn replied.

Calypso stumbled forward and grabbed onto a branch. "Y-you can talk?"

"All animals can talk if you take the time to listen. Now, who are you?"

"I am Calypso...um...Princess of West Ivoria. And who are you?"

"I am Arabella, royal consort of the unicorns. What are you

doing in the Enchanted Woods? I have never known a human to venture this far."

Bowing her head, the princess answered, "I am searching for my grandmother. I have lost her." Taking a deep breath, she retold the events that had transpired over the past twenty-four hours. When she finished, a look of fear spread across Arabella's face.

"If you are the Princess of West Ivoria, then you must turn around at once. The Enchanted Woods exist as the halfway point between east and west. To go farther would put your life in peril."

"Why?" asked Calypso, puzzled.

"You have heard of the tale of Willa and Estelle?"

The princess nodded.

"When their father died, Estelle used evil ways to obtain the throne, whereas Willa tried to use kindness and reason. This is why the realm is divided and this agreement has remained in place for centuries. No citizen of either West Ivoria or East Ivoria can cross through the woods, for such an act would be considered the start of a new war. It appears that something as monumental as your intrusion has already occurred.

"What are you talking about?" asked Calypso.

"Who is on the throne in West Ivoria while you are frolicking in the woods?" asked the unicorn.

"I am not sure. No one, I guess. I am the only heir to the throne."

"No one is ruling West Ivoria? You must go back!"

"I am not going anywhere. I have to find my grandmother," replied Calypso, crossing her arms. "Besides, I do not want to be queen."

"Why do you not wish to be queen?"

"Because being queen means I cannot do any of the things that bring me joy."

"Well, then, you must go see The Fairy Countess of the Forest, Ellerie. She will give you guidance on how to solve your dilemma. But you must hurry. The Queen of East Ivoria is powerful in the art of evil magic. It will not take long for her to realize the throne of West Ivoria is open for the taking."

"I do not know how to find the Fairy Countess," replied the young princess.

"I will go with you. She lives in the heart of the forest. I have some questions to ask of my own."

Together the princess and unicorn walked through the green foliage until they reached a small pond. Lily pads rested on the surface, and cattails framed the edges of the water. Small frogs jumped about as they came closer. Nearby grew a tall weeping willow tree. Its long thin tendrils filled with leaves swept downward, obscuring the trunk and trailing their reflections into the waves.

"We are here," announced Arabella. "This is the heart of the forest."

Walking through the elongated leaves, Arabella disappeared as if in a mist. Stunned by the vision, Calypso looked around and then followed.

To her surprise she found herself inside a secret hideaway far from the outside world. Calypso entered into the domain and stood next to Arabella. A heart was carved in the center of the willow's trunk. Reaching up, Calypso brushed her fingers along the image, feeling the rough grain of the bark against her skin.

"Hello!" a light-hearted voice called.

Calypso looked up to see a beautiful fairy sitting high in the branches. Ellerie the Fairy Countess was clothed in an off-the-shoulder white dress. A choker of rubies glittered around her neck, and ruby cuffs decorated her upper arm and ankles. Hair clips of gold shaped like leaves decorated her brown hair. Protruding from her back were two large elegant wings that were transparent with sparks of color flashing pink and gold.

"O, Fairy Countess, we seek your wisdom," replied Arabella.

Fluttering her long wings, Ellerie flew off her perch and hovered before them until she settled on the ground. "A unicorn and a human asking for my guidance, how interesting. Wait a minute. I know both of you. You are the Princess of West Ivoria, Calypso, and you are one of the royals of the unicorn court, Arabella."

"How do you know who we are?" asked Calypso.

"I know everything," replied the fairy. "Including the reasons why you are here."

Ellerie looked from unicorn to princess then took a deep breath.

"Your fear of becoming queen has brought Evil to your doorstep, Calypso. The peddler woman who gave you the golden pear was Magdelone, the Queen of East Ivoria. The bite you took from the pear was the Magic of Transformation that turned your grandmother into a unicorn."

"I don't understand," interrupted Calypso, "that was not my heart's desire."

"One thing you must learn, child," replied Ellerie, "expecting others to have the same heart as you, will break you. Evil twists your desires into outcomes that benefit it, not you. As for the reasoning behind your grandmother's transformation, I cannot answer that. But I can answer for you, Arabella. The unicorns are disappearing because Magdelone's army is capturing them. Unicorn blood carries strength and power in its golden liquid. The Queen of East Ivoria wishes to drink an elixir filled with the blood of unicorns to gain the dominance to rule the entire realm of Ivoria."

"How catastrophic! What kind of evil magic is that?" whispered Calypso.

"What is even more terrible is the state your grandmother is in right now," replied Ellerie.

Calypso clasped her hands over her mouth.

"Yes," continued the fairy. "Drinking your enemy's blood will allow conquest. You must find your grandmother before Magdelone's army captures her. Travel to the Fields of Marzanna to find Queen Hylzarie. From there you must head to the castle of East Ivoria. I leave you with a gift."

She handed Calypso a bow and one arrow.

Calypso held the weapons in her hands. Memories flooded her mind.

"If I remember correctly, you were at one time quite a skilled archer, Princess."

The princess smiled. "Yes, I used to shoot targets all the time until my grandmother forbade it. As she did everything else." She felt a sense of resentment wash over her. *A princess does not shoot arrows, a princess does not grow plants. This is why we hire people. A princess must partake in royal duties so she may rule the kingdom.* Her grandmother's words flooded her brain. She cleared her throat. "Only one arrow?"

"Why have a clutch of arrows when it takes only one to succeed. Many times in life, we have only one chance to grasp what we want more than anything, and we must take a risk. You will know what to do when that moment arrives."

The fairy waved her hand over the objects. The bow and arrow collapsed into a gold bracelet with charms that mirrored the objects they represented. The chain wrapped itself around the princess's wrist.

"When the right moment presents itself," continued Ellerie. "Touch the bracelet, and the objects will become their proper size. But remember, you will have only one opportunity, so make your shot count."

The fairy stepped back and fluttered her beautiful wings. "Best of luck to both of you. Now that the balance has been tipped, hopefully you can restore the scales in your favor. For if Evil takes control of West Ivoria, the land will perish."

Flapping her crystalline wings, she flew to the tops of the trees. Once again Calypso and Arabella continued their journey.

Walking along the pathway towards the Fields of Marzanna, Calypso's brain swirled with the words of the beautiful fairy.

"If you don't mind me asking," said Arabella, her hooves clopping on the stones. "What did you mean when you said being queen meant you cannot do the things that bring you joy?"

The princess took a deep breath. "Becoming queen means giving up everything I love. I want to be a botanist, but my grandmother says that as royals, we have people to do those kinds of employments. I will be too focused on running the kingdom. I used to like archery, too, but she made me give it up as well."

"Why can't you have both?" asked Arabella.

"Because it's not what royals do," replied Calypso surveying the forest.

"But if you are queen, don't you get to make the rules?"

The princess was silent.

"We wish to forge our own paths but we fear disappointing those who are closest to us. Many times, in childhood, families push their own agendas and fill young minds with their own desires. We do not see that we have choices and our happiness matters. You, Princess Calypso, can do whatever you want as Queen of West Ivoria."

Before Calypso could answer, birds chirped above. The song brought forth a distant memory. Her mind flashed back to a time when her mother, her grandmother, and she were gardening among the castle flowers. They had gotten dirty planting various blooms as the birds chirped in the trees above them. She remembered her grandmother's beautiful smile. It had been a long time since she had seen her grandmother smile like that. After her mother died, her grandmother had never set foot in the garden again.

"She wasn't always so strict," she muttered to herself. "There was a time when she was happy." The princess cleared her throat. "What about you? I do not know much about the unicorn clan."

"Unicorns are peaceful creatures. We do not bother anyone. However, it appears everyone likes to bother us because of our blood and horns. Our blood has been known to bring superhuman strength and power. Our horns can cure illness. I noticed the unicorns disappearing. Now I know Magdelone has been behind their absence. We have lived in solitude for many years with no one causing trouble in our lives until now. As one of the highest members of our clan, it is my duty to make sure everyone is safe. I only hope we can find your grandmother, restore her to human form and rescue all of my fellow unicorns."

"I am so sorry. I hope we can fix all of this, too." Calypso looked out at the trees. Where could her grandmother be? "Do you think my grandmother is in the Field of Marzanna with the other unicorns?"

"All of the forest is our home. The fields are deep in the forest where many humans would not venture. The Field of Marzanna is the best place for the most delicious fruits and grass."

Arabella paused. A rustle could be heard in the bushes nearby.

The princess's breath caught in her throat, and her heart beat louder.

Appearing from under a leafy branch, the two companions watched a creature half man and half horse reveal himself. His expression was gentle and his eyes were kind. As he stepped onto the path before them, the princess's eyes widened. He was a centaur.

Arabella neighed, "Gwydion."

Gwydion, the young centaur, smiled in return. He was bare-chested, and the filtered light from the trees reflected on his muscular frame. He had a tattoo that ran from his right arm across his chest. It was an array of symbols and designs that Calypso did not recognize. He ran his hand through his sandy brown hair and stomped his hooves into the dirt. His lower body was that of a pinto horse with splashes of white and brown. Slung across his back was a knapsack, and a bow was clutched in his human hand.

"Greetings, Arabella, how are you, fair unicorn?" replied Gwydion. "Who are you walking with? A human? We do not see many of them around these parts."

"This is Princess Calypso of West Ivoria."

"Pleasure to meet you, Your Highness." Gwydion nodded his head.

"We are on a mission to find Calypso's grandmother, The Queen of West Ivoria. She has been turned into a unicorn by dark magic from East Ivoria. The Queen of East Ivoria is also capturing the unicorns from my clan."

"Has the battle between West Ivoria and East Ivoria reignited again?" asked Gwydion raising his eyebrows.

"It was always ongoing, my friend, as is life. It was just dormant for a while."

"Well, then, you are going to need all the help you can get. I would be happy to offer my services. Anything to keep Ivoria at peace."

Arabella was about to reply, when Calypso shouted, "There she is!"

At the end of the path stood a unicorn wearing a gold crown. It was the Queen of West Ivoria. Calypso began running towards her beloved grandmother whose eyes were full of fear and confusion.

"Grandma!" She shouted. "It's me, Calypso! Wait! Stop!"

Before Calypso could get closer to grasp the escapee's mane, the equine took off and ran through a gap in the bushes. Tears began to brim.

"Calypso, you must not startle the queen," cried Arabella as she and Gwydion galloped up behind her.

"Why doesn't she recognize me? Why is she not talking like you do?" moaned the princess.

"Your grandmother is not a unicorn by birth. She does not understand the magic of the clan. She is frightened and has appeared to have taken on animalistic traits. When she is not consumed by fear, she will slowly begin to recognize you," replied Arabella.

Gwydion reached into his backpack and pulled out a rope. "If we can get close enough, we can use this to capture her and keep her safe. Come. Her tracks show she has gone this way."

They pushed through the gap in the bushes which opened into a beautiful meadow.

"Where are we?" asked Calypso.

"This is the Field of Marzanna," answered Gwydion.

Various spices of flowers stretched across the grasslands into a distant abyss. At the perimeter were bushes filled with berries. Unicorns of every shape and size grazed before them.

"I see her!" cried Calypso, pointing towards her grandmother. The unicorn with the golden crown had found shelter in the center of the clan. The queen raised her head and snorted. Then she began to gallop away with some of the other unicorns.

"Hurry! She is getting away!"

The three companions took off after Queen Hylzarie. Calypso darted in and out among the unicorns. She brushed past hindquarters and withers. Tail hair flicked in her face, and she felt suffocated from the closeness of the equine bodies. Soon she broke free from the herd of unicorns, and cool air found its way into her lungs. She saw her grandmother galloping along the edge of the forest. Other unicorns ran in front of her.

Calypso paused, her chest heaving, and then she froze. "Grandma!" she called.

However, Queen Hylzarie ignored her and continued to run among the grasses.

A dark shadow fell across the sun, and Calypso looked up to see a figure sweeping through the sky. It landed with authority in the center of the field. A large creature with the upper body of an eagle and lower body of a lion, its wings spread wide flapped violently causing the unicorns to scurry. It was a griffin.

A harness was attached to the creature's body and connected to a large wooden cage on wheels. Riding on the griffin's back were soldiers. The knights hopped to the ground and began herding some of the unicorns into the cage. One of the unicorns was her grandmother!

"No!" cried Calypso. She began to run to the soldiers, but Gwydion grabbed her and pulled her into the bushes.

"Now is not the time for foolishness. Those are the soldiers of East Ivoria. There are too many of them. We must wait," the centaur informed her.

The princess watched in horror as the soldiers herded her grand-mother and five other unicorns into the cage. Then they jumped back onto the griffin. The terrifying creature took to the skies, pulling the wheeled cage fluttering behind it like a flag.

Calypso felt her cheeks grow hot. How were they going to rescue her grandmother? One task turned into two more tasks, multiple upon multiple problems needed to be solved. What if something happened to the queen? What if she never saw her again? She thought back to her last conversation with her grandmother and a gloom overcame her. An argument. Words spoken in anger. She did not mean it. What if she never got the chance ever again to speak to the one person in the world who was her family?

"I should have never said I hated her," whispered Calypso. A great pain gripped her heart.

"Calypso, everything is going to be alright," Arabella's voice came to her.

The princess turned. "No, it is not. Everything is a mess. It is all my fault. If I had not made that stupid wish, my grandmother would still be in human form." Her voice was tight with tears and her words felt smothered in her throat.

"Ah, princess, we all are guilty of falling victim to the selfishness of others. But now we must work together to right these wrongs, or West Ivoria will be in great peril."

"What is our next step?"

"We must go to the Castle of East Ivoria to free the unicorns and rescue Queen Hylzarie. Once there, we will face Magdelone. I just hope she has not taken any of the unicorn blood until we get there. It will be much harder to defeat a human who has taken such a powerful potion."

Nodding, Calypso turned to Gwydion. "Are you going to come with us?"

"Of course! It appears that you need all the help you can get. I am prepared for a battle against Evil. It is a part of my centaurian nature."

Arabella looked at the sky. "We must head east. The road to Magdelone's castle is paved with challenges and we must keep our wits about us."

With Calypso riding on Arabella's back, it took them a day to reach the end of the Enchanted Woods. As they moved out into the open, leaving the trees far behind, they were greeted with a deep ravine that stretched before them. Looking down into its darkness, there was no bottom. Reaching across the wide gaping chasm was a rickety narrow bridge. Only about three feet wide, the vines woven into the crossing seemed a mile long. The boards that covered the floor of the bridge were worn, and some were missing. The ropes holding the entire edifice seemed slightly frayed. The scene before them was one of inevitable doom.

"There is no way that bridge is going to hold all of us," announced Calypso.

"We have no choice," replied Gwydion. "I will go first. Calypso will go second, and Arabella will go last. That way we can spread out the weight."

The centaur took to the bridge and put his hooves on the first board. The bridge sagged but held his weight. The princess followed, then the unicorn.

Every muscle in Calypso's body felt tense as she lightly tapped each board before putting her weight on it. Her breath felt strangled and she gripped the ropes so tightly her knuckles were white. At one point, one of the boards snapped and fell into the abyss. Arabella pulled her back to keep her from pitching forward into the gorge.

"This is taking forever," groaned the princess.

Calypso felt her mind begin to wander. She hoped her grandmother was alright.

"We are nearly at the end of this troublesome impediment," Arabella's musical voice broke the princess from her thoughts. The opposite edge that anchored the bridge was feet from their arrival.

Crack!

Looking behind them, Calypso saw one of the ancient frayed ropes had snapped, causing part of the woven branches to collapse. As the boards fell one after another in a domino effect, the trio managed to reach safety on the opposite side. As their feet and hooves touched land, they watched the rest of the ancient twigs and vines fall into the chasm.

"That was too close for comfort," said Gwydion brushing off his hindquarters.

Arabella raised her head as the wind blew her mane and tail. "The breeze whispers that Magdelone grows stronger. Her evil aura has begun to invade the land, creating chaos. We must keep moving."

They began to follow the path that led to East Ivoria. The way to the castle wove in and out of giant boulders before transforming into flat land. Calypso noticed that East Ivoria lived up to its reputation of being a place of evil. The ground beneath their feet was cracked, and there was not a blade of grass in sight. The trees were barren and dead. There were no flowers or bushes, only skeletal images of what had been plants. There were no animals. The foliage around them seemed to be in desperate need of water, food, and love. Soon the princess could see the turrets peeking out from above the dead pine trees. She hoped she and her friends would reach the castle in time before the evil queen drank her grandmother's blood.

They rounded the corner, and beheld the full scale of East

Ivoria's castle. The edifice stood twice the size of her castle. Made of black stone that absorbed light, moss as dark as the deepest swamp grew on one side. Multiple turrets stood tall as if trying to pierce the sky with their points. A moat surrounded the castle, and a large wall encircled the entire fortress protecting it from outsiders. The barrier connected to a long stone drawbridge led to open iron gates.

"Where are the soldiers?" asked Gwydion. "It seems noticeably quiet for a kingdom that is about to raise chaos."

"That is because they have left to fulfill the wishes of Queen Magdelone to ride to the dominion where no ruler reigns and seize the defenseless realm," a voice crackled. A figure moved from under the stone bridge and blocked the path before them. It was an ogre.

"Besides, the queen can handle the three of you. You are no match for her powers. Also, I told her I wouldn't mind guarding the bridge until the soldiers returned, for a price, of course."

Standing about seven feet tall, the ogre had long hair down its back. A pointy nose protruded from his face, and ears as large as turnips grew on both sides of its head. Long yellow nails flashed like claws from its fingertips, and a foul smell came from the creature.

"Who are you?" boomed the guardian. It sniffed the air. "Ah, I smell a princess, but not one from this side. It appears that you are letting your kingdom get away."

"That is not true!" yelled Calypso.

The creature shrugged, "I don't care. All I know is if you pay me some gold, Queen Magdelone does not have to know you are here. It will be as if I never saw you, but if you do not wish to pay, then I will bring you to the queen myself. She will love to know you have arrived in her domain."

Calypso looked over at Arabella. It seemed East Ivoria held true to its reputation of being evil. Lies, deceit, and betrayal ran rampant throughout its borders.

"We do not have any gold," replied the princess. "We have traveled a long way to face the queen so you might as well tell us..."

She was interrupted by Gwydion's voice. "Well, if it is gold you seek, then it is gold you shall have," The centaur reached into his knapsack and pulled out a velvet bag. He opened the pouch and pulled out a shiny gold coin. The object glistened in the sunlight.

The gatekeepers' eyes widened. "Yes! Give it here!"

Placing the coin back in the bag, Gwydion smiled. "If you want it, go and get it."

He threw the bag of coins into the moat. The ogre dove after it.

"Hurry!" Gwydion motioned for them to cross the drawbridge. As they hurried into the castle, the greedy guardian plunged into the muddy water of the moat.

"Gwydion! How could you do that? You shouldn't have had to give your gold on my account," cried Calypso.

"Asking him to lead us directly to the queen was not a good idea. We do not know what we are up against. I feel the lack of authority is a trap. Also, I did not lose anything. The bag may have been full of gold, but it was not real. For only a fool full of greed would try to take something from another and in turn end up with nothing."

After crossing the drawbridge, they hid behind a stack of crates piled in the open marketplace surrounding the castle. For a few moments they stopped to assess their situation. Before them was the courtyard. People were bustling among the different booths at the public square. Children played near a fountain, and soldiers stood against the castle wall.

"There are too many people," whispered Calypso. The fact her friends were a unicorn and a centaur would be difficult to disguise.

"I see the stables," pointed Gwydion. "Hopefully the unicorns and your grandmother are there."

"How do we not draw attention to ourselves?" asked the princess.

"With unicorn magic," replied Arabella. The tip of her horn glowed. She reached forward and touched Calypso and Gwydion's chests with her point. "A spell of invisibility I place on you."

The princess looked down and saw her body begin to turn gray. Arabella and Gwydion became the same shade.

"We can see each other because we are all under the same spell," continued the unicorn. "However, we must hurry because the spell will only last about a minute. Evil magic works against us, and a unicorn's powers never function properly in East Ivoria."

The three friends wove their way in and out of the crowd until they reached the safety of the stable. Gwydion and Calypso closed the stable doors. As the princess clicked the lock into place, her hands returned to their original color.

In the stable there were a few workers putting away shovels and brooms. Their eyes widened when they saw the unexpected visitors. Arabella raised her head high and her horn began to shine. The servants' eyes drooped, and they slumped over into a slumber.

"Phew, that was close," replied Gwydion. "I still feel like this is too easy, and it is a trap. We must be careful."

As they walked down the rows of stalls, the unicorns' cries for help greeted them.

"Arabella, you're here!" called out one of the unicorns.

"We knew you would save us," declared another.

Calypso and Gwydion hurried through the motions of unbolting the stalls and freeing the captive creatures. With each passing stall, Calypso hoped she would see her grandmother, but the queen was not there. Soon all the unicorns were crowded into the aisle.

"Where is she?" pleaded Calypso. "Why is she not with the rest of the unicorns?"

"You mean the unicorn with the crown?" cried a captive with green eyes.

"She is not here. The guard took her up to the castle," chimed in another with sparkly hooves. "She did not say much. It was almost as if she was in a trance."

"We have to get into the castle," said the princess, glancing toward the entrance.

"First, we must get my clan out of here," declared Arabella. "That way Magdelone won't have a source anymore. Evil magic is clever. I need everyone to concentrate."

The princess watched as the unicorns came together and began to hum. They closed their eyes in concentration. The tip of Arabella's horn began to glow with a bright light. Bending downward, she touched her horn to the dirt floor and a hole opened.

"Hurry!" called Arabella.

One by one the unicorns jumped into the hole before it closed.

"What a brilliant display of magic," complimented Gwydion.

"When we unicorns gather as one, we can create magic. This

portal will lead them to Kiano Meadow in the Enchanted Woods where they will be safe."

"Why couldn't you have created a portal for us to come here?" joked Gwydion.

"As head of the royal court, I have special powers; however, those powers do not work well in East Ivoria. I wanted to save my magic for the right moment and not drain myself. Humans and other creatures have persecuted us for years. They have taken our blood and tried to take our horns, but our magic they can never take. Now that the captives of our unicorn kingdom are safe, we three must find a way to get into the castle so we can rescue your grandmother."

Arabella was able to summon enough magic to create an invisibility shield that allowed them to get across the courtyard into Magdelone's domain.

As they returned to visibility, Calypso realized the vast interior was very quiet. All the soldiers were outside, yet none seemed to be inside. The palace was silent.

"I do not have a good feeling about this," repeated Gwydion.

They walked down the hall and entered the throne room. Again silence greeted them. There was no sign of the Queen of East Ivoria, nor any of the servants.

"Oh, this is not good," muttered Calypso. "How is it that everyone is outside but no one is inside?"

"It seems Queen Magdelone is trying to trick us, we must tread carefully," advised Gwydion.

Calypso noticed a door behind the throne that was slightly ajar. "I think we should check in there."

Sniffing the air, Arabella nodded, "I sense the presence of a unicorn behind those doors."

"What if it is a trick to lure us in?" asked Gwydion.

"We have no choice. I need to find my grandmother. I have to make things right," replied Calypso.

Approaching with caution, the intrepid royal trio moved through the door and down a set of winding stone steps that led them to a secret lair. At the center was a work table filled with herbs, keys, potions, burners, and glass flasks. A fireplace with a bubbling cauldron was behind the table, and there were shelves upon shelves with books, and labeled jars. In the gloomy room, they found Queen Hylzarie chained to one wall. On the work table were two vials of what appeared to be unicorn blood.

"Grandma!" cried Calypso running over to the unicorn and throwing her arms around its neck. Seated on a gold rug, the Queen of West Ivoria seemed to be lost in a trance. The princess noticed a cloth wrapped around her fetlock. "Her blood has been taken. Quick, Arabella! Open the portal."

Arabella shook her head. "I cannot do that. Queen Hylzarie is not a unicorn."

"Then we must get her out of here," demanded the determined princess. Looking around, she saw mysterious keys sitting on the bench. Grabbing them, she jammed one key into the lock that held her grandmother captive. It turned easily and the chains fell away.

"Do not worry, Grandma," she whispered, stroking the unicorn's head. "Everything will be alright."

"Well, well, well, who has invaded my lair? Why, if it is not the royals from West Ivoria!" a voice boomed.

Calypso whirled around to see a tall slender woman standing in the doorway. She had straight black hair framing her face, accentuating her high cheekbones. Her dark eyes, rimmed in eyeliner, sent chills down the princess's spine. Queen Magdelone waved her hand, and the door clicked shut.

Swaggering with defiance to each of the intruders in her alchemy chamber, she cackled. "Here we have Princess Calypso of West Ivoria." She turned to Gwydion. "I have no idea who you are." She waltzed over to Arabella. "You are the Royal Consort of the Unicorns." Lastly, her eyes fell onto the Queen of West Ivoria. "And everyone knows Queen Hylzarie, who has seen better days. Once a vibrant queen, she is now a beast of the forest, thanks to her impudent granddaughter."

Calypso felt her face grow hot as she stroked her grandmother's muzzle. "You tricked me!" she hissed to Magedelone.

Placing her hand on her own chest, the evil woman laughed. "Me? Trick you? Now why would I do a thing like that?" She waved her hand and her image transformed into the beautiful blonde peasant woman from the market. "What is the heart's desire?" Then she morphed back into her true self and cackled.

"You did trick me!" snarled Calypso.

"I did nothing of the sort. I believe I said 'one's heart's desire shall come from eating this pear, which includes you and me. In fact, you should be thanking me, Calypso. Don't you see? I gave you everything you ever wanted. Your heart's desire was not to be queen. By turning your grandmother into a unicorn, you did not have to feel obligated to take a destiny you did not want. By right of the royal treaty signed by our two kingdoms, if no royal is on the throne in West Ivoria, the absence allows me to take over and become the one and only Queen of both kingdoms! So, we both get what we want. You grow your little plants you love so much, and I shall be queen!"

Calypso looked in horror at the malignant queen. *What have I done?* she thought, *If West Ivoria were to fall into the hands of this woman, the realm would be doomed. The balance and harmony would be destroyed.* Her grandmother did not deserve this fate. *How selfish I have become. After all, she raised me when my parents died.* Then the princess remembered how rigid her grandmother had become.

"In times of grief, people can turn into someone they are not. Pain has a way of forcing us to build a barrier to those we love most," whispered Arabella who stood beside her. The princess glanced at the unicorn. Her friend had read her mind.

"Ah! You all have been so stupid," continued Magdelone. "You walked right into my trap. You really thought the castle was abandoned? No servants, no soldiers, everyone outside but no one inside." She laughed. "I have half my army waiting near the castle of West Ivoria, fully prepared to take over a castle that currently has no queen on the throne."

"Where is the other half of your army?" sneered Gwydion.

"Whose horse is this?" asked Magdelone.

"He is a centaur," snapped Calypso.

"A centaur should know better than to question the Queen of all of Ivoria. The other half of my army is lying in wait ready for my command." She cackled. "I allowed you to rescue the unicorns. I did not need them when I had the grand prize: Queen Hylzarie. Unicorn's blood is special. It gives superhuman strength and power.

It creates a psychic and instinctive sense. It can cure illness and chase off weakness. With my supply of unicorn blood, I will be the most powerful being in all of the realm. And unicorn blood is even more valuable when it comes from an enemy queen in unicorn form."

Moving towards the large fireplace set into the opposite wall, Magdelone reached for a rock and flint. "When I strike this, it will light a fire that will send thick dark smoke into the sky to inform my leaders at West Ivoria to begin the ambush and take over the castle. However, this can all be avoided, Calypso, if you simply give up the throne. After all, you have always hated to become queen. If you let me have the throne voluntarily, then you can live your life as a normal Ivorian botanist and be happy. Then you will truly have your heart's desire. What do you say, girl?"

Wringing her hands, Calypso turned toward her grandmother who was pawing the ground with her hoof. The princess saw she was favoring her bandaged leg. Her eyes showed pain.

"Return my grandmother to her human form," Calypso yelled.

"I beg your pardon?" said Magdelone

"I said, return my grandmother to her human form!"

"Only if you give up the throne." The evil queen sneered at her.

Calypso could tell by the look in Magdelone's eyes she was lying. After all, if Queen Hylzarie were returned to human form, that would mean West Ivoria still had a queen. A flash of images whirled through Calypso's brain. Visions of her grandmother, her mother, and herself gardening. Visions of her father and herself shooting arrows on the lawn while her grandmother watched. The two activities that had once brought her so much joy had been taken from her. However, they had been taken away because of the grief that death had imposed upon her grandmother. While Calypso loved these activities because they had made her feel close to her parents, they brought too much pain to her grandmother.

We all grieve differently, Arabella's voice whispered to her. The princess thought back to her earlier conversation with the unicorn. *I thought queens made the rules. Why can't you have both? Why can't you be a botanist and a queen?*

"No," whispered Calypso.

"What was that, girl?" hissed Magdelone.

Her grandmother had never tried to hurt her. She did not want to be around the things that made her miss Calypso's parents so much. But as queen, Calypso could change that. She could associate her parents' memory with joy instead of sadness.

"I said no!" yelled Calypso.

"Well, then, I guess West Ivoria is about to be in for a surprise awakening." The Queen of East Ivoria reached for the flint and stone. At that moment, a beam of light shot out of Arabella's horn. The beam hit the ceiling causing a portion of it to collapse around the fireplace, sealing it from Magdelone's touch.

"Oh, you think that is going to stop me?" hissed Magdelone. "You are going to give me that throne one way or another."

"No, I'm not!" yelled Calypso. She turned towards her grandmother. "I am the Queen of West Ivoria."

The crown on her grandmother's head began to glow. With trembling hands, Calypso took the coronet and placed it on her own head. "I claim my birthright to the throne of West Ivoria."

"Well, if you want to be queen so badly, then fight for it, Princess," hissed Magdelone. Her slender fingers grasped one of the vials that held her grandmother's blood. In a swift motion, Queen Magdelone raised the glass to her lips and drank the contents in one gulp.

Calypso froze, "She drank my grandmother's blood!"

"Oh, this is not good," moaned Gwydion. "With Queen Hylzarie's blood in her body, the evil monarch is unstoppable."

Watching in horror, the princess, unicorn, and centaur witnessed a red glow form around Magdelone. Flames illuminated in her palms, then absorbed into her body. The queen ripped a fragment of the stone out of the wall and threw it at Calypso. Dodging the missile, Calypso tripped and slammed against the table.

As she steadied herself, her eyes fell upon the other vial that sat before her. This was the vial that held her grandmother's blood. If Magdelone wanted to play games, she could play them, too. Without hesitating, Calypso brought the glass to her lips and swallowed the liquid.

She winced. To her surprise, the contents was a mixture of sweet, salty, and metallic elements. Her chest tightened as she clasped her hands to her heart. The glass dropped to the floor shattering into pieces.

Placing one hand on the table to steady herself as she bent over, Calypso felt a tingling sensation move throughout her body. Muscles contracted in her arms and legs. She felt stronger. Her feet wanted to run faster. Light, the source of magic, began to glow from her hands. The sensation subsided and the princess knew something was different. She was different. While she looked the same, she had been given superhuman speed, strength, skill, and magic.

Righting herself, she turned to see everyone staring at her.

Turning around she walked to the wall, pulled a giant stone from it and threw it at the locked door. The large stone smashed the wood.

"Quick!" yelled Calypso, "get Grandma out of here."

Magdelone was about to interfere, but Calypso picked up the table and threw it at her. Magdelone dodged the object with rapid speed. This distraction allowed Gwydion and Arabella to get Queen Hylzarie out of the lair, up the stairs, and into the throne room.

"Oh, you thought you could defeat me by drinking the blood, too. Well, my dear, you are wrong, I am going to destroy you. But first I will get rid of that unicorn!" Magdelone waved her hand sending a bolt of light towards Calypso. The princess dodged it. Magdelone ran out of the lair followed by Calypso moving at the speed of lightning.

Halting at the entrance to the throne room, the malicious queen stopped a moment. Calypso tackled her from behind. The two women separated. Calypso looked around at the throne and gasped. Some of the guards who had been left behind were trying to capture her friends. However, Arabella and Gwydion were fighting back. To her surprise, Calypso saw her grandmother kicking and biting the soldiers. She was grateful the rest of the army was in West Ivoria, waiting for a signal that would not arrive.

A snap sounded above her, and Calypso looked up to see a blue light shoot from Magdelone's palms and connect with the ceiling. Calypso jumped out of the way before a portion collapsed down on her head. She glared at Magdelone who stood across from her.

Both women launched into a magic battle for control of the throne. Magdelone shot more blue light at her, which Calypso deflected. Then the princess threw purple beams at the evil queen who batted them aside like annoying flies. She returned fire with a yellow bolt, and Calypso jumped out of the way before it made an immense hole in the wall. Spells that had missed their target rammed into the floor, ripping up the tiles. Some spells even connected with the furniture that overturned chairs, disintegrated statues, and tore the stuffing out of pillows.

Since both women had drunk the same amount of blood, they were evenly matched with superhuman speed, strength, skill, and magic. Neither of them seemed to tire. Calypso began to worry this battle would go on forever.

At one point, Magdelone hurled a fire bolt at Calypso. The princess ducked behind a statue. The spell deflected off the statue and collided with the ceiling, causing a portion of it to collapse. Some of the debris fell onto her grandmother's back and the unicorn's legs buckled under the weight. She fell to the floor, unconscious.

"Grandma!" yelled Calypso.

Arabella reared on her hindlegs. A spark illuminated from her horn and shot a firebolt at the wall causing a section to fall, sealing the soldiers off from the throne room. It was now Calypso, Arabella, Queen Hylzarie, Gwydion, and Magdelone left to fight the battle of their lives.

Looking at the heavy mountain of debris, Calypso could hear the soldiers on the other side, yelling and scurrying for tools to try to break through the rocky heap.

Arabella turned and looked at Calypso. A moment of secret knowledge passed between them, and they both understood the next task. Arabella had eliminated the guards, but she could not eliminate Magdelone. That was Calypso's fate. Calypso would have to repair her own mistakes.

The princess clenched her jaw and threw her own firebolt at the crystal chandelier that hung above Magdelone's head.

The vile queen leaped out of the way as the chandelier came crashing to the floor, sending a slew of glass and crystals everywhere. Magdelone tripped and fell.

Calypso felt a jingling against her wrist. She looked down to see the bracelet with the bow and arrow charm.

Ellerie's words rang in her ears, *Many times in life we have only one chance and we must take a risk. You will know what to do when that moment arrives.*

The princess waved her hands over the charms, the trinkets became whole, and a real bow with an arrow was in her hands.

Gripping the wooden weapon, Calypso felt a warmth pass through her and thought back to when her father had taught her how to shoot on the castle lawns. Quickly she came to reality.

Magdelone was getting up from her fall and was brushing pieces of glass off her dress. The moment of distraction was the perfect opportunity.

Calypso notched the arrow and pulled the bow back. She jumped out from behind the statue and pointed the tip of the arrow at Magdelone's heart. Releasing the bowstring, she let the arrow fly.

The unicorn blood flowing through Magdelone's veins gave her an instinctive psychic sense. Magdelone raised her head and with the flick of her hand, she swatted the arrow away as if it were a pesky mosquito. Her hand sent the arrow in the opposite direction. Right towards the princess' wounded grandmother lying on the throne floor with her legs curled beneath her.

Calypso's eyes widened. The arrow was going to kill her grandmother.

"No!" screamed Calypso, using her superhuman speed, she raced across the room and threw herself on her grandmother, covering the queen's body with her own. Instead of the arrow hitting the ruler of West Ivoria, it buried its point into Calypso's side.

The princess felt the arrow penetrate her skin and slice it open. She gasped and clenched her fists. Pain swept through her body followed by numbness. Was this the end? If only she had never eaten the golden pear. Her grandmother was saved, but would she be, as well? A wetness clung to her dress and she knew it was her blood. Her arms grew weak, and she did not have the desire to lift her body off her grandmother. Tears began to well up in her eyes, and her brain was foggy.

"I am so sorry, Grandma, I did not mean for this to happen, I was so wrong. I'm so sorry." As Calypso's eyes began to close, the tears that clung to her lashes were set free and fell onto her grandmother's fur.

Calypso blinked and the room started to come into view. She wasn't sure what had happened. She must have blacked out for a moment. She was still lying on her grandmother but as she moved her palms, she no longer felt unicorn fur. Instead, she felt human skin, and the softness of regal garments.

Pushing herself off her grandmother, Calypso sat up and cried in delight. For before her lay Queen Hylzarie in human form. No longer a unicorn, the leader of West Ivoria had returned. The queen blinked, and sat up.

"Grandma!" cried Calypso, throwing her arms around her. "You are alright."

"Oh, Calypso, you saved me. I saw how brave you were to rescue me. I was aware of everything going on. The spell cast on me would not allow me to speak."

"I am so sorry, Grandma,"

The queen hushed her. "I know."

It was then Calypso remembered how she had been impaled by the arrow before her blackout, yet she did not feel any pain. Her hands flew to her side. There was no wound; she was healed. The arrow was gone. Looking down, Calypso saw the same arrow that had almost killed her reappear at her feet. It was stained with her blood. The princess picked it up and stuck it in her pocket as she helped her grandmother to her feet.

"This is impossible!" screamed Magdelone bringing the princess back to the present. "That spell was supposed to keep Queen Hylzarie as a unicorn forever. The spell could not be broken."

Calypso realized that during her moment of saving her grand-mother, everyone in the room had stopped fighting in order to watch the action.

"Ah, Magdelone," replied Queen Hylzarie, "this is where you are wrong. For the most powerful magic in the world is the magic of Love. When Love is given in sacrifice and in a moment of selflessness, it can break any spell of Evil."

"The magic of Love will forever be more powerful than the blood of any unicorn," chimed in Arabella

"Blood and bones!" yelled Magdelone, "then I will destroy both of you!" A fire bolt gathered in her hands; it grew bigger in her palms. Then the Queen of East Ivoria shot the spell towards Calypso and her grandmother.

Watching the fireball come towards her, Calypso pulled the arrow from her pocket. Reaching her arm back, the princess threw the arrow towards the oncoming fireball. The arrow zoomed at a fast pace and cut through the fireball causing it to self-combust into smoke. The arrow continued on its journey and finally reached its target, Queen Magdelone, burying itself into her chest. Calypso's blood stained on the arrow mixed with Magdelone's blood. The combination of Good and Evil.

Screaming, Magdelone doubled over and burst into flames that stretched from floor to ceiling before evaporating into thin air. The whole castle began to shake violently. Pieces of ceiling and walls began to fall.

"We must get out of here!" yelled Arabella. Calypso hopped onto the unicorn's back while Queen Hylzarie got onto Gwydion's. Sparks bounced off the walls as the group escaped from the castle. As they stood on the barren ground in the distance, they watched as the giant edifice collapsed. Piles of stone, beams, and furniture disintegrated. Then the fire began to morph. Flames twisted upward, looking like branches. Parts of the castle merged together into the trunk of a tree stretching high towards the sky as the fire disappeared. The base of the tree turned brown and the leaves transformed into a bright green. Surrounding it in a gold light, Calypso saw the barren ground beneath her feet turn green as grass burst through the dirt. On the soil in front of the tree, a circular mosaic of red, black, and gold appeared in the shape of a rose.

Looking around, the brave warriors of West Ivoria saw dead trees surrounding the former castle sprout leaves and come alive. Flowers bloomed and bushes sprouted from the ground. The Enchanted Woods would now forever bloom in East Ivoria. Plants appeared all around them as the former kingdom became a place of greenery instead of a barren wasteland.

"Calypso, you did it," cried Gwydion, "Ivoria is rid of that villainous woman."

"Ah, Gwydion," replied Arabella, "there will always be evil in the realm. That is life. But now we celebrate as Ivoria is whole again under one monarch."

Calypso looked at the mosaic embroidered in the dirt. It was the exact replica of the image in her solarium at West Ivoria Castle.

Ivoria is whole now, just like the pieces of the mosaic, thought Calypso. Even though the pieces were broken, when molded together, they made a beautiful display. Just as hearts that are broken can one day find peace and happiness.

"Either way, I am glad the realm is safe," Gwydion's voice brought Calypso out of her thoughts.

"Yes, all of Ivoria is grateful. You risked your lives and chose Good over Evil. You did not let your grief consume you, unlike me." Queen Hylzarie's voice chimed in.

Arabella looked from the queen to the princess. "We will give you two a minute." The unicorn and the centaur walked off.

Calypso turned towards her grandmother. The queen's long white hair had come out of her chignon and flowed in the breeze. Her dress was tattered. She pulled her shawl tighter around her body. Looking down at her own regal garments that were torn and burned, the princess realized her long hair was tangled, too.

"Grandma, I'm so sorry," blurted out Calypso. "I have been a fool, I was so angry at you for taking away all the things I loved. I should never have wished away my duty as queen. It was I who ate the pear given to me by Magdelone that turned you into a unicorn. I should have known better."

Her grandmother took her hand. "Hush, my dear, I too am sorry. When I lost your mother and her husband, I wanted to rid myself of everything that reminded me of them. I see now it was wrong to take my sorrows out on you. I should never have forced you to give up archery and botany. Those activities brought you closer to your parents, while for me, they brought pain. But we should be honoring your parents' legacy by continuing these passions, not hiding them away."

"Yes, Grandma, I miss my mother and father so much. And I do want to be queen. I just do not feel I should have to lose myself to become the leader of our realm."

The queen smiled. "It is important to have variety when ruling a kingdom, my dear. I feel archery and botany can be worked into your schedule. I would love to see the work you have been doing in the solarium."

Calypso threw her arms around her grandmother. "Then I accept my birthright to be queen."

Hylzarie adjusted the symbol of royalty on Queen Calypso's head.

"And the crown looks good on you, too."

EPILOGUE

West and East Ivoria merged into one kingdom with Calypso on the throne. The Enchanted Woods were no longer under a dark spell. Now the animals and magical creatures had more land to roam in East Ivoria. The princess maintained her friendship with Arabella and Gwydion, and they visited her often. The bond between granddaughter and grandmother became stronger, and they spent many afternoons gardening in the solarium together. Archery became a favorite sport among the inhabitants of the castle. The memory of those who had been lost was honored instead of hidden, proving that even when the heart is broken, the pieces can be mended into a joyous whole, and happiness can be had by all.

ABOUT THE AUTHOR

N.D.T. Casale is an Italian-American author who lives in the United States. She creates magical realms for others to escape to and enjoy.

When she is not hard at work writing, N.D.T. Casale spends her time riding horses, working out, traveling, snowboarding, and looking for her next adventure. She is fluent in multiple languages and always ends her day with a cup of tea.

Follow more of N.D.T. Casale's storytelling adventures on Instagram: @ndtcasale

Acknowledgments: Mom, Dad, Ashley, and Edith thank you for everything. Love you!

Dimension of the Sasquatch

Donna White

M ercury Dawn Walker stepped out of the green mist that floated around her body. She was perfecting the art of walking from dimension to dimension. It was a genetic ability, unknown until recent events warranted her special talents. She left her training exercises from a palatial ballroom in Egypt and stepped onto an asphalt-paved road. The black ribbon of hardened tar was straddled between a wall made of stone blocks overlooking an ocean that stretched to the horizon, and a sequoia forest with tall, cinnamon-colored trees that reached to the sky. The ground around the trunks was blanketed with soft tree debris in a dustier shade of pale cinnamon. The forest was silent. The sound of gentle waves lapping at the sand below and the cries of the sea gulls flying above the deep blue ocean made her smile. She was tempted to climb down to the sea and dip her toes in the salty chill.

In the distance she could hear the beautiful beast sounds of a finely-tuned engine snarling out angry revs around the curves. She stood on the road waiting for what would come. *Do other dimensions have cars?*

As the sound got closer, she could tell it was going at a great clip. She stepped to the side of the road and was surprised to see a scalding, hell-fire green Mercedes AMG-GT roll up beside her.

A man in a black linen shirt and matching pants exited the car. His bearing was gracious, grooming meticulous, and his style unmatched.

"Nice color," Mercury Dawn commented.

"It is. The previous driver had it custom painted to match her reanimated-from-the-dead, evil brand. I'm taking it out of this dimension and back to where it belongs."

Mercury Dawn nodded. "I came as you asked, Thaddeus. No bug repellent. No jewelry. No weapons. I have boots, utility pants, lightweight jacket, hair in a braid down my back. I feel like Tomb Raider."

The man laughed. "You look like Tomb Raider! As expected after your dimension training started, your martial arts skills moved beyond human levels, and that makes you qualified for dimension walking. Take this." He opened the trunk of the car and produced a canvas backpack. "It contains basic supplies: food, water, first aid kit, a folded cotton bag, and a compass. The compass not only shows your orientation, it is a direct link to me."

She rooted through the bag and held up the minuscule tool. It had a round dial, set in a diamond-shaped block of honey-colored wood. A ring of green gemstones glittered around the edge of the dial. Thaddeus held up his arm. The watch he was wearing was a perfect match for the compass, including the ring of gemstones around the bezel.

"Remember the healing stones I used on your shoulder after our little adventure in July?" asked Thaddeus. "These are the same stones, and this is the watch I used. You may not have noticed it. You were in considerable pain at the time."

He dropped his arm. "Dimension walkers can step out of this world at any time. Your task is to find a grove of a certain type of tree unique to this dimension and collect enough seed cones to fill your bag. The appearance of these trees is very similar to the Giant Sequoias of your dimension, but there are crucial differences. These differences will become apparent to you soon enough."

Mercury Dawn raised an eyebrow at him. She didn't like the sound of that. It could mean the trees were animated or fanged or just plain oozing with death to humans. "Are the differences dangerous?"

"They could be."

"Could you clue me in on what I'm up against?"

"This is your training period. You learn to solve problems as they arise in the dimensions. There are no textbooks, nor maps. This is a mild dimension. There are dangers, but as long as you use common sense you won't die. Your super-power is walking. You walk out of the dimension when you need to. The gemstones in my watch will pull you back to wherever I am when you've collected the seed cones.

"That watch of yours is a pretty neat piece. It can heal wounds and pull people through dimensions. Where did you get it?"

Thaddeus twitched his lips signaling the conversation was over. "Do you understand what you have to do?"

"I do. I arrived here on my own. Now I find a grove of mutant Giant Sequoias and collect the seed cones. Then I return to you by way of the secret powers of a do-it-all watch."

"It's as easy as that." Thaddeus smiled as he opened the car door. His eyes reflected the cinnamon color of the tree trunks as he sank into the leather seat.

He started the beast Benz and glided down the road. She watched him disappear behind a curve and could hear the downshifting of the engine. She pulled out her blade, a Bowie knife. *No weapons allowed, but this is only a tool.*

Mercury Dawn took out her compass and headed straight north.

There was an over-clean scent of pine with a faint whiff of decaying wood creeping around the edges. There was no path, but plenty of open space for tramping through the forest. She passed an occasional patch of green undergrowth. It was too quiet, and no wind blew across her exposed skin. It wasn't unpleasant. She just wondered why the local wildlife was not scolding her. She continued north while memorizing the features of the forest.

Her senses were alert. In a forest in her own dimension; birds and animals would have warned her of another presence. Here, she had to rely on her own sharpened senses. As she hiked along, she heard a soft crunch of tree needles. She listened for a moment and moved further into the forest. Faint grunts and a crack of a fallen branch stopped her in her tracks. She wasn't sure when these sounds turned from natural forest noises into someone following her, but they were getting clumsy in their chase. Up ahead was a thick patch of vegetation. The footfalls behind her were moving faster. She ducked into the fern-like plants and crawled her way over spongy ground. She stopped and turned her head over her shoulder and listened. No sound. *Where are the animals? Birds? Why aren't they screeching at me or whoever is chasing me?* What she saw next did not make sense. She turned her head to look forward and came nose to nose with a simian-faced creature covered in dark fur. It was larger than any human or gorilla she'd ever met. Mercury Dawn tumbled backwards as the creature took a swipe at her. She rolled to the side, pushed her body up, and ran.

Forget direction! Just move! She tore through the undergrowth, terrified. *Sasquatch! Sasquatch!* She remembered she was a dimension walker and made for Thaddeus Fernhawth's ballroom. Only there was no green mist and there were no posh settees to hide behind. Shocked at her only safety net not working, Mercury Dawn chided herself for not bringing any weapons. *Knife!* She reached into her utility pocket the same moment a hard shove connected with her back. Her hands shot out before her face hit the soft ground, and she somersaulted her way into a standing position. In a flash, she took in the terrifying visage. A human shaped animal in faded black, silky fur gazed down at her from twice her height. It would have been less scary if its face was gorilla-like. Instead, this unusual monster looked something like a wild man with calculating eyes that could read what she was about to do next. Unsheathing the knife, Mercury Dawn swiped at her attacker as it reached out to her.

The sasquatch roared as the knife cut into its hand. She took another swipe and caught its other arm. Bigfoot bolted from her, making deep, enraged sounds. The forest area was now filled with answering calls and wood beating against wood. She was surrounded, but she could only hear their positions, not see them. She chose a clear area to run. For the life of her, she could not get out of this blasted dimension. She heard a sole hoot behind her, then hoots to her left and right. She realized they were counting her and passing the message along the line. She headed for a slope and plunged down, sliding with all the tree needles and keeping the barest hint of balance. Down below she could see a river. A grizzled, scowling sasquatch was bent over a rough wooden canoe sitting near the edge of the water.

Mercury Dawn smiled and picked up her pace as the land levelled off. She barreled down and used her momentum as she planted her left foot, swung her right leg into her side kick chamber and jumped. As she flew through the air, the cranky sasquatch stood at full height and faced her with a look of confusion. Mercury Dawn hit him full on the chest, and he was knocked to the ground. She landed in a crouch and used that upward motion to push the canoe into the river. She jumped in and paddled into the flow of the water. She could hear the angry cries of her pursuers. Remembering the long, thick arms of the sasquatch with hands the size of dinner plates, she paddled harder to get out of the way of anything these monsters could hurl down on her. Within moments of this thought, large rocks splashed into the water behind her. *Paddle faster than the sasquatch horde can run down the bank.*

Mercury Dawn wondered if there were more canoes on her tail. She doubted she could outrun them. The calls of the sasquatches began to die down. She still paddled long enough for the sun's position to change over the trees. Nothing stirred. No animal noises. She pulled the canoe out of the water on the far side of the river and pushed it underneath some brush, hoping there was no sasquatch colony in the area. Several deerskins were piled in the far end of the canoe. She picked through them out of curiosity and uncovered a... sleeping sasquatch child! "Oh man!" *What am I going to do? I've taken it too far away from the colony!*

Mercury Dawn held her breath and placed the deerskins back over the sleeping child and rubbed her forehead with the heels of her hands. She climbed out of the canoe and sat on a large boulder to munch on a chocolate chip granola bar. The pile of deerskin blankets stirred and the furry creature, about the size of a petite teenager flipped them over and popped its head up, startling her. The big-eyed sasquatch cocked its head to the side and looked at her. Mercury Dawn smiled at the creature and extended the granola bar in friendship. It clambered over the canoe and snatched the snack out of her hand, then retreated back to the pile of blankets. As the child sniffed then nibbled the treat, Mercury noticed the silky, caramel fur, and realized it was a female. It was a little-girl sasquatch! She took her time as she broke off small bites and chewed with the relish of a connoisseur of fine cheese. Mercury Dawn pulled out a package of dried fruits and began to bite into a mango strip. The young sasquatch sniffed the air and walked closer. She looked at the yellow treat in Mercury Dawn's hand and grunted. Mercury Dawn smiled and handed her the snack. She thought about what she should call the sasquatch baby. *Baby Bigfoot! B.B. for short.*

B.B. sniffed at the mango and jumped around. A big bite, and B.B. was in heaven! She gobbled it down and ran up to Mercury Dawn who pulled out another mango strip as she said in a soft, gentle voice, "Mango," and pointed to the food.

B.B. stepped back and cocked her head. Mercury Dawn pointed at the food again. "Mango."

B.B. took the mango and ate it in a few bites.

Mercury pointed to herself. "Mercury Dawn," she said.

B.B. cocked her head as Mercury Dawn repeated her name and actions. B.B. pointed to herself and made a guttural noise. Mercury Dawn tried to imitate the sound but failed. B.B. laughed out loud like an unruly monkey and rolled over backwards onto the soft ground. After the laughing fit was over B.B. tried to teach Mercury Dawn her name again. She was just incapable of making the sounds, so Mercury Dawn pointed at Baby Bigfoot's chest and said, "B.B."

B.B. grunted, but it didn't seem like a complaint. Mercury fished out another granola bar and the pair ate nuts, dried fruit, and granola. Mercury Dawn drank from a water bottle while B.B. drank from a clear stream that flowed into the river.

Mercury Dawn pushed the canoe back to the river. "I'm going to take you to the other side."

B.B. did not understand what Mercury Dawn said, but she seemed to know what pushing the canoe back to the water meant. B.B. leaped in and grabbed a paddle. The human and Baby Bigfoot synchronized their paddling. Mercury Dawn in the front and B.B. in the back. It was a soothing, gentle ride down the wide river. Up ahead was a sandy bank that was just right for a landing. Mercury pointed it out, but B.B. raised her paddle and dipped it into the water on the other side of the canoe. They moved away from the landing.

"Why not?"

B.B. didn't answer. She straightened the boat on the water. It became clear that B.B. did not want to land the canoe. The sun was getting low, and Mercury Dawn did not have gear to stay the night.

B.B. dropped her paddle inside the canoe and snuggled into the deerskins. Mercury kept them moving until she found a safe spot. She was not sure why B.B. refused to come ashore. This was not a dimension she knew. *Caution, girl.*

She hid the canoe in some dense brush and peeled a few deerskins off B.B. to make a halfway-decent soft spot in the bottom of the boat. There were no animal sounds. She wondered about this strange land where animals did not scold newcomers or sound a warning to the forest community. She sat there peering through the brush at thick, cinnamon tree trunks. In her own dimension, Giant Sequoia trees were the largest living thing on her planet. The smell was that clean, evergreen scent mixed with the earthy soil packed with dried plant needles that carpeted the ground. It was a pleasant evening, so she took a moment to breathe it in and marvel at the solitude. Her breathing slowed and her mind calmed. She caught the sound of river water burbling around the rocks. Her senses were so tuned into the natural world that she was surprised when a blunt object knocked her out of the canoe.

"Ahhh" escaped her lips as the breath was knocked out of her. The strike across her back lifted her out of the canoe. She sprawled on the ground, scared and in pain. Her assailant lunged in for another attack. B.B. jumped from the boat and bowled over the strange attacker. If Morticia Addams and a tree had a baby, that's what this creature would be! Long green moss topped a tree that was the height and rough shape of a human. Several branches stuck out at different angles, and they were flexible. Not to mention, it had super walloping powers. Its core was a trunk, but a slight bend was noticeable. It ended with octopus-style roots as its feet, much like Morticia Addams and her black-clad tentacles.

B.B. wasted no time pushing the tree creature over and rolling it to the river. It seemed to be shocked and threw its branch-arms out in a failed attempt to stop rolling down the bank. It splashed into the water and bobbed on the surface. B.B. ran down to the water's edge and gave it a shove towards the current, but the grasping root-toes grabbed her arm and pulled her along for the ride. B.B. gurgled and sputtered as she kept her head above the water. She grasped along the sandy bank with her free arm, desperate to climb back to safety. Water was kicking up all over her head, blocking her vision. She heard Mercury Dawn's voice loud with panic. She felt the air swoosh near her face and the vibration of the thud as a branch swung down and hit the tree creature just above the roots. The roots popped open and B.B. broke free. She scrambled up the bank and watched as Mercury Dawn poled the tree creature out of their reach to float down the river. The creature let out a thin screech like tearing paper.

In the time it took for the two of them to run back to the canoe, the forest was overrun with swift, human-sized trees moving towards them with their tentacle-like roots. Mercury Dawn was horror-struck and abandoned the canoe as did B.B. Not knowing where to go, she followed the young sasquatch. B.B. could run much faster than the tree creatures. Her pursuers gave up the chase and turned back to Mercury Dawn who had been running from the trees behind her. Now she had to dodge the tree creatures in front of her. She saw an opening and took it. As she passed a tree, it whipped out a long, spiky branch and punctured her arm. She dropped down and grabbed her mangled flesh to stop the bleeding. Blood was pouring, and then pain slammed her head. She saw black with tiny stars as she began to pass out, and the faint green mist covered her face. It was pulling her out of danger.

B.B.'s howls sliced through the pain in her head. Furry arms grasped her shoulders and her vision turned from black to green. Solid green. There was no feeling. No sound. Nothing was there, only her thoughts. *Am I dead? Is death supposed to be green?*

From the outside corners of her vision, blackness appeared and it crept to the center, and she knew no more...

Mercury Dawn woke in a pile of sumptuous, white Egyptian cotton. Dull pain thudded all over her body. She groaned and pushed herself upright. The room was stark white adorned with dark, curved furniture. Yards of gossamer curtains framed large windows overlooking a rose garden full of red, pink, peach, and yellow blossoms. Roses in full bloom were sipping up clean water in crystal vases throughout the room. She watched a bee buzzing outside of the window as she tried to remember how she got to this place. Mercury Dawn picked up a glass bottle of mineral water from the bedside table and chugged it. She was dressed in the clothing she had on when she was attacked, although the jacket was gone and her arm bandaged. Her boots were also missing. It was too hard to think, so she eased herself back into the soft pillows and fell asleep.

It only seemed as if minutes had gone by before she felt something poking and pulling on her good arm. "Stop. Go away. I'm sleeping," she said as she pulled her arm over her head. The poking continued until she opened her droopy eyes and saw a familiar furry face. "Ack!" Mercury Dawn scrambled up and back from B.B. who was grinning at her. She clutched at her heart and calmed her startled breathing. "Good grief B.B.! You almost gave me a heart attack!"

B.B. bounced on the bed and made her happy, grunting noises. Mercury placed her hand on B.B.'s arm to settle the bouncing and her other hand on the back of her throbbing head. B.B. heard the footsteps before the injured woman and hopped off the cloud of comforters to open the bedroom door wide. A thin, elderly lady dressed in a tailored, black dress stood at the door. "Good evening Dr. Walker. I'm glad to see you awake. I'm Madre Rose. I'm in charge of the rose cottage that belongs to Thaddeus Fernhawth."

"Oh, that's where I'm at. I'm in Egypt."

Madre Rose looked at the floor. A grin spread across her face.

She took a deep breath and spoke. "No ma'am. You're in California."

"Oh, uh, I wasn't expecting this. Um, did Thaddeus explain about my uh... way of transportation?"

"I know you are a dimension walker. I am experienced enough to help you. First, you need feeding up. Let's start you on some bone broth and go from there. Would you like to eat in bed or try coming to the kitchen?"

"I need to get moving. I'll follow you." Mercury peeled herself from the bed and touched her feet to the cool stone floor, the color of the softest, palest gold. B.B. took hold of her hand and led her to a white kitchen with big windows covered in gauzy curtains and blinds. The stone floor was the same gold, and the hardware, lighting fixtures, and accents were gold. Plush chairs and Persian rugs were pale pink, matching the fresh roses scattered throughout the room. Mercury Dawn and B.B. sat at the table and Madre Rose served them bone broth in white porcelain bowls with gold spoons. B.B. ignored the spoon and drank from the bowl. Mercury Dawn shrugged and followed suit.

"Instead of you asking questions, I'm going to tell you how you got here, the extent of your injuries, and what your little friend and I have been doing." Madre Rose said as she made herself a cup of

Darjeeling tea. "I am no expert on dimension walking. Thaddeus Fernhawth has begun your education based on the type of dimension walker that he thinks you are. It often takes many journeys to understand how each unique individual works," Madre Rose said.

Madre Rose added some olives to a platter and placed it on the breakfast table with some plates and forks. Madre Rose filled a plate for B.B. with pita bread, herb-topped hummus, grilled tomatoes, avocado, and salty olives. "I am considered a dimension traveler," Madre Rose said. "That means that skilled dimension walkers can put me in certain places. I can't move to dimensions on my own. I have the ability to be pushed or pulled into all of the properties that are owned by Thaddeus Fernhawth. Mr. Fernhawth and I were at this property when he got a call from his Egyptian home saying that you had arrived in the ballroom hurt and unconscious, with a Bigfoot in tow. The staff was unable to get near you because this little creature here stood over you and bared her teeth. Mr. Fernhawth was able to pull you into this cottage through dimension travel, and as the green mist appeared, Princess Bigfoot grabbed onto you and was pulled through too. She was terrified and you were hurt. Thaddeus had to calm her down before we were able to tend to your wounds. Thankfully, you did not have a concussion. We cleaned your wound and I added some stitches to your arm. You were waking and we medicated you". Madre Rose paused and sipped her tea. Mercury Dawn nibbled on the food before her. B.B. was on her second helping.

"This special little princess wanted to stay near you while you slept, so I took that time to teach her some sign language. Watch this," Madre Rose pointed at Mercury Dawn. "B.B. what's the sign for Mercury Dawn?"

B.B. dropped her toasted pita on the plate and made the "M" and "D" signs with her hands. Mercury's mouth fell open and after a second or two she cheered and clapped. "That's amazing!"

"We had time for one more sign before she got restless and wanted to explore. She finally trusted me enough to care for you. B.B., show Mercury Dawn, hungry!"

The furry hand formed a "c" and traced from her neck down to her tummy.

"Bravo B.B.! You've got the most important words!" All three of them smiled at one another.

"Thank you so much for caring for me. I can't thank you enough for your kindness to me and B.B. Is there anything I can do for you?" Mercury Dawn asked.

Madre Rose shook her head and removed the dishes from the table. "Just give yourself a rest before you go out again."

Mercury Dawn's smile faltered. She had a task to complete, and she still didn't know where to find these seed cones Thaddeus wanted her to harvest. Mercury Dawn stared off into the distance. "Do you have a picture of a giant sequoia tree that I can show B.B.?"

"There may be one in the library in a book."

"Even better."

"Follow me." Madre Rose took B.B. by the hand. They walked out of the kitchen where they were treated to a stunning view of the ocean. Mercury Dawn sprinted to one of the massive windows. The home was situated on a hill that sloped down green and lush to a sandy beach trimmed with curling waves.

"Wow," she breathed. Madre Rose beckoned her out to the large white and tan living room with long plush sofas and tables and lamps that looked as if they had been scrubbed in the gritty, wet sand themselves. She led Mercury Dawn up a modern-style wood, open-step staircase that appeared to float in the air, just caressing the tall windows overlooking a row of manicured Cyprus trees. They reached the landing and were greeted by a sitting area with more of the white, plush sofas and scrubbed tables. Madre Rose opened a door to a small library with books lining the same type of ocean-washed shelves that matched the wood in the sitting area. She found the section of nature books, which she let Mercury Dawn peruse at her leisure. B.B. trotted to the sitting area and pulled out a wooden puzzle from a basket of toys. She sat with Madre Rose on the faux-fur rug and they began to examine the pieces.

Mercury Dawn found a book about giant Sequoia trees. She brought the book into the sitting area and watched her new friends bond over playtime. B.B. found a pad and pencil from the toy basket. Madre Rose showed her how to hold the pencil and draw a line. It was apparent that she had drawn with sticks in the dirt or charcoal on rocks. Mercury Dawn took this opportunity to show B.B. the picture of the trees she was seeking. The little sasquatch frowned at the photo. She grabbed the pencil and added lower limbs with clawed hands to the picture in the books. Mercury groaned and sank into a soft chair covering her face with her hands. "Claws, I knew those trees had to have claws. Teeth, B.B.?" she uncovered one eye and peered over at B.B. hard at work on her drawing. She couldn't see, so she pushed herself up and dropped to her knees to get a good look at the photo on the coffee table. B.B. was busy drawing roots above ground at the bottom of the trees.

"Oh, I see! We were attacked by smaller versions of the Giant sequoias. That means we were getting close to where I needed to be," Mercury Dawn let out a long whistle. "I need to talk to Thaddeus. Can you call him or summon him here?"

"At the moment, no. Mr. Fernhawth has business on the other side of the world. He won't be available for some time."

"Um, he sent me on a quest, and it turned out to be a lot more dangerous than he thought, plus I accidentally kidnapped a young sasquatch. Her parents have got to be frantic. I don't know what he's doing, but I need his help."

Madre Rose considered Mercury Dawn for a moment and glanced down at B.B.'s stylized tree. Mercury Dawn padded back to the library. She was determined to get B.B. back to her family. She wasn't sure what she was looking for, but she flipped through the books anyway, hoping to find anything that would help her fight through those slasher trees.

"Hey! Madre Rose!"

Madre Rose walked to the doorway of the library, her narrowed eyes peered down her nose and her demeanor was frosty. *One does not yell through the homes of Mr. Thaddeus Fernhawth.* "Yes Dr. Walker?"

"It's Mercury Dawn. Does Thaddeus keep a flamethrower on this property?"

She gave Mercury Dawn a sour look. "He does not. You are mistaking Mr. Fernhawth for the ladies of the Whitmere Legacy."

Mercury Dawn gave her a warning look. She was not about to

hear an unkind word about her mentors, the women with both fierce warrior spirits and kind hearts.

"I have to go back to the dimension, with or without Fernhawth. I need weapons. Specifically weapons that will take out rogue trees."

"Oh my goodness no, no, NO! Mr. Fernhawth was explicit about dimension travel and weapons... Dear me! Let me see. Oh yes, I need to call a friend. I'll be right back! Don't leave! I'll get this sorted."

Mercury shrugged and headed for her suite of rooms and the large shower. The bathroom was stocked with tiny bottles packed with beauty elixirs behind endless rows of cabinets. She ignored the waterfall feature due to the stitches in her arm, and turned on the water jets to massage her sore muscles. With the hand-held spray, she washed as fast as was possible under the circumstances. The towels were fluffy and were of a variety of colors that matched the roses outside. She selected a silky, red robe that matched the towel that wrapped her hair on top of her head. She dotted some coconut oil on her skin and ran a few strokes of a gua sha stone over her face and neck. Even during a quest, she realized she had only one skin and was determined to take care of it.

She stepped into her bedroom and guzzled a bottle of water while she stared out the window. The riot of colorful blooms served as a beautiful backdrop as she planned the next step of her quest. *How do I safely return B.B. to her family and harvest some seed cones without losing a limb or an eye?* Mercury Dawn ran through a series of possible situations in her mind. She didn't yet have a plan, but all she could hope for was that for every challenge, there would be a solution.

She left her hair damp and rubbed some bamboo oil into her tresses for her trademark shiny, raven-dark locks. Her clothes were clean and folded on her bed. She dressed and strode out of the room in search of Madre Rose. She was ready to return to the dimension and needed her boots. The old woman was coming down the stairs with a small box in her hand as Mercury Dawn walked into the living room.

"Sit."

Mercury Dawn chose one of the white couches. Madre Rose pulled up a rather furry, white pouf with tan spots and sat in front of her. She smoothed out her skirt. Then she placed the black box with a matching ribbon tied in a bow in her lap. "I have sorted it out," Madre Rose said with a bit of triumph in her voice. "Mr. Fernhawth says no weapons. It is no secret that the Whitmere ladies are fierce fighters. You are no doubt training under their tutelage."

Mercury Dawn nodded.

Madre Rose sat up taller. "They are fine ladies with gracious manners, and a few of them are caring souls. From what I hear, you have the capacity for great compassion yourself."

"I may. What have you got for me?"

Madre Rose raised an eyebrow but continued. "My sources tell me that the Whitmere gemstones affect certain people's personalities. On the right person, pearls bring out their softer side." At this she untied the ribbon and opened the box, displaying a small round pearl on a short platinum chain.

Mercury lifted the necklace. "Yes, I'm one of the few who react to the pearls. I don't see how compassion is going to help me get past giant, slashing trees. "What am I going to do, give them a hug and ask for their seed cones? I'd come back a lot worse than this!" she gestured at her bandaged arm.

"Do you trust Thaddeus?"

"Not really."

"He is training you to be a dimension walker."

"I didn't ask to be a dimension walker. Had I not gotten injured and the green mist pulled me here, one of those slasher trees could have decapitated me in a second! I don't think the green mist could preserve my life without my head!"

Madre Rose looked down at her hands in her lap. "No, dear, I don't suppose it could."

Mercury Dawn moved to the crystal-like window. The blue of the ocean was hypnotic. "What do you suggest I do?"

"Wear the pearl. Unleash the compassion that will show what to do with these creatures with whom you cannot communicate."

Mercury Dawn glanced at the delicate chain draped across her fingers and clasped the necklace around her neck. Madre Rose opened a door off the side of the living room where B.B. sat watching a children's video on sign language. She was forming her hands and making the movements like the actors on the screen, she was practicing the "yes" and "no" hand signs.

Mercury Dawn turned to Madre Rose, "B.B. is learning at a remarkably fast rate."

"Well if you think about it, the sasquatch has eluded humans for centuries. They must either be highly intelligent or have the ability to disappear."

Madre Rose had shown B.B. the vocal word for yes and no earlier by using food as something she wanted or didn't want while Mercury Dawn was in the shower. Mercury practiced the signs along with B.B. until she felt her whole body itch to get moving. She turned off the television and brought B.B. back to the book of the Giant Sequoia trees with the hand-drawn claws and tentacled feet. Madre Rose taught them both the sign for big tree. Mercury Dawn touched the picture and took her hand as if to leave. B.B. got the message pretty quick and did the sign language for "no". She was quite adamant that she did not want to take Mercury Dawn anywhere near those trees. Mercury Dawn insisted and pulled B.B. away from the table and out the door. Madre Rose ran up with the small, lightweight pack that contained a few essentials.

"I think B.B. can find those trees," Mercury Dawn said.

"I think she can too. You are going to complete this quest. Goodbye, Dr. Walker. I hope to see you again," Madre Rose said as she reached out to hug B.B. "Goodbye my little friend." B.B. crossed her fists over her chest and Madre Rose melted with joy and tears. She hugged the sasquatch child. "You understood what it means to hug! I'm so happy." B.B. hugged her back with her long arms.

"Dr. Walker, someday I want to visit this dear one again. I know you can find a way."

Mercury Dawn's voice caught in her throat and tears welled up in her eyes. She didn't know what to say. She did not know if she was even going to be alive in an hour.

Mercury Dawn was not moving, but green mist started to surround her. *What is happening? I didn't start the process!* She lunged for B.B. and gripped her around the shoulders. The mist swirled towards the sky, and she felt the light sensation of being lifted upward. B.B. had no weight at all. They linked their arms together as they floated in the mist. They couldn't even see one another, and then they felt crunchy evergreen needles beneath their feet.

T he mist disappeared, and Mercury Dawn recognized the area where they stood. It was the place where her arm had been slashed. She scanned the area for any attackers. Her heart beat fast. B.B. took both of Mercury's hands and pulled her down into a sitting position. Mercury Dawn protested, but B.B. insisted and patted her head. B.B. stood and held Mercury Dawn's hand as she sat on the ground with her legs crossed. B.B. called out to the forest in a loud voice with a growl and some strange hooting. Mercury Dawn was not sure this was a good idea. B.B. bent down and grasped the pearl around Mercury Dawn's throat and made a series of grunts.

"You think the pearl of compassion will keep us safe?"

B.B. did not understand, but she patted Mercury Dawn's hand. She continued to call out to the forest. The only answer was silence, and anxiety grew in Mercury Dawn. She wasn't on good terms with either the slashing trees or the sasquatch colony. Then in the distance, they heard an answering call. It did not sound scary. It sounded full of concern. B.B.'s reply was a long string of vocalizations that almost sounded like a coyote howling, only with a much deeper voice. The answer was closer to them and came in short barks. Mercury Dawn tried to get up, but B.B. held her down and gave the hand signal for "no".

The little sasquatch made occasional loud grunts that were followed by animal noises getting ever closer to them. It seemed like forever before they heard the faintest sounds of the forest floor crackling and twigs snapping. Mercury Dawn thought it was much more ruckus than that one voice ought to be making. B.B. would not let Mercury Dawn stand. Within moments they were surrounded by sasquatch and B.B. kept both hands pushing down on Mercury Dawn's shoulders, keeping her from rising as B.B. communicated with her kinfolk. The sasquatches were silent as they listened to her long tale. B.B. stopped, and a very old, gray leader answered in his barky, growling tongue.

Mercury Dawn kept her hard-as-steel demeanor while sitting on the ground as the colony decided what they were going to do with her. Inside her brain she worked out a strategy for hamstringing fifty super-tall, legendary beasts with a sharp rock. The two of them talked back and forth until the leader was satisfied. B.B. smiled at Mercury Dawn and pulled her from the ground and over to the leader. He grunted at her and the colony grunted back in agreement. They turned and walked deeper into the woods. B.B. led her with the other sasquatches as they traipsed through the forest.

She was surprised at the outcome and wondered if her pearl of compassion saved her carcass from being roasted over the leader's fire pit for dinner. She felt the tiny gemstone and marveled that a simple adornment could have that kind of effect on her compassion rather than her combative nature.

She lengthened her stride to keep up with the long-legged sasquatches. They glided through the forest, passing taller and taller trees. The bases were gaining in girth, in fact, she'd never seen such large trees in her dimension.

The group stopped before a tower of a tree with a broad opening at the base. Parts of the bark were missing. Holes were open all the way to the center. She looked up to the full height of the tree. It looked like natural windows were dotted about like a house, and it appeared as if a wooden skeleton was holding it upright. The dead heartwood had been removed, and the sasquatches built a series of platforms with sturdy ladders made of rough branches inside the tree to keep it from falling over and damaging the rest of the forest. The vital outer layer of sapwood remained, feeding the tree with water and minerals.

With great ceremony the leader grunted and waved his arms, inviting Mercury Dawn into the towering tree with the diameter of the base greater than the length of a school bus. Light spilled through the window-like openings. The first floor was rough wood covered in animal skins. A low table was piled with whole roasted fish from the river, tree collards, mushrooms, and wild grapes. B.B., the leader, and a few other important-looking sasquatches sat with Mercury Dawn in silence and gorged on food. Mercury loved the fish, but the vegetables were a tad bitter for her tastes. She was not sure of the safety of the mushrooms, so she avoided them.

After the feast, the leader led her up into the towering rooms. Each level was filled with soft layers, but no food. She guessed they were sleeping chambers. The top was at a dizzying height. She peered out a large hole that overlooked the ocean. It was similar to the view at the Rose Cottage. Only this view was adorned with the giant seed cones hanging from neighboring healthy trees. B.B. slapped her cheeks and pointed to the seed cones. She pulled on the leader's arm and implored him to come down the stairs with her at a quick trot. She kept up a high-pitched chatter while the leader answered her in grunts and low sounds. The delegation followed B.B. to one of the strong, vibrant trees where seed cones littered the ground at its base.

The old leader picked up one as Mercury Dawn held out her backpack. It was so large that she could manage only one. The weight and size of a large watermelon were more than either she or Thaddeus planned for. She couldn't close the zipper, and after some struggle she gave up, hoping that the partially-opened pack would be secure enough to get her back to her dimension.

The green mist started curling around her body. The watch of the secret powers that seemed to do everything was preparing to bring her back to her own dimension. She smiled at the leader. B.B. gave the sign for 'hug', but did not come forward. Mercury Dawn returned the hug sign. She watched the old sasquatch hug B.B. She was struck by the thought that the leader was in fact B.B.'s grandfather. She had no hope of discerning sasquatch-family-resemblance, but they both had a regalness about them. Then she disappeared in thick green fog. The shadow of a hand reached for her, and she grasped it. She was pulled through the dimension and ended up on the beach that could have been the one she had been looking at moments before.

Thaddeus Fernhawth stood before her, dressed in a wetsuit with a surfboard stuck in the sand. His shoulder-length dark hair sported beachy waves from the salt water that dripped from his hands and face.

"I didn't know a fellow like you had fun. I thought all you did was get mixed up in protecting the world from ancient foes and looking after a family of super beings."

He smiled. "Madre Rose should have lunch ready. We can talk about your adventures over gumbo."

"Gumbo? Have the Whitmere ladies gotten you into that?"

"I've been eating some form of gumbo for centuries."

The two walked up the path towards the Rose Cottage. They went their separate ways to change. Mercury Dawn pulled on a long, x-back dress she found in the guest room bedroom and a pair of seashell studded sandals. The yellow of the dress made her tanned skin pop. She shook out her braid and let her hair fall down her back. She made her way to the veranda overlooking the sea. The air was warm with just a hint of breeze. Thaddeus joined her wearing light pants and a white linen shirt, carrying a crystal pitcher of iced tea. Madre Rose followed with a tureen of seafood gumbo.

Pleasantries were made and Mercury Dawn dived right for the French bread wrapped in a kitchen towel and the Irish butter shaped into shells. Even though she had eaten not long ago, she could always make room for gumbo. Thaddeus ladled the rich, brown broth with crab and vegetables over a pile of white rice. Madre Rose skewered some shrimp and dropped them over her salad.

Mercury Dawn dabbed the crumbs from her lips with a cotton napkin. "Thaddeus, did you know there were sasquatches in that dimension?"

"I did not until Madre Rose told me after your first trip. Had I known this, I would have sent a more experienced dimension walker to retrieve the seed cone. I apologize, although I was right about you having the skills to deal with unforeseen incidents."

"I could have died! Why couldn't I walk out of the area the first time when the colony was chasing me?"

"That was inexperience and pressure. Your mind must develop."

"You know you don't make any sense sometimes."

"You will learn in time, Dr. Walker."

"It's Mercury Dawn or Mercury, please. So why do you need this seed cone?"

"Natural dimension walkers produce the green mist themselves without any help from outside sources. Seed cones from trees in certain dimensions produce the mist that is used when one cannot produce the mist oneself. The mist is used for a variety of reasons other than travel." Thaddeus took a sip of iced tea and dug into the gumbo.

"I suppose I will learn about the other functions of the mist in time."

"Yes."

The trio finished lunch and carried the dishes to the dishwasher. Mercury Dawn removed the pearl necklace and handed it to Madre Rose. "Thank you for the necklace. I didn't even skewer one sasquatch. Without it, I probably would have gotten into a massive brawl with them and would have ended up dead."

Madre Rose laughed. "No, no my dear. All that constraint was you! This is my necklace from a plain-Jane jewelry store, no amped-up powers here."

"You mean you sent me out to a sasquatch dimension under the impression I was safe with one of the Whitmere pearls?"

"I would not send you anywhere if I didn't think you were capable. The compassion is inside you. You are capable of so much more goodness than any gemstone can bring to the surface."

Mercury Dawn fell silent. She pondered this for a while then walked out to the veranda where she found Thaddeus. He looked up from the book he was reading. "I want you to work from the Rose Cottage for a few weeks."

"Not in Egypt? I do like it here. Can you send me a wetsuit and surfboard?"

"The wetsuit arrived before you did, along with several surfboards. They are in the shed by the beach. I ordered a new wardrobe for jaunts to the sasquatch dimension and for your stay here. I see you found the yellow dress. Don't ask for katana blades."

"Rats! You know me so well. Can I get a car?"

"You can use either of the Lamborghinis in the garage, Urus or SVJ. Don't lose them in another dimension."

"What am I supposed to do here?"

"Make friends with the sasquatch colony. Find out where and why they move to other dimensions, and if it's natural or through tree mist. Learn to communicate with them, with Rose's help. You know she is a dimension traveler. Take her with you."

"It's funny, Thaddeus. This whole time humans have been trying to capture Bigfoot, and I accidentally stumbled upon their secret as I was learning to be exactly what they are, dimension walkers."

Mercury Dawn looked out over the ocean and squinted her eyes. "Well I earned today's paycheck. I can answer the question about whether or not the sasquatches can cross into our dimension."

She pointed out to the sea and Thaddeus came to her side. He squinted. Three, overly-large, furry individuals sat on bobbing surfboards waiting for a good wave. "Ya know Thaddeus, I'm looking forward to this assignment," she said as she bounced down the path toward the beach. "I get paid to surf!"

Author's Note

Follow Mercury Dawn's story in The Whitmere Legacy series
By Donna White. Available here: http://www.amazon.com/
author/donnawhitethewhitmerelegacy

About the Author

Donna White is the author of The Whitmere Legacy series. She was born and raised in the South and moved to Southern California as a young adult. She splits her time between her husband, children, large dogs, and her passion for nature photography. She writes epic paranormal stories of gracious women with enhanced martial arts skills in exotic locations. Charm and humor are her trademarks while keeping the scare factor at bay.

You can catch Donna on Instagram: @whitmerelegacy

Read the first few chapters of her books for free, or purchase them, on her Amazon page: http://amazon.com/author/donnawhitethewhitmerelegacy

THE FERN FLOWER

ELENA SHELEST

To release the tension in her chest, Miray took a big breath of the warm midsummer air. After the morning thunderstorm, it was filled with the sweet aroma of cedar trees and the earthy scent of moss. This old forest was the only place where she could be herself, never rejecting her as people did. Its leafy arms were always open. In their embrace, surrounded by the soft murmur of leaves and trills of birds, the young woman could forget for a moment how different she was from others. Sometimes she even heard her mother's songs woven into the soothing melody of nature and hummed the tunes of her distant childhood when no one could overhear.

Today these sights and sounds wooed her with renewed strength. It would have been easy to get lost between the trees and never return.

"You don't have to go tonight if you don't want to." Olena's voice was an unwelcome reminder that she wasn't alone. The woman was the closest thing Miray had to a friend and a very adamant one at that. "Still, think about it. How would you even know if you like it or not? You've never attended. And what if you miss out on something important?"

"Like what?" Miray only half-listened, more interested in a little chickadee bird that was hopping around the bush and chirping. It looked like the one she brought home in spring with a broken wing.

What a silly thought!

"Well, it's the night of Ivana Kupala," Olena continued. "When I was about your age, I put a wreath on the water during the celebration. It went all the way down the stream. That meant my marriage would be happy and long. A few days later, I met Yakiv and didn't even think twice when he eventually asked for my hand. Of course, he was also handsome and the most desirable groom in our region."

Miray let Olena talk, keeping her eyes on the basket of herbs she was gathering, filled with bitter sagebrush and prickly nettle to match her mood. Her back ached from walking stooped to the ground for hours in search of healing grasses, but any task was better than being forced to join the festivities. She avoided large crowds like the plague.

Savko will be there.

Heat engulfed Miray's cheeks at the thought. The young man had been coming to their *hutir* over the last six months to pick up broken equipment or bring back repaired tools from the local blacksmith. Miray always watched him from a distance and only came closer when she was sure he wouldn't notice. Everything about Savko fascinated her: the confidence in his movements, the merriment of his contagious laughter. She was drawn despite herself. He seemed so full of life and vigor, while her existence was but a shadow.

He'll never pay attention to me. Especially not when every girl in the area will be there. Forget him. Forget the festival.

A few steps away from her, chamomiles spread over a small clearing. They would have been perfect for the wreath, but Miray wasn't making one. Neither today nor for years to come. She averted her eyes from the blooms and met her companion's narrowed gaze instead.

"Why are you not with other girls picking flowers for the wreath, singing, playing games?" Olena demanded. "Don't you like to sing? What are you doing here with me all day if not hiding? I sure don't need your help."

Miray smiled softly. "You never do. But it doesn't mean I can be idle while everyone is working."

Olena never shared her load of responsibilities, bubbling with excess energy even after having four children. The older two, both hardy girls, were chasing each other between the cedars nearby. The woman was not only strong but beautiful with her long braid of chestnut hair, alabaster skin, and healthy curves.

So unlike me...

At seventeen, Miray looked rather fragile and slim, like a young willow battered by the harsh storms or a small fig tree replanted into foreign soil without enough sunshine. She tugged on her raven black curls to cover the left side of her face. An old burn scar snaked down from her cheek to her neck, disappearing in the embroidered collar of her shirt. Miray usually covered the disfigurement with silky scarves wrapped around her head. She wore one now despite the hot weather and the fact that she was a maiden. Flowers and colorful ribbons should have adorned her hair instead, but that could never be.

Olena tugged on Miray's chin, lifting it up so they could face each other. "Listen, I don't care what you do, as long as it's what you truly want. Don't let fear keep you from living your life to the fullest."

How can a jar ever get filled if it has a crack? Olena would never understand.

Miray's eyes burned, but she swallowed the tears that had been threatening to spill over since she woke up. The truth was, no matter how terrifying large gatherings seemed, she always longed to take a peek at the midsummer celebration, to watch the carefree youths, if only from a safe distance. She wished to be a bird and observe it all from above.

"Hey!" Olena snapped her fingers, bringing Miray back to reality. "Stop dreaming and just do it."

The young woman sighed. "You're right. I shouldn't avoid things."

Olena had a smug look on her face. "I'm always right. Just ask my husband. He'll tell you it's not worth arguing with me."

"Still, I hate noisy events like this and—"

"No, no, no. Promise me you'll go. Promise you'll enjoy yourself today."

Olena will never let up unless I agree.

Miray gave her a small smile. "I'll try. After I finish this and help with the meal for the workers."

They hurried to complete their task, but by the time they found all the needed herbs, the sun was already setting. Sweat covered Miray's brow and ran down her back when they returned to the homestead. The path led them through the green pastures to the cluster of one-story whitewashed houses with thatched roofs. They passed the crane well and the orchard, entering the main *hata* building through the back door.

Galina Mihailovna, Olena's mother-in-law and mistress of the estate, sat at the head of a large wooden table, sorting through the herbs with several female servants. A few more women made porridge in the oversized cauldron on the stove. Galina was regal but stern, holding the large household in her tight grip. Even on a big holiday like this, everything ran smoothly and peacefully under her watchful gaze.

Olena's third child, a boy of three, jumped off the bench and ran to embrace his mother while she cooed over the crib where her youngest slept. Miray hid in the corner, trying to stay out of everyone's way, and grabbed a bucket of potatoes to peel.

"What took you so long? We returned hours ago," the older woman said, glancing up from her task. "There is no reason for you to be breaking your back like a commoner. Better watch after my grandchildren. And healing grasses are only useful if you gather them in the morning, don't you know that?"

"Oh, *Mamo*, stop complaining," Olena retorted. "I know you're keeping yourself busy as well. We are all trying to forget that our men are on yet another campaign."

Galina Mihailovna threw a sharp glance at Miray as if it were her fault that the Cossacks were at war again. The girl shrank further into the shadows. She was a foreigner, a dark-skinned child of the Turks, rescued by Galina's husband out of the flames when his unit stormed Kefe eight years ago and ambushed the largest slave market to free the Slavs. It wasn't that unusual for Cossacks to bring foreign wives from such trips, but no one ever returned with an injured child. After raising four healthy sons and losing three of them to war, Galina wasn't too keen to care for the sickly girl.

Locals took a while to warm up to Miray too, calling her *busurmanka*. Maybe it was her own fault. She learned the language and let them rename her Maria but kept at a distance from people who were used to open doors and open hearts. Boryslav Sergeevich Koval, her savior, was the only one who earned her trust. The man had a rough exterior but was as soft as melted wax on the inside. When he first brought her home, she was like a small feral animal, hiding in tight corners and refusing to come out unless he was around. With time everyone learned to ignore her. Everyone except Olena, who found a way to break through her walls. No one could deny that woman anything she set her mind on. Unfortunately, it included the idea of Miray finally attending the yearly midsummer celebration.

After helping for a bit, Olena scooped up her one-year-old, took the toddler by the hand, and turned to Miray. "Come. I need to get you ready for tonight."

Galina Mihailovna raised an eyebrow but didn't stop them. Olena marched through the garden that surrounded the main house, her children following like little ducklings. Miray trudged along, wondering with a trembling heart if "get you ready" meant more than just washing off the grime of the day's work. They walked past the pens with livestock, storage buildings, and barley fields where workers hurried to finish the daily tasks before the start of the festivities. The homestead where they lived was large. Boryslav Sergeevich poured all his war spoils into it. He was also shrewd, raising cattle and horses for the Zaporizhska Sich garrison. His only surviving son joined his efforts. A small village sprung up around his wealth.

Miray enjoyed exploring the place as a child and spending time with farm animals. They were so much easier to understand than people. She had a knack for horses too, could calm a spooked one and nurse the lame back to health. Boryslav Sergeevich was quick to shower her with praise for her skills, but others eyed it with suspicion, calling her a witch behind her back.

Soon they came to the house where Olena lived with her husband and children. A one-story structure with bright-blue shutters and embroidered curtains was roomy and light. It always smelled of freshly baked bread. An elderly nanny and a young servant girl met them at the door.

"Feed and wash them, especially these two." Olena smiled at her muddy daughters, who jumped around, showing off their finds from the forest. Their brother joined the excited chatter and even the baby bounced in Olena's arms when she handed him over. "I swear these little monsters never get tired."

She turned to Miray with her hands on her hips, her gaze sweeping over the young woman's disheveled appearance.

"I will... I'll go get changed too," Miray said, turning toward the door.

"Not a chance. You're not leaving until I make you presentable." Olena grabbed her by the elbow and pulled her toward the room in the back, signaling for the servant girl to follow.

Horrified, Miray watched as they filled the basin with water, set out towels and a lavender-scented bar of soap. By habit, her hand went up to the scar on her neck, tugging the hair down. "I'm not... You can't... Let me do it myself!"

Olena frowned, then her determined gaze softened. "Fine. But don't you dare put your dusty clothes back on. I won't let you go back to your place either, or you'll never come out. You'll wear something of mine."

She went over to the large embossed trunk and threw the lid open. After digging through piles of clothes, Olena picked a white embroidered garment and set it on a chair. "This should fit you just fine if we trim a bit at the hem and sides. I wore it for my wedding before these children made me twice my size. No one would recognize the dress now."

Miray waited until everyone left her alone and locked the door. She washed herself as quickly as she could without risking Olena's disapproval in the amount of cleanliness. God forbid she would demand to do it over. The young woman could hardly bear to look at herself, and she would have rather died than let another person see her unclothed. The fire that trapped her mother in the house, silencing her beautiful voice forever, left a constant reminder of that horrid day on Miray's body. She would not have survived if it wasn't for the healer Boryslav Sergeevich found.

The warped, discolored skin still covered her left shoulder and part of her arm, continuing its uneven pattern on her abdomen, hip, and down the leg. Her burns didn't circle the limbs, leaving her movements intact. The healer said she should have been thankful for keeping all her fingers and toes as well as her sight. She also said being alive was a gift, but that truth was hard to swallow sometimes. Over the years, Miray's external wounds healed, but those that went deeper than her skin kept pestering, constantly reopened by the taunts of her peers.

What am I doing? I shouldn't be going anywhere. I should be content with what I have. At least here I'm safe.

Miray reached for her discarded clothes when Olena knocked on the door. "You better be wearing my wedding dress or I'll change you myself!"

Biting her lip, Miray grabbed the white linen *vyshyvanka* dress

Olena left for her. Beautiful red and black embroidery of floral motifs covered the high collar, went down the long cuffed sleeves, and circled the hem that dragged on the floor.

When Miray opened the door, Olena smiled approvingly. "This dress was made by the best needleworker on this side of the Dnipro River. And it suits you well. Now sit and let us do the rest."

Ignoring her protests, Olena and her servant went to work, trimming down and tucking in loose parts of the garment. They wrapped the wide red belt over Miray's tiny waist, fit her into the shiny red boots, and hung the bright jewelry around her neck. Miray fought so hard with the last piece of her wardrobe that they finally settled on one string of red coral beads. The servant girl brushed out her tangled dark curls, letting them fall over her left shoulder in a wave that covered the scarred side of her face. Olena ran out and came back with a small wreath made of white yarrow, purple mallow, blue forget-me-nots, and red poppy flowers.

"It's beautiful." Miray sighed. "But I can't—"

"I knew you weren't going to make one anyway," Olena said. "So I had Galina prepare it. You can't refuse. It's a gift."

She placed the flowery crown over Miray's head and attached a few silky ribbons of different colors in the back. "You look lovely. May it bring you a blessing tonight."

Miray's heart lightened at her kind words. Maybe there was a bit of happiness left for her in this world after all.

Savko crouched low in the grass, surrounded by the buzzing of insects and the soft exhales of horses in the enclosure nearby. Four more of his friends hid along the fence with him. The sun had already set, but it was still light enough for the men left guarding the property to spot them.

"Are you sure we should do this?" the young man closest to him whispered. "Koval is the second man after the *hetman* himself. If we get caught..."

"Hey, what glory is there in playing tricks on regular folk?" Savko interrupted. "Who was impressed last year when we placed Danylo's cart on his roof? Or left Bohdan's boat at the church doors? But when we took Pavlo's gate to the main road, people talked about it for months. The strongest Cossack in the area got outsmarted."

Savko chuckled at the memory, loud enough for others to shush him.

"Well, you almost got whipped for it," one of his friends mumbled. "Despite being related to the man."

"We can get hanged for stealing horses," someone else said.

"Hogwash." Savko scoffed. "We ain't stealing. We are upholding the holiday tradition, observing the rituals, keeping the evil powers at bay like the responsible members of the community we are. Or would you rather have wood goblins do our work for us tonight?"

Savko's voice dripped with jest, but his friends didn't seem to share the same festive mood.

"I've heard all Koval's people are armed, half of 'em former Cossacks," another young man said. "A few years ago, they shot a band of horse thieves on the spot."

"Most of them had gone to the gathering at the bonfires," Savko retorted. "Or brought in *gorilka* and are falling asleep as we speak."

Everyone still fretted.

"We're missing out too."

"If Koval ever finds out, you won't have any chances of joining Cossacks next year."

"Even with a brother-in-law high in the ranks."

"Bad idea, I tell ya."

"I am sensing trouble."

"Isn't his adopted daughter a witch or something?"

"What if she curses us?"

"I can see now I've made a mistake," Savko grumbled, getting off the ground and standing to his full height. His friends breathed an audible sigh of relief, but it was short-lived. "I brought a bunch of terrified children here with me. You can sit here and whine or go back to the riverbank. I'll do this myself."

No one moved. A smirk pulled at Savko's lips. He didn't mind having an audience to tell the tale. Not that people wouldn't still hear the rumors, but it was better to have witnesses. The good food was waiting for them, so he wanted to hurry and be done with this.

He would do it alone too and take all the fame, but such a task required a few helpers.

Maybe Danylo will finally tire of my roistering and let me take some real risks on the battlefield.

There was nothing Savko desired more. He wanted to be a warrior, not a blacksmith like Danylo, who hung up his saber years ago. At least, he got enough money to build a house, start his own workshop, and marry a girl he fancied. Savko wouldn't settle for less than that.

"So, who's with me?"

His four friends nodded or mumbled their agreement. They reiterated the plan one more time and moved swiftly along the pen with a few dozen horses, all chosen stallions and mares, the best ones in the area. Anyone in the village would recognize whom they belonged to. Savko wasn't going to take them far, just let them loose around the property and hopefully not get shot in the process. It would be a waste. He was planning to let Tatars or Nogais take an aim first. But if luck was on his side, he'd survive and take back the riches the slave raiders accumulated on the backs of his people. He promised his brother to wait one more year. Just another five months now until he turned nineteen, then no one could stop him from signing up to the regiment.

"Ready?" He turned to his friends, crouched low behind him. Despite the dusk of the evening, he could still see the tension in their faces. "Relax. Let's do this quickly so you can go chase the skirts at the festival."

As they spread out, the horses began to pace inside the enclosure, beating their hooves and snorting louder at the closeness of the strangers. A few herdsmen sat nearby, and Savko tried to stay out of their view. The plan was to lure the men away from the gates first. Earlier in the day, he delivered the repaired tools and left the back window of the shed open. Now his two friends were on their way to create a ruckus inside before locking the workers in. Ideally, without getting caught in the process.

Savko scarcely breathed as he squatted behind several large barrels, his heart beating faster in anticipation. Loud noises from the shed startled the workers. They ran inside, swearing and yelling while the horses squealed in earnest. It was his cue to act.

Savko swung over the fence into a paddock, bolting aside to avoid getting kicked by a frantic mare. His two remaining friends dashed to the gate and threw it open. They ran along the fence, whistling and hooting at the frenzied animals that quickly found the exit. Savko roped one and jumped on its back. The other young men followed suit, galloping out of the enclosure. Savko glanced back. The workers had broken down the door of the shed and piled out with rifles at the ready. He took out a piece of white cloth from his belt and waved it in the air. One of his friends took his shirt off and twisted it above his head with a boisterous whistle.

A few of their pursuers threw their hats on the ground in frustration and spat, others lowered their weapons, waving their fists instead. Savko laughed and nudged his horse forward as others scattered around the property. It took a certain skill to ride with a rope halter and without a saddle, but Savko had enough practice. The stallion under him was eager, racing like the wind. Fresh evening air filled his lungs and blood rushed through his veins. He hoped Pavlo would let him borrow a horse like that once he started the service. Or maybe he would save enough money to make a purchase.

Savko pressed the horse's side, turning it between the structures at full speed, away from the shouts of men. A crowd must have already gathered to hunt them down. He would get to the edge of the property, let the animal loose, then escape into the steppe.

A flicker of white interrupted his thoughts a few yards ahead as a small figure ran in front of him, blocking the route.

"Get out! Whoa!" In panic Savko yelled at the stupid girl and the horse at the same time. He had no bridle and no time to stop. But instead of moving away, she raised her hands up. The stallion under him reared up, throwing him off despite his desperate grip on its mane. Savko's back hit the ground, knocking all the air out. It took him a moment to come to his senses. Fearing for the girl, Savko forced himself to get up only to find her kissing the horse's nose while the traitor snorted happily. He shook the dirt off his new *sharovary* purchased for the holiday and frowned. They were ruined now.

"At first I thought you were a ghost," he grumbled. "But it looks like you're just a senseless child."

"I... I'm not a child."

He stepped closer. It was hard to see in the dark between the buildings, but she was definitely not a child. Just small. For a moment, the young woman stared at him, her mouth half-opened, then turned away and hid her face in the horse's mane.

"Why are you racing Thunder like a madman?" she asked with reproachful notes in her voice.

"I was taking him for a ride," Savko replied smoothly.

"Then why is everyone shouting? And other horses are on the loose." She was still focused on the animal, rubbing its neck.

"My friends and I, eh... We dared each other to take the horses out for a quick ride."

The young woman looked up, her dark eyebrows knitted together. "Without permission? Then you should know Thunder only listens to me. He will throw you off if you try to climb onto him again."

Savko laughed. "Is that so? The two of us were doing just fine until you showed up."

The young man wasn't sure why he was standing there, trying to explain himself to this wisp of a girl when he had an angry mob at his heels. Something about her drew his curiosity. She was well dressed, from what he could tell, but everyone prettied themselves for the celebration. Her face was unusual. Beautiful but foreign with bewitching midnight eyes that seemed almost too large, a slender nose with a high arch, and full lips, which she currently pouted. Flowers adorned the dark wave of her tresses. Her voice was strangely melodic too, almost as if she were singing the words while she spoke.

"I don't understand. Why would you do this?" She must have asked this a few times before the words registered.

"You must not be from here," Savko said, shaking off the spell. "It's a tradition of sorts, to steal something impossible on this day. But we return it later, usually in odd places. You know what else gets stolen on Ivana Kupala?"

"What?"

Savko grinned at her naivety, then stooped down and claimed her soft lips. He must have shocked her for a moment because she didn't resist. Or maybe she enjoyed the kiss as much as he did. Her mouth was sweet, and her slender body melted against him when he wrapped his arm around her waist and drew her close. But he was mistaken about her eagerness. The girl bit his lip. Hard. Savko let go, wiping blood off his mouth and grinning like a fool.

A feisty little thing.

Angry voices brought him back to reality. He barely had enough time to dash behind an overturned cart when the men appeared with torches.

"Maria! What are you doing here?" one of them barked. "We have spooked horses running around the property. It's not safe."

Savko's heart froze with dread. Maria? Koval's ward, that's who the girl was!

You've dug your own grave this time!

"Isn't she a horse whisperer?" another man sneered. "Maybe we should let her collect 'em."

Savko frowned at the way these men talked to her and almost stepped out to tell them to clip their tongues when she spoke.

"I-I'd be happy to."

The young woman hugged herself, trembling. Was it because of what he'd done? Other girls usually didn't mind him stealing kisses, on holiday or otherwise. But she seemed... different. He wouldn't blame her now for turning him in. She threw a glance to where he was hiding, as if contemplating this herself.

"If I catch these rascals, I'll whip 'em 'til I draw blood," one of the men grumbled. "I'll make sure they remember this day for a while. Now we have to gather the herd instead of resting."

"I-I will help." Throwing one last glance at Savko's hiding place, the young woman shook her head slightly as if to chide him and moved in the opposite direction, taking the men with her.

Savko should have felt guilty, but given a chance, he'd do the same thing over and kiss her again. She felt so small and helpless in his arms. An overwhelming desire to protect her thrummed inside him, and the memory of their closeness still boiled his blood despite the throbbing lip.

Don't be daft. She's definitely *not for you.*

Besides, there was currently only one maiden he wanted to pledge his loyalty to, and soon she would be within his reach.

Savko waited a few more minutes then snuck out. It was a mad dash to the outer fence where his friends huddled safe and sound. They had a good laugh, patting each other on the back for another successful stunt and feeling rather heroic, then went to the festival to find more things to conquer. A food-eating contest sounded like a good idea at the moment. Savko's stomach growled when they got close enough to catch the smell of fried meat carried by the breeze from the river. A few neighboring villages and estates gathered at the large field near the water, lighting a multitude of fires along the bank. People spread over the area, visiting, dancing, and playing games. The sounds of music and laughter carried for miles.

Everyone brought food, and Savko quickly found a few familiar faces and several willing hands to load him up with all sorts of delicacies. His friends scattered about, and for a moment he stood, deciding what to do next. That was when he saw *her*.

Ruslana was hard to miss, already surrounded by a crowd of young men. She laughed and teased, playing with a lock of her blonde hair that fell loose over her perfect shoulders. With a flower wreath to adorn her, firelight reflecting in her bright eyes, and blush coloring her cheeks, she looked like *rysalka*, a water nymph in the flesh. He sure wouldn't mind being lured away by her charms.

You already have been.

Ruslana caught his gaze, and one side of her crimson lips curved up. Was she mocking his open-mouthed stare or inviting him to join the pathetic ranks of her admirers? Savko swore under his breath and looked away. He couldn't blame her for looking down at the lowly apprentice of a blacksmith. But she would be sure to accept a decorated Cossack once he returned from the war with fame and riches to lay at her feet. A new determination filled him.

Soon you'll be mine.

I t was dark by the time they rounded the horses, but Miray kept to her decision to attend the Midsummer festival. She promised herself to give it a try. Olena stayed home with children, not wanting to go without her husband.

"I would have loved to come with you," she said. "But it seems wrong to enjoy myself while Yakiv is putting his life in danger to keep us safe. I'll just end up ruining your evening."

Miray knew the way to the river, but even if she didn't, the wind carried the echo of the celebration all the way to their homestead. After what happened to her earlier, she happily agreed to have an entourage take her to the festivities. It wasn't the safest day to be wandering around alone. Savko proved as much. She couldn't stop thinking about him on the way while the servant girls by her side chatted and laughed, excited to be finally released from their household duties. Miray wondered if Savko was planning on stealing other girls' kisses, then reprimanded herself for such thoughts.

Stay away from him.

She sighed. Why did this brazen young man fascinate her so? Even Olena noticed it and nudged her a few times to talk to him. Now they'd done more than talk! The heat of Savko's body when he pressed her close still surged through her, his demanding mouth still made her breath hitch. She always avoided being touched at all costs, but somehow this was different. His embrace felt... right. But when his fingers brushed her hair, fear compelled her to stop him. Seeing Savko recoil if he found her scars would have been too much to bear. Miray berated herself for giving in to this moment, for dwelling on it even now. Her first kiss was all a game for this young man, nothing but a momentary whim.

I'd be better off letting this go. No one would want someone like me in earnest. Definitely not after being bitten!

As they got closer, the noises became louder. Miray came out to the clearing and froze. The young women who came with her ran ahead and quickly disappeared into the large crowd. The sights and sounds overwhelmed her. It was all too much: the drumming of tambourines, the cheerful whistles of *sopilka*, the strumming of *bandura* mixed with singing, laughter, and shouts. And fire, it was everywhere. She wanted to shut her eyes, plug her ears, and run away into the silence of the forest.

I have to do this... for myself. And I promised Olena. Enough hiding.

Swallowing against her dry throat, Miray forced herself to move forward and was instantly swept up by the movement of people. Someone grabbed her hand and pulled her into the fast *horovod*. She was soon out of breath and broke away. A stranger put a drink in her hand and a kind woman gave her a cheese pastry, but Miray couldn't swallow a single bite. A boisterous group of young women drew her attention. They defended a small birch tree decorated with ribbons and flowers, splashing with water and swatting young men who tried to steal these trinkets from the branches. Both sides seemed to enjoy the confrontation and constantly provoked each other, eliciting laughter and shouts of victory.

Miray's heart jumped in her chest when she noticed Savko with a crooked smirk playing on his lips and eyes shining. His chestnut hair was disheveled. The embroidered shirt he wore was half-tucked into the leather belt, and his sleeves were rolled up, showing off his tanned muscular arms. But her excitement quickly dwindled when she noticed the looks he gave to a stunning young woman standing between him and the tree. With her hands on her curvy hips, she smiled at him playfully, as if daring him to get past her. Savko prowled around. Enthralled, Miray watched his smooth movements. She couldn't look away even if it made an ache grow inside her chest. A moment later, he ducked under the girl's arm and snatched a ribbon off the tree. A crowd of her squealing comrades descended upon him with buckets of water and soaked him to the bone. Laughing, Savko handed the ribbon back to the blonde beauty with a slight bow. The "defenders" snuck hooded gazes at the wet shirt that clung to his lean torso and smiled coyly.

"What's the prize for taking the ribbon?" he asked, leaning closer. The girl crossed her arms, but her bright-red lips spread into a seductive smile.

No!

Miray must have made some sort of a sound because Savko's gaze darted in her direction. Surprise registered in his eyes. She turned and ran, her cheeks engulfed in heat from embarrassment and annoyance at herself and at him. No, she would not be like all of these girls, throwing longing glances at this prideful boy! He was ready to add another kiss to the collection. That moment they shared meant nothing. A scornful laugh escaped her lips. How could it? And after what she'd done, he would never try again. Then why did her stupid heart feel like it was breaking into pieces?

What am I when he can have any of these colorful birds? A little mouse he happened to catch in an alley. But I won't go back to hide in my hole! And I'm not here because of him.

Miray didn't stop until she was clear to the other side of the gathering. With every step, a new determination grew stronger inside her to see this night through. For once, Miray wanted to prove to Olena and to herself that she could overcome her fears. In the past, her awkward attempts to join her peers usually ended in rejection. This time, she wanted things to be different. Just another hour or so and she would leave with her chin held high, not because she was scared or intimidated, but on her own accord. She would not run away now, no matter what anyone said or did.

Miray forced herself to look up at people's faces, catching a few that were familiar. Some nodded and even waved. A man tipped his hat in her direction. A woman stopped her to ask about Olena. The tension in her shoulders eased a little. Resolved to see all the activities, the young woman moved toward another group of people who gathered around the bonfire. She kept her distance, watching while they jumped over the flames, some alone, some holding hands. The reddish-orange blaze was high, licking their feet and throwing sparks after them. Miray's body trembled as they leaped over and over again. Someone nudged her forward.

"Your turn now, sweetie." A young woman smiled next to her.

Another one took her hand and pulled her closer, but Miray dug her heels in.

"Are you waiting for your intended to jump together?" she asked.

Miray shook her head. "I-I don't want to."

"Everyone has to do it," a third girl chimed in.

"Can't you see? She's not of our people," someone joined in.

"C-mon, it's safe," the first girl repeated. "I'll show you."

People pressed all around her and propelled her forward before she could escape. The bonfire was so close now, the heat of the flames hit Miray's face. The blaze whispered, crackled, and hissed like a fiery monster, filling her nostrils with the sharp odor of smoke. Her mind burst with memories. Encouraging voices around her morphed into blood-curdling screams. The nauseating stench of burning flesh brought acid to her throat. Roaring flames trapped her. She was inside the burning house again, charred carcasses of its frame caving in on her head. Pain seared her body. Sobbing and bucking, Miray clawed like a wild animal against the hands that held her.

"A witch! She is a witch! She's afraid of the fire!" Shouts broke through the haze of Miray's flashback. She opened her eyes, staring at an angry mob that was now pulling and pushing all around her. Her wreath was knocked off in the commotion and trampled underfoot. One sleeve tore off, catching on something as she slumped to the ground and covered her face with her hands, trembling with fright. She tried to reach for a safe place inside herself and regain control of her body, imagining that she was in her beloved forest, but it wasn't working to calm her this time.

"Enough!" Savko's voice thundered close by, silencing the clamor. "You're a bunch of superstitious idiots! Can't you see you're scaring the girl half to death?"

"Have her jump through the fire to prove that she's not a witch!"

"Jump with her if you want to!"

Other shouts followed in agreement. Savko kneeled in front of Miray and she reached for him with a shaky hand. She could barely see him through the tears, but the warmth of his fingers circling hers gave her a surge of strength.

"Everything will be all right," he murmured, smoothing her hair. "I won't let them hurt you. They would have to go through me first. You saved me once, now it's my turn."

He tried to fix her torn sleeve with his free hand and stopped, his fingers flexing into a fist.

"The girl's burned," he bit out. "Of course, she doesn't want to jump through your stupid fire."

In the hushed silence that followed, a few women next to Miray let out strangled gasps and several people murmured apologies, but her eyes were on Savko. His gaze reflected what she hated most—pity. No, she couldn't bear that look. Not from him. It would have been better if the crowd tore her to pieces or if she had died in that fire years ago. Miray backed away, scrambled to her feet, and ran. People parted to make a passage for her.

"Wait!"

The sounds of the festivities drowned Savko's voice, but the pounding in her head was even louder. Miray begged it to stop before realizing that it was the frantic beating of her own wretched heart. Blindly the young woman ran forward until she finally got to the edge of the field where the noises were overrun by the chirping of crickets and bright lights gave way to darkness. The sky was clear and the moon bright enough to illuminate a path for her. Miray continued at a brisk pace despite the burning in her lungs.

"Where are you running to, girly?" a drunken slur came out to her right. A man separated from the shadow of a tree and stumbled toward her.

Miray sucked in a ragged breath and quickened her steps.

"Heeey, hold up. The c-celebration's not over yet."

She dashed away, but somehow the man's steps drew closer behind her. Panic constricted her throat. It had been a mistake to come here, and an even bigger one to leave in a hurry like this, with no entourage. She should have found the servants and forced them to take her home. But it was too late now. Miray broke into a run, fear giving her tired feet new strength. The forest drew closer, and she crashed into the trees without a second thought, seeking solace in their deep shadows. This was her refuge, her place of security, and it would save her now.

The heavy footsteps didn't let up. Branches snapped as someone pressed at her heels. Maybe she should have stayed on the main path. She might have met other people on the way. No one would hear her or come to her rescue now. Miray strangled back a sob and pushed through the foliage, branches tugging on her clothes as if to hold her back. She stumbled over the root and fell but pushed herself back up and forced her body to move forward.

"Stop! Wait!"

The voice was familiar, but it couldn't be. Her mind was playing tricks on her. Miray stumbled again, and this time didn't hit the ground when a strong arm caught her. She shrieked and fought to break free.

"Stop it, you wild thing!" Savko hissed into her tangled hair, breathless and irritated. "Why are you making it so hard to rescue you?"

She stilled, but her heart raced even faster, nearly jumping out of her chest.

A chuckle rippled behind her. "It's the second time I'm saving you today, so you owe me now."

The girl stiffened in his arms, then trembled with sobs. Savko had never seen a person cry like this in complete silence. It made his throat tighten.

"Don't... please. You're safe. I was just trying to help."

He scooped her closer, and she hid her face in his shirt. Her shoulders shook and her tears soaked through the thin linen that was still damp from the cold soak he received earlier. He held her tight, giving her time to let it all out, once again stricken by the desire to protect her. That's why he went after her, unsettled after watching her run off. As Savko suspected, the ignorant girl left the celebration alone. He had followed at a distance, determined to see her make it safely home. Then the drunk spooked her and she sprinted into the forest like a frightened doe. She was surprisingly fast, and by the time he caught up, they were deep in.

"I hope you knew where you were running to because I have no idea how to get out of here," he said with a chuckle. She lifted her dark eyes at him and chewed on her lip, the gesture making his heart beat a little faster. The only answer he received was a sniffle and a shrug. "I see. You don't know where we are either. Well, we can try to find our way out, but I'm afraid we might have to wait till morning. Then I can solemnly swear that I haven't done anything unsuitable, or we can bribe another girl to vouch for you. Unless, of course, your family organizes a search party and finds us first."

"Th-they might get worried."

Savko rubbed his neck. "Great. Then I'd get that whipping after all."

"I won't let them."

Determination rang in her voice and reflected on her face. Savko laughed. He tucked the girl's tangled locks behind her ears, his hand brushing against the uneven skin of her left cheek. She froze then jerked away.

The burn.

"I'm sorry." Savko meant it, but the comment made her shrink into herself even more. His heart prickled uncomfortably on her behalf as she wrapped her arms around her torso. Savko wished he had a jacket to cover her ruined dress, but it was probably not the cooler temperatures that made the young woman shiver. His fingers flexed into a fist when he remembered seeing her on the ground, scared and confused, people shouting over her. He wanted to beat them all senseless, then scoop her up and carry her away in front of everyone.

"Let's try to find our way out, shall we?"

Savko reached for her hand. She gave it willingly, her small fingers warm in his grip. He moved forward, shoving the branches aside and slowing his steps to allow the young woman to keep up, but he had no sense of direction. It was the same forest all around them, the trees high enough to cover the stars, leaving only small pieces of the night sky to peek here and there. The air was still and silent, filled with the fresh odor of pine. Everything seemed peaceful, but Savko kept his senses sharp. He did not believe in all the silly tales that surrounded this night, about the dwellers of the rivers and forests coming out to meddle in the affairs of people. But there were other real dangers to worry about.

"I'm Savko," he said, breaking the silence. "I come to your—"

"I know."

"Oh..." He wondered if the girl would tell Koval about his stunt with the horses later and if his older brother would have to answer for it, but none of that mattered at the moment. First, they had to find their way out. "So your name is Maria?"

"It's not my real name."

"What is it then?"

"Miray."

"Pretty. Does it mean anything?"

"The moon."

Savko chuckled. "Would you mind shining a bit of light on our path then? I might end up flat on the ground soon and take you along with me."

Miray let out a gentle laugh, like the sound of a chiming bell. It made him smile until another thought entered his head. He was never the one to listen to the rumors, but a well-known person such as Koval could hardly escape them. Everyone still wondered why the man brought the child of their adversaries home, and Savko was curious now.

"You're not from here," he said.

"I'm from Kefe."

"I see. Ottoman's domain then."

Miray tried to wiggle her hand out of his, but Savko held it tight. He turned to look at her but couldn't see her face well. Still, the girl was clearly upset.

"I'm not judging you," he said softly. "No one chooses where to be born."

"I understand why you might hate me. I've heard enough about steppe raiders capturing people here and selling them in my city. It shouldn't be like that."

He pressed her fingers. "I certainly don't hate you! None of it is your doing."

She let out a shuddering sigh. "Not all Turks own slaves. It's just a way of life for the rich. But my father was a shoemaker, and my mother taught music. They... they did not deserve to die."

She choked on the last words. Savko stopped and turned around, but she avoided his gaze even in the dark.

"How did it happen?" he asked quietly.

"It was an accident. A fire broke through the city when the Cossacks stormed it. We were hiding in our house."

"Is that how..."

She nodded ever so slightly. "Boryslav Sergeevich must have passed by when he heard my cries. He saved me. It was years ago, but I still remember. It's as vivid in my mind as if it happened yesterday.

Sometimes I even see it in my dreams. And sometimes... what you saw by the bonfire... It's like I am there again." Her gaze fluttered to him, glistening with tears. "I-I've never told anyone."

"I'm sorry."

Her expression hardened. "Stop saying you're sorry. I don't need your pity."

She turned away and marched past him.

Savko groaned and stomped after her. "Ok, I'm not sorry. What am I supposed to say? You shouldn't be ashamed of what happened to you, it wasn't your fault."

"I'm not!" For the first time, her voice lost its gentleness. She sounded angry now.

"And there is nothing wrong with having scars," he pressed on. "I have them all over my body. I burn myself all the time in the smithy. And I have plenty of other marks to commemorate all the stupid things I've attempted in my life. If you want, I can show you."

Miray halted so suddenly he almost ran into her. She studied him with her big eyes. Savko wanted to look into them longer, wanted to know what other thoughts ran inside that pretty head. He never had conversations like these with other women, not even with men. No one ever bared their very soul to him like that, and he wanted to do something in return. Maybe it was the strangeness of being lost in the forest together. On impulse, he grabbed her hand, then untucked his shirt and pulled her forward until her fingers touched the knotted skin on the left side of his abdomen. She gasped but didn't pull away. He suppressed an involuntary shiver when she traced the ragged scar up to his chest.

"I almost died that day." Savko's voice came out strangled. Miray finally stopped exploring, letting him breathe easier.

"What happened?" she murmured.

"My friends and I made a rope to jump into the river. Not a very sturdy one, as I discovered." He chuckled. "Let's just say I didn't make it into the water. My mother was in hysterics. That was worse than getting stitched up after. I swore to never scare her like that again."

A small stream of moonlight illuminated Miray's smile. "Seems like you're bad at keeping promises."

He grinned back. "I only take calculated risks now."

"So, did you plan to fall off my horse then?"

Savko laughed at the mischief twinkling in her eyes. He liked it better than seeing tears in them.

"Well, I usually don't do anything life-threatening. Unless you count chasing a wild girl into the dark woods. I was half-expecting you to turn into a nymph and lure me to my death."

A tree branch snapped nearby, and Miray clung tighter to him. Savko might have enjoyed this more under different circumstances, but he detected movement in the foliage, his body tensing with a sense of danger. Then he saw it. A fiery glow from a pair of eyes, then another. He stepped back toward a wide tree, pulling Miray along.

"Climb up. I'll help you."

"I'm not leaving you," she said firmly.

"Don't be silly. What will you do? Wolves rarely attack. You'll stay up there until they leave. Just in case."

She shook her head "no", and Savko swore under his breath. For someone who had been trembling in his arms a few minutes ago, she was incredibly stubborn. It was summer though, so the pack should have been well fed. Probably just curious. He changed his mind when the shiny eyes circled them, and low growls came from between the trees.

"I don't know what's wrong with them, but this doesn't sound too friendly. Stay back, let me try to scare them off."

Savko wasn't sure anymore where "back" was. The animals might have been all around them. Carefully, he stooped down and searched the ground, picking up a few branches and stones, and throwing them between the trees. He yelled and stomped too for good measure. The eyes disappeared for a few moments then turned up even closer. He broke a bigger branch off and pointed it at the beasts tentatively moving toward them.

"Go up that tree," he ordered.

Miray's fingers dug into his arm, and she only pressed herself closer to his side. One step away from him, a wolf bared its teeth.

"They don't like you," she whispered.

"I can tell," he muttered, lunging forward and shoving the branch into the animal's angry muzzle.

If only I had a torch...

His thought was cut off when another beast grabbed and pulled at his pants, ripping them to shreds. Savko swung the branch but missed as the animal jumped away. Another wolf grabbed the end with its teeth and tugged with a low growl. A third one readied to attack his open side. Before it did, Miray was between him and the wolf, throwing her hands out as she had with the horse. Savko's heart leaped.

"No!" she yelled.

The beast stopped mid-sprint and crouched low to the ground with its tail between its legs. And then it whined. Savko watched in amazement as the rest of the pack stopped and did the same thing. One even lay on its belly and scooted until its muzzle was next to Miray's foot. She squatted and reached out to pet the beast.

"Miray!"

The animal growled at the sound of Savko's warning.

Miray laughed, then rubbed behind the monster's ears. "I told you they don't like you. I think they were trying to protect me from you."

"The savage is wagging its tail like a dog!" Savko exclaimed. "How do you do this?"

She shrugged. "Don't know. Just didn't want them to hurt you or themselves. I've always had a way with animals." Her voice hitched. "But people, they say things..."

Savko stepped closer and drew Miray up to her feet. Ignoring the renewed growls from the wolves, he cupped her face. "Don't mind what others say. I think you're incredibly brave."

Miray's heart raced as Savko's fingers ran gently over the outline of her chin and his gaze dipped to her lips. The wolf behind her shifted and whined, forcing her to look back. It paced in a strange dance, jumping backward with each step as if begging them to follow.

"I think he wants to show us a way out," she said.

"Yeah, right." Savko scoffed but followed.

They really had no other option. There were no people to rescue them, and either way, animals were always friendly and more helpful to her. Why would it be any different this time?

They followed the wolf, the rest of the pack trotting along, heeding his lead. At least Miray thought it was a "he". The animal was the largest of them all and looked familiar. A few years ago, she had found a wolf on the edge of the forest with a paw caught in a trap. It had the same white coloring of fur on its chest. She freed the poor thing and wrapped the wound. Maybe it was trying to thank her now.

Would a wild animal remember something like that?

The wolf proceeded at a slow enough pace for them to keep up. His pack stayed close by, keeping Savko on his toes. Unlike him, Miray finally relaxed and could breathe easier. The longer they hiked through mossy pines and wide oaks, the better she felt. She could have walked like this for hours, enjoying the earthy fragrances and occasional crunch of twigs underfoot. Miray was always more alive in the forest, and this time it loosened her tongue too. She was surprised at the conversation that passed between her and Savko earlier, at the things they had revealed to each other. He also reclaimed her hand, and it seemed so natural that she didn't even think to break away, nor did she want to.

"I guess we are even again," Savko said. "Now you saved me twice."

"I'm not sure I really needed saving the second time. No one followed me into the forest aside from you, and we were both equally lost as a result." The teasing notes in her voice surprised Miray. What were Savko and this night doing to her? She never talked like that, but now the words kept coming. "It seems I have a personal entourage to lead me out, and your presence will only compromise me if we are seen together so late at night."

Savko twirled her around, causing the wolves to grumble again and her heart to drum an uneven rhythm as she faced him.

"Hey, if you keep up with such accusations, I might actually do something compromising." His lips spread into a shameless smirk, sending heat to her cheeks. Then he was serious again. "And just to make this clear, I don't mind being indebted to you."

Forever?

Miray swallowed hard and stepped away, appalled at her own thoughts as they continued to walk. Friends. They were only friends. Or at least they were starting to be. And she was thankful for that. She would cherish their time together for as long as she lived, storing Savko's kind words in her heart. Things would be different now. Whenever he visited their homestead again, she would no longer avoid him. Instead, they could talk and laugh about this odd experience. She might even show him her favorite spot in the forest, a clearing full of flowers with a happy little stream where she spent hours alone. The idea of having another person to share it with filled her heart with warmth.

And then she remembered the golden-haired girl. He probably wanted to sit around with her instead and weave flowers into her long tresses. It was silly for Miray to imagine that Savko would want to waste his time on someone like her. He wasn't repelled by her burns, but he couldn't possibly be attracted to a feeble, battered creature when a goddess was sending approving smiles his way. It would be ridiculous to even imagine such things.

"What's wrong?" Savko slowed down and pressed Miray's fingers as if sensing her changing mood.

"It's nothing."

"You're not a good liar," he teased. "Should practice more."

"Usually, I don't say anything at all."

Not counting tonight. I haven't said this many words in months!

"That's not right. You should speak up if you feel the need."

"Says a boy."

"A man."

Miray huffed. "Exactly my point. And you probably haven't been called an infidel to your face either."

"I would have punched the face of the person who said it."

"Do I look like I can go around punching everyone?"

"I can punch them for you!"

"But you can't stop people from talking."

"True. Then maybe we should ignore them."

"We?" Exasperation rose inside Miray. For the second time now. Somehow Savko brought all kinds of emotions out from the depths of her soul where she had been hiding them for years. Usually she pushed them away, hoping that whatever upset her would disappear if hidden below the smooth surface. But for some reason, tonight she couldn't hold back the torrent.

"What do you know about such things?" Her voice trembled but the words kept tumbling out. "You seem well liked by your peers and able to defend yourself against those who might have something against you. You can't possibly understand, so don't pretend to!"

Wolves growled. Miray tried to pull her hand away for the umpteenth time this evening, but Savko held it in a firm grip, forcing her to face him again. She was now appalled at this splash of indignation and looked up to see if he was equally shocked. But there was no judgment in his steady gaze and not even a shred of the dreaded pity.

"I do understand, Miray," he said softly, pulling her along when their guides moved forward. "And I know about wanting to fit in. I grew up poor. Until I was about eleven, we barely had enough to eat. My older brother worked hard to provide for us, but with so many mouths to fill, it wasn't enough. My mother kept her pride and never asked anyone for help after my father died. I was a scrawny boy and wore ill-fitting clothes. Other children constantly made fun of me, but I learned to either fight back or laugh it off. Then my brother joined the Cossacks, and everything changed. That's why I will serve too."

Miray pressed Savko's hand to show her support while he talked, even though her heart ached at the thought of him stepping into the dangerous life of a warrior. They slowed their steps as if trying to postpone the end of their walk together despite the animals prancing impatiently ahead. For a moment, they walked in companionable silence, each deep in their thoughts. Miray recalled her own childhood. She lacked nothing then and was certainly thankful for everything Boryslav Sergeevich did for her now. The man was like a father to her, protective and caring. And here was a boy who grew up without one, having to fend for himself, even though his older brother stepped into that role.

"I've never told this to anyone either," Savko finally said.

Not even to the blonde-haired siren? she wanted to ask but bit her tongue. Maybe there were some girls for kissing and others for talking. But he had done both of these things to her. Then what was she to him?

"Thank you," Miray said instead. "For sharing. And for listening too."

"You know what I'm thinking? People might find they ain't that much different from each other if they do just that." He glanced back with a smug grin.

"You know what *I* am thinking?" she asked with a smile. "It isn't so bad to be a little different if you find someone who understands."

Savko halted and searched her face. Once again Miray caught herself craving his touch. She was no longer worried about Savko seeing her scars. For the first time in her life, she wanted to be held by a young man. Timidly, Miray placed her palm on his chest, and his breath hitched underneath. Savko drew her close, scalding her once again with a wave of heat that overwhelmed her senses. This time she did not fight his embrace but looked up and met his eyes, filled with surprise and... longing. She thought he would kiss her right then and there, and her heart leaped into her throat. But the darn wolves howled all around them as if they caught a scent of prey. The pack rushed ahead, and they had no other choice but to follow in haste.

"It seems we've been walking for a while. Much longer than it took me to catch up with you," Savko muttered.

Miray could barely keep up with his long strides, even though he constantly turned to check on her. "Maybe they are taking me all the way home."

"How would they know where you live?"

She shrugged, then spotted a flickering light between the trees. "Look! A lantern! We must be almost there."

As they moved through a thick foliage, fireflies appeared all around them. They floated in a strange dance as if responding to a silent melody. Then Miray could hear it too. The whole forest hummed, the sound getting stronger with every step. Mesmerized, she opened her hand to see if one of the fireflies would land on her palm, but they darted away.

"Do you hear it?" she whispered.

"What?"

Savko tensed next to her. She looked past him. A small clearing with an overgrowth of fern bushes opened up ahead of them. It was filled with moonlight. Hidden among the leaves, something pulsed with red light like a beating heart. It sounded like one too, coming toward them in waves and resonating inside Miray's chest as if a giant drum was being played nearby.

The wolves stopped at the edge of the clearing, and Miray glanced up at Savko. He stood still, staring at the scene before them as if spellbound. Then he let go of her hand for the first time and ran forward, kneeling in front of the strange light. Miray followed cautiously and stood close by while he moved away the greenery, uncovering a flower bud the size of his hand. It was elongated like a lily. Red light tried to break out of it, swaying the shell slightly as if a swarm of fireflies was stuck on the inside.

Miray grabbed Savko's shoulder. "Don't touch it. I have a bad feeling about it."

He turned toward her with an awestruck look on his face. "Do you not know what this is? It's a fern flower!"

She furrowed her brow in confusion. "Ferns don't have flowers."

"It blooms only once a year on this exact day, but I thought it was only a myth! Somehow your wolves led us to it."

"Why?" she asked, trying to fight the unease inside.

"It... It's like finding a treasure. Even better. Whoever plucks this flower, can see all the treasures hidden deep in the earth and open any lock. Its owner will be the richest person ever!"

A sinking feeling struck Miray. "Is this what you really want?"

"To never worry about money? Of course! Who doesn't want that?" He laughed, his eyes shining. "But that's not all. Although the rest of these things sound too crazy. I've heard it can help people understand animals, gain unlimited knowledge and wisdom, become invisible, even change their appearance. Hard to believe, I know. But the treasure... It has to be real!"

His excitement was almost feverish. It seemed to overshadow any common sense. How can a flower, even as unusual as this one, point to treasure? Maybe she didn't understand what it meant to grow up poor and what such discovery truly meant for Savko, but something about it didn't feel right. If she could use this wander-plant, she would have picked a different gift. To understand animals would have been nice.

Miray...

She stiffened. It was her mother's voice.

Miray, come.

She turned in the direction from which the voice came and took a step forward, but Savko grabbed her. "Where are you going? We have to stay here and wait until it blooms."

Miray, come. Help me.

The voice was more urgent, even distressed. "I am... I'm hearing something," she said, pulling away again. "Maybe someone is lost and needs our help."

Miray... hurry!

The wolves howled, and she dashed toward the voice, somehow breaking Savko's hold. "I'm coming."

"No! Miray!" He scrambled after her and grabbed her arm.

"I have to go. You don't understand." She didn't understand

either, but somehow her mother was nearby, and she was in trouble. "It's my mother. She's hurt. I need to help her."

Savko gripped her shoulders and turned her so she could face him. "It is not your mother, Miray. You're being tricked. Whatever this is, it's luring you away from here."

Miray, help! I can't get out! Help me, please.

The desperate call tore through any logic and pierced her heart.

"Geliyorum, anne! Geliyorum!"

She screamed "I'm coming, Mother" in the tongue of her childhood until her voice turned hoarse. She pleaded with Savko to let her go, fighting out of his embrace with all her strength. He carried her back to the ferns and held her tight, wrapping his big arms around her and restraining her as if she were a little child. Reality slipped. Miray was in the burning house again, trapped while her mother was calling for help, but she couldn't get to her, couldn't save her.

"It's not your fault, it's not your fault," Savko kept repeating, gently rocking Miray in his embrace until she passed out from exhaustion.

The young woman slept in his arms, her face now relaxed in the moonlight, all suffering erased from her peaceful countenance. She was beautifully fragile, like the fern flower that was opening next to him. But the promise of endless riches no longer had the same appeal. Savko shuddered, thinking what could have happened to Miray if he had let her slip away while distracted. He had heard other stories about this flower, of people going mad or becoming forever lost in the depth of the forest, of evil spirits stealing their souls. Miray was right to be wary of it.

I almost lost her...

And then the flower opened, taking his breath away. Savko stared at the red light bursting before his eyes as if a setting sun descended into a bloom. The fiery hues swirled and changed like burning coals. He wanted to wake Miray so she could see it too but decided not to disturb her after what happened earlier. From what he had heard, the bloom only stayed open for a short time, and he reached out to pluck it.

"Are you sure you want to do this, boy?"

Savko knew better than to listen to some crackly old voice. It wouldn't fool him.

"A sacrifice would be required of you," someone said again.

Savko gritted his teeth. "Begone now, would you?"

"A sacrifice from the very depths of your heart."

He glanced over his shoulder then, his arm tightening protectively around Miray. A woman wrapped in a long cloak stood at the edge of the forest. The wolves that had guided them earlier gathered around her. In her bony hand, she held a staff with a blue light on its end. It illuminated her mirthless smirk and crooked nose, not quite reaching her eyes underneath the hood. But he knew who she was. The stories circled around enough times to get ingrained into him since childhood. The forest witch, Baba Yaga, stood before him as real as could be.

"I bet you want this flower for yourself, old hag," he said, shifting so he could see the bloom and not miss the moment when it started to fade away. "You don't scare me."

The witch cackled, showing off her uneven teeth. "I can get as many of these as I want, but what's the use? They serve me no purpose. I know the tongues of animals. I can see all the treasures in the depth of the earth. And I can change my appearance at will."

Baba Yaga hit her staff on the ground and her face transformed into that of a fair maiden. She hit it again and was back to her grotesque appearance.

"I think this look makes a deeper impression." She smiled, but it looked more like a scowl.

"What do you want then?" Savko bit out.

"Leave the girl to me and you can have the fern flower."

Savko tried to hide his surprise at such a request, forcing his voice to come out even, but worry clawd on the inside. "It's not yours to give. I can take it myself."

And Miray is not mine to give either.

"You won't be able to walk away with it."

The wolves rose at her side and growled. *Traitors.*

"Then why ask me at all?" Despair now made its way into his heart. He wouldn't be able to outrun them, and he would never leave Miray behind. But what could he possibly do to stop the witch and her beasts?

"Miray won't stay willingly unless you make her," the old woman continued. "I need you to break her heart."

"You must be out of your mind, crone!"

The young woman stirred in his arms, and he stilled, forgetting about the wander-flower, forgetting the witch. Almost. Baba Yaga was quick to remind him of her presence, resuming her ridiculous demands.

"Can't you see? She is unhappy as it is, unable to fit among your people. I know, because she comes to the edge of the forest often, seeking solace from plants, birds, and animals. The girl can't find it elsewhere. She will have nothing but more heartbreak in your world."

"That's not true. There are people who care for her, who would miss her." He looked at Miray and paused, realization dawning on him. "*I* would miss her."

The sorceress laughed. "Aren't you planning to get rich and marry the most spoiled girl in the region? What do you need Miray for? To follow you like a puppy? You would only prolong her suffering. Better make a clean cut and end it now. Plus, you'd get something in return. Something you *really* want."

Right now he wanted nothing more than to protect the sleeping young woman in his arms. "What do you need her for?"

"She's got a gift," Baba Yaga said, almost tenderly, then she scoffed. "A brainless stump like you would never appreciate it. This girl has a gentle spirit, a way with animals and plants. She'll be my apprentice, my helper, my successor when it comes to that. Only in pursuing her purpose can she find her true happiness. You can never give her that. But she is blind with love and would never believe me."

Love?

Could it be that Miray loved him? How did that happen? When? She couldn't possibly have fallen for him so fast. The young woman had a sensible head on her shoulders.

"She watched you for a while," the witch said, as if reading his thoughts. "But you were blind. Your vanity made you oblivious to what was right in front of your nose."

Her crackly laugh cut deep into his heart. No wonder Miray never approached him. He could see now how shallow he was, how full of himself. The evil spirits couldn't even tempt him to follow any voices. Yes, he cared for his siblings, his mother. He'd die for them if needed. But all his friendships and even infatuations went only as far as he could benefit from them. He was always trying to win, to prove himself, to outshine others. Even his interest in Ruslana started because of a challenge she presented. He wanted to prove that he could have the prettiest girl if he wanted to.

Miray was different. She seemed selfless, willing to help, to stand up for others. For him. For any living creature. She thought so little of herself. Too little... The girl was bashful because of her scars, but with all his good looks, he didn't deserve her affection. Somehow, he wanted to be different, to change for Miray, and to help her pursue the things she enjoyed instead of going after riches or fame. But first, he had to get her to safety. There was no talking the witch out of her crazy ideas, so Savko kept an eye on the flower and played along to buy more time.

"What do you need me to do?"

"Ah, that's better!" She rubbed her hands together with a tooth-less smirk. "When Miray wakes, tell her you got the flower—which you will, don't worry—and that you don't need her help anymore. Tell her that you've used her to find it because of the rumors that she is a witch. You thought she might know the forest well and followed so she could lead you here. Now that you have what you were after, you don't need her anymore. For good measure, tell her she is ugly and pathetic, and that you couldn't wait to be rid of her. Then you'll leave her crying here, and I will come to comfort her and to offer her this lucrative position in a place she enjoys."

"I see," Savko deadpanned, even though his insides twisted painfully at her words. "Sounds very reasonable to me. But you won't harm her?"

"Never! Even if I tried, the entire forest would rebel against me. It loves her dearly."

"Good." Swiftly, Savko plucked the flower, the nature around him releasing an audible sigh.

He paused, holding it up in his fist, its light blinding him. He knew what he was about to do, but in that split second, Savko also understood something profound. Something deep. As if he could see into his own heart and the future itself. That future was with the slender young woman he cradled in his arms. He didn't care about her scars nor what others thought of her. In that moment he could see right into her bright soul, see the damage that every negative word or cold stare did to the tender sprout of a girl and the lies she had told herself as a result. Over the years, this dimmed her true light, causing Miray to hide her gifts. Savko wished for nothing more than to become a wall between her and all the arrows directed at her heart. He had no doubt what needed to transpire.

"One other thing I've heard about the fern flower," he said. "It has the power to heal and bring inner peace. And my only wish is that it would do this for Miray."

He placed the flower on her chest. Baba Yaga launched forward with an angry howl, but the wolves grabbed at her cloak and pulled her back into the forest while she cursed and hit them with her staff. The trees groaned as they swallowed their struggle.

Savko sighed with relief and turned his attention back to Miray. The fern flower shimmered with many colors like a precious stone on her chest until it faded away slowly, dissolving through her skin. For a moment it was Miray who glowed, beautiful like the morning sun that was now peeking through the thick branches. Savko brushed her hair away, running his fingers over the smooth skin of her face. Her bare left shoulder where the dress was torn did not have any scars either.

"You were wrong, witch," he whispered. "She doesn't need to stay broken to find herself. There are those who love and care for her, a family she belongs to... I will be your family if you'll have me, Miray."

Gently, he kissed her forehead and stood up, the young woman still sound asleep in his arms. She was light as a feather, and Savko held her tighter. He could have carried her like this for hours with her warm cheek against his shoulder and her soft breath on his neck. A desire to shield Miray from pain made his chest hurt. It now felt like the most important purpose in his life, and this girl... more valuable than any riches he could have found. Savko chuckled, realizing something.

"The fern flower fulfilled its purpose," he whispered into Miray's tangled locks. "It pointed me to the biggest treasure."

As he walked away, their four-legged friend made another appearance and led him in the right direction this time, stopping only when they reached the edge of the forest. When Savko stepped out from under the trees, he found himself on the road to Miray's house. He looked back at the noble pines, powerful oaks, and elegant birches. In their green crowns, birds raised their cheerful chorus, and he wondered whether the entire forest conspired to reveal its biggest secret to help one slender girl who appreciated its beauty.

Miray didn't know how she ended up in bed in Olena's house. Slowly, the events of the previous night came to her memory, hazy like a dream. She did dream of Savko sometimes, of walking together and having conversations when in reality she was afraid to come close enough to utter a greeting. But this time it was real! They had done all of that and more. He told her things about himself no one else knew, and she also shared her heart. But how did they get out of the forest? She couldn't remember. Did she fall asleep on the way and he carried her home? What would others think of that? Her cheeks engulfed in flames, and at that very moment Olena burst through the doors.

"Get up, sleepyhead," she chirped, throwing the shutters open. "Sounds like you had too much entertainment last night."

Miray shielded her eyes from the bright light. "What time is it?"

"Almost noon."

"What?!" Miray sat up, blinking. "How did I sleep so long? And how did I get here?"

Olena winked. "I caught a very handsome young man carrying

you home when I went to the well this morning. Be thankful no one else saw him."

Miray opened and closed her mouth, stunned at Olena's nonchalance.

"I won't tell Mother, don't worry," she said. "If anyone asks, I'll say you slept in my house. I told you it was worth going to the festival last night."

"But we didn't... We're not... There was nothing..."

"Oh, there was something!" Olena laughed. "He insisted on taking you all the way into my house and handed you over as if he was giving up some great treasure. He better treat you as one and do what is right now, or he'll have to answer to me!"

Miray fell back in bed and covered her head with a pillow. "I will never come out of this room." She groaned, but joy filled her heart at the realization of what happened. For Savko to carry her all the way to the house, and out in the open like this, could have only meant one thing.

"Are you sure you won't come out?" Olena teased. "Because there is someone waiting for you at the door already. Very impatiently. I don't think that lad had any sleep at all."

"No! This can't... he can't still be here."

"What? You think I imagined it?" Olena arched her brow when Miray sat up and stared at her. "Tall, handsome, dark hair, blacksmith's apprentice, I believe."

Miray scrambled out of the bed while Olena laughed and called in the servant girl to bring fresh water and a set of clothes. Miray apologized profusely for the ruined dress. Olena told her not to worry and that all of this was worth the ripped sleeve, which made Miray's cheeks heat up once again. She pushed the women out of the room and slipped her clothes off. Cold water sent goosebumps up her arms as Miray scrubbed herself hastily with the soaked washcloth, pausing when her fingers brushed over the left side of her neck. Her breath hitched. She touched it again, slower, her palm sliding up against the smooth skin of her cheek where the scar had been.

Miray usually avoided looking at herself, but she did this time and scarcely believed her own eyes at what she found. Tears ran down her face. Could this really be true? The scars that held her chained to

the tragedy of her past and crippled her future had vanished! And
not only that. There was no more guilt, no overbearing loneliness
that threw her into melancholy, no self-loathing. Her heart felt light.
It had wings now, and each feather was a kind word, a smile, a pat on
her cheek, a sunny day, a horse's wet nose, a chirp of a bird, a rustle of
a green leaf, a fragrant flower... a kiss. How could she not see how full
her life had been? No, it had not been the scars keeping her from
enjoying all of this, but her own faulty beliefs that she wasn't worthy
of happiness.

What occured last night? Savko! He would know.

Miray dressed in a hurry, then sat impatiently, letting Olena
brush her hair and twist it into a pretty braid. This was the first time
she dared to wear her tresses up, and happy tears spilled again. Olena
kissed her and told her she was silly to cry over a hairdo, then forced
her to put on a string of corals.

"Olena," Miray asked timidly. "Don't you find it strange?"

"What, silly goose?"

"My scars..."

Olena gave her a quizzical glance. "Your scars?"

"Yes. They are gone!"

No matter what Miray said, Olena and even the servant girl
insisted they could not recall her having any scars. Finally, Olena
ordered her to stop speaking nonsense and focus on getting ready.
The young woman pinched herself to make sure all of this was real.
Whatever caused her skin to clear must have removed the memory of
her disfigurement from others. Part of her was saddened by this
strange occurrence. Would her benefactor Boryslav Sergeevich not be
able to recall his own heroic feats in saving her? Somehow, she didn't
mind the scars anymore and wanted at least someone to remember
them. They were part of her story, of the things she had to overcome
when she fought for her life and sanity. She might have even worn
them with pride now. Savko didn't seem to mind. He thought she
was courageous, and Miray started to believe that too.

Olena handed her a small mirror. The young woman couldn't
peel her eyes away from her face in the reflection that seemed to glow
with delight from the inside, shining eyes staring back at her. But
maybe it was from the anticipation of seeing Savko again. Blush

spread over her cheeks in the mirror at the thought. Miray hugged Olena and ran out, slowing her steps once she reached the door. Her heart was about to jump out of her chest as she stepped into the bright light of the warm summer day and noticed Savko on the ground.

He was leaning on the wall with his eyes closed, hair falling haphazardly over his forehead. She allowed her gaze to linger on his chiseled features. He must have fallen asleep waiting for her. Smiling, Miray walked closer and knelt next to Savko in the grass, unable to stop herself from moving his unruly locks out of his face. He caught her hand and brought it to his lips, smiling against her palm.

"How did you know it was me and not some random girl?" she demanded.

He opened one eye, squinting at her, then pulled her into his lap. She yelped and tried to get up, burning with embarrassment, but he held her close and buried his face in her hair.

"You smell like the forest, that's how I knew."

She finally gave up and settled in his embrace, praying no one would spot them. "What happened last night, Savko, tell me. I don't remember anything besides getting lost, following the wolves, then..."

"Then I found the greatest treasure." He cupped her cheek and smiled.

She caught his hand that caressed her skin. "What... what happened to my scars?" Her eyes widened. "The fern flower! You did something!"

He lifted her chin, his face somber. "I didn't need to, Miray. You were as beautiful then as you are now. But when I plucked that flower, I understood something. I saw... you, I really did! And I want you to know something. The scars don't define you. And you can't hide behind them anymore."

"You remember then," Miray murmured, tears running out of her eyes.

Savko wiped them off, fervently promising that he would never let anyone or anything make her cry again. Shyness overcame her at his burning gaze. She tried to get up, but Savko held her even closer.

"I'm not letting you go, so don't even try." He chuckled, then looked worried again, searching her face. "Unless you want to leave. Ugh, I'm such a fool, thinking I could... Assuming you'd want me. There is not much I could offer you aside from myself, Miray, if you agree to marry me. And you're worthy of so much more."

She touched his cheek, tears burning in her eyes again, and shook her head. "No. I want to be with you."

He had given her so much already, she could hardly put it into words.

Savko let out a breath he must have been holding, his gray eyes overfilling with glee. "Then no one would be able to take you away from me like they can't take away the moon from the sky."

He claimed Miray's lips, and her heart burst with a melody of her own making.

Author's Note

This story is set in the 17th century, during the time when Ukraine was still dealing with frequent Crimean-Nogai slave raids. It is estimated that several million Slavs were taken to the Ottoman Empire as a result. Zaporizhska Sich was formed by the Cossacks to defend that area. The raid of Kefe (Caffa) was a real historical event that resulted in the freedom of thousands.

Now more than 130 nationalities and ethnic groups call Ukraine their home, including many Turks and Tatars who migrated there over the years and stayed. The Ukrainian government formally recognized Crimean Tatars as indigenous people of that region in 2021 legislation. At this moment Turkey, along with other countries, is helping Ukraine defend its freedom from the Russian invasion. It accepted thousands of refugees fleeing the war zones.

During these difficult times, writing stories about Ukrainian history, folklore, and culture mixed with some hope-filled fantasy became an outlet for me. Several more stories set in the fictional village near Khortytsia Island in Zaporizhia are scheduled to be released. To be the first one to read them, sign up here: https://www.subscribepage.com/slavic_fantasy

About the Author

Elena Shelest immigrated to the U.S. from Ukraine at the age of 15. She currently resides in the Pacific Northwest with her husband, two busy kids, and three pets.

Elena is a full-time nurse, an artist, and an avid reader of fantasy and inspirational books. She is hoping to encourage her readers to be able to look beyond what's possible and believe again that everyday miracles do happen.

Her contemporary fantasies about dreams coming true, *The Seven Lives of Grace* and *Sweets Make Everything Better* can be found on Amazon along with other books. To receive updates, words of encouragement, fun historical facts, and book discounts from Elena once a month, sign up for her newsletter: https://www.subscribepage.com/fantasy_signups

WILLOW DAUGHTER

ASTRID V.J.

I am an old man now, but once I was as young and foolish as you are, my child. Then, when my back was strong and my mind weak, I came upon a creature of legend that brought me the adventure of a lifetime. With my axe strapped over one shoulder I dared to venture into the oldest part of the forest. On the whim of youth, I went deep among the gnarled trees, where every creak and whisper makes our human bones tingle. I should have known better. The tales about the deep places of the world where the Wild Ones roam are all cautionary. I thought I was more quick-witted and skillful.

The place was thick with magic—heavy with mysteries being born, where The Impossible walks by the canopy's twilight. There, among those ancient pillars of the ageless woods, I heard a song. It was sweeter than the clearest brook, more melodic than that of the fairest bird, and it tugged at my heartstrings, drawing me ever deeper into the gloom. It was thus I met the willow's daughter—the only name I ever knew her by.

As I stepped through the gnarled and grasping hands of the thicket, I stumbled forwards into a clearing beside a whispering creek. The bubbling water danced along a bed of pebbles, fringed with emerald grass and deep green moss. Daffodils bobbed their sunlight trumpets at the water's edge, holding hands in *ring-o-roses* around the mightiest willow I have ever seen.

The trunk was wide. It spanned the arm's length of at least five men and the gullies the bark made in its surface were so deep they spoke of centuries. The tree was tall; I could not see its top even as I craned my neck to spy the sight of blue between its blade-like leaves.

And on its lowest branch, which was still higher than I could reach, with feet dangling right above the brook, sat the most beautiful maiden. Her flaming red hair danced in a breeze that whispered in the willow's crown, but never touched the breathless air below where I stood. Her skin was like alabaster, paler even than the praised towers of Erdalbad by the sea. Blazing green eyes captured me and I could not see past their inner flame.

She sang, and although the words escaped me, the meaning hummed in my bones. It made me both joyful and sad all at once. Her song carried memories laden with homesickness and I saw before my eyes fleeting images of towering black mountains, clothed in skirts of green so very unlike this gnarled old forest where I lived. There was something youthful and life-giving about the vision she shared with me, and her lament drove deep into my heart.

The song, and the images of a place I'd never known existed before, along with the flickers of emberlight in her impossibly green eyes, muddled my mind. I coasted along in a flood of impressions where my whole life lost its meaning. Night and day ceased to have any influence upon my existence. The forest and its untamable forces, and my own human nature that battled to bring the Wild to heel with that steel axe, still strapped to my back and useless in that moment—all of it paled into insignificance before that girl.

Her lips sealed and even as her song stopped, my heart cried out. I was filled with loss and heartache, and a feeling that I would never hear such a sweet sound again. The agony of having that beauty revealed and then stolen away from me provoked some primordial beast to raise its head in my chest. I could not leave this maiden behind when I returned to the realm of men. I had to take her with me. The need became so strong, it consumed me.

The girl still held my gaze and the ripple of fire within those emeralds loosened my tongue so I could speak even as the rest of me remained bewitched, bound to that being whose song still echoed in my mind and that I yearned to hear again for every single one of my remaining days.

"Will you come down and speak with me?"

The gems of her eyes blazed as she shook her head, and then she turned away, releasing me from her power and leaving me bereft, lost and adrift. Her voice, weighed with melancholy, floated down to where I stood.

"I cannot."

The echo of her song and its deep sadness tugged at my heart. "Why not?" I asked, more forcefully than I expected, yearning for her to gaze upon me once more so that I might catch a glimpse of her striking beauty. I needed to see it, even if for a fleeting moment, just like a thirsting man needs a single dewdrop although he knows it can never slake his thirst.

I shuffled a few steps closer, coming under the shadow of that great tree and its long tendrils swishing like a gown to within reach of my outstretched fingertips. "I wish only to converse with you so you might tell me what weighs upon your heart so. Your song is filled with sadness. Please come down," I gestured to the grass glowing in the sun.

"I can *not*."

The emphasis was final. Her tone sparked to anger that beast within my chest, and it reared its head, eyes flashing, horns gleaming —ready for a fight.

"Cannot or will not?" rage tinged my voice and resentment added its note. She still had her back turned to me, leaving me craving the bewitching power of her eyes. For the first time, I became aware of her attire. She wore a brown shift with green trimmings along the hem and sleeves. It was so simple, even plainer than what most of the young women in my village wore. Their blouses were embroidered in rich patterns and bright colours. In contrast, this simple outfit brought out the girl's aethereal beauty and revealed her as a queen—classed above all others.

As if reading my thoughts, those blazing green eyes I craved a glimpse of looked down at me along the girl's aquiline nose. In a biting tone she said, "I will not lower myself for the likes of you."

Even as her head turned again, my mind knew it was a jibe— deliberate barb placed with perfect accuracy. All the same, the realisation could not stop the rampaging beast within my heart whose frenzy wiped away all reason.

I had come here, drawn by her song. No one else was here, so I knew it had not served to lure others to this place. I was here, in this forgotten spot at the heart of the forest. Did that not make me better than any other?

Before I even understood what I was doing, I'd unclasped the axe from my back and let the smooth haft fall into my hands. The head weighed heavy, tugging towards the ground with its familiar heftiness.

"If you won't come down, and I cannot climb up, then I will fell the tree so I might reach you." I covered the distance between me and the gnarled trunk, crushing daffodils under my boots.

She laughed, the sound soothing my heart with its melody and at the same time piercing me with the depth of her disdain. She pinned me with those eyes once more, a challenge glowing in them. "I'd like to see you try."

The barb, again, was obvious, but I could not sway the fury it called forth. With a howl of anger, I drove the axe into the tree with all my might. The metal rang out in protest as a shock of resistance coursed up my arms, leaving my bones shuddering.

"You see," she said, her voice dripping with derision. "Less than worthy."

An animalistic bellow rumbled out of my chest as I swung once more, refusing to accept her belittlement. I would show her—would prove myself. With all the force at my disposal, I rammed the sharp blade into the trunk. The tree was so solid, its resistance sent numbing pain up my arms and all the way to my shoulders. I let go of the axe, my fingers useless against the strength of such a mighty tree. The blade stuck. It had gone in little more than an inch and had barely traversed the bark, but it held firm even without my arms to steady it.

I looked up into the branches, expecting to see the fire-haired maiden laughing at me. Instead, her attention was focused on the axe, or to be more precise, on the damage the axe had made to the tree trunk.

Her eyes glittered with something akin to anger.

No, it was resentment.

Or was it hate?

Before my mind could fully grasp what the emotion was exactly—and the fact she did not direct her animosity at me, but at the tree—the girl drew her arms back and a blast of fire tore from her fingers, slamming into the opening my axe had made on the tree trunk.

The heat made me stumble backwards even as it consumed my axe. I didn't know what was happening and watched in blank disbelief as flames billowed from the girl and devoured that massive willow trunk from the inside out. The flames did not reach the fire-haired maiden's branch and I wondered at the blaze consuming the tall tree's column while leaving all else intact.

The maiden's face was etched with fury, turning the once beautiful visage into something truly terrible to behold. Heart in my throat, I took another step away, wondering what would happen to me if she turned those blazing emerald eyes onto me once more.

Another step back brought me out of the tree's shadow, but returning to the afternoon's glow did little to calm my terror. I looked up to see a cloud of smoke belching out of the top of the tree, consuming the highest branches and leaves. Within moments the blue of the sky was supplanted by the grey cloud of ash—the sun's light blotted out in the blinking of an eye.

I stumbled a few more steps backwards, not daring to tear my gaze away from the horrendous sight. Blood pounded in my ears, each thrum a reminder that I would be next, for it was clear this vengeful Fury—nothing more than a slip of a girl but with such unfathomable power—would not stop with the destruction of the tree. For my insolence and the presumptuousness of having dared speak to her, let alone wished to converse with her, was probably enough to warrant my death.

When you live near the ancient places of the world, you learn from a young age to respect the locations of the Wild Ones, but here I'd blundered into such a glade without even thinking of the consequences. My fear squeezed all the life out of me, turning my limbs to jelly.

The conflagration stopped.

The crackling of flames as they licked out the insides of the tree whispered into oblivion and only the blackened husk of the once proud willow remained. The fire-sprite, for the maiden could be nothing else, turned her flame-green eyes upon me and I stumbled backwards only to lose my footing. My backside hit the ground sending a jolt up my spine that made my eyes water.

I knew my end was nigh and merely watched in stupefaction as the emberlight dimmed in her eyes, which turned a kinder shade of verdigris. The flames snuffed out and she jumped from that impossible height with grace. The softest *thump* announced her landing.

She was thin—graceful as a willow switch. And she walked towards me, out of her tree, quite visibly capable of descending from that height without any help at all. The only thing running through my mind at that moment—apart from my abject terror, of course —was: *why?*

Nothing made sense. My head hurt trying to understand what was going on. Why had she first denied me and then destroyed the tree? Why did she come down now after that display of power, when she could simply crisp me from the vantage of her high branch?

"Come, human," she murmured, her lilting tone reminding me of her spellbinding song.

I was still stuck in the whirlwind of my tumultuous thoughts, and all I could say was, "Why?"

She stopped, tilting her head to one side. The crimson strands of hair framed her oval face and made those impossibly green eyes sparkle even more brightly. Her gaze travelled down to my crotch, and I realised, to my utter humiliation, that warm liquid spread its way through the fabric of my trousers. I dropped my gaze, squirming under her scrutiny, but strange creature as she was, the fire-sprite didn't laugh or draw attention to my embarrassingly weak bladder. Instead, she stretched out her hand and when I looked up, raising my arm to accept the gesture, she pulled me to my feet. I was head and shoulders taller than her, but still, her show of power reverberated in my mind, and I knew my physical prowess would never match what she could do with her little finger.

"The lord of this forest comes, and it would be best if we were far away from here before he arrives." Even though the meaning of her words carried urgency, her demeanour showed no such thing. Nonchalantly, almost as though she didn't have a care in the world, the fire-sprite walked in the direction from which I'd come into the glade.

Even as I turned to follow, my ears caught the sound of rustling leaves and crackling twigs on the other side of the clearing, beyond the burned willow tree. Glancing over my shoulder, I saw the tops of the trees swaying. Something big was coming—and it was moving fast. Ready to flee, I launched myself forwards, only to knock into the fire-sprite, her hair tickling my cheek as my weight jostled her and almost brought us both crashing to the ground.

As we each caught our balance and righted ourselves, I noticed her eyes were wide. She stared at something coming through the forest where we'd hoped to escape. The trees there shook from a similar movement of some massive beast coming at great speed, accompanied by a symphony of cracking branches and scattering leaves.

"Too late," the girl whispered, but there was a twinkle in her eyes that contradicted the lament. Then she looked at me, really saw me, and her tone changed. "I am sorry I dragged you into this quarrel between me and the Forest Father. I had hoped you'd have more time to escape."

What?

Before my addled mind could formulate a coherent question to begin understanding what was going on, the trees ahead of us parted to reveal a dog the size of a large horse, its eyes as big as small plates. A huge pink tongue dangled from a black snout and amber eyes peered down at the two of us. The beast glimmered copper in the sun's light.

The cracking of trees behind us intensified and I spun around just in time to see an even bigger dog, closer to the size of a small house lope into the clearing beside the willow tree. This one had liquid silver eyes, the size of mill wheels and its coat was pale cream.

More rustling drew my attention to the area of the forest off to my right and even as I glanced between the two other dogs, wondering what would happen next, a third one of these gigantic canines came into sight above the treeline, its golden head so high up I shuddered to think of the creature's size. The whole forest groaned at the passage of this beast and my bladder gave way, even though it was already empty. As things were, there was nothing left but for my heart to speed off at a painful gallop, while my limbs froze. My eyes bounced from one canine to the next while I struggled to absorb what I was seeing.

A thunderous growl shook the air, accompanied by the forest's creaking protest as the biggest of the canines drew closer. I wanted to run, but my legs had grown firm roots. I was stuck there, forced to face whatever this was.

Something grabbed my arm and I jumped. The girl from the willow tree clutched at me and I noticed her fingers trembling. I glanced down at her eyes, the set of her jaw and the way she fixated her gaze on the tree line where there weren't any dogs. I deduced it was anger, not fear that quivered in her veins. I looked over in the direction she was staring, and sure enough, the trees parted moments later to reveal a creature older even than the forest.

The animal that stepped through into the glade matched the size of the second dog, but this one's head was crowned with a rack of antlers. Its coat was pristine as snow and glittered when the animal stepped forwards. Massive cloven hoofs pawed the ground as midnight eyes settled upon us, two tiny insects in the Wild One's domain.

It was my turn to quake. My knees felt weak and in a strange turn of events, it was the small female beside me, who propped me up in the face of this apparition, stepping out of myth and taking on true form right before my eyes. I know we've been taught to disbelieve the existence of these ancient ones. Our belief in the One True God makes the creatures of magic out to be a trick of our ancestors' imaginations. Well, god or no, the Wild One is terrifying. I could feel the power coming off him, the one we used to call Somrenouc before he was reduced to a creature of the Wild.

Even as my legs gave way beneath me and I crashed into the soft grass, I could not help but wonder: What quarrel could this tiny fire-sprite have with the ruler of the forest? I wanted to ask, but my voice had taken flight to some place beyond my reach.

Next, the stag shimmered. For the briefest moment, the massive form of Somrenouc faded into the intangible and in the next heart-beat he moved forwards on two legs, the antlers reduced and now crowning the head of a man. I blinked, my mind disbelieving what my eyes perceived. Two cloven hooves still rested on the ground, although they had shrunk quite dramatically. Silver hair coated both legs, which reminded me of the limbs of a goat. From the waist up, he was bare-chested and very much a man.

I knelt where I was, the coolness of the ground seeping in through the knees of my trousers while the Wild One strode forwards, throwing his arms wide and gazing upon my companion. Somrenouc flicked his eyes towards me for the space of a breath before fixing them upon the fire-sprite once more.

"What have you done, Willow Daughter?" The timbre of his voice was deep—ancient like the very willow the girl had burned to a crisp. There was also sadness and reproach in his voice.

Emberlight blazed in the fire-sprite's eyes. "I am no daughter of your race," her voice was low and quivered with suppressed rage. "You stole me from my people and bound me to this forest-prison, holding my magic captive too. Well, no more." She flung her arms out in agitation. Her tone was almost petulant when she continued, "I lured this human here and channelled my anger into them. Then I used their axe to break the barrier on my magic. Now you hinder my escape, so I will repay you for the treatment I have received in this infernal forest of yours."

"Don't be hasty, little Emberling. Remember, you were sent back with us as a surety. Your people would stop burning my forests and—"

The fire-sprite stamped her foot. "You stole me and used me against my people!" Her hands clenched and unclenched. "But you know, I realised something while you had me chained to your willow. The people of Ember are nothing when compared to the destructive power of the humans. They think of naught but themselves, and you have overlooked the true danger to your forest, oh, Ancient One. Now, I shall see to it that they succeed faster, because the sooner you are stripped of your powers, the better. Although, after what you've put me through, I'm going to enjoy watching you suffer before the end." Emberlight flickered in her eyes, and she raised a hand. The ripple of power she sent out spread tingles all over my skin and made the hairs on my arms prickle.

"Stop her!" Somrenouc gestured towards her even as he shifted back into his stag form, head lowered with his antlers pointed right at her frail body and waves of power shimmering from his figure.

The fire-sprite laughed as a ball of flames shielded her from the oncoming creatures of the Wild, all four of which backed away from the heat radiating off that barrier. The dog behind me whimpered. Through the crackling flames, I heard her chanting and the stag danced about a few times before flickering back into his humanoid shape, arms extended towards the fire-sprite.

"Come now, Emberling," he pleaded. "We can come to some agreement."

The chanting behind the blockade of flames stopped. All was

still except for the whispering fire dancing in the air and turning to coal the grass beneath the fire-sprite's feet.

A howl to my right jolted me upright. It was followed by a similar cry from the dog behind me. The silver-eyed canine joined in the chorus, and I clapped my hands over my ears to dampen the intensity of their yowling. Somrenouc joined in with a shriek of his own and then an even deeper shattering tore through the glade as something profound within the earth rent asunder.

I cowered down, my eyes firmly shut, my hands clamped over my ears. At length, the clamour subsided. All was still.

Cracking open an eye, I saw the Wild One on his furry knees a few steps away from me. His humanoid torso rose and fell with deep breaths while the green-eyed sprite stepped forwards, her flaming shield snuffing out with a hiss. She strode past the afflicted Somrenouc and stretched out her hands towards the burned-out willow tree. Her chanting started up again and I noticed the brook had stopped flowing. A dried-out gully was all that remained of the babbling stream. More tearing resounded from deep underground and the whole forest seemed to groan with whatever the fire-sprite was doing.

The stag-man clutched his chest, moaning and rocking backwards and forwards. At one point, his eyes flashed obsidian and he lurched to his feet. With a bellow, Somrenouc launched himself at the fire-sprite, but she held the flat of her hand out before her, stopping the Wild One in his tracks. The ancient guardian of the forest hit an invisible wall and slid to his knees once more, a trail of moss-green blood dripping from one nostril.

Once again, the force of the magic sent a ripple of energy over my skin, and I suppressed a shudder. Behind me, an ear-splitting whine tore into my bones, freezing them to the marrow. I turned, crossing my legs in the motion, and looked upon the copper-coated dog doubled over, its eyes wide in agony. It looked to its master, but even as I followed its gaze to see what Somrenouc's reaction would be to this new development, the canine whined, and my attention was drawn back to it. The animal's nostrils flared wide, its stomach clenched, a wail tore from its throat, and then it retched.

In a tinkling cascade, coins rolled out of the beast's open maw.

By this time, I was taking the abnormalities in my stride. Yes, Somrenouc's dog belched coins. One bounced against my foot, and I picked it up. It shimmered copper and was larger than any penny I'd ever seen, fitting neatly into the hollow when I touched my thumb and forefinger together.

Before I could even begin to fathom the immensity of the copper wave coating the ground in front of me, I heard similar sounds of distress coming from beside the tree. The second dog, the one with shoulders brushing the branches of that immense willow, yelped and retched a fountain of silver coins. Less than a heartbeat later, I heard the thunderous whimper from the third canine who sat by the tree line to my right. An avalanche of gold spewed into the clearing, creating a mountain of glinting coins.

"What have you done?" Somrenouc's eyes were wide. He struggled to his feet and took a step towards the fire-sprite.

She giggled. It was both spiteful and childlike, and then she danced around the tree. "I have bound the Treasures of the Forest to this place. They no longer serve you, oh, mighty Forest Father." She pranced up to the Wild One. "Your three Treasures can only be summoned by this." In the flat of her palm, she held out a little silver box. I couldn't make out much more than that from where I sat.

Somrenouc stretched out a hand, long fingers reaching for the device, but before he could grasp it, a spark flashed from the box and ignited his hand. With a yell, he floundered backwards and punched the flaming appendage into the ground.

"Oh, no," the fire-sprite said, her voice dancing to the tune of glee. "This is not meant for you to wield—nor any other of your forest folk." She grinned in the face of Somrenouc's hard obsidian stare. "This," she tossed the silver receptacle in the air, watching it arc into the sky, the sunlight glinting off it. "This is meant for the humans. They shall wield power over the Treasures, and you can do nothing about it." She caught the box and pranced over towards me.

I shrank back a little. Her actions had been so confusing, I didn't know if she meant me well or not. I did understand that she had used me to get out of whatever prison she'd been held captive in, and the knowledge she had been magically chained to that tree sat like fermented grains in my stomach; but at the same time, even though I barely understood what she was doing, something about her actions sent shivers coursing up and down my spine.

"Do not fear," she said, her voice losing its edge of spite. "This is my gift to you," she said, holding up the silver box. It was rectangular, with the edges cut off. The lid depicted three dogs, sitting in a row with a large one in the middle and a smaller one on either side. She lifted the lid, saying, "This is a tinderbox, something my people have shared with the humans far away from here. You have probably never seen its like, so I will explain how it works." The inside was divided into three compartments. The first contained some wood chips, the second and third two different types of dark stone. The sprite lifted the two stones from the box and handed them to me.

"Strike them together."

I hit the one with the other and a spark, like the one that ignited Somrenouc's hand, drifted onto the pile of copper coins at my feet.

With a rush of wind and a prickling against my skin, the horse-sized dog sat before me, eyes wide. I jumped backwards and almost lost my footing on the slick surface of loose coins, which tinkled as they cascaded around my feet.

The fire-sprite leaned forwards, grabbing my shirt front to steady me. When I'd found my footing again, she gestured to the stones I'd dropped at her feet. "One strike summons this one," she patted the dog's leg. "Two strikes for the silver," she pointed to the dog by the tree. "And three strikes for the fine mutt over there," she gestured with her head up towards the gigantic canine behind the hill of gold coins to my right. Pulling my hand forwards, she placed the box into my palm. Its cool surface drew my attention to the chips of wood.

"What is the timber for?" My voice rasped, brittle at the back of my throat.

She dropped down onto her haunches and scooped up the two stones. When she straightened, she smiled. "They are how you use the spark from these." The fire-sprite dropped the stones into their compartments. "When you make a fire, you strike the stones and allow the spark to fall on the kindling. But this tinderbox is special as it now also commands the forest's Treasures." She patted my arm and I swallowed. The emberlight flickered back to life in the depths of her emerald eyes when she said, "This is my gift to you, in recompense for drawing you into this muddle. You can call upon these three at any time it suits you, and you may bid them do whatever pleases you. They are bound to serve the wielder of this box now and will not be able to leave this glade in any other way."

My first instinct was to reject the gift. It contained too much power and not knowing the full extent of the goings-on meant I really didn't know if I even wanted to have such might. In the next heartbeat I considered what the fire-sprite might do if I rejected the gift. At least this way I might get out of the situation with my life intact.

The copper dog whined, drawing my attention away from the short sprite before me. The animal's eyes twitched from the fire-sprite to a movement behind her. In the next breath, a shadow fell upon her and Somrenouc's head and antlers towered above the redhead. She let out a squeal as his hands, one of them blackened and barely able to grasp, gripped her arms and I shuddered at the anger blazing in those obsidian eyes.

"You will undo this curse, Emberling." The Wild One spun her around to face him.

I watched her form stiffen when she flared in reply, "I will not."

Somrenouc shook his head. "Don't you understand that doing this will throw the land out of balance. The Treasures are meant to guard the forests. Their duty is to the ley lines and the magic in the land. Without them channelling the power of sacred places, The People will have more work to do keeping everything in balance. The chances of disasters will increase. With the forest vanishing, all the peoples, even those of Ember, will be affected. The Balance is a circle." He shook her, as if trying to impart the importance of this last. "If you break a single link in the chain, it ripples through the whole round, bringing decay to all. You must reverse this."

Raising her chin and looking the perturbed Somrenouc straight in the eye, the sprite affirmed, "I care not. You and yours will pay for what you've done to me and mine. Your forest will fall under the axes of the humans and burn before the fury of Ember. If nothing remains of your sea of trees, I will be glad for it. Do me your worst! I won't undo the enchantment."

The stag-man closed his eyes. He took several breaths before he spoke, voice trembling with the effort of remaining calm. "You may have caught me off guard today and now I shall pay for that over-sight. You have tied the Treasures here, and so I bind you to this place, Emberling. You will remain here, chained to the forest and its fate. You may call on me when you change your mind and are willing to retract your spell. Until then, Willow Daughter, you will remain here." He leaned forwards and whispered something in the fire-sprite's pointed ear.

I heard her gasp but couldn't see the expression on her face when she looked up into the antlered being's face. Less than a heartbeat later, a shriek tore from her as power crackled over her form, throwing her arms up and taking a hold of her body. I watched in stupefaction as the fire-sprite's arms contracted and shrank, changing colour to a bright green. My heart thudded as I watched her fingers fuse together; they curled up into a tight spiral at their tips. Flaming hair contorted and contracted into five petals, crimson points reaching for the sun. Another heartbeat. The simple shift fell to the ground as what remained of the fire-sprite's frame disappeared into a tremulous green stem.

Looking down upon the flower she'd become, I quaked. What would happen to me now? I was not a party to this except for her doing, and now she could not protect me anymore.

I tore my eyes from the flower that had once been a fire-sprite and dared to meet the gaze of the Wild One. Somrenouc was still focused on the bloom. Sadness poured off him. Tears pricked in my eyes in response to that weight. Then the Ancient One, whom my forebears honoured as a god, stepped over the blossom and reached for me.

"I know you did not come here to desecrate the forest, human. I understand the Willow Daughter lured you, and I cannot fault you for what has happened here. I will give you free passage through my wood, back to your home under two conditions." His eyes bored into me, and I swallowed. It didn't really matter what his conditions were. I would accept them, for I knew from the stone-like severity in his black eyes that I would not be allowed to live if I did not accept his terms.

Somrenouc nodded as if satisfied with the conclusion of my thoughts and continued. "Firstly, you will leave that infernal tinderbox in this glade, preferably in a place no one can find it. I suppose down that hollow tree will do well." He gestured towards what was left of the willow tree. "And secondly, you will promise under penalty of death never to return here."

I nodded, knowing I could not refuse, but at the same time, the existence of all those riches suddenly weighed on my mind. In this moment, when I stood on the brink of losing all of it, the immensity of the treasure spilling onto this clearing in the woods sank in.

Before I could even consider the consequences of speaking, I said, "I will do as you wish, Lord of Forests, but I request that one of the dogs carry me from this place and you allow me to take some gold with me to see to my future and that of my family.

The antlered head bowed in acquiescence. "It shall be done. Now, leave the tinderbox, gather your treasures, and begone."

Not wanting to try the Wild One's patience, I strode closer to the tree, took aim, and tossed the silver box into the air. It arced high and dropped out of sight in the burned-out trunk of the willow, a soft *thunk* echoing up to where we stood. Next, I glanced about. How was I going to carry the gold with me? My gaze fell upon the fire-sprite's shift and without thinking, I grabbed the brown homespun and set about tying it into a sack-like shape. Once ready, I crossed over to the mountain of gold and filled as much as I could into my pockets and the pouch I'd just made myself. Magic still hung heavy in the air, and I do not know how it came to be, but the scrap of fabric that the fire-sprite had worn would not fill. I piled more and more gold into it, working my way through that mountain by the handful, and, still, it did not fill up. Glancing inside, I could see the gold within, but from the outside the bag appeared half full at most.

I kept on pouring gold into that bag until there were no more gold coins left. I lifted the pouch, expecting it to remain stuck on the ground, but to my utter surprise, it came free from the grass to the accompanying chime of coins clinking within.

From the corner of my eye, I observed the thundercloud stare the Wild One gave me and decided not to pursue any more riches. That mountain of gold was enough, and it has seen to my success and provided for your future, my dearest one.

The copper dog was closest to me, and I remembered the fire-sprite saying that once I'd struck the tinderbox and summoned the dog it had to do my bidding. So, I ordered it to carry me home, which it did. In just a few bounds we were out of the deep forest and, not long after, it dropped me off outside the hovel that I'd been living in.

Well, I can assure you, much has changed since then, but the only thing I regret is having left that tinderbox down the hollow tree. I have tried to find the glade, but the magic binding me is strong and I have not managed. But you, granddaughter, who have not been bound by the might of Somrenouc, you could do this. Listen carefully, and I will share with you what I remember of how to get there. That tinderbox is your birthright and I want you to have it.

Author's Note

Thank you for reading *Willow Daughter* and for supporting *Enchanted Forests*. Your donation towards rainforest conservation is very much appreciated. If you would like to find out how these events spiral out of control and affect the wider world, you can pre-order *Johara's Choice* my upcoming retelling of Hans Christian Andersen's fairy tale, *The Tinderbox*.

In the meantime, you are welcome to dive into this realm of fairy tale retellings with the other tales in this series: *The Siblings' Tale*, a two-part retelling of the Grimm tale, *Brother and Sister*, *Gisela's Passion*, a retelling of the ballet *Giselle*, and *Naiya's Wish*, a retelling of *The Nixie of the Mill-pond*. Available here: www.amazon.com/dp/B089M2C4NP

ACKNOWLEDGMENTS

As always, there are so many people I would like to thank for their support of my writing, and particularly, I am grateful for this truly inspirational group of authors I've had the honour of working with on this anthology. You are amazing and, on those days, where I wanted to give up, you were there to pick me up and help me through it. Thank you.

However, more than anyone else, I would like to thank the musicians without whose inspiration this little tale could not exist: Erutan, with their fantastic song *The Willow Maid*; and Damh the Bard's thought-provoking *Green and Grey*. Thank you for the music!

ABOUT THE AUTHOR

Award-winning and USA Today Bestselling Author, Astrid V.J. was born in South Africa. She is a trained social anthropologist and certified transformational life coach. She currently resides in Sweden with her husband and their two children. In early childhood, she showed an interest in reading and languages—interests which her family encouraged. Astrid started writing her first novel at age 12 and now writes fantasy in a variety of subgenres, exploring her passion for cultures and languages. When she isn't writing, Astrid likes to read, take walks in nature, play silly games with her children, do embroidery, and play music.

Astrid writes transformation fiction: incorporating transformation principles in novels, rather than writing another self-help book. She loves exploring the human capacity for transformation and potential to achieve success in the face of adversity. With her background in social anthropology, Astrid is interested in minority group questions, considerations on social standards of beauty and the negative consequences these have, and would like to make the fantasy genre accessible to people of non-white, non-Christian backgrounds. Astrid feels the fantasy genre has become too restrictive with limited representations of race, ethnicity and culture.

She seeks to explore other paths on this writing journey, incorporating her background in anthropology and psychology to create engaging experiences, which also provide food for thought on the diverse topics she finds most important. These include: racism, minority rights, cultural diversity, culture change, intolerance, humanity's environmental impact, the representation of people on the autism spectrum among the general populace, the human capacity for transformation, and much more.

Find out more about Astrid, her books, her current writing projects and where to connect with her here: https://www. elisabethandedvard.com/

One Fair Eve

Lyndsey Hall

CHAPTER 1

March 20th, 1880
Hartwood, England

P ip dashed up the street, slipping on the wet cobblestones. He held the envelope up to his eyes, but rain still streamed down his round, horn-rimmed glasses. When he breathed out, they clouded over and he almost ran into Mrs. Baker as she crossed the road with Fergus, her yapping little dog.

Apologising over his shoulder, he hurried on towards the tall, narrow house with the brass plate beside the door. He was late for his piano lesson. His tutor, Mister Ericsson, would *tut* and make him play the Bach piece again.

Unless...

He clutched the letter from the Axton Conservatory tighter and rapped on the door with his knuckles, hopping from foot to foot.

The door opened to reveal a tall, green-eyed man wearing a brown, knitted cardigan and woollen trousers. "Master Reed, you're late. Again."

Pip stepped inside and hung his dripping coat on the rack before wiping his glasses on a handkerchief from his pocket. "I know, I'm sorry, Mister Ericsson. I was waiting for this." He brandished the letter.

His tutor's eyebrows rose almost imperceptibly and his mood seemed to lighten. He ushered Pip into the small room at the front of the house, which was predominantly taken up by an elegant piano. "Well, let's see then. What does it say?"

"I waited to open it with you, Mister Ericsson. I thought you'd want to be the first to know if I got in."

The grey-haired, Swedish music teacher nodded and Pip felt a rush of satisfaction at having made the right decision. They both took their usual seats in the practice room—Pip on the piano bench and his tutor in a wing-backed chair by the window—and Pip tore the envelope open. He slid the single sheet of paper out and read the brief letter thanking him for applying to the conservatory.

And politely rejecting his application.

The ground seemed to crumble away beneath Pip and he felt as though he were falling.

Rejected? It couldn't be. He'd done well in his interview and performance. Hadn't he?

Sure, he'd been nervous. Wasn't everyone when they auditioned for the thing that meant the most to them?

"Well?" Mister Ericsson asked, reaching for the paper. Pip let him take it, his hand dropping into his lap like a dead weight. He'd ruined his only chance; he would never get another audition. He wouldn't be going to the most prestigious music school for miles around. He wouldn't play at the world's most famous concert halls in Paris and Vienna, or stand on stage at the Royal Albert Hall, performing his favourite piece—Beethoven's Moonlight Sonata—for an audience of thousands.

His blood ran cold. He'd be forced to join his father down the mine.

As the only son, he'd been expected to follow in his father's footsteps and provide for the family when he came of age, but his musical talent had given him hope for a different future. A better, safer future, where he could still afford to support his mother and sisters financially, but without the risk of being killed in a cave-in, or an explosion. Or getting lost inside the mine and starving to death before he could find his way out—

He shuddered.

Mister Ericsson finished reading the letter and folded it up neatly, tucking it into the inside pocket of his waistcoat. "Well. I am surprised, and more than a little disappointed."

Pip's heart sank. He hated disappointing his tutor.

Viktor Ericsson had been a world-renowned pianist before retiring to rural England to become a music tutor. He was a very particular, exacting teacher, never letting Pip get away with a single mistake. In some lessons, Pip had played the same piece dozens of times, restarting every time he missed a note or his timing was off. It was exhausting, but it had made him into the talented, dedicated musician he was today.

Or so Pip had thought.

"Which piece did you play—the Beethoven?"

Pip nodded.

"Show me."

He nodded, his pulse picking up speed as he moved to the bench and lifted the cover on the piano-forte. He didn't think he'd made any mistakes in his performance, but why else would the panel have rejected him?

He straightened the sheet music, took a deep breath, and began.

The notes flowed from his fingers like second nature. He'd played this sonata so many times he knew it inside out. Could have played it backwards, if asked. His hands danced over the keys as the intensity built, the music filling the room and carrying him on a wave of melody—a feeling as familiar as breathing.

When he finished and the final note died in the air between him and Mister Ericsson, he couldn't bring himself to turn and face his tutor.

A small sigh came from the teacher, and finally Pip swivelled round on the bench to meet his eye. His tutor wasn't smiling, but neither was he frowning.

"Well, that was certainly a very precise representation of Beethoven's Sonata Number Fourteen." Pip felt a tiny swell of pride in his chest, but the fact that Mister Ericsson still wasn't smiling made him falter. "It is not talent or skill that you are lacking, Master Reed. It is heart. Passion." All of the air rushed out of Pip's lungs in one silent gasp. He had passion. Didn't he? "You play the notes with familiarity and comfort. You know the piece almost too well. If this is how you performed at the interview, then I'm afraid I'm not surprised you did not get in."

A crushing weight pressed down on Pip as the dream he'd built up around himself came crashing down. He'd have to go home and tell his parents that he hadn't gotten into the conservatory. He'd have to look at his father's stern face as he told him that, come September, he'd be joining him down the mine.

Tears pressed at the backs of his eyes and he forced them away angrily. He might have to accept his depressing fate, but he would not let Mister Ericsson see how distraught he was. He picked at the threadbare cushion on the bench, pulling a loose thread and refusing to look up until the threat of tears was gone.

The tutor clasped his hands in front of him, leaning forwards to close the distance between them. When he spoke, his voice was low and had taken on a strange timbre Pip had never heard coming from the man.

"Philip, I know you feel disappointed. There isn't anything you wouldn't do to get into the conservatory, is there?"

Pip looked up, confused, and shook his head. "I'd do anything. Do you think they'd give me another chance?"

The older man rubbed a hand over his short, grey beard, eyes narrowed. He appeared to be wrestling with something internally, his jaw taut. Finally, he sat back, expression clearing. "My piano needs a new string. Today is the Hartwood market, up in the big field. If you go to the market and find Master Dobson's stall and purchase a new string for me, I will write to the conservatory and explain your circumstances. I will see if I can arrange for you to repeat the performance part of the interview. How does that sound?"

Pip leapt up from the bench, hope and desperation making him giddy. "Really, Mister Ericsson? You would do that? Thank you, sir, thank you. I'll go to the market right away."

He started to gather his things and put his damp coat back on, wanting to leave before the tutor could change his mind and take back his offer.

Mister Ericsson took a small leather pouch out of his trouser pocket and placed it in Pip's palm, but instead of letting go, his other hand gripped Pip's wrist tightly. His green eyes were a shade darker as he leaned close, towering over Pip and casting him into shadow.

"Be sure that this is what you want, Philip Reed. If you have even an ounce of doubt that this is the future you truly desire, then I will say good day and wish you well. But if you are sure that the conservatory is your destiny, then I wish you only good luck."

Pip stared at the man for several seconds, mouth dry as the words tumbled over one another in his mind. The conservatory was his only dream. He would do anything—give anything—to have the chance to attend. To escape his fate in the mine. To escape Hartwood.

"It is what I want, Mister Ericsson. I'm sure."

The piano teacher let go of the coin pouch and released Pip's wrist, stepping backward and taking the shadows with him.

As Pip stepped outside and turned to thank his tutor one more time, he caught the faraway look on the man's face as his gaze turned towards the field where the market was held. "Give Master Dobson my best." And he shut the door, leaving Pip standing in the street, a peculiar feeling settling over him.

CHAPTER 2

The walk up to the market didn't take long. Hartwood was a small village bordered by acres of farmland; little more than a cluster of houses, a church, post office, school, and the small train station that carried the miners to and from Axton and the surrounding towns. On the other side of the field where the market was held lay Hartwood pit, the iron mine where Pip's father worked, and where Pip was destined to spend his life—if Mister Ericsson's plan was unsuccessful.

And beyond the pit head was dense forest as far as the eye could see.

Pip trudged up the hill and through the open farm gate, feeling the weight of the coin purse jostling in his coat pocket. It had been years since he'd visited the market. Usually his mother did the shopping, coming home each Saturday with baskets full of fresh fruit and vegetables, balls of wool for knitting and lace collars to brighten up his sisters' old dresses. Pip hadn't even known there was a stall that sold musical instruments and equipment.

As he reached the big field, the market spread out before him. A variety of horse-drawn carts and canvas-covered wagons stood behind tables laden with the sellers' wares. Horses were tethered loosely, munching on the long grass while they waited to take their owner's home. Hand carts and large wheelbarrows stood behind some stalls, some still laden with excess produce.

Pip's worn leather boots slipped on the wet grass as he passed tables spread with jars of homemade jams and preserves, leather goods and lace-trimmed tablecloths. Heaps of carrots, their leafy green tops brushing the muddy ground, sat next to baskets of mushrooms and garlic bulbs. A ruddy-faced woman in a pinafore fussed over heads of lettuce, broccoli, cauliflower and cabbage in every shade of green, red and purple.

Shouts from the sellers and the rhythmic clang of metal on metal coming from the blacksmith's stall filled the air, which was still heavy with moisture despite the rain having eased. As he passed, the green-grocer cried out and attempted to *shoo* one of the horses who had taken a fancy to her carrots.

Pip pushed his glasses up his nose with his forefinger and chewed the inside of his cheek. He'd purchase the string, go straight back to Mister Ericsson's house and practice the Beethoven piece until his fingers bled. He would put as much passion into it as he could, and hopefully that would be enough to convince the panel at Axton Conservatory. He couldn't let this be it; he couldn't let his chance at following his dreams and playing music for the rest of his life be dashed on the cobblestones, along with his future.

He wouldn't let himself be sent down that mine to die.

Pip passed another stall, this one laden with knitted scarves and mittens, and squinted to see just two more tables ahead. It would be just his luck if the stall he needed wasn't present this week.

The final stall was a painted caravan, set a little away from the rest of the market, with a wooden sign bearing the name Master Dobson and Company in gold leaf. Pip's heart leapt into his throat and he picked up his pace, one hand going to his pocket where the bag of coins weighed heavy, full of promise.

There didn't appear to be anyone manning the stall as Pip approached. He stood in front of the caravan's hatch, taking in the neat stacks of sheet music tied with red ribbon, the rows of shiny metal tools and wooden implements, some of which Pip recognised from tuning the piano.

"Hello?" Pip called, peering deeper into the caravan.

A head popped into view; fuzzy, grey hair sticking out from the sides, matching the grey broom-shaped moustache that sat above a thin-lipped mouth. The man was a good few inches shorter than Pip —who himself wasn't the tallest tree in the forest—and he wore a dark-green suit with a brocade waist-coat, a silver pocket-watch chain hanging from his chest pocket.

"Oh, my apologies, young sir. I didn't see you there. How can I help you, this fine Spring Equinox?" The man's accent sounded strange to Pip's ears; he couldn't place it. Most of the miners and traders who travelled to Hartwood for work came from Axton, but the city accent was sharper and more clipped than the villagers'. This gentleman's voice sounded like he was one note away from bursting into song.

"Mister Ericsson sent me. He needs a new string for his piano."

The little man's brows rose. "Mister Ericsson? Indeed, indeed." He studied Pip with a watery but intense gaze from under straggly, grey eyebrows. "How is Viktor?"

"He's well, thank you."

Master Dobson hummed and stroked his moustache with his thumb and forefinger, still studying Pip. Icy cold fingers raked down Pip's spine and his flesh broke out in goosebumps. He resisted the urge to rub the back of his neck or shuffle his feet under the strange man's scrutiny.

"Teaching you the piano, is he?"

Pip nodded. "I'm hoping to attend Axton Conservatory, but—" He wasn't sure why he said it, but Master Dobson's curiosity seemed to have been piqued. He leaned forward, dark eyes sparkling as a sudden ray of sunlight broke through the clouds, casting the field in a golden glow and limning the odd little man.

"Go on, lad. But?" When Pip didn't respond straight away, he supplied the answer himself. "You're worried you won't get in?"

Pip chewed his bottom lip, forehead furrowing. "I failed my interview. My application was rejected. The letter came this morning."

Master Dobson nodded eagerly, to Pip's dismay. He appeared altogether too excited to hear of Pip's abject failure. "Is that so? And Viktor sent you to my stall, did he?"

Unsure how the two were connected, Pip nodded.

"Interesting, interesting. Well, I believe I may be able to help you, young sir."

"You have a piano string?"

Master Dobson chuckled and the sound sent a shudder through Pip, like a cat's claws on a chalkboard. "Oh yes, I certainly have a piano string or two. But that isn't all." He rubbed his hands together, his dark eyes shining, the pupils seeming to swallow the irises so they looked entirely black. "What would you say if I told you there was a way to make your dream of becoming a world-renowned musician come true?"

"What do you mean? Mister Ericsson is going to petition the conservatory to give me a second chance. If I practise really hard, they might still let me in. Is that what you mean? Do you know someone on the panel?"

Master Dobson shook his head. "What I'm offering has nothing to do with practising, Master Reed. If you're amenable, you can leave here today and every time you play your instrument—every single piece will be the most beautiful, *most exquisite* piece of music any listener has ever heard. You will be celebrated as a musical prodigy; a genius. Your talent will know no bounds."

"How is that possible?" Pip's voice was little more than an exhale.

"*Magic*, Master Reed."

Everything went still, as though the world had stopped turning for a fraction of a second. Pip held his breath. Master Dobson's face broke into a slow, wide smile, his crooked teeth like fence posts beneath that brush of a moustache.

"Magic?"

"That's right. *Magic*. Your greatest desire at your fingertips. For a price, of course."

"But, isn't that cheating?"

Master Dobson chortled. "My, you're an honourable young lad. But I don't believe it is cheating, no. No more than possessing natural talent, or the privilege of a great tutor, the time to practise and the opportunity to audition for such a prestigious conservatory. You already have an advantage over so many young musicians,

Master Reed, why not use every resource at your disposal to achieve your dream?"

Pip turned the man's words over in his mind. It was true, he was lucky—privileged even—to have had the opportunity to learn a musical instrument. His parents had paid for his lessons, and they'd indulged him when he had shown real talent, rather than forcing him to put childish dreams aside and face the reality of his future as a miner. If there were some way to show them they had made the right choice by encouraging and supporting him, didn't he owe it to his parents, and Mister Ericsson, to take it?

"What would I have to do?"

Master Dobson's eyes glistened greedily and he ran his tongue over his thin lips, snatching up a piece of paper that Pip had presumed to be sheet music, but he now saw was a letter.

"All you need to do today is to sign your name here, and the rest will be taken care of."

Hesitantly, Pip took the pen and paper that Master Dobson proffered, reading the elegant, cursive hand and understanding less than half of the elaborate language. "What does it say?"

Master Dobson waved a hand dismissively. "Oh, nothing much. Just that you agree to the terms and are willing to accept the conditions, and in exchange you will be furnished with musical ability the likes the world has never borne witness to."

That sounded like exactly what Pip dreamed of, to be the most talented piano player to ever live. To escape Hartwood and his fate as a miner, and the grey, impoverished future he dreaded. He could scarcely believe all it would take was a signature on a piece of paper.

He paused, pen hovering over the paper. "And I'll get to audition for the conservatory again?"

"That much is up to Mister Ericsson, young man, but if he is still the persuasive and eloquent gentleman I remember him to be, then I doubt there is anything he could not arrange."

The little, grey-haired man loomed over Pip as he scrawled his name in black ink on the bottom of the page. As soon as the final flourish of his signature was done, a clap of thunder sounded overhead and the sky darkened. A chill ran down Pip's spine as a breeze lifted his hair and rustled Master Dobson's moustache. The man's pupils were so large now that there was barely any white visible, and his teeth glittered like blades in the low light. Master Dobson snatched the paper from Pip's hands and folded it into his pocket before handing Pip a brown paper packet containing a new piano string.

Pip stumbled back a step, a growing sense of unease in the pit of his stomach. His hand went to the coin purse in his coat pocket. "Here," he said, setting the pouch on the caravan's shelf. "For the string, and the magic."

"No payment necessary," said the man from within the caravan, slamming drawers and rattling locks as he prepared to leave.

Pip frowned and followed Master Dobson round to the front of the caravan where two pure white horses were harnessed. "But I thought you said there was a price for the magic?"

Master Dobson hopped up onto the seat and took the horses' reins in his hands before looking down at Pip, a terrifying grin on his suddenly sharp, strange features. The man was barely recognisable now, his skin had taken on a greenish-grey hue and he appeared almost monstrous as he hissed, "There is a price indeed, Master Reed, but not in coin. Your dreams will be made reality, young sir, but only until the day of the Spring Equinox the year after you turn eighteen. On that day, we will call in your debt and you will join us in the Fair Realm for the remainder of your days. Best of luck, Master Reed. I'll be seeing you soon."

At that, the man snapped the reins and the horses took off, pulling the caravan at a speed Pip wouldn't have believed possible if he hadn't seen it with his own eyes. He shouted to the man to stop, but within moments the caravan had disappeared into the vast forest on the edge of the field.

A weight dropped into the pit of Pip's stomach and he started to shake as the sky broke and fat raindrops began to fall.

What had he done?

CHAPTER 3

March 20th, 1882
Vienna, Austria

Pip stood in the wings at the Wiener Musikverein, one of the grand, newly-built concert halls in Vienna, and listened to the rapturous applause coming from the stalls. Verity had just finished her violin performance—a stirring rendition of Vivaldi's Concerto in G Minor—and was curtsying to the audience as bouquets of flowers were thrown at her feet. She turned to walk off stage and caught sight of him, a shy smile playing at her lips as their eyes met.

Her dark hair was pinned up in a fashionable style, but fine strands had fallen down to frame her face and a light flush warmed her cheeks. Heat rushed through Pip's veins and his mouth went dry. She was the most exquisite creature he had ever set eyes upon.

On stage, the lights had dimmed as four stagehands brought out the pianoforte and positioned it in the centre, ready for his performance.

"Good luck, Philip," Verity murmured as she passed, placing her hand on his arm momentarily before continuing to the backstage area. A shiver went through him at the touch.

"Thank you," Pip replied, but she was already out of earshot. It was just him now. He turned to the stage, where the piano and the audience both waited in silence. He ran a hand through his wavy, light-brown hair.

This was it. No turning back.

He took a deep, steadying breath, pushed his horn-rimmed glasses up with his forefinger, and walked towards his instrument. A polite smattering of applause met his appearance on stage, but he kept his eyes on the piano. He swept his coat tails out behind him and sat on the stool, lifted the cover and placed his fingers on the keys. One more deep inhale, and on the exhale, he began to play.

The music flowed from his fingers with ease, rising and falling with his breath, surging up from his very core. It filled the concert hall, swelling to reach every corner, taking on a life of its own. Pip closed his eyes and felt the music take over. He was just a conduit, channelling the composer's exquisite combination of notes. A vessel for the beauty and precision of the piece.

His fingers flew over the keys as the music built to a crescendo, never missing a single note. The tiny hairs on his arms and the back of his neck stood on end, as though an electrical current surged through him, charging the air around him as his hands moved faster and faster, his foot pushing the pedals, sweat beading on his brow and sliding down the back of his crisp, white shirt.

When the piece was finished and the final note had faded from the air, Pip took a shuddering breath without opening his eyes. As he exhaled, calmness expanded in his chest where before the tension and nerves had been bundled tightly. Now, he felt light. Unburdened.

The audience exploded into applause and Pip finally opened his eyes. Chairs screeched as one by one the spectators got to their feet and gave him a standing ovation. Pride rushed in to replace the calm, and a satisfied smile spread across Pip's face. He stood, bowed to the audience, and left the stage, applause and shouts of "bravo!" still ringing in his wake.

Just before he stepped behind the curtain, he thought he recognised one of the faces in the front row, but when he glanced back at the audience the seat was empty.

Outside the concert hall, Pip adjusted his cashmere scarf and shivered at the chill in the air. Despite spring having officially begun that very day, no one had thought to tell the weather in Vienna.

The door swung open and Verity appeared, carrying her violin case and wearing a heavy cloak with a rabbit fur trim. Pip rushed forwards.

"Let me help you with that, Miss Whitley." He took the violin case in his left hand and offered her his right arm. She took it with a smile.

"Thank you, Philip. And, as always, please call me Verity."

A blush warmed Pip's cheeks and suddenly he was grateful for the cold air. They walked together through the lamp-lit streets, admiring the elegant architecture and commenting on the sights, sounds and smells of the city. The glistening pavements were a world away from the dull cobblestones of Hartwood. A light fog hovered preternaturally above the ground, clinging to their ankles and giving the city an ethereal ambience.

Verity squeezed his arm. "Can you believe it, Philip? We're really here, in the city where both Beethoven and Mozart lived and composed. You can almost feel it in the air, can't you? The inspiration, the magic."

A shiver ran through Pip at the word 'magic'. He'd tried his hardest to forget the strange man at the market in Hartwood, but each year, as the days had crept closer to the Spring Equinox his mind had turned to the contract he had signed, the promise Master Dobson had made. The payment the man had demanded in return.

He hadn't believed it at first. He'd returned to Mister Ericsson's house with the piano string to practise his piece for the repeat audition. At his next lesson, his tutor had been somewhat gentler with his criticisms and more generous with his praise than Pip was used to, but he put that down to the rejection letter and Ericsson's kindness rather than any enchantment.

He had charmed the panel at the conservatory with his second audition, playing a more difficult Bach piece after hours and hours of perfecting his performance. So when the acceptance letter had arrived it had been easy to convince himself that he'd gotten in on pure talent and hard work. Since then, he'd only grown in his abilities and confidence, as was to be expected now that he was a student of one of the finest musical institutions in England.

And yet, he still couldn't suppress a shudder at the mere mention of magic.

"Indeed. I feel incredibly lucky to be here. Especially in your company, Miss Whit—Verity."

Verity beamed at him and a bubble of anxious excitement rose in his throat. He swallowed it down.

Residents and visitors of Vienna hurried past, clutching their coats about them and quickening their steps to get home and out of the cold. Pip felt his feet slowing as they approached the guest house where Verity and the other female students from the six British conservatories were staying.

They came to a stop in front of the building's ornate edifice. Pip breathed in deeply, inhaling the cold Viennese air with its scents of rain and wood smoke. If he closed his eyes, he could have been standing in Hartwood, the smoke from the chimneys mingling with the metallic tang from the iron mine.

"Verity, I—"

Something darted into the shadows between the guest house and the next building and Pip jolted. He stepped in front of Verity, one arm holding her back as he squinted into the darkness.

"What is it?" Verity asked, leaning to peer over his shoulder. Her breath tickled his ear and moved the short hairs at the nape of his neck, and Pip's skin broke out in goosebumps.

"I'm not sure, perhaps a fox or a stray dog. You should hurry inside to be safe. But before you do—"

It had to be now, or he might never have the courage to do it again.

Standing beneath a flickering gaslamp, Pip took Verity's left hand. He slid the rabbit fur-lined glove off and brought her knuckle to his lips, his eyes never leaving her face. Surprise widened her eyes, but a smile played about her mouth.

"Miss Verity Whitley, ever since the first time I heard you play, I have been enchanted by you. Your talent; your beauty. And from the first moment you smiled at me, I have been bewitched. I am yours, completely. If you will have me."

Pip took a deep breath. Verity's eyes shimmered with silver and the smile that had teased her lips now shone brightly.

"Oh, Philip," she breathed.

"Verity, will you do me the honour of becoming my wife?"

For a moment, it was as though time had frozen. Pip held his breath as snowflakes began to fall around them. The sounds of horse's hooves, and a train whistling as it pulled out of the nearby station, fell away. The world shrank down to just the two of them, standing there in the circle of light from the gaslamp. Standing at a fork in the road, choosing their own destiny.

When she didn't respond right away, Pip's heart felt as if it might burst out of his chest. "I haven't got a ring—not yet—and I haven't spoken to your father, but I will. Verity, I—"

"Yes."

Pip's throat constricted and he had to swallow before he could speak. When he did, his voice came out an octave higher than usual. "Pardon me?"

Verity's eyes danced. "Yes, I will marry you, Philip."

Grinning, Pip removed his glasses and wiped them with his pocket square. Once they were back in position on his face, Verity pressed a kiss to his cheek and bid him goodnight, a beatific smile on her face as she stepped out of the ethereal glow cast by the lamplight and disappeared into the guest house.

"Master Reed," came a strange voice from the shadows.

"Who's there?" Pip's voice quavered only slightly and he squinted into the darkness between the buildings. He thought he recognised the lilting accent, but he couldn't quite place it.

"One year, Master Reed. Enjoy your success. In one year's time you'll be leaving all of this behind. Oh, and congratulations on your engagement."

Pip's blood chilled, his limbs frozen in place. "Master Dobson?"

But there was no response, and when Pip's body thawed and he leapt into the shadows to discover the source of the voice, the alley was empty.

CHAPTER 4

March 18th, 1883
Hartwood, England

For months, Pip had tried to think of a way to escape his terrible bargain, to remain in the Human Realm with his beloved Verity, but to no avail.

He couldn't remember the wording of the contract—he hadn't been able to decipher much of the convoluted language at the time—but he felt as though he was trapped in a deal with the devil. His only conclusion was to stay as far away from Hartwood as possible. But then, Master Dobson, or one of his lackeys, had come to Pip in Austria and seemed to have no trouble discovering his whereabouts or following him across the globe.

And in the end, it didn't matter much anyway. At the beginning of March in Pip's eighteenth year, a letter had arrived at the conservatory dormitory addressed to Pip, written in his mother's hand. His father had taken ill and he was needed at home in Hartwood at his earliest convenience.

"We'll take a carriage to the station," Verity had said when he informed her, packing her violin into its silk-lined case and pulling on her gloves.

"What do you mean? I can't ask you to accompany me, Verity, this is my burden to bear."

His fiancée had given him a withering look. "What's yours is mine now, darling. For better or worse. Or, at least, it soon will be."

Pip had forced a small smile. Delaying the wedding date until his bargain had passed hadn't been difficult. Verity had agreed they should wait until they had both finished their studies, it would give her enough time to plan an extravagant affair with every bell and whistle, whilst they both continued to study and perform regularly.

Pip felt tremendous guilt for deceiving her, but he couldn't bear the thought of marrying her only to be torn away from her and held prisoner by the creatures with whom he'd made the ill-fated bargain. That would be a much worse stain on her honour than a broken engagement.

"Fine," he had said, giving her a conciliatory smile. "My mother and sisters will be pleased to see you. We'd better hurry, the next train to Hartwood is at ten past the hour."

Inside the velvet-draped carriage, Verity had removed the glove from her left hand, admired the gold filigree and opal engagement ring Pip had bought with his earnings, and twined her long fingers through Pip's. The warmth of her small hand contrasted with Pip's large, cool one, and he had brushed his thumb over her skin, soaking in her heat.

He'd been glad she was joining him. Her presence grounded him and gave him strength—something he'd only ever felt before when his fingers were on the ivory keys of his instrument.

Pip's father lay under a thin blanket, a sheen of sweat on his ashen face. His chest made a terrible rasping sound and a hollow appeared beneath his ribcage with every breath.

"What happened?" Pip asked his mother quietly as she poured tea into faded, porcelain teacups.

Verity took hers with a grateful smile, added a dash of milk from the jug, and sipped. "Delicious. Thank you, Mrs Reed."

Pip's mother nodded at his fiancée before sitting down and picking up her own cup.

"It was an unfortunate accident," she said with a shake of her head. "He was working late last Thursday night. The others had already gone on to the pub and he was closing the pit down for the day. He tripped on something or other and fell into the pit. Luckily it was quite a shallow part or he'd have been killed, but he lay there in the freezing cold unable to move all night, until the men on the early shift arrived the next morning. His workmates thought he'd decided to come straight home and I—well, I thought he was just having a drink and lost track of time. I never imagined—" She took a handkerchief from the inside of her sleeve and dabbed at her eyes and nose. Verity reached over and put a reassuring hand on his mother's shaking one, the teacup rattling in its saucer. Pip's mother pressed her lips into a thin smile that emphasised the new wrinkles she'd formed since he last saw her. It occurred to him that both of his parents had aged significantly in the past two years, their hair that had been thick and dark before he'd left was now streaked with grey, their skin had become sallow and lined, their bodies frail.

How had his leaving caused them to change so dramatically?

He took in his sisters, sitting on the threadbare settee in the lounge, Lucy reading a social pamphlet while Eleanor darned a pair of stockings. They wore elegant dresses adorned with beaded, lace collars, draped over jutting collarbones. Pip, on the other hand, had gained weight from the rich food served at the conservatory and the few treats he could afford with his income from performing for the upper classes at their lavish parties. He sent as much as he could back home to his parents, only keeping enough to support himself and putting a little away each month for his future with Verity, but perhaps it wasn't enough?

And now that his father was unable to work it certainly would not be.

"How will you manage without Father's salary? Do you need more money? I could send more, whatever I make is yours."

His mother dabbed at her nose with the handkerchief and

lowered her voice. "After paying our dues, buying the girls' new dresses and putting away enough money for decent dowries, things are tight." She tucked the handkerchief back inside her sleeve. "We'll manage, Pip. We always do. You're a good boy. You keep your money, you've earned it. Treat this lovely girl of yours." She squeezed Verity's hand and smiled, eyes shining with unshed tears.

But Pip couldn't conjure more than a grimace.

Whatever happened, he could not go through with the bargain. He needed to find a way out of it, and soon. Before it was too late for everyone.

Pip dropped the last book on the gnarled wooden table with a thump. He'd scoured every single book on fairies and folklore and magic in Hartwood library and found nothing about breaking a bargain with a fairy creature.

The Spring Equinox was almost here and he had no way to stop Master Dobson from taking him. He slammed the cover of the large tome he'd been studying, causing the petite, white-haired librarian to *shush* him sternly, but he didn't care. He cursed the day he'd set eyes on the strange, little man and his colourful caravan. He'd been stupid and greedy and arrogant to accept the man's dark promise. He wished he'd never gone to buy the piano string for Mister Ericsson—

Mister Ericsson. That was it! His tutor had been the one to suggest Pip visit Master Dobson's stall. That must mean he knew the man and had had some dealings with him in the past. Perhaps he would know something that could help Pip escape the agreement.

CHAPTER 5

"Philip, I am sorry, but I know nothing of what you're asking. A fairy bargain? *Magic?*" Mister Ericsson wrung his hands and shook his head, a tense expression on his face. "It sounds—well, forgive me, but you sound a little crazy. Is everything alright at home? I heard about your father. I'm very sorry for what happened to him."

Pip stared at his music tutor, a wave of disappointment and dread rendering him temporarily mute. Mister Ericsson had been his last hope, his one final chance to unravel the magical contract and avoid Master Dobson's payment terms. And now he was hours away from being forced to leave his family and join the man in—what had he called it, the Fair Realm? For the rest of his days, if Master Dobson was to be believed.

He rested his elbows on his knees and dropped his head into his hands, a sob threatening to choke him if he didn't let it out. What would he do now? Run? Fight? He had never been particularly adept at either.

Perhaps if he pretended to join Master Dobson willingly, he could try to find a way out, a way to escape the bargain.

He rubbed a hand over his face, grazing the stubble that had formed on his jaw and cheeks. It was hopeless. Utterly hopeless.

"Thank you, Mister Ericsson," Pip said, getting up to leave, despondency heavy upon his shoulders. "I'll bid you farewell and hope to see you again someday."

Ericsson's expression was conflicted as he showed Pip to the door. As he crossed the threshold, Pip turned and studied his tutor for a moment.

"You truly don't know anything of Master Dobson and his magical contracts?"

Ericsson's hand tightened on the door handle, his knuckles turning bone-white; and a muscle in his jaw leapt before his expression smoothed into a tight smile. "I'm afraid not. Best of luck, Master Reed."

P ip sat at his parents' kitchen table that night, a glass of whisky in his hand and one eye on the carriage clock his father had been given the previous year, on his thirtieth anniversary of working at the pit. He took a sip and swallowed it with a wince. He hadn't acquired a taste for alcohol yet, but he needed something to steady his nerves.

The clock read five past eleven. The Spring Equinox was less than an hour away. His time had almost run out.

After his conversation with his tutor, Pip had begun to question whether he had in fact imagined the entire thing. The pressure of getting into the conservatory and being regarded as a great musician could well have gotten to him. Perhaps he had gone, as Mister Ericsson had said, a little crazy.

"Philip?" Pip leapt out of his seat, spilling whisky on the table.

"Verity. What are you still doing up?"

She pursed her lips and pulled out the chair opposite him. She wore a midnight blue nightgown and robe, her long, dark hair hanging over her shoulders in loose waves. His heart ached at the sight of her beauty. He did not deserve her.

"Worrying about you. You haven't been yourself these past weeks. What's the matter, darling? Whatever it is, we'll face it together." She reached across the table and took his hand. "Is it your father? The household finances? Tell me."

Pip sighed and swallowed the rest of his whisky. Perhaps he should tell her. She might be able to convince him the entire scenario was nothing more than a figment of his imagination. Or maybe she knew something about fairies and their infernal bargains that could help him?

As the clock ticked towards midnight and the Spring Equinox drew closer, he told Verity the entire sorry tale, from his failure to get into the conservatory on first try, to Master Dobson's caravan and the piece of paper he had signed, to the unsettling encounter in Vienna after he had asked her to marry him. Finally, he told her of Mister Ericsson's odd behaviour when he'd confronted the man about his connection to Master Dobson. Pip hadn't failed to sense his tutor's nervous reaction to his questions. He felt sure his tutor knew more than he was letting on, but what could he do?

The only thing left to do was wait and see if Master Dobson would appear and take what was rightfully his—Pip.

Verity's eyes shone silver as he reached the end of the story. The clock read a quarter past midnight, and there hadn't been so much as a knock at the door.

"Oh Philip, why didn't you tell me all of this sooner?"

"I'm sorry, my love. I understand if you wish to end our engagement and have nothing further to do with me."

He dropped his head, but Verity gripped his chin gently and lifted his eyes to hers. "I meant what I said, Philip Reed. For better or worse. Now, tell me what the library books said on the subject, and perhaps between us we can come up with a way out of this mess."

CHAPTER 6

Pip jolted awake to the sound of floorboards creaking and rain pattering on the window panes. He had fallen asleep on the settee, Verity beside him, note paper scattered across the low coffee table where they had tried to think of a way out of Pip's deal.

He sat bolt upright as his ears caught the sound of whispering voices.

"Who's there?"

Three small men appeared from the shadows as if they had taken corporeal form when called. He recognised Master Dobson, but the others were new to him—just as strange and grotesque as the market stall holder, short in stature with long limbs, large noses and pointed ears. Their eyes glittered black in the early morning light, sending a shiver through Pip. He opened his mouth to—he wasn't sure what. Shout? Wake his family?

"It would be better for all involved if you were to come quietly, Master Reed. Our magic can only do so much here. It would be an awful shame if we were forced to harm your loved ones." The man's casually threatening tone was enough to make Pip close his mouth.

Despite hours of going over what Pip could remember of his initial encounter with Master Dobson, they had failed to come up with a single idea they believed could get Pip out of the bargain. He had no choice but to go along with these frightening creatures, and forcing his family to watch him be dragged away would do no good.

With a hard swallow, Pip nodded and got to his feet. He moved slowly, his joints were stiff from sleeping in an upright position on the settee, and he wanted to spend just one minute more in the company of his beloved Verity before he said goodbye forever. He draped a blanket over her sleeping form and glanced at the papers on the table.

"Can I leave a note?"

Master Dobson's lips thinned, but he nodded. "Quickly."

Pip scrawled a short note saying goodbye and apologising for the mess he had gotten himself into, and for the black mark his disappearance would leave on her honour. He asked her to forgive him, and thanked her for loving him. He signed the note 'Your Philip' and placed it in Verity's hand, careful not to wake her.

"Alright. I'm ready."

Pip followed the creatures from the house, through the deserted streets of Hartwood, and up towards the pit where his father had worked. Something occurred to him at the sight of it.

"Were you responsible for my father's accident? Was that your way of getting me to Hartwood? So that I'd be here when the time came for you to take me?"

Master Dobson chuckled darkly and said without turning, "No, boy. That was simply a happy coincidence."

Pip wasn't sure he believed it.

They passed the pit, Pip's hair and clothes growing damp and heavy from the constant drizzle, and entered the vast forest that bordered Hartwood village. The scent of wet leaves and living things hit Pip as they picked their way through the underbrush. It was almost as though he could smell the colour green.

Eventually, they reached a clearing where a pair of gnarled trees had grown twisted together, forming a natural arch. There was nothing especially remarkable about the spot, but Pip got the sense this was where they were heading.

"Where are you taking me? What do you want? I don't know why you're doing this, I never meant for any of this."

Dobson stopped and turned to face Pip, who stood in the centre of the clearing, surrounded by these odd creatures and wishing he had tried harder to get away.

"Would you go back and erase the bargain, if you could?" Dobson asked, one eyebrow raised. "Never taste success, never meet your beautiful Verity? Would you stay in Hartwood and take care of your family and never play your music for audiences of thousands? Would you sacrifice everything you've had these past three years to avoid your fate?"

Pip's breath caught in his throat. Would he? He tried to imagine living the life he'd always dreaded instead of the miraculous, wondrous life he'd enjoyed since he signed Dobson's contract. Could he honestly say he would rather live that small, quiet, safe life and never know the magic of performing in Europe's most prestigious concert halls? Never fall for the most exquisite and talented girl he had ever met?

"Is that possible?" He held his breath as Dobson's expression turned devilish.

"No. I was merely curious. Now, come along, we haven't got all day. Through the portal, if you please."

"What?" Pip's brows furrowed, but only for a moment, as the two other creatures each grabbed an arm and dragged him towards the archway between the trees. A peculiar sensation washed over Pip as they passed beneath the arch, and a second later he stood on lush, green grass in another clearing altogether, where the sky was streaked with pink, gold and orange as the sun rose on a mild, dry day. Nothing like the wet, gloomy morning they had left behind in Hartwood.

"Where are we?"

"The Fair Realm, Master Reed. And, as to your other questions, we are taking you to our home in the Gnome Kingdom. When you signed our bargain you agreed to become the new goblin king and join us in this realm forevermore. All we ask of you is to play your beloved piano for our enjoyment and remain with us until the day you die, or another goblin king is chosen."

Fair Realm? Gnome Kingdom? *Goblin king?* Pip's head swam and he staggered on his feet, but the two creatures—goblins, he now realised—still held his arms and kept him upright. He glanced at them and noticed that their features had become even more distorted and hideous. He questioned how he had ever believed them to be human.

"You can't be serious."

"Oh, but I am Master Reed. I never joke about matters as serious as this."

They walked on until they reached a place where the trees thinned and a small, grass-covered hillock rose out of the earth. There was a small wooden door into the mound, roughly the height of the goblins and far too small for Pip himself. Luckily, they didn't seem to be leading him towards the underground dwelling. He followed Master Dobson up a stone path that led to the top of the hillock, where a large courtyard spread before him, and at its centre stood an elegantly carved piano.

"If you please, Master Reed." Dobson gestured to the instrument and Pip frowned.

"You want me to play for you?"

Dobson nodded and stepped forward to pull out the bench so Pip could take a seat.

Sitting on the velvet cushioned bench, Pip felt utterly bewildered. This was surreal. There was no sheet music, and the keys had been worn smooth by the fingers of his predecessors. He tried to imagine the musicians who had played this instrument before him, who they had been in their real lives, and how they had ended up in this place. Had they been tricked into fairy bargains, like him?

"What do you want me to play?"

Dobson shrugged, affecting nonchalance, but his black eyes glimmered with mischief. "Whatever comes to mind. Your favourite piece. Anything you want. Just play."

Pip pressed down on the F key, held it and let the note fade away, listening to the way it sounded as it died. Next, he played a quick scale, testing the instrument's consistency. Satisfied, he pushed his glasses up his nose with his forefinger and lay his hands upon the keys. With a deep breath in and out, he began to play a simple Chopin piece, one he had always enjoyed and found to be a good measure of any new instrument.

As he played, Dobson and his lackeys began to dance. It was

somewhat incongruous, after the threatening way they had brought him here. He hadn't expected to have to perform straight away, but at least they seemed to be enjoying the music. While they were distracted, he might have a chance of finding a way to escape.

More of the creatures appeared, climbing the path to the courtyard, males, females and children filling the space and joining the others in their dance. By the time the piece was finished, there were dozens of goblins surrounding the piano and dancing, their long limbs flailing, large feet tapping.

As the final note rang out, Pip launched into another piece, this one by Schubert. Except, Pip hadn't meant to keep playing, he hadn't even consciously chosen the piece. He tried to stop playing and found that he couldn't—his fingers kept moving across the keyboard, his foot working the pedal and the goblins kept dancing.

What was going on here? Had Dobson enchanted the instrument so that Pip would be unable to stop playing until Dobson decided it was time?

The Schubert piece ended and Pip's fingers played Beethoven. Then Bach, then Chopin again followed by Mozart.

Pip's fingers were beginning to ache and the panic that had risen up in his chest was beginning to consume him. Would Dobson ever let him stop playing, or would he die on this very bench, starved and sleep-deprived?

Hours had gone by, Pip still played the piano and the goblins still danced, apparently unfatigued. Tears ran down Pip's cheeks in a constant stream. He understood now that he wouldn't be able to stop until the curse that had been placed on him came to an end. His mind ran over and over everything that had happened, searching for the smallest hint or clue that could get him out of this nightmare. Dobson had said he was obliged to remain here and entertain the goblins until he died. Or another goblin king was chosen. That was it!

But, how would he find another goblin king to take his place? And how could he, in good conscience, condemn another to the very same fate he was trying to escape?

A shout went up and some of the goblins scattered as a figure appeared in the courtyard. Two figures, Pip thought, though his vision was obscured by his tears.

"Philip!" Verity rushed towards him and took his face in her hands. She was a sight for sore eyes, her cheeks flushed and her hair wild. Her breath came in short pants, like she'd been running full pelt. He wanted to kiss her, but he couldn't stop playing.

"Philip?" She looked from his tear-stained face to his dancing fingers and realisation dawned on her face. She tried to stop his hands from moving, but it was no use—the magic seemed to prevent any interference. She gave up and put her hands on his shoulders. "It's all going to be alright, darling. I brought Mister Ericsson with me. He's going to make everything right. I promise, you'll be home safe soon."

Mister Ericsson was here? Pip looked to where the goblins were still dancing, albeit hesitantly now, the wild abandon they'd previously shown displaced by this unexpected interruption. Mister Ericsson was noticeable by his height—the goblins barely reaching his chest—and by his stillness. He was speaking with Master Dobson, who had also paused his dancing. Ericsson's palms were spread, as though he were pleading with Dobson. Begging for Pip's release? He hoped upon hope that's what the exchange was about.

Finally, Dobson nodded, a resigned look on his twisted features. Ericsson closed his eyes for a moment, a shuddering sigh racking his body. Then he looked up and locked eyes with Pip. An unspoken understanding passed between them. The music tutor crossed to the piano and took a seat beside Pip on the bench.

"I'm sorry Philip, for everything. This was my curse, not yours. I was afraid before, but I'm ready now. I'm ready to accept my fate."

Pip didn't understand what his music tutor was telling him. The bargain had been meant for him? Ericsson joined in with the Bach piece Pip was playing and after a moment, Pip felt something intangible rush through him, like a shiver, a pressure lifting somehow, and his fingers stopped playing. He slumped, exhausted, and Verity caught him. She was much stronger than she appeared, years of practising the violin for hours had given her a physical fortitude he'd never recognised before.

Ericsson looked to Pip, fingers moving expertly across the keys, his expression grim. "Go now, quickly, and forget this place. Forget me, Philip. You never needed the magic. You were always talented. You were my best student. Please forgive me."

When Pip only stared at his tutor, frozen in fear and confusion, Ericsson raised his voice. "Go! Before it's too late. And don't come back."

With Verity's help, Pip got to his feet and stumbled across the courtyard, weaving through the horde of revelling goblins. None looked his way, absorbed in the beautiful music coming from the piano and the silver-haired man now sitting in Pip's place. Before they descended the hillock and lost sight of the gathering of goblins, Pip looked back one last time to see his music tutor playing the piano with his eyes closed, a calm expression on his handsome, ageing face. He looked serene, at peace.

They hurried through the forest, searching for the archway that had allowed them to step through into this realm, Pip clinging to Verity's arm as he stumbled along. He had so many questions, he scarcely knew which to ask first.

"How did you find me?"

"There was knocking at the door, and when I opened my eyes you were gone. Your tutor came looking for you. He was devastated when he saw he'd arrived too late. He was babbling about a curse and I realised he knew who had taken you. He told me he'd been a foolish, arrogant young man and had sought out the goblins, looking for a way to guarantee his success. They had promised him talent and fortune, the likes of which he couldn't imagine, for three years, and in return he would be compelled to join them in the Fair Realm forevermore. But he negotiated with the goblins. He offered to send them talented young musicians in his stead, and they agreed."

Pip stared at Verity, wide eyed. He'd been handed to the goblins as payment for Ericsson's own bargain? He couldn't believe what he was hearing. The man who had taught him the piano—his greatest passion and the thing that brought him the most joy—since he had been eight years old, had given him up to a fate worse than death in exchange for his own freedom?

And yet, Mister Ericsson had come to take his place and let Pip go in the end. What courage it must have taken to knowingly resign himself to the fate that he had sent many young musicians before him.

Pip found that he couldn't hate his tutor for what he had done. Hadn't Pip wanted the exact same things? Fame. Fortune. To be the world's most brilliant piano player, no matter what. In the end, greed and arrogance had been the downfall of them both. Now, thanks to Mister Ericsson, Pip had a chance to make amends for his past self-ishness. He only hoped he would be worthy of his tutor's sacrifice.

Pip and Verity staggered into the clearing where the trees entwined, forming the arched doorway, and without a glance behind them, stepped through.

EPILOGUE

Viktor's fingers were numb from hours of playing, but he knew he had done the right thing this time.

Pip hadn't been the first young musician he had condemned to this fate, there had been others before him. Viktor had moved on each time a student had disappeared—it helped that the youngsters had become erratic and nonsensical in the days and weeks running up to their disappearances. Babbling about fairy creatures and magical contracts. Nobody suspected Viktor of any wrong-doing, and he was able to set up a new practice in the next town with no dark cloud hanging over his name.

But this time had been different. Philip Reed was unlike the grasping young people he'd sent to Master Dobson in the past. His ambition was not born from a selfish place. He had only wanted to escape the desolate future that lay before him in Hartwood, and to provide for his family by making a living doing what he loved. Viktor had respected his student's admirable intentions.

Unfortunately, Viktor had become desperate. It had been years since he had sent a student to Master Dobson. He'd needed a sacrificial lamb, and Philip with his rejection letter and broken spirit had been too perfect.

But after years of sending young musicians to a fate worse than death, he had begun to feel—something. Shame? Regret? Or perhaps all the years of moving around, running from his fate, had finally caught up with him. Whatever it was, he could no longer live with his decision.

As he played, the goblins began to fall asleep one by one, collapsing from exhaustion, until the entire courtyard was filled with their snoring, unconscious figures. The spell was temporarily broken and Viktor stretched his fingers, arching his back and rolling his neck. He stood up and pushed the bench under the piano, then found a shady, peaceful spot on the grassy hillock to lay down. He needed some rest. As soon as the goblins awoke he would be compelled to play for them until they slept once more. And every day, until he could play no more.

The time had come to accept his fate.

About the Author

Lyndsey Hall lives on the edge of Sherwood Forest, one of the most magical places in England's history, and the inspiration for her debut novel, *The Fair Queen*. She grew up surrounded by books, and loved to write from a young age.

She loves to travel and try her hand at new things, but is most at home when curled up in a chair with a cup of tea and a good book, usually accompanied by at least one dog. She's fortunate enough to share her home with two cherished humans and two beloved dogs.

Find Lyndsey online here: https://www.lyndseyhallwrites.com

Find out more about *The Fair Queen* .

ACKNOWLEDGMENTS

We would like to thank Alice for getting us all together. Without you, Alice, the Enchanted Anthologies wouldn't exist, and we are deeply grateful for this opportunity to work together. You are an inspiration to us all.

Our thanks go to Astrid who has done an exceptional job being head organizer of this anthology and we thank her for all her time and effort especially when spinning many plates.

Elena, thank you so much for your incredible illustrations. They are absolutely breath-taking, and we are blown away by your contribution to this anthology. You have truly brought every character to life!

We didn't just want to write and publish our stories but wanted to also do some good on a larger scale. Since this is an anthology about magical forests and the creatures living in them, we decided to pick a rainforest conservation charity because all of us working on Enchanted Forests agreed that the state of the planet's rainforests is something we are deeply worried about. It did take us a long time to decide on which charity to choose, and because of all the deliberation that went into our choice, we would like to take this opportunity to thank Rainforest Foundation for everything this organisation does, particularly when it comes to working together with indigenous peoples to protect their habitats.

Defending rainforest biodiversity and protecting these regions from logging and other human activities, and to ensure sustainability, are mammoth tasks and Rainforest Foundation does an incredible job of achieving the goals they've set towards reducing our human impact on the rainforests.

Special thanks go to the early birds of our street team. Thank you for being behind us every step of the way! Oksana Klindukhova, Debajyoti Banerjee, Iris Vélez, Sharon Brown, Crystal White, Megan Holbrook, Jade, Vyshnavi, Mareli Thalwitzer, Emily Downey, Maria Ashley, Patricia, Divya Ramji, Sylvia, Lenise, Aaron Arm, Breanna Schwab, Cheryl Phillip, Nguyễn Tú Anh, Shenali Tissera, Jessica Rinaudo, Alyson Raven, Madam Crystal Butterfly, Mel Wright, Rebecca Benson, Kara Schmidt, Lisa P Hughes, Samantha, Brittany Caraballo, Ash C, Shruti Zunje, Cassandra Arnold, Alyssa, Simpu, Sharlene, Rahdika Karuppannan, Derek Callahan, Arya Rai, Chelsea Fox, Yajna Ramnath, Shagun Varma, Caroline Silver, Madison Horton, Bianca Rogers, Ellen Read, Jenny Leverett, Angana Premarathne, Lelita Baldock, Jan Foster, Triin, Olivia Castetter, Allie Eldridge, Angelina, Suz, Devenial Dream, Julie Jenny, Kristin, Rachel Wilkinson, Megare, Giselle Schneider, Amanda Cino, Makarena Fuentealba, Ellie Sanders, Robin Ginther-Venneri, Seher Mohsin, Ivy Whitaker, E.J. Yerzak, Candice, Linda Darlison, Kassie Simonis, D'Linda Pearson, Zara G, Ashley Clark, Carol Hand, Jahara Morris, Emma Durphey, Ingunn Helgemo, Stephanie Dulac, Sarah Elyse Rodriguez, Kathryn Norton, Madeleine Booth-Smits, Ashwati Biju, Sarah Festa, Natali, Albert Gamundi Sr., Sintia, Caoimhe Rogers, Shelley Anderson, Laura Billingham, Jess, Ashley Snow, Rebekah Franks, Sarah Westdorp, Conny Hegeman, Ashley Duncan, Denise Winchell, Holly, Stephanie, Kelly Hill, Kitten lewis, Tiffany, Natasha Wheeler, Kaia Yang, TaniaRina Perry, Kimberly Ann, Natasha Leighton, Kaitlyn Parker, Diane Dicke, Angela Sanford, Stephanie Cotta, Akash Dadwal, Ruth Hinojos, Judith Cohen, Brittni Kelly, Mandy Dawn, Rida Ashraf, Caroline, Maria, Kelsey Josund, Eunice Carbone, Pamela Anne Reinert, Natalia Navarro, Wilsey Zahner, Desiree Heltzel-Baylin, Anindita Ghosh, Abigail McMillon, Angela Hughes, Meethi, Sherrie Wood, Luca Szijjártó, Ruth Mitchell, Jennifer Macaulay, Emily Katzenberger, Beth, P.L. Stuart, Olivia Jayne, Regine, Nil, Anushka, Aditi, Kari Frazier, Catherine Green, Riley Hlatshwayo, John Irvin, Alexander Giant, Steven S P, Larissa Porsche, Jess Ross, Kelly Ussery, Musaiyyeb Bin Mujib, Nicole Sanchez, Fathima, Mathew Joben Thomas, Aathira S Sunil, Alexandra Antipa, Sofia Kouloufakou,

Alexis Mills, Katrin, Hannelore Adler Gailwin, Ellie Stevens, Sara, Louise Murchie, Bhoomika, Michael DeConzo, Kari Carter, Carmen Alicea, Ria, Alex Stubblefield, Jennifer Peavey, Barbara Harrison, Cassandra Stevens, Angie Hardesty, Amber Herbert, Elle Hartford, Susan Doumont, Darrah Steffen, Mary E Jung, Adelle, Emily Butler, Vanessa, Irene Kroon, Shreya Pillai, Madison, Toluwalope Oyedele, Utkarsha Kalambe, Lia, Kim Beebe, Leah, Crystal Anne Mitchell, Sheryl Bird, Tanya Robinson, Kelly, Carmen Capoziello, Selena, Danna Gzz, Nikki Brooke, Rebecca Karlsson, Adena Lee, Rudra, Dounia, Amorina Arlton, Anna Lindgren, Gia Guido, Lauren, Elena Carter, Sameeksha Varshney, Priyanka Chakraborty, Anjali Panikar, Holly, Naina Rajput, Derzsi Ana-Maria, Jimena, Shana Dow, Charlotte Valentine, Muntaaha Rahman, Tanya, A.M. McPherson, Ashlyn Watkins, Kübra, Elsie Bea, Rachel, Hannah, Ruth V Jarvis, Katie O'Sullivan, Maya, Aanya Verma, Emma Berger, Yvonne Ziblut, Corrissa, Cristiana Harkness, Jessica Dapper, Angela, Sharimila K, Tifany Ness, Nicola McKenna, Sara Scully, Madi Healey, SN Lindsi, Robyn Barebo, Dana Flanders, Rachel Dailey, Odysseus, K. Sneha, Priyanka Gunasekaran, Caitlin Sheppard, Silpi Srivastava, Jess, Gladia Joseph, Maia, Jewel, Alexis Gibbings, Gerard, Haley Sywak, Abbi Gibson, Hannah Baller, Linda McCutcheon, Kristin Blazer, Dina Husseini, Rachel, Yana Metro, Ishita Dey, BitsandBobsandBooks, Stella Hlivkova, Megan Wilcox, Rachel Pelkey, Lea, Sucharita Biswas, Paula, Alexis Skurdall, Anushka, Stefanie, LaChanda Collins, Katie Cathey, Kourtney, Chelsea Warren, Olive Katz, Lenore Borja, Carmen, Sayantika Adhikary, Tejaswini, Lipi, V.P. Morris, Corey, Hepzibah Becca Jael, Sara Lawson, Sarah Elyse Rodriguez, Jessica Woznick, Stephanie Brandt, Shivani, Shannon Coley, Chad Barrus, Ronel Janse van Vuuren, Linda, Katrina Bjerky, Loni Greyson, Elaine Kane, Carol Brandon, Jo, Kristina Gehrls, Amena Jamali, Kritika Dharia, Marie Reed, Marlena Smith, Aniya Saunders, Marie Sinadjan, Evgeniia, Theresa Hodge, Nel E., Miranda Krause-Chivers, Susan Stradiotto, Leanne Wilkinson, Amber Peterson, Sohini Dasgupta, Akshita Agrawal, Magda Smith, Amy Friedman, Leslie Manlapig, Cheyenne Clause, Vannezza Aranas, Kendall Victoria, Ember S., Zola, Sydney

Tomac, Juliet Ann Tio, Moira Siobhan, Laurel, Grant Webster, and Sam.

To all the other members of our street team, we would also like to thank you for your support of Enchanted Forests.

We also want to thank Emily from Emily's World of Design for donating this beautiful cover towards the anthology.

And to all the editors involved, thank you! Carolyn Gent, Melissa Cole, Amanda Nicoler, Kereah Keller and Astrid V.J., thank you!

OTHER BOOKS IN THIS SERIES

Enchanted Waters is a collection of ten short illustrated fantasy stories about magical water creatures. All proceeds of this book benefit Oceana, an ocean protection organization.

Stories include:

Daughter of the Selkie King - Lyndsey Hall
Merrily Merrily - Jennifer Kropf
The Kelpie of Loch Linnhe - Alice Ivinya
The Bridge - Ben Lang
Kiss the Frog - Sky Sommers
Sea Ghost of the Isle - N.D.T. Casale
The Naiad's Curse - Astrid V.J.
The Arctic Mermaid - N.D.T. Casale
Heartless Melody - Alice Ivinya
The Wishing Well - Elena Shelest

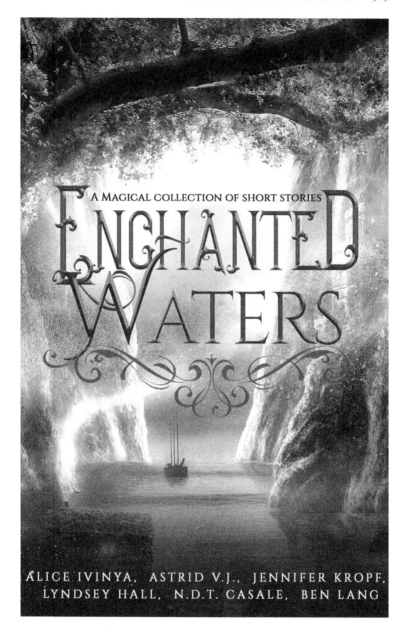

314 OTHER BOOKS IN THIS SERIES

Enchanted Flames is the next book in this series of anthologies. All proceeds of this book will go to benefit a charity dedicated to conservation relating to forest fires. The charity will be announced in the autumn of 2022 and the book releases on June 18, 2023. Join our Facebook fan group to see the cover reveal on August 24, 2022. And pre-order your copy for the early-bird price of $0.99 (due to go up to $2.99 in December 2022).

A MAGICAL COLLECTION OF SHORT STORIES

ENCHANTED
FLAMES

Printed in Great Britain
by Amazon